A GHOST IN THE MACHINE

A GHOST IN THE MACHINE

Caroline Graham

 St. Martin's Minotaur ☒ New York

www.minotaurbooks.com

ISBN 0-312-32421-9
EAN 978-0312-32421-6

First published in Great Britain by Headline Book Publishing, a division of Hodder Headline PLC.

First St. Martin's Minotaur Edition: August 2004

10 9 8 7 6 5 4 3 2 1

For Jane,
the sister I never had.
And for Bob and Rebecca.

GLENDOWER: I can call spirits from the vasty deep.

HOTSPUR: Why, so can I, or so can any man;
But will they come when you do call for them?

Henry IV Part One, Act III, scene i

THE WAR ROOM

CHAPTER ONE

Mallory Lawson's aunt had been a relative in a million. Throughout his childhood her large, rambling house and semi-wild garden had afforded unlimited scope for adventurous games during the school holidays. Aunt Carey seemed to know instinctively when he wanted to be left alone and when he wanted company. She fed him drippingly scrumptious, massively calorific food that would have had his mother fainting with horror. Frequently, when leaving, more money was slipped into his pocket than he would earn in a year washing the family car. Kindest of all, when Mallory was fourteen she had encouraged him to smoke one of her special Havana Cohiba cigars to the very end, which made him so violently sick he was never able to touch tobacco again.

And now, peacefully in her sleep during her eighty-ninth year, the old lady had died. As perceptive and understanding as ever, she had accomplished this just as her beloved nephew's mental and physical health was at breaking point. He thought then and for a long time afterwards that coming into his inheritance when he did saved his sanity. Perhaps even his life.

The news of his aunt's death broke in the middle of a family argument. Kate, Mallory's wife, was putting all the difficult, row-inducing points that anxious parents feel sometimes compelled to put to their children, even when such children are officially adults. This burden, for some time now, had fallen upon her. Mallory, even if he had not spoiled their daughter since the day she was born, was too broken-backed to enter even the mildest affray.

Polly had just completed her second year at the London School of Economics, reading Accounting and Finance. Though the Lawsons' house was a mere fifteen minutes from the LSE by Tube, she had insisted on finding her own place to live. For the first year this had meant staying in the halls of residence. Then, after the long vac, she had found a flat share in Dalston. Her allowance was enough to cover the rent and food, with a modest amount left over for pocket money.

During the first twelve months her parents had seen little of Polly. Mallory had been extremely hurt but Kate had understood. Their daughter was on the threshold of a new world, a new life, and Kate regarded it as a compliment that Polly couldn't wait to run out on to the high board, hold her nose and jump in at the deep end. She was bright, extremely pretty and confident. Psychologically speaking, she could swim. But financially? Well, that was something else. And that was what this set-to was all about.

Polly apparently now planned to move again. She had found a two-bedroom flat in Shoreditch. Her intention was to let both rooms to cover the rent. The agency wanted a three-month deposit to be returned when giving up the tenancy and a quarter's rent in advance.

'So where will you sleep?' asked her mother.

'There's a space I can cram a futon in – roll it up during the day. They do it all the time in Japan.' Polly, never patient, took a long, slow breath. The discussion, which had already been going on for half an hour, was proving tougher than she had expected. If only her mother wasn't here. 'Don't look so appalled. Anyone'd think I was going to sleep on the Embankment.'

'Is it furnished?'

'No . . .'

'So you'll need extra money on top of—'

'I'm *saving* you money, for Christ's sake!'

'Don't talk to your mother like that, Polly.' Mallory frowned, the deeply graven lines between his brows drawing together. His fingers plucked nervously at his shirt cuffs. 'She's worried about you.'

'But, don't you see, it means you won't have to pay my rent any more?'

'So you're doing it for us?'

'There's no need to be sarcastic.'

Kate could have bitten her tongue. She thought, why am I like this? Mal can be patient with her – listening, understanding. Giving way more often than not and receiving hugs and kisses in return. But herself – the slightest criticism, any attempt to stand firm against unreasonable demands or establish even a modest degree of routine or discipline, even when Polly was small, had brought the constant accusation from the child that her mother had never really loved her. More often it seemed to Kate the other way round. Still, her remark had been uncalled for. She was about to apologise when Mallory spoke.

'About this furniture—'

' "This furniture". I'm not going to Heal's. Just round skips and junk shops.'

'You can't charge two hundred pounds a week for bedsits full of rubbish—'

'They're not bedsits!' Polly stopped, took a deep breath and counted aloud to ten. 'I *told* you – it'll be a flat share.'

Kate hesitated. She had always thought flat shares were cheaper than bedsits. And wasn't it usually a month's deposit people wanted?

'Anyway, you know nothing about skip culture. People throw the most amazing things away.'

'We'd have to have a look at it,' said Kate.

'Why?' Then, when her mother looked taken aback: 'I'm asking

4

for a measly ten grand. I'll repay it – with interest, if that's what you want.'

'Don't be ridiculous.'

'And what's it to you? It won't be your money.'

It could well be, thought Kate. For she was still working practically full time. But she didn't care about that. Her concern was over what the money was really for. She remembered an item on a radio programme only days ago saying that something like seventy per cent of the banknotes circulating in the banking area of the inner City showed traces of cocaine. If Polly, God forbid, needed money for that . . .

'It would be nice, though, love,' Mallory tried to ease the tension, 'to see where you're going to live.'

'The thing is . . .' Polly looked frankly at both her parents, looked them warmly straight in the eye. She did not know that, since she was very small, her mother had recognised this as a sure sign that her daughter was lying. 'There are still people in there. It won't actually be vacant for a couple of weeks.'

Kate said, 'I still don't see any point—'

'I want a bigger place, all right? More room.'

'But if there's three of you—'

'Oh, sod this. I'm sick of being cross-questioned as if I'm some sort of criminal. If you don't want to lend me the money just say so and I'll piss off.'

'Sounds familiar.'

'What's that supposed to mean?'

This remark was the opener to a long harangue about since when had either of them ever offered anybody any real support or genuine concern in their entire self-centred lives. And now there was a chance to do something to help someone, and that person their only daughter, but she should have known – they'd always been so bloody tight-fisted. Well, she would just have to borrow from the bank and when she was hopelessly in debt because of the astronomical rate of—

That was when the telephone rang. The Lawsons' answerphone, always on even when they were there, bleeped and wheezed. Distressed cries and squawks could be heard.

'It's Benny!' Mallory rushed to the phone. Listened and gently spoke. His wife and daughter saw his face suddenly transformed by shock and sorrow, and their anger evaporated into thin air.

The funeral was held on a rather breezy summer's afternoon. Mallory, Kate and Polly accepted condolences as a packed church slowly emptied and the organist played 'The day Thou gavest, Lord, is ended'.

Almost all the village had been present, as well as those of Aunt Carey's friends and relatives that still survived. One elderly man in a wheelchair had been driven down from Aberdeen. Mallory was moved but not surprised at this group display of affectionate mourning. His aunt, though perhaps not easy to love, was almost impossible to dislike.

The Lawsons stood at the graveside for a little while when everyone else either went home or over to Appleby House. And Mallory, who had always thought the knowledge that someone had had a long and largely happy life would make their death easier to bear, discovered he was wrong. But he was glad it had been sudden even as he regretted this meant he had had no chance to say goodbye. She would not have coped well with a slow and painful decline. He sensed that Kate, who had been very fond of the old lady, was silently crying. Polly, only there because of what she described as 'emotional arm-wrestling', stood a few feet away from her parents, trying to look sympathetic while impatiently chewing her bottom lip. Genuine sorrow was beyond her, for she had not seen her great-aunt for some years and was not into faking stuff just to make other people feel better.

They made their slow way back to where the baked meats were being consumed along with stone jars of apple wine made from fruit gathered in the orchard that gave the house its name. Everything had been organised by Benny Frayle, companion to the deceased, who had refused all help. Benny was desperate for something to fill these first days. The worst days. She had whirled and bustled and flung herself about; a grief-stricken Dervish, never still.

Though the already extremely large rooms on the ground floor had had their dividing louvre doors folded back, people had started spilling out on to the terrace and into the garden. Two girls from the village in jeans and Oasis T-shirts were handing round trays of knobbly-looking dark brown bits and greyish twists of pastry. Most people were drinking, though the punchbowl, holding a non-alcoholic fruit cup, had been hardly touched. Everyone seemed to be knocking back the home-made apple wine. Fair enough. Most of the mourners would be walking home and those who had travelled some distance would be returning to their hotel at nearby Princes Risborough by cab.

You could not mistake the fact, thought Kate, looking about her at the far from soberly dressed crowd, that most of the people present seemed to be rather enjoying themselves. What was it about funerals? The obvious answer – that everyone present had been suddenly shocked into gratified elation at their own survival – was surely not all there was to it. Anyway, sorrow could wear more than one face. There was Mrs Crudge, cleaner at Appleby House for thirty years. Just a few hours ago crying her heart out in the kitchen; now smiling and chatting while nervously twitching at folds of black veiling clumsily pinned to a shapeless felt hat.

The Lawsons had been down at Forbes Abbot for five days. Already Kate, taking some wine over to Mallory, noticed the difference in him. It was infinitesimal in such a short time – no one else would mark it – but she touched his forearm, and the tendons, taut as violin strings for as long as she could remember, gave a little under her hand.

'That stuff is utterly disabling,' said Mallory, nevertheless taking the glass. 'I know it of old.'

'Do you think we should circulate?' asked Kate.

'As chief mourners I think people should come and file past us,' said Polly. 'Like at a Greek wedding.'

Perhaps if she stood still long enough and smiled sweetly enough someone might come and pin money on her. It would have to be a lot of money because she owed a lot of money. An awful lot. With compound interest making it awfuller by the day, if not the hour. Swelling, like a monstrous succubus in a jar. Angrily Polly attempted to wrench her thoughts back to the present. She had vowed to keep . . . what? Fear? No, Polly had never been afraid. Let's just say to keep the image of the reptilian Billy Slaughter at bay. Squat, flat-eyed, repulsive to the touch. A flash from a childhood rhyme: 'I know a man. What man? The man with the power. What power? The power of voodoo . . .'

Polly grappled with her mind, pinned it still, screwed it down and forced it to pay attention to the assembled throng. She took in every detail – clothes, jewellery, mannerisms, voices – and decided they were a bunch of real saddoes. Average age seventy; not so much dressed as upholstered and held together with Steradent. At the thought of all those clacking dentures Polly burst out laughing.

'Polly!'

'Whoops. Sorry. Sorry, Dad.'

He looked dreadfully upset. Polly, suddenly contrite, vowed to make amends. What would please him most? Make him proud of her? She decided to mingle. She would not only mingle she would be absolutely charming to everyone, no matter how decayed or unintelligible. And if it made her father more amenable next time she asked for help – well, that would be a bonus. Her face, now transformed, became wanly sensitive. Her smile almost spiritual. She murmured, 'Catch you later,' to her parents and melted into the throng.

Polly knew hardly any of the people present, though several remembered her visiting her great-aunt as a little girl. One or two reminisced about this, often at interminable length. At one point she sat next to an extremely eccentric cousin of Carey's for a full five minutes, leaning deferentially close and noting the old woman's phrases and mannerisms, planning to imitate them later for the entertainment of others.

The vicar hove to – a portly figure, neither old nor young. He had a lot of soft, light brown hair of the sort described on shampoo bottles as flyaway. It certainly seemed to be doing its best at the moment, lifting and stirring about his head like a lively halo. He laid a damp hand on Polly's wrist.

'Would you believe, my dear, Mrs Crudge just asked me if I was enjoying the reception?'

Polly tried to look incredulous but found it hard. The question seemed to her both inoffensive and appropriate.

'Whatever happened to the word "wake"?'

'I don't understand.'

'Exactly! Totally "out of print" today.' He hooked quotation marks out of the air with his free hand. 'And yet, how metaphysically apropos. For it is but a single letter removed from that happy state that dear Miss Lawson presently enjoys. A-wake in the arms of her Heavenly Father.'

Jesus, thought Polly. She removed the vicar's hand from her arm.

'Look at Polly.' Mallory's tone was fond. Plainly his daughter had already more than compensated for her earlier thoughtless behaviour.

'I think more than enough people are looking at Polly as it is.'

This was true. Nearly everyone – and not only the men – were looking at Polly while pretending not to. Mainly they were looking at her slender, never-ending legs in their sheeny black tights. She also wore a black linen, long-line jacket apparently over nothing at all. Polly's skirt, usually no deeper than a cake frill, no doubt in deference to the gravity of the occasion was somewhat longer than usual. This one could almost have supported a soufflé.

Kate felt awkward then, feeling her terse comment had indicated resentment or, worse, jealousy of her daughter. Surely this couldn't be true? As a small, gingery man came towards them across the grass she smiled a relieved greeting, welcoming the distraction.

'Dennis!' Mallory spoke with great warmth. 'It's good to see you.'

'We'll be meeting tomorrow, as you know. But I just wanted to offer my sympathy. Mallory – my dear fellow.' Dennis Brinkley held out his hand, the back of which was lightly stroked with reddish-gold hairs. 'Your aunt really was a quite exceptional person.'

'Shall I take those for you?' Kate offered to relieve Dennis of his half-full plate. She had tasted the walnut swirls and sausage twists as Benny was arranging them in the kitchen.

'No, indeed.' Dennis gripped his plate. 'I shall eat up every bit.'

You'll be the only one who does then, thought Kate. We'll be finding twists and swirls in the garden urns and undergrowth for years to come. Archeologists, centuries hence, would be chipping away at the extraordinary shapes, bewildered as to what use they could ever have been put. Kate, long familiar with Benny's culinary skills, had brought down several boxes of party bits from Marks and Spencer, taking care to explain they were for emergencies only. Before leaving for the church she had discreetly placed them on an out-of-the-way table in the shrubbery. Long before her return all had vanished.

Mallory was thanking Dennis for his help at the time of Carey's death.

For taking charge of what he called 'all the technical stuff'. He was also thinking how fit and full of vitality Dennis appeared. There were nine years between them and Mallory couldn't help thinking a stranger could well guess wrongly which way the difference lay.

Mallory had been eleven when Dennis Brinkley had first come to his aunt's house to check over some details on her foreign investments. Newly attached to a brokerage house and financial consultancy, Dennis was extremely intelligent and articulate when it came to discussing figures, but otherwise paralysingly shy. The firm was then known as Fallon and Pearson, though the latter had long since died. By the time George Fallon retired Dennis had been with the firm thirty years, for the last twenty as a full partner. Inevitably he had opened up and become more confident over such a long period but there were still few people to whom he was really close. Mallory was one. Benny Frayle, another.

'Is a morning appointment all right for you, Kate? I expect there'll be a lot of . . . um . . . straightening-up to do.' Dennis sounded uncertain, not quite sure what 'straightening' involved. He himself was extremely neat and tidy, both about his person and his affairs. His daily cleaner – that same Mrs Crudge – and excellent secretary were hardly run off their feet.

Kate assured him that the morning would be fine.

A sudden burst of raucous jollity, quickly shushed, caused all three to turn their heads.

'Ah,' said Mallory. 'I see Drew and Gilda have been kind enough to come and pay their respects.'

'Not at my invitation, I assure you.' The absence of any trace of warmth in Dennis's voice said it all. Andrew Latham was the other partner at what had now become Brinkley and Latham. He had never had any dealings with Mallory's aunt. Indeed, as she rarely went into the office, they had probably not even met.

'No doubt he has his reasons.' Mallory's tone was dry in its turn.

'Oh, yes. He'll have those all right.'

Kate murmured an excuse and turned again towards the assembled company, hoping to be of some use rather than simply absorb yet more consoling sound bites.

She saw David and Helen Morrison standing by themselves and looking rather isolated. They were representing Pippins Direct, the firm that had rented the orchard from Carey for the past twenty years, maintained it and sold the apples and their juice. Kate knew that Mallory was keen for this arrangement to continue. But as she started to make her way towards them another couple beat her to it, introduced themselves and all four started talking.

One of the Oasis T-shirts was sitting under a monkey puzzle tree drinking apple wine and had plainly been doing so for some time. Kate sighed and looked about for the other, who seemed to have disappeared. But she could see Benny's wig with its fat, golden curls like brass sausages, bobbing about. Benny herself, hot and flustered, was collecting plates and glasses, and stacking them on a nearby tray.

'Mother!' Polly sprang up as Kate approached, abandoning Brigadier Ruff-Bunney, the elderly, wheelchair-bound relative from Aberdeen. The poor man, vividly describing his cataract operation under local anaesthetic, was left in mid-scrape.

'It was so nice talking to you.' Polly gave him a brilliant smile, took Kate's arm and pulled her away. 'Hope I die before I get old.'

'Bet The Who aren't singing that today. Have you seen that girl who's supposed to be helping?'

'You mean the one getting legless under the monkey tree?'

'No. I mean the other one.'

'Uh-huh.'

'Someone should give poor Benny a hand.'

Benny Frayle had been 'poor Benny' for as long as Polly could remember. As a little girl she had run the words together, thinking this one long sound was Benny's true name. One day Kate overheard her, explained, then asked Polly not to do it again as it might be thought hurtful.

Now Polly watched her mother relieving Great-aunt Carey's companion of a heavy tray. Noticed how she managed to do it casually without fuss; without the slightest implication that Benny had taken on more than she could handle. She was good at that. Polly could never imagine her mother deliberately setting out to make someone feel small. To find their weakest point and jab and jab. Her father either, come to that. Sometimes Polly, excellently versed in both these activities, wondered where she got it from.

'I'll come and help.' She called out the offer on impulse to Kate, just now passing within hearing distance. Then was immediately resentful at making a decision so much to her own disadvantage. Still, at least she'd be out of the crumblies' bony reach. Quite honestly, for one or two it hardly seemed worth the trip back from the graveyard.

'Fine,' Kate shouted back, trying not to sound surprised. 'See you in a minute, then.'

She made her way towards the house via the vegetable garden and across the croquet lawn. The kitchen opened off a rather grand, iron-ribbed Edwardian conservatory. A few people, all strangers to Kate, lolled, lightly comatose, on steamer chairs and a huge, rattan sofa. She smiled in a friendly and sympathetic manner as she climbed over their feet.

The kitchen was empty apart from Croydon, Aunt Carey's cat, asleep in his basket on which Benny had tied a black silk bow. Kate remembered the day Carey brought the animal home. Mallory's aunt had been making a visit to a friend that necessitated changing trains at Croydon where she found it in a wicker basket, jammed behind a stack of wooden crates. Both cat and carrier were absolutely filthy. Carey had described later how the half-starved creature had sat upright and with great dignity in piles of mess, looking hopefully about him and mewing.

After raging at the station staff for ten minutes without repeating herself Carey took a cab to the town centre, bought a basket, food, a dish and some towels, cancelled the rest of her journey and took the cat home. Cleaned, it proved to be extremely beautiful, with a cream and amber freckled coat, a reddish orange ruff and huge golden eyes. It proved as grateful as a cat could be – which admittedly isn't saying a lot – purring extensively and sitting on her lap whenever she wanted to work at her tapestry or read the papers.

Kate bent down and stroked Croydon. She said, 'Don't be sad,' but the cat just yawned. It was hard to know whether it was sad or not. Cats' faces don't change much.

Kate pulled on a pair of rubber gloves, squirted some washing-up liquid into the sink and turned the taps full on. The glasses were rather beautiful and she didn't want to risk them in the machine. When the sink was half full she placed them gently into the sparkling suds and carefully washed them up. There was no sign of Polly. Kate had never really thought there would be. So, why offer? And what was Polly doing instead?

Even as she chided herself at the pettiness of such an exercise, Kate retreated to the dining room and through it to the terrace steps. She saw Polly straight away, sitting on a low wooden stool, talking, laughing, tossing her hair back from her face. She was with Ashley Parnell, Appleby House's nearest neighbour. He was in a green and white striped deck-chair; resting as he always was, his state of health not being conducive to leaping about. But even at a distance, and not at all well, his beauty was still remarkable. Kate watched as he replied to Polly, who immediately became gravely attentive, locking her glance into his. Resting her chin in the palm of her hand and leaning forward.

Kate saw Ashley's wife, Judith, moving towards the couple, walking rather urgently as if in a hurry. She stood over them, brusquely interrupting their discourse and gesturing towards the lane. Then, half helping, half tugging her husband up from his chair they walked away, Ashley turning to smile goodbye.

Polly waved, then immediately got up and lay back in the deckchair he had just vacated. She didn't move for a long while. Just sat and sat, as if in a daze, gazing up at the clear blue sky.

Half an hour later and Judith Parnell was just beginning to recover, though still feeling somewhat shaky.

'Sorry about that – dragging you away. I really felt quite strange.'

'Are you all right now?'

'Fine. Just needed a rest.'

Judith looked across to where her husband was sitting in a high-backed wicker chair, an angora blanket thrown across his knees despite the heat of the day. He was gazing, rather longingly it seemed to her, across their front garden in the direction of Appleby House.

Judith observed his shining dark blue eyes, the elegant plane of his cheek and perfect jaw and momentarily felt sick in earnest. So far the ravages of this mysterious illness were slight. But these were early days – only three months since the first symptoms appeared. Unable to help herself Judith crossed the room and laid a hand on his soft, pale yellow hair. Ashley jerked his head away.

'Sorry, darling.' Lately he had begun to hate being touched. Judith frequently forgot this and now recalled that she had also tried to hold his hand at breakfast.

'No, I'm sorry.' He wrapped her fingers round his own and squeezed them gently. 'My scalp hurts today, that's all.'

'Poor Ash.'

Could that be the real reason? Was a tender scalp a symptom of his illness? As they had still not discovered what that illness was, it proved impossible to say. He could be making it up, using it to keep her at a distance. Perhaps he was falling out of love.

There was a time she could have touched him anywhere and everywhere at any hour of the day or night. They had sex once in his office, sprawled across the desk behind unlocked doors minutes before a Japanese business delegation was due to be shown in. Now he had not approached her for weeks.

Judith would never admit to anyone, and had only once, in a painfully sharp moment of insight, admitted to herself, that she was glad Ashley was ill. Ill meant out of circulation. She wanted him to get better – of course she did – but perhaps not a hundred per cent better. Not restored to his former Apollonian strength and beauty, for then she would be back on the old treadmill. Jealously assessing every woman he looked at or spoke to, needing to denigrate everything about them: their hair, their skin, their eyes, their clothes. Not aloud, of course. It would never do for Ashley to become aware that she was terrified of losing him; to put the idea in his mind.

Judith's thoughts flew nervously back to the wake in Carey Lawson's garden. Tired as he was, Ashley had seemed really happy to be out and about, mixing with people. And genuinely regretful when she had dragged him home on the pretence of a sudden attack of nausea. Of course that might have been because of the Lawsons' ghastly daughter flashing her legs and teeth at him, half naked like a tart in a brothel. Teasing surely, for what interest could an ailing middle-aged man have for a young, strong, lovely . . .? Judith fought to remain calm, breathing slowly and evenly. She had got him away – that was the main thing. The girl was here for the funeral; a day or two would see the back of her.

But rumour in the village already had it that her parents might be moving down for good. So Kate, with her freckled, apricot skin and soft ash-blonde hair pinned up any-old-how, would be a stone's throw away. In her late forties she looked, in spite of the dreadful time she had been having with Mallory, a good ten years younger. Ashley had always liked Kate. She was gentle and intelligent, quite sexy in a school-marmish sort of way – oh sod it.

'What's the matter?'

'I'm all right.'

'Are you sure?' Ashley looked worried. He started nervously brushing the skin on his arms. 'Maybe you could put off this meeting tonight, Jude. Say you're not well.'

'Better not. It's a new contact. Don't want to make a bad impression.'

'What does he do again?'

'Manufactures surgical instruments. A small firm but apparently stable. Seems his accountant's retiring so he's looking round.'

'Isn't it strange you're not meeting at the factory?'

'Not at all. Business meetings often take place at hotels.'

Just then the fax began chattering in Judith's office, a tiny, dark place next to the stairs. 'The visitor's parlour', they had larkily christened it when first moving into their Victorian villa. Where the gentry would have presented their cards and been offered a dry sherry and a caraway biscuit before moving into the larger sitting room to exchange discreet gossip. They had seen themselves entertaining too in a modest way but somehow it had never come about. And now, with every spare penny going on Ashley's health, they couldn't afford it

'I know who it is.' She moved away from the window, widening the space between herself and her husband. Giving Ashley what he called 'room to breathe'. 'It's slimy Alec.'

'Is that any way to speak of a client?'

'Faxing his phoney expenses. He's claiming for a new Alfa Romeo, which was stolen almost as soon as it was delivered. Alas—'

'The paperwork was still in the glove compartment.'

'You're way ahead of me.'

'Tell him to chuck it.'

Judith made her way reluctantly into the hall, marvelling at the casual ease with which the solution had been offered. It wasn't Ashley's fault. He had no idea how difficult, desperate even, their plight had become. He thought his wife had given up her Aylesbury office and laid off her clerk purely so she could work from home and look after him. But that was only part of it.

The heart of the problem was that, until Ashley's illness had been properly diagnosed, his insurance would not pay out and the disability allowance people had also dug their heels in. And Judith could not afford to keep them both and also pay rent for an office and wages.

An unforeseen by-product of the decision to work from home had been a suggestion from one high-profile customer that, as her overheads

13

would now be so much lower, his fees should be reduced. Instead of explaining the circumstances behind her decision, worry and nervous strain provoked a quick, sharply worded refusal. He transferred his account elsewhere.

The foot-and-mouth crisis in British farming took its toll and several of her agricultural clients chose this year to give up. Then there was the young couple with a thriving specialist food business who decided, with advice and support from the Internet, to go it alone.

So there was no question, thought Judith, watching the neatly perforated pages of immaculately printed lies falling softly into her in-tray, of telling slimy Alec to chuck it.

Meanwhile, at a much more glamorous residence just a few miles south in the village of Bunting St Clare, the Lathams had arrived back from Carey Lawson's interment.

Gilda began to undo a glittery black lace coat, which was practically splitting apart under the strain of trying to decently constrain her massive bust. You could almost hear it sighing with relief as the buttons popped. Underneath lay several acres of taffeta, ruched rather in the manner of an Austrian blind: a dress as wide as it was short. Flesh coloured, it appeared briefly, to her husband's startled gaze, horribly like a crumpled version of the real thing. She pirouetted slowly.

'How do I look?'

'A credit to your mortician, my love.'

'Don't mumble. I've told you before.' She pulled down the hem of her dress. It sprang up again. She sighed. 'If that wasn't a waste of a beautiful afternoon perhaps you'd tell me what is?'

Recognising his wife's remark as an opening salvo rather than a serious question Andrew did not immediately reply. He was a man with a headful of turbulent thoughts – gross, violent, implacable – and a mouthful of ever-ready platitudes – polite, conciliatory, gutless. Sometimes these two achievements coincided, as they did now.

'I'm sorry you didn't enjoy it, sweetheart.'

Define the waste of a beautiful afternoon. Well, there was dragging the Mountfield over the bloody lawn while the trouble and strife lay in an overstuffed hammock crushing chocolate brazils between her fearsome mandibles and telling you your stripes weren't straight. Or there was having a highly expensive lunch out with a partner very much not of your choice, who masticated with her mouth open, gobbling three-quarters of every course before complaining that it tasted peculiar and sending it back to the kitchen. But actually the worst, the very, very worst waste of a beautiful afternoon Andrew Latham dare not entertain in his mind even for a second for fear the thought might be catching.

'And what did I say before we left?' asked Gilda.

'Does my bum look big in this?'

'There you go again. Mumbling.' She was removing a hatpin as long as a skewer with a lump of amber stuck on the end. 'I said, they won't want any of your pathetic, quote, jokes, unquote.'

'Did you?' Andrew couldn't take his eyes off the pin. The lump looked to him like the glossy turd of a small mammal fed entirely on butterscotch.

'When that poor old man told us he'd recently lost his wife and you offered to help him look I didn't know where to put myself.'

'I misunderstood—'

'Rubbish. I know you think you've got to be the life and soul of every party but this was a funeral, for heaven's sake.'

'A *funeral*!!?'

'Don't start.' She took the hat off. It was a black, gauzy affair, built rather like a flying saucer with a riot of strangely coloured vegetation dangling from the rim. 'I don't see why we had to drag ourselves there in the first place. She was Dennis's client, not yours.' She laid the hat carefully on a gold Dralon sofa the size of a barge. 'He won't think any more of you.'

For a fraction of a second Andrew lost it. 'I don't give a monkey's arse what he thinks of me.'

'Language,' cried Gilda, delighted.

'Yes, well – that's what I use when I wish to communicate. Call me old-fashioned—'

'It's not as if you need to tout for business.'

Tout? Ah well, common is as common does.

'And who do you have to thank for that, Andrew?'

'You, my little bonbon.'

'And what do I get in return?'

Automaton man, that's what you get. A smiling skull. A mind full of loathing that's always somewhere else. Mechanical sex. If you were a human being you'd know the difference.

He murmured, 'Gilly . . .' Her bottom lip pushed forward, full and shiny like a scarlet sausage. 'Gill*eee* . . .' He crossed the room, bent down and kissed her cheek. The skin was dry and slightly pitted. Her hair smelled of dead flowers. 'Why don't you go and put those tooties up? And Drew will bring you a nice G and T.'

'You think that's the answer to everything.'

To her husband it was the answer to everything. Without it he certainly could not have got up in the morning, forced down his greasy breakfast, transported himself to the office and sat there most of the day, let alone dragged himself home. He said: 'What would you like then, angel?'

Without a trace of affection or even interest Gilda told him what she would like.

'And a good one this time. For once.'

She walked off, holding her glittery lace coat between two fingers, trailing it across the carpet like someone on a catwalk. All sorts of people

15

had seemingly once told her she should be a model. She had even done a course but then Daddy put his foot down. Andrew had sympathised, shaking his head. It seemed to him Gilda would have made an excellent model. Twelve stone lighter, thirty years younger plus a million quids' worth of plastic surgery and Kate Moss would have been throwing herself off Beachy Head.

He selected a tumbler, iced it, gurgled in the gin. Then took a long swallow and waited, gauging the effect. Balance was all. Happiness on the head of a pin. He was aiming for the point at which faith arose. That exquisite, almost mystical moment offering a powerful convincement that only good times were round the corner and the future was shiny with hope. Another swig. And a third. Why not? Why fucking not? One thing was certain – he could never give her a good one sober.

And yet, and yet . . .

Once upon a time, and that barely a decade ago, Andrew Latham had imagined, in marrying Gilda Berryman, he had landed himself the bargain of the century.

Starving people are prepared to cope with anything as long as food is part of the deal. Andrew had never been starving, of course – he'd never even been really hungry – but he had been minus all the things that, to him, made life worth living. His own home, a decent car, really good clothes, travel, money – not just in your pocket but in your life. Fine wine, eating in swanky places, flagging down a taxi to travel spitting distance.

To hear Andrew talk it wasn't really his fault he lacked all these things. He hadn't had the luck, that was the truth of it. He'd had energy, enthusiasm, ideas – gosh, the ideas he'd had. The businesses he'd started, the dreams. To meet him you'd swear here was a man born for success. And nearly always you'd be right, for success attended most of Andrew's ventures. The trouble was, after a while it became clear that the price of this success was the loss of everything that made existence fun. No time for a drink with the lads or a bet on the gee-gees. When the sun did come out no chance to lie in it. Up every morning at some ungodly hour, which meant no all-night casinos. Then there were women – more time-consuming than anything else in the world, but oh, how very much more worthwhile. Problem being, you had to be there for them. Take them out, talk to them, listen to them, go to the movies and for walks and drives and picnics. Dance them, schmooze them, kiss them a lot. How was a man supposed to do all this and run a business?

Not that the businesses were always legitimate. Indeed, for a while he sailed very close to the wind. Someone he went to the races with lent him a few hundred quid to put on a dead cert that turned out to be a dead loss. Stony-broke, he was invited to assist this man in whatever way proved necessary for as long as it took to pay it off. The harsh alternative having no appeal – Andrew rather liked his knees – he agreed. It wasn't so bad.

16

Sometimes he drove a van, usually at night, to an appointed spot, waited while boxes of various sizes were loaded, then drove to another address where they would be rapidly unloaded. Several times he took heavy suitcases to a dry-cleaners in Limehouse, where they were received without thanks or comment. From time to time he was a lookout man and it was during one of these occasions that the arrangements between himself and his erstwhile creditor came to sudden grief.

At the time Andrew was in the garden of a large house near Highgate, keeping an eye open for visitors, dogs, roving police cars. The house had been dark when the thief he was covering entered but, after a while, a light came on in an upstairs room. Soon after that there was a lot of shouting and almost simultaneously a siren wailed.

The burglar came racing out of the house, pausing only to stuff something into Andrew's pocket and drop a bag at his feet before vaulting over the shrubbery wall and vanishing into the night. Andrew watched the police car turn into the gates, saw the officers admitted to the house, then ran like the clappers. He left the bag, which contained tools, having no wish to be charged with 'going equipped to steal' and, as soon as the first Tube started running, hopped on to the Piccadilly Line and left London as well.

He still had his 'souvenir' of that unpleasant experience – the burglar's picks thrust into his pocket. If asked why he'd kept them Andrew couldn't have told you. Certainly he never intended to take up a life of crime. That one close call had completely flaked him out.

Eventually the Tube had fetched up in Uxbridge. With just the clothes he stood up in he registered at an employment agency and the next day started the first of what was to prove a long line of undemanding semi-clerical jobs. He rented a room and then a studio flat, eventually braving a trip back to the Smoke to collect the things he had left behind. But the work was so dreary it drove him half mad with ennui. This naturally led to absenteeism, extended lunch hours and constant sackings. The fact that computers bored him witless didn't help. They were like a foreign landscape without a map, though he could, just about, cope with simple word processing.

What to do? Andrew had often thought that the most pleasant way out of his dilemma was to meet a rich *patronne* – someone who would support him in the manner to which he hoped to become accustomed in exchange for witty conversation, immense respect and a lifetime of devotion and gratitude. Now, instead of just dreaming he decided to do something about it. He began to advertise in the lonely hearts columns, describing himself as a managing director (GSOH, own home and car) so no one would think he was after their money. Naturally he was contacted by lots of women who did not have their own home, had a car that wouldn't start and such a GSOH they laughed like drains when discovering his real circumstances. Apart from the one who threw Bailey's Irish Cream all

17

down his tie. He was on the point of jumping off the nearest railway bridge when he met Gilda.

At the time he was working at the extremely upmarket Palm Springs Hotel and had been there nearly two months. The main part of his job was liaising on the telephone between the restaurant chefs and their many suppliers, taking the flak from both sides when something went wrong, which was every day.

Attached to the hotel was a health club and spa. The subscription, ostentatiously costly, kept the numbers down and the riffraff out. Although there were stern rules against any mingling with the guests, when he thought himself unobserved Drew would slip into the changing rooms, disguise himself in expensive goggles and discreet unlogoed trunks, and swim in the pool.

He watched the women while seeming not to. The majority were well preserved rather than young: too thin, baked to a hard caramel under the sun lamps and clanking with money. He caught sight of one doing the crawl, her arm breaking the water and curving upwards, dazzling bracelets falling away from her wrist, then tumbling back as the arm plunged down. She wore rings on every finger, including a wedding ring. They nearly all did.

Gilda stood out from the rest. Even then she was plump. Around a hundred and fifty pounds, Andrew thought as he sat, balanced nicely on a tickling jet, in the Jacuzzi, and watched Gilda walk across artificial grass towards the pool. She wore a heavily boned flowered swimsuit with a frilly skirt attached. Standing at the edge for several minutes she finally attempted a dive but only succeeded in falling clumsily into the water. She swam in circles using a splashy dog paddle.

Andrew began to assess the possibilities. She wore no ring but that didn't necessarily signify. Her skin was creamy pale, she had a lot of flossy, fair hair and while never likely to turn heads, was not entirely unattractive. He dressed, slipped out of the fire exit and waited for her to leave. As she crossed the hotel car park someone waved and called, 'Hi, Gilda,' so then he knew her name. She drove away in a mouthwatering BMW 328i. Andrew looked up her details in the club file and very promising they were too. She was single and lived on Mount Pleasant, a gated cluster of large, many-roomed houses surrounded by lawns and beautifully designed gardens and known locally as Millionaires' Row. The telephone number was included on the card but the box for her age was blank.

Fraternising with guests and club members might have been forbidden but gossip between members of the staff about them was not. It was rife, and jollied up their mundane office hours no end. Drew had only to mention the magnificent car to hear all about the Berrymans, *père et fille*.

He was a self-made man. Started with a single broker's yard in the early seventies, expanded into a chain, sold that. Bought into sports equipment and did very well. Went into business with a couple of creative youths looking for backing for their virtual reality games. One of these took off into the stratosphere, making Charlie Berryman a fortune but leaving the lads somewhat bewildered as to the modesty of their own profits. After this Berryman played the markets, investing shrewdly and selling his investments even more shrewdly.

So far, thought Andrew, so satisfactory. But what of Gilda? Why wasn't there a husband in the picture? Was a wedding perhaps imminent? Tania Travis, Foreign Booking, was able to put Drew straight on that score. Goes without saying with all that money, men came sniffing round. She'd go out with them for a bit, Gilda, then something always went wrong. Obviously Tarn couldn't say exactly what, not being in the picture, so to speak. What was Gilda like? Well, like most rich people everything had to go her way and she could be a bit sharp if it didn't. But Tarn'd come across worse. Take that cow Melanie Bradstock . . .

Andrew went out to view the house but without much success. The estate was surrounded by a circular twelve-foot-high wall joined by huge, ornately styled gates. These hung between bronze pillars and in one of them was set an electronic checking system. Close by stood a sentry box. When Drew, in his shabby Fiesta, prepared to park for a closer look, a man in a uniform came out of the box, stared at him and wrote something down in a little book.

Effecting an introduction to Gilda seemed impossible. The circles in which they moved could hardly be further apart. He would have to rely on the old bumping into her 'accidentally on purpose' trick. This wasn't easy either. He had one day off a week and spent it parked in Mount Pleasant Drive, planning to tail her when she came out. He did this for a month: result nil.

Then he decided to follow her next time she came to the club. This would involve leaving work in the middle of a shift, which would mean the sack, but there was everything to play for and it was a crap job anyway.

Gilda drove into Amersham to have her hair dried at Mane Line after the swim. Drew blocked her way on the narrow pavement just as she was coming out. They dodged one way then the other, saying, 'Sorry.'

'My fault,' said Andrew. Then: 'Haven't we . . . that is . . . I'm sure I've seen you. Was it at the Springs Hotel? It's . . . Gilda, right?'

And that was that, more or less. Amazing how it never fails. People are rarely suspicious if you call them by their name. Which is incredible when you think how easy it is to get hold of a person's name – and all their other details come to that.

He explained he had nearly an hour to kill before an appointment. Would she possibly be kind enough . . . awful cheek, really . . . to have some coffee with him?

Gilda came over all fluttery but agreed, yes she would.

19

After this first meeting their courtship proceeded at a slowish pace but in a very satisfactory manner. She was lonely and vulnerable. Andrew, an expert in the art of seduction, played the part of an affectionate friend. Only gradually, as their meetings became more frequent, was he seen to be falling in love.

Meanwhile, between times, he worked on his cover story. He was staying with an ex-colleague while looking for a house, having sold his London flat in the Barbican. His business was property development, mainly on the coast of Southern Italy and in Capri. Rather more glamorous than Spain and not quite so easy to check up on.

He managed to get a five-thousand-pound loan from his bank. Dumping the Fiesta, he hired a smarter car and began to wine and dine Gilda. He bought one beautiful suit and prayed it wasn't money down the drain. He met her father and disliked him on sight.

There are all sorts of self-made men and Charlie Berryman was the sort who rubbed your nose in it. Within the first ten minutes you knew more about his humble beginnings than was almost decent. You knew about his contempt for the silver spoon brigade, equalled only by that for the spongers and creepers and crawlers at the bottom of the heap. As for the so-called asylum seekers – cram 'em in a ship with all the layabouts and do-gooders, tow it out to sea and blow the lot to smithereens.

His face was as ugly as his opinions and almost as ugly as his furniture. Andrew, knowing how much hung on this foul creature's opinion of him, tried to be pleasant without appearing ingratiating. He nodded and smiled from time to time and occasionally exchanged affectionate glances with Gilda. He felt almost fond of her at that moment, and certainly sympathetic. What a life, he thought, growing up with this God-awful cretin. It's remarkable she's as nice as she is.

When he judged the time to be right i.e. when he was down to his last two hundred quid – Andrew proposed. Gilda radiantly accepted, her happiness palpable. So much so that Andrew had to make quite an effort to detach himself emotionally. Such joy made him quite uncomfortable.

Quickly summoned to Mount Pleasant, as he approached the house he heard, through an open window, Berryman bellowing and Gilda weeping. She cried out: 'You do . . . you know you do . . . every time . . .'

Andrew rang the bell. It was almost ten minutes before the door was opened. Berryman jerked his head, walked back into the huge, thickly carpeted hall and stood leaning on a marble table with one hand inside his jacket, resting against his chest like Napoleon. Behind him a job lot of large, gilt-framed oil paintings – mayors, aldermen or other civic worthies – lined the walls of the stairwell. No doubt one was meant to assume they were Berryman's ancestors. If it hadn't been such a crucially important moment in his life Andrew would have laughed in the man's face.

'Mr Berryman.'

'I understand you want to marry Gilda.'

'Yes. I promise to try—'

'And I can promise you something, sunshine. The day you marry her is the last day she gets a penny out of me. Alive or dead. And that goes for you an' all.' His speech finished, he stood there, watching Andrew closely.

Andrew could see, in spite of the belligerence of his words, that Berryman wasn't really angry. His eyes sparkled with spite, his lips kept tweaking at the corners into a grin.

Andrew fought to keep his expression blank while his mind ran around like a rat in a cage. Was Berryman's threat truly meant? Would he hold fast to it if Gilda defied him? Or was it bluff – designed to test his, Andrew's, motives?

Memory spoke and he suddenly heard Tania talking about Gilda's boyfriends. 'She'd go out with them for a bit but then something always went wrong.' This is it, thought Andrew. This is what goes wrong.

So, what to do now? He wouldn't let go – not at this stage. He had made an investment, both serious and costly, in his future. He couldn't abandon it – he couldn't go back to the costive blood-letting jobs in hellish offices for rotten money. Or dreams and schemes that fate decided would always be stillborn. He would call the bastard's bluff and play the cards as they came.

'I don't want your money, Mr Berryman. I want Gilda. I love her.'

He heard a soft, plaintive cry then, a little whimper from behind a door, half open at the far end of the hall. She must have been standing there all the time.

'My daughter's got expensive tastes.'

'I'll look after her.' Andrew, about to run expressively on, checked himself. Quit while you're ahead, boyo. While you can still sound sincere.

'You'll have to look after her. 'Cause I shan't lift a bloody finger.'

'Frankly, Mr Berryman,' said Andrew, 'I don't give a damn.'

At this Gilda had come charging across the shag pile and into his arms. Then she turned and seared the distance between herself and her father with a hate-filled glance.

He bared his teeth and said, 'Plenty of time.'

Gilda wanted the date set straight away. The earliest the registrar's offices were available was in one month less three days; as it happened Andrew's birthday. He returned to the bank in Causton for another loan. Unsurprisingly, as he had made not a single repayment on the previous one, it was refused. He explained that the present application was for wedding expenses and mentioned the bride's name. Magic! The forms materialised as if conjured from the air, as did a cup of Earl Grey and some chocolate Bath Olivers, or would he rather have a sherry? Andrew chose the sherry, agreed that five thousand pounds was nothing for a wedding these days and accepted double.

Afterwards he stood on the pavement in Causton High Street and seriously considered doing a runner. He was ten grand up and he still had the suit. Within days, if not hours, the money would start seeping out of his wallet on its way to enrich caterers, florists, printers and car-hire merchants. And all for nothing. Wasn't it?

Andrew bought a copy of *The Times* and slipped into the Soft Shoe Café for a cappuccino and a bit of a think. He had gambled all his life. As a child he could not even play conkers without betting on the outcome. Now here he was at the last crap table in town.

The choices were limited. He could risk going through with the whole grisly procedure, betting on a change of heart from Berryman once he realised Gilda was getting married anyway, even without a penny piece to her name. He could go through with it accepting that Berryman might well not come round for a very long time, if at all. Unless . . . weren't grandchildren supposed to heal rifts of this nature? At the very thought Andrew's lips congealed. He nearly regurgitated his coffee. There would be no children. He *loathed* children. Final option, he could just scarper.

Even as he brought this idea forward Andrew knew it was a no-no. He had never, ever been this close to this much money in his whole life and he knew the odds against it happening again were astronomical. So he went along with it, admired invitation cards embossed with silver bells and ribbons, discussed the merits of mignonette as opposed to gypsophila to accompany pink rosebuds, and struggled to stay awake as Gilda went in and out of fitting rooms wearing various outfits, size eighteen. When he proposed she had been a sixteen but every day since, she admitted coyly, had somehow added a pound or two of sheer happiness. In the few hours she had to spare they looked at houses.

He wondered more than once during this waiting period what, if anything, Gilda might be bringing to the marriage in her own right. Savings, jewellery, a share portfolio. Did the BMW actually belong to her? Far too canny to ask even the most oblique questions in this regard, Andrew kept his fingers crossed as more days ticked by.

Then, a few hours before the wedding eve, there was a message that Charlie Berryman wanted to see him. This time the meeting was at a solicitor's office in Uxbridge. Andrew presented himself – not too apprehensive. He was marrying money in two days' time and believed no one could stop him.

It was Berryman himself who sat behind the desk; the solicitor leaned up against the water cooler. Andrew was not asked to sit down. It was explained to him that he had been investigated and found wanting on the matter of property ownership in foreign parts – or anywhere else come to that. As regarded financial or any other sort of integrity his reputation stank.

'You're a gold-digging tosser,' concluded Berryman. 'But my daughter loves you. And, unlike the others, you seem prepared to see this farce through to the bitter end to get your snout in the trough.'

'That's not fair!' cried Andrew. 'I shall marry her even if—'

'Spare me the bullshit. We both know what you are.' Charlie beckoned the solicitor, who came forward and handed a paper to Andrew. 'Sign that.'

'What is it?' He made no attempt to read the document.

'A pre-nuptial agreement,' explained the solicitor. 'In the event of irrevocable marital breakdown or divorce you are entitled to nothing.'

'Not a bleeding penny,' said Berryman.

'Well,' Andrew, his heartbeat quickening, threw the paper on the desk, 'as you've cast her off without "a bleeding penny", this is hardly relevant.'

'Gilda won't want for anything, I'll make sure of that. Sign it.'

Andrew shrugged, the epitome of cool. But his fingers, hardly able to hold the pen for excitement and relief, gave him away. He signed.

Berryman took back the contract. 'You're a heap of shit, Latham. And I hope before I snuff it I see you back in the gutter where you belong.'

Alas for Charlie's hopes, he died of a stroke followed by a brain haemorrhage just three years later. But he lived long enough to be reconciled to his daughter, who eventually had to agree that he had had her best interests at heart.

It was unfortunate for Andrew that the old man lived so long. Coming across the pre-nuptial amongst Berryman's papers Gilda returned it to the family solicitor with the instruction that it should still stand. Up to a year after the wedding or perhaps even a little longer, she might have torn it up, but by this time, in spite of Andrew's untiring, exhaustive efforts to act the part of devoted husband and lover, even she was beginning to see cracks in the façade, and sense behind them fear, greed and, worse of all, a massive indifference as to her welfare and happiness.

They lived comfortably, at least in material terms, in a handsome ranch-style bungalow with green shutters and a wide veranda. Ten rooms surrounded by an acre of attractive gardens and an open-air pool. The house, which Gilda had christened Bellissima, was in her name. She also had a decent allowance – enough, anyway, to buy Andrew a car on his forty-second birthday – a yellow Punto, R reg, but in pretty fair condition. The cream coupé, which she still drove, turned out to belong to Berryman and he refused to reinsure it to include another driver.

Andrew was expected to earn his living. At his age and with his work record there seemed – and here Berryman jabbed a callused finger hard into his son-in-law's solar plexus – little point in writing letters and seeking interviews.

George Fallon of Fallon and Brinkley, who had handled Berryman's affairs since he was heaving scrap iron about in the early seventies, was on the point of retiring. Charlie got his account safely transferred to Dennis Brinkley, then made an offer for Fallon's half of the business. As a fellow Lion and member of the Rotary Club he knew his approach would be favoured over several others.

There were two reasons for this purchase, neither even faintly altruistic. First, the company had grown to about ten strong and was doing extremely well, making the acquisition a good investment. And second, Gilda was becoming extremely uncomfortable at having a husband who either sat about the house all day or insisted on accompanying her wherever she went, even if it was just to see a girl friend. 'Also,' she further explained to her father, 'people are talking. I overheard this attendant at the pool – she was calling Andy a sycophantic leech.' Berryman did not know sycophantic but he knew leech all right and thought the smart little tottie had got it in one.

It took a long time for Gilda's disillusionment to become complete. Finally having found someone who loved her for herself alone, even when she started to suspect this was not true she could not bear to let the illusion go. She hung on through the discovery of her husband's lies about the past, his secret gambling and mounting debts. And through her never proven suspicions of other women. But each revelation gnawed and nibbled away at the heart of her earlier bewitchment until she awoke one morning and found that the illusion was no more and love had gone. And the dieback had been so gradual that this final discovery didn't even hurt.

Freedom felt strange at first, clean and empty like a cavity when a rotten tooth has been drawn. But, the human mind being what it is, the cavity did not remain empty for long. And in Gilda's case it was filled, degree by slow pleasurable degree, with the understanding that she now had another human being completely in her power. Without her Andrew, by now in his late forties, had nothing. No home, no food, no money. And no prospects of getting any of these either. His weakness, his inability ever to get his act together, had left him stranded. All washed up like the soft-shelled creatures left helpless on their backs when the tide goes out. Very occasionally he would murmur a request – perhaps for a new jacket, or some books. Or, even more occasionally, he might make a mild complaint when it would be briskly pointed out that if he didn't like the way things were round here he could always go. Except that he couldn't because he had nowhere to go.

Not a happy state of affairs. Gilda sometimes thought she might never experience happiness again – had indeed almost forgotten what it felt like. But one thing she did know: if you couldn't have happiness power was definitely the next best thing.

CHAPTER TWO

The Lawsons' appointment, already referred to by Dennis Brinkley, was for 10.30. At 10 a.m. Polly was still not up. She had been called twice and replied twice that she was getting dressed. Finally, instead of calling, Kate went into her room to find Polly still in bed. She wasn't even pretending to be asleep; just lying on her back and gazing at the ceiling.

'You know we're due in Causton at half-past ten.'

'No, I didn't.'

'I told you when I brought your tea.'

'So?' Polly sat up, shaking her dark curly hair. Scratching her scalp. Sighing. 'Why do I have to come anyway?'

'Because you have a bequest in her will.'

'Bequest.' The word was a scornful snort. 'Bet it's that rubbish cameo—'

'Listen!' Kate seized her daughter by the arm and half dragged her off the mattress. 'Don't you ever talk about Carey or her things like that. Especially in front of your father.'

'OK . . . OK . . .'

'You know how much he loved her.' Kate, exhausted by the previous day's activity and comforting her husband through a sleepless night, struggled to banish tears of weakness. 'I want you downstairs and ready to leave in ten minutes.'

In fact they were only slightly late for their appointment. It was 10.35 when they entered the light and elegant reception area, to be welcomed by a smartly dressed buxom woman with a slightly too gracious manner. An inscribed wooden Toblerone explained that she wished to be known as Gail Fuller. Next to the sign was a large bouquet of roses and creamy lilies in a crystal vase. Polly was impressed. She had pictured Dennis all on his own in a poky little hole surrounded by dusty box files and a prehistoric Amstrad.

Her impressedness deepened as they were led through the main office, which was large and open plan, taking up the whole floor of the building. Here were lots more desks, all personalised in some way: photographs, a smart executive toy, a plant, a stuffed animal, a cartoon. Each supported an iMac, the keyboards of which were pretty busy. A photocopier hummed. At diagonal corners of this space were two quite large glassed-in enclosures. Gail Fuller opened the door of the one with Dennis's name on and announced them.

Polly apologised prettily to Dennis as soon as they were all seated. She said their late arrival was all her fault and he must forgive her. This was said with much eyelash fluttering which, to Kate's secret satisfaction, hardly seemed to register.

'This is so exciting,' trilled Polly, thinking Dennis must be older than he looked. She remembered him, of course. As a child she had rather admired his red-gold, close-cropped hair, freckly countenance and chestnut-brown moustache. He had reminded her of Squirrel Nutkin. Now the gingery paws were opening a heavy crimson envelope; easing out the will. Dennis smoothed the heavy parchment, pinning it down under a butterfly paperweight. In spite of her totally negligible expectations Polly couldn't help a sudden tightening in her throat. It was like a scene in one of those old-fashioned crime stories that turned up sometimes on the box. Except then there would've been a murder first. Now that would liven things up. Dennis had started speaking.

'As I know you are already aware,' he smiled directly at Mallory, 'Appleby House and all the grounds pass without entail directly to yourself. I hope the arrangement with Pippins Direct will continue.'

'We've already spoken,' said Mallory. 'They're happy to carry on. And I'll be confirming it in writing later this week.'

'The rent at ten thousand pounds is modest but they are a small firm, organic and deeply conscientious. Your aunt would have been pleased at your decision.'

Polly wondered what profits this 'small firm' were actually raking in. It sounded to her as if the old lady had been a pushover and they were now creaming it. Maybe she could get her dad to take a closer look.

'There follows a number of small bequests,' continued Dennis, 'which, as executor, I will be glad to undertake.'

He started to list these in a droning monotone. Polly switched off and began to look about her, observing the activity outside. She pictured herself this time next year in the heart of the City in just such an environment and wondered what she would put on her desk. Something cool, certainly. No clacking silver balls – that was for sure. No photographs either – who would she want a photograph of? And if there was any green stuff it would definitely not be some run-of-the-mill garden centre takeaway.

As she mused along the lines of what form her rare exotic plant might take – weren't orchids rather common? And didn't they need a particular environment? – the door of the other private office opened. A man came out and strode across the room. A shortish dark man, somewhat younger than Dennis as well as much better-looking. She recognised him from the funeral where he had been laughing immoderately and drinking too much. She could see papers in his hand and watched as he gave them to a girl at the photocopier with a wide smile. All his actions appeared vigorous and lively, yet there was a strange artificiality about them as if he were acting a vitality he didn't really feel.

Polly wondered about him but in a detached, disinterested way. No man could possibly attract her at the moment. Overnight she had become immune to that particular virus.

Tuning back into the meeting (surely it must be her turn soon?) Polly heard Dennis says, 'After these bequests have been paid the residue of your aunt's estate, including her portfolio of investment trusts, is valued at just over three hundred thousand pounds.'

'I had no idea . . .' Mallory stumbled over the words. 'That is . . . thank you.'

'Regarding Benny Frayle—'

'Shouldn't she be here with us?' asked Kate.

'I've already talked to Benny, soon after Miss Lawson's death. Although Carey frequently attempted to reassure her as to her future, you know how . . . um . . .'

Utterly stupid? suggested Polly silently. Like, dim as a camel.

'. . . apprehensive she can be. I was able to reassure her. For as long as she wishes she may live in her flat over the stables. Should conditions arise that necessitate the sale of the house . . .' Dennis ended on an upwards inflection, his eyebrows twitching into auburn crescents.

'There's no question of that.' Kate reached out and took her husband's hand. 'We have plans.'

'Excellent. But should it ever come about, funds must be found to purchase comparable accommodation, which must then be put in her name.'

Mallory said, 'I understand.'

Polly gave a soft whistle.

Kate glared at Polly.

'Her pension fund, even allowing for the somewhat volatile market, is still very healthy. She should be able to live in a reasonable degree of comfort on the annuity. There is also a sizeable sum available in blue chips. In the case of her—' Dennis stopped speaking and stared bleakly for a moment into space. Then cleared his throat to continue – 'shall we say, demise, this money will revert to the estate.

'Finally, Polly.' He smiled at her and waited a moment before speaking. He had the air of a man with one hand behind his back and that hand holding an exciting surprise. If he had not been such a nice person one would have said he looked sly.

Polly smiled back and, in spite of herself, felt again that flicker of excitement. She knew what the chances were of getting any serious money but even a mouldy old cameo brooch might fetch something. What if it turned out to be incredibly rare and famous, like that timepiece in *Only Fools and Horses*?

'Just over five years ago I advised your aunt to realise a portfolio of shares which were offering only mediocre returns and to invest the proceeds in pharmaceuticals. These have succeeded almost beyond my wildest expectations.'

There was an hiatus. No one liked to ask how wild these expectations had been in the first place. Not even Polly.

'Your aunt's instructions were that these shares, valued as to the market's closing index on the day of her death were to go to her great-niece—'

Polly sucked in air, a great indrawn gasp. Then apologetically covered her mouth with her hand. She did not breathe out.

'– on the occasion of her twenty-first birthday. The sum presently stands at a little over sixty thousand pounds.'

No one spoke. Dennis beamed kindly at Polly. Mallory smiled too, overwhelmed by this example of his aunt's generosity. Kate did not smile. Even as she chided herself for meanness of spirit her heart sank. Polly exhaled with a 'whoosh', then started to laugh.

'God . . .' She thrust her hands through the air, reaching above her head. A triumphant winner's gesture, seizing a crown. 'I don't believe it! Sixty K . . .'

'Congratulations, my dear,' said Dennis.

'And as I'm nearly twenty-one—'

'You were twenty last month,' snapped Kate.

The others looked at her. Even Mallory could not conceal his disappointment at this deliberate puncturing of such an exciting moment. He said 'We'll have to celebrate, Poll.'

'Let's get some champagne on the way home.' Polly had stopped laughing but her voice was still unstable with merriment. It seemed that any minute it might tip over into a giggle. 'And tonight we can go somewhere really super for dinner.' She paused then, perhaps becoming aware that such levity might be seen as insensitive, placed both hands in her lap and regarded them soberly. Mentally she counted to five, then looked up, her face grave.

'How very kind of Great-aunt Carey to remember me in this way.'

This sudden volte-face, unconvincing even to Mallory, led to a somewhat awkward pause.

Dennis skilfully bridged the gap. 'You mentioned plans earlier,' he murmured, looking at Kate and Mallory in turn. 'For the house?'

'Oh, yes,' said Kate, her face slowly lighting up with pleasure. 'We've always had this dream—'

'Kate's dream really,' explained Mallory.

'Of setting up our own business. Publishing good, really good fiction.'

'Been on the back burner for ages.'

'We were beginning to think it might never happen.'

'A big step,' said Dennis. 'Needs careful planning. And sound financial advice.'

'Well, as to that . . .'

Kate and Mallory regarded Dennis with hopeful confidence. Polly turned her attention once more to the outer world. She had heard about her mother's wonderful dream *ad nauseam*. A loser if ever there was one. Polly had better things to think about. Like how near, how wonderfully near was her escape now from the strangling grip of debt. But she certainly couldn't afford to wait another ten months, not with compound interest at twenty-five per cent piling up. So how to get around such a stupid restriction?

The next morning Mallory returned to London. Polly, who was to have gone back with him, unaccountably now wanted to stay on and help her mother 'sort things out and tidy up'.

Kate was disappointed. She had anticipated a quiet, pleasant if inevitably melancholy two or three days with Benny. She had pictured them going through Carey's things, remembering when she had last worn a certain dress, read a certain book. They would comfort each other and, no doubt, weep a little. Now everything would be different. Kate had realised for a long time that she loved her daughter more when Polly wasn't there. Now she struggled with the dreadful possibility that she didn't love Polly at all unless she wasn't there.

The annoying thing was Kate knew perfectly well that whatever reason Polly had for staying on it had nothing to do with sorting anything. Of course, she had no intention of provoking a row by saying so. Or by trying to discover the real reason, a hopeless task in any case. You couldn't get Polly's opinion on the weather if she didn't choose to give it.

Suddenly Kate remembered the brief episode she had witnessed in the garden the day before yesterday between Polly and Ashley Parnell. Even from a distance Kate had sensed the scene's extraordinary intensity. And then afterwards Polly's stillness, her dreaming silence. She hoped with all her heart that Polly, young, vigorous, determined, beautiful, had not set her sights on even a mild flirtation with the poor man.

She and Benny planned to work for two hours, then stop for coffee. Kate decided to stay in the kitchen and check out the china and glass. There were masses of both and quite a lot of it was chipped or cracked. Polly agreed to sort through the two sideboards and huge chest of drawers in the dining room. These were full of napkins, embroidered place mats, runners and tablecloths.

Benny had offered to tackle the linen cupboard. As she trotted across the bare, polished boards of the landing she caught sight of the closed door of Carey's bedroom and turned her head quickly away. She had been in there only once since Carey died, to strip the bed, throw out all the pills and medicines and do a quick tidy. It had hurt so much, handling her friend's special things. The beautiful Chinese bowls and collection of elephants. The silver-framed photographs of family and friends – so many, and even more in the rooms downstairs. And the novel, *The Flight from the Enchanter*, which Benny had been reading aloud the last night of Carey's life. Still open at page 176.

'Stop there,' Carey had said. 'We're nearly at my favourite bit – that wonderful shareholders' meeting with the mad old ladies. Let's save it for tomorrow.'

Recalling this Benny, suddenly overcome by grief and loneliness, started to cry. She ran to the nearest bedroom and buried her face in her apron to stifle the noise. Kate had more than enough to do without mopping up after moaning minnies. Also, Benny thought she might upset Polly. She was sure the girl must be taking Carey's death much harder than she let on. Not everyone chose to make a display of their feelings.

Kate had opened a deep drawer containing nothing but tea towels. Crisp, white, perfectly ironed. At the very bottom there was a separate stack tied neatly with ribbon. As soft and weightless as beautifully darned tissue paper. As she delicately lifted them out Kate sensed someone standing in the doorway.

'Oh, Polly. Just look at these.'

'Mm,' said Polly. 'Is it time for coffee?'

'No. We've only been going half an hour.'

'I've finished.' Polly wandered over to the window and stared out at a hot blue sky. 'What a fabulous day.'

'What would you like to tackle next, then?'

'I shall definitely spend much more time down here.'

'There are two huge boxes of cutlery—'

'I thought I might go for a walk.'

'Right.'

'That sounded a bit tight-lipped.' Then, when Kate did not respond: 'See you soon.'

'Why don't you—'

But she was gone. Kate was going to suggest Polly put a jacket on. She knew the girl's clothes were none of her business. Polly had worn exactly what she liked for as long as her mother could remember. But Forbes Abbot was not London. Kate hated the thought of Polly being talked about behind her back. Laughed at, even. Thought no better than she should be. Ridiculous archaism but people still used it. And everyone knew what it meant.

Polly had gone out wearing a tight white sleeveless top with a large triangle cut out of the front, revealing the top half of her breasts and a strange skirt made of assorted floaty panels, longer one side than the other but still pretty short. Though not quite transparent it was far from opaque. Round her neck she had slung a purse in the shape of a tiny star made of silver beads on a leather thong. Strangely the fact that she knew Polly would be totally indifferent to village opinion did not make Kate feel any less protective on her behalf.

She moved to the large sash window over the sink. Ashamed of herself for spying but driven just the same, Kate watched her daughter pass through the tall iron gates. Polly turned right and walked away. She hadn't even glanced at the house opposite. Becoming irritated with herself now as well as ashamed, Kate wondered if she had imagined emotion that simply hadn't been there in the scene at Carey's funeral. Willing this to be so, then wanting to shake it from her mind, she decided to stop for coffee after all. She went into the hall to call Benny. There was no reply. Then she heard soft little whining noises, muffled as if through several fabric folds, and ran quickly upstairs.

Polly strolled along Forbes Abbot High Street, which was a pretty low street compared to, say, the King's Road, but not without its charms. A stranger in a small community always provokes interest and although a lot of people, because of the funeral, remembered who Polly was, she still remained a relatively unknown quantity. So a few heads turned as she passed and one or two people said, 'Good morning,' but there was nothing like the amount of interest, admiration and resentment that Polly expected. Then she noticed how people were talking together in groups of two or three, their faces grave but also somewhat excited. This did not disturb Polly overmuch. She presumed it was some trivial local matter blown up out of all proportion by people who had nothing better to do with their time.

Like almost everything else Polly undertook in her life this mid-morning amble was index-linked and had a dual purpose. Primarily there was the hope of bumping into the man she had met at the funeral – and no sooner met than, if not loved, fancied extremely. Reeling him in shouldn't be a problem. Polly had never wanted a man who had not wanted her. And she had energy enough for two should things get deliciously out of hand.

Strangely, though she had thought of little else since yesterday, when she tried to recall his face feature by feature it proved impossible. But Polly remembered the look of Ashley, his golden hair and wasted, slender hands. She wondered what precisely was wrong with him. There was no doubt that, in the early stages, illness could be quite romantic. And in the later stages too on occasion – look at those illustrations in Victorian novels. Huge-eyed, wistful creatures lifting heavenwards on pillowy clouds, drifting gently from this life surrounded by heartbroken mourners, weeping and wringing their hands. Not that Polly would want any truck with the illness itself. Administering pills and medicines, giving jabs or mopping-up of any sort were definitely out. Especially the mopping-up.

But the object of her affection seemed not to be about. Polly passed the little tea shop, the Secret Garden, and glanced through the windows but without any real hope of success. Not much point in coming out for scones and a cuppa when you were three minutes away from access to your own. She had higher expectations from the village store, which doubled as post office and newsagent, but he was not in there either. Pricked on by disappointment, and wanting to upset someone, if only slightly, she asked for a copy of the *Financial Times*. Of course they only had it to order. Polly sighed and shook her head as the owner apologised, bought a small bottle of sparkling water and continued on her way, stopping occasionally to take a drink.

Polly's second reason for being abroad was much more down to earth. She planned to call on Dennis Brinkley. There had been no point at all in attempting to establish any sort of relationship, business or otherwise, the previous day when her parents had been present. No point in attempting to soften up Dennis, to display how knowledgeable and skilled she could be in fiscal matters. In other words, how pointless it was to make her wait a full ten months before releasing money that, in any case, already belonged to her. No, she would need to be on her own with him for that.

These reflections inevitably brought Billy Slaughter to mind. Slimy, slithy, slippery Billy with his black heart and veins running with gold and venom. Polly's thoughts took refuge, as they so often did, in an attitude of cruel superiority. She pictured herself now, tossing the money at his feet. Laughing to show her contempt as he struggled to get past his great belly to bend down and pick it up. What insults, selected and polished again and again during wasted hours of angry resentment, she would fling in his face. And then turn her back and slowly, insolently stroll away.

Although Polly did not remember the exact location of Dennis's house she did know it was a conversion of the old village primary school and so should be easy enough to find. But so strange was its present appearance – rather like a towered fortress with high, arrow-slit windows – that she walked straight past and eventually had to ask someone.

While ringing the front doorbell Polly was already reconsidering her approach. Although it would certainly be sensible to appear confident, might it not also be a good idea to ask Dennis's advice on handling her money? Of course she wouldn't take it but what man was not susceptible to flattery?

Though she could hear the bell ringing loudly inside the house no one came to the door. A low wheezing sound, which Polly guessed came from a vacuum cleaner, unnerved her. Surely Dennis would not be doing his own housework?

She wandered round the side of the house and into the garage. It was almost empty. Just a few boxes, neatly stacked and some gardening tools. Right at the back was a pegboard on the wall with several keys. While Polly was reading the clearly written labels tied to these and wondering at the trusting foolishness of country dwellers the hoovering stopped. A door reinforced with steely mesh led directly into the house. Polly tapped gently on it. Receiving no response she tapped more loudly, then stepped inside.

A woman stood at a kitchen sink, clattering dishes about. A beefy, slab-faced woman with piggy eyes, one of which was turned firmly inwards, giving it a nice clear view of the bridge of her nose. The other glared at the stranger in the doorway.

'Oh!' cried Polly, blinking in surprise, then throwing away one of her freshest and most guileless smiles. 'Hello.'

'Ain't you never heard of knocking?'

'I did but I don't think you—'

'What d'you want?'

Well really, thought Polly. To be spoken to in such a manner. And by someone who was presumably a cleaner. To add to her discomfort she was sure she had met the woman before but could not think where. She said firmly, 'I'm here to see Mr Brinkley.'

'He know you're comin'?'

'Naturally.'

'Funny he's gone to work then.'

'Ah . . . yes . . .' Polly snapped her fingers while cursing that she had not thought to check. In the city no one worked on Saturday. 'I remember now. He did say to meet in Causton.'

The turned-out eye roved over Polly, coming to rest eventually on the deeply revealing triangle. 'Business, is it?'

'Mr Brinkley is my financial advisor, yes.' Why am I talking to this ghastly person? I don't have to explain myself to her. Poor Dennis. Fancy having to put up with this cross-eyed, ill-mannered lump trundling about the place.

The woman folded solid forearms gauntleted with sparkly foam. She didn't speak again. Just stood very still and carried on staring.

Polly turned crisply on her heel and left. When she got to the gate and turned to close it the hideous old bat had come to the garage entrance, no doubt to see her safely off the premises. Polly was furious. Bloody cheek. And it wasn't as if she could return to Appleby House and offload her anger. She had no intention of letting her mother know she was planning to soften up Dennis.

But by the time she had returned home Polly's whole mood had changed. Hearing voices in the garden of the house opposite (the garden of the wondrously fanciable man), she began to slow her steps until, passing the gate, she had practically reached a standstill.

The Parnells were having lunch at a table on the lawn beneath the shade of a large flowered umbrella. Alas, it was Judith who was facing the hot, dusty road.

Polly gave a false but brilliant smile and waved, receiving a curt nod in response. Quite unput out – she had expected nothing else – she called: 'Hi! Isn't it a brilliant day?'

Ashley turned slowly in his chair to see who was speaking, looked out across the grass and recognised her immediately. Polly smiled again, this time with warm, pleasurable anticipation. Then sauntered slowly away.

* * *

33

'Pretty girl,' said Judith, grasping the nettle. She sounded detached, slightly amused, as if talking about an attractive child. 'Clever too.' Her magnanimity knew no bounds. 'Mallory said she was at the LSE.'

'That's right. She was telling me about it at the funeral. Sounds a bit of a bear pit.'

'I've no doubt she'll cope. When you're that young everything's a challenge.'

Now the years between the girl and herself and Ashley yawned. The girl was half their age. I should have more faith, thought Judith. She smiled across at him and struggled to believe herself truly loved.

Ashley said, 'You still haven't told me how your meeting went the other night.'

'Meeting?' Judith frowned, repeating the word with vague puzzlement as if she had forgotten its meaning.

'Peacock Hotel. New client. Surgical instruments.'

'Oh, that. Nothing to tell really.'

Nothing to tell? Only that it had been the most disagreeable experience of her entire life and was still fresh and foul and hot in her memory. Only that she had spent hours afterwards soaking and scrubbing herself in a scented bath and still felt filthy when she slipped into bed beside Ashley. Inevitably her recollection of the experience would fade but Judith knew she would never forget entirely. How did you scour the inside of your head?

He had seemed pleasant enough – a stout, middle-aged man with a stiff little grey moustache and rather smeary half-moon spectacles. His suit, brown pinstripe worn with a pink shirt, was too tight. He was sitting at a banquette in front of a tankard of beer, next to which lay his wallet. After they had shaken hands he stood up and pulled the table out. When she squeezed past him and sat down he pushed it back, which left Judith wedged into a corner. She opened her briefcase.

'So, Mr Paulson—'

'Polson. With an O.' He exaggerated his wet, red mouth into the sound, then inserted his little finger in and ran the tip around his lips gradually widening the opening.

'Remind you of anything?'

'I'm sorry – I don't—'

'Just my bit of fun. What've you got for me then?'

Judith produced a folder and handed him a four-page glossy brochure describing her services. He glanced down and handed it back, moving unnecessarily closer to do so.

He said, 'The photo doesn't do you justice.'

'So how do you think I can help, Mr Polson?' Judith made her voice very firm and brisk. 'Do you have an accountant at present?'

'I do.' He was staring at the opening of her shirt.

'May I ask why you're thinking of changing?'

34

'I'm not thinking of changing.'

'Then I don't quite see what I can do for you.' Judith spoke tersely. She had left Ashley feeling not at all well and driven ten miles for this meeting. She put the material back in her case and snapped it smartly shut.

'I do,' said Mr Polson. He opened the wallet and handed it over. 'Try one of these for size.'

Judith reached out without thinking. She saw neat rows of condoms. There must have been thirty . . . forty perhaps. Not a very pleasant experience but hardly likely to leave one poleaxed. She looked at them long enough to show her indifference, then handed the wallet back.

'I see you're an optimist, Mr Polson.' Then, feeling the first stirrings of anger at the insult she added: 'Try looking in the mirror sometime.'

A spasm twisted his mouth. Immediately Judith was sorry and not just because of the deliberate wounding. Apprehension was present too. His face had darkened, becoming suffused with blood. Judith looked about her.

The room was very large and, at 6.30 in the evening, sparsely occupied. Half a dozen dark-suited men were grouped around a table stacked with glasses at the far end. They huddled, murmuring, occasionally throwing their heads back with harsh guffaws of laughter. Two youngish women were on bar stools chatting to the barman. And there were two or three scattered couples, also engrossed in conversation.

Judith was trapped. Polson blocked one side, the angle of the banquette as it turned a corner blocked the other. She pushed slightly at the table then realised his metal documents case was jammed firmly against it. He closed the gap between them. Pressed his leg against her own. Breathed his plaguey breath into her face. Poured a stream of filth into her ear.

Gagging for it she was he knew he could tell her name was a byword a byword open up for anybody thought he was ugly? he wasn't ugly down there down there where it mattered they were all the same down there they could go upstairs he'd got this film get her going five of them five and this tart thirteen she said what? thirteen? knew it all couldn't wait got on this bloke's shoulders then all the others queued up acting crying she was good at that acting crying this bloke he said pretend it's a lollipop, laugh. Then he put his . . .

Afterwards Judith could never understand why she just sat there unable to move. Embarrassment didn't come into it. It was as if the area between and around them was as solid and impenetrable as thick ribbed ice. His hand, which had been resting on her knee, slipped over to lie on the inside of her thigh. The thumb separated itself, pointing upwards.

Then Judith noticed someone making their way over the acres of carpet in their direction. She caught the man's gaze, locked her own into it lest he should walk on by, then glanced despairingly sideways at her tormentor.

Polson saw what was coming. He stood up, collected his case and said loudly, 'Look forward to doing business with you then. Until next week?'

As he strode off Judith closed her eyes. She was conscious of the second man sitting down but couldn't look at him. She sat there as seconds and then minutes dragged past. The frozen skin on her face began to soften. She became conscious of her heartbeat and that tears were rolling down her cheeks. The man went away, then came back with a large brandy. 'Drink this.' He put her hands around the bowl. 'Come on, Mrs Parnell.'

'I can't.'

'You must. One swallow at a time.' Judith drank, spluttered. Drank some more. 'Good. You know, you should go to the police about this.'

The thought of it! The thought of describing him, having to repeat what he had said perhaps over and over again. Nausea swept over Judith. Brandy mixed with bile filled her mouth.

'Excuse me a moment.' He got up. 'I'll get some water.'

'I must go.'

'No – that's just what you mustn't do. And you certainly can't drive.'

'All right.'

She gave in straight away even while acknowledging how spineless this was. How utterly pathetic. Yet the relief was overwhelming. She could just sit here, quiet and small and, above all, safe. Eventually she would stop feeling faint, the mortified muscles in her legs would flex into life and she would be able to stand upright and make her way to the door. How wise and kind this man was. This stranger she had never seen before and yet who, unaccountably, knew her name.

CHAPTER THREE

As now even Sunday had a late afternoon rush hour, Kate's plan was to leave Appleby House about midday to avoid the weekenders streaming back to their city homes. She put several boxes of lovely garden vegetables in the boot of the Golf, planning to drive home via Tesco where she could fill up with diesel.

Polly, of a sudden bored to tears with rural life, went back with her mother, spending the whole journey in bad-tempered silence. Unable to banish from her mind the infuriating contretemps at Dennis's house she was sure the village had, by now, received a well-embroidered account of the situation. Personally Polly didn't give a stuff about this but hated the idea of being at a disadvantage with Dennis. Of course, there was always the slight chance that the woman with the corned beef complexion hadn't told him.

It had been a mistake, though, casually wandering round to his place like that. Next time, say in a week – she daren't leave it much longer – she would make a proper appointment And borrow something boringly respectable to wear. Polly saw herself in a dark, sober and creakingly dull ensemble asking Dennis's advice on her sudden windfall and laughing up her sleeve.

The other reason for her sulks was the divine Ashley. Far from being able to follow up their first meeting Polly had been thwarted at every turn. She had not even managed a casual word over the garden gate. Discovering from Kate that his wife worked from home was quite a blow. On the other hand, Polly reasoned, Judith must leave the house sometimes, if only to shop and go to the post. Not a bit of it. In two whole days Judith did not budge. Then Polly saw her handing a stack of letters over to the postman. A request to her mother that the Parnells be asked over for a drink as they were all going to be neighbours now met with a very sharp response.

Kate had asked Benny also to come to London and stay a while. But Benny refused and could not be persuaded. What about Croydon? Someone would feed the animal, certainly. But how cruel to abandon him so soon after his dear mistress had also unaccountably vanished. Plus there was the threat of burglars. An unoccupied house was an open invitation to the criminal element. Thieves could break in and steal Carey's lovely things.

And so, when Kate and Polly drove away, Benny was left at the tall iron gate calling, 'Goodbye,' and fluttering her handkerchief. Squinting and blinking through her pebbly glasses she waved and waved until the dark blue car was out of sight. Then hesitated, feeling suddenly bereft.

She noticed Judith coming out of her back door and called, 'Cooeee!' When Judith nodded back Benny started to make her way across the lane for a few words, putting off the moment when she had to go back indoors. But by the time she had reached the opposite fence Judith had disappeared so Benny had little choice but to retrace her steps. Once back inside she drifted into the vast, shabby kitchen and stood in the centre vaguely looking round.

For the first time that she could ever remember she was quite by herself in Appleby House. A terrible quietness seemed to have crept inside. Now, instead of feeling comfortably familiar, it felt strangely cold and full of nothing to do.

Benny began to feel nervous. The building was very large and, it seemed to her, very detached. On its far right was the fifteenth-century church of St Anselm's, separated from the house by a large graveyard. Roughly half of the three-acre apple orchard curved around the other side. The remainder stretched right away behind the walled garden at the back. In fact you could truthfully say, and Benny murmured as much to herself aloud, that the place was pretty well cut off. Of course there was a telephone, but not in every room. And what if someone did break in and she couldn't get to it in time?

Benny stood motionless, listening. Gradually she became aware that the surrounding silence, with which she had previously always been at ease, was not really silence at all. For instance, there were the rooks in the elm trees flanking the church walk, an unmusical background to all her waking hours. She heard them now as if for the first time. Carey had told her that a gathering would be called 'a parliament of rooks'. Considering the ugly sounds they made, forever scrawking and scraping, it seemed entirely appropriate.

Benny recalled once, after she had put some flowers on a grave, stepping back on to a dead one. It had given softly beneath her foot, a splodge of stiff feathers, dark red gluey stuff and heaving white worms. Benny had broken into a cold sweat of repulsion. She felt it again now: a creeping, nauseous chill.

A cup of tea was the thing. Though she was careful – unnecessarily now, for Carey was no longer ill upstairs – each of Benny's movements seemed to give rise to an astonishing amount of noise. Water gushed from the heavy brass tap, china cup and saucer clattered against each other in her hand. Then the elderly fridge, tall, dirty cream with a rusting chrome handle, suddenly rumbaed into vibrating life. Shudder and shake it went. Shudder and shake.

Benny sat down at the kitchen table. She put the radio on, then immediately switched it off, realising that if anyone did approach the house, she would not be able to hear them. Above her a wooden airer, winched up to the ceiling and draped with towels, creaked slightly. Now that was odd, thought Benny, tipping back her head and staring upwards fearfully. Why on earth should it be moving? There were no windows open. No draught. Yet it definitely was. Almost swaying actually . . .

Carey had said once that Benny would be lost without something to worry about. Certainly Benny could never remember a time when she had not been struggling to keep her head above a positive ocean of free-floating anxiety. The words 'what if?' ruled her life. She could not help investing the most harmless, innocent situations with lurking terror. And any fleeting moment of happiness would immediately be tarnished by a deep apprehension as to what the next might reveal.

No one, Benny least of all, could understand why this was so. According to the psychology textbooks, she should be as carefree as a bird. A wanted child, she had been lovingly if unimaginatively brought up by stolid, kindly parents. Shy, incurious and outwardly placid, she went to school and did her homework, played tennis sometimes – though she always preferred reading to games – and made a few humdrum friends in a humdrum sort of way.

As a teenager she had occasionally gone to local dances where her earnest, bumpy moon face and thin straggles of mousy hair (after a severe attack of ringworm it had never grown properly again) attracted little attention. She was hardly ever asked to dance and, in any case, always left well before the end to make sure of getting home safely. Even so, the fear was always with her. Always. *What if. . .?*

Once she had got off the school bus, convinced her home was on fire. She tried to walk normally down the road but was unable to stop breaking into a run. She raced along, heart thumping, satchel banging into the small of her back, weeping frightened tears. She saw the great orange crackling framework of the house, sagging and swaying on the point of collapse. Firemen, shouting urgently, ran across the pavement, dragging hoses, and vanished into billowing smoke. A woman was screaming. So vivid was this hellish premonition that, hurtling round the corner of Laburnum Crescent, Benny stopped dead, blinking in disbelief at the serene row of unscorched semis dreaming away in the afternoon sun.

A sudden shriek. Lost in recollection Benny shrieked as well, springing up, her chair falling backwards. But it was only the kettle. She righted the chair and went to make her drink, glad there was no one present to witness such foolishness. She could get another kettle now. A nice silent one that you could plug in. Carey had insisted on the whistler since Benny had let an older kettle boil so dry the bottom had fallen out.

Sitting down and sipping Earl Grey, Benny made an effort to think about supper. Mallory, who had foreseen a slide into sorrowful inertia once his aunt's companion found herself alone, had urged her to eat properly. And Kate had stocked up at the supermarket before leaving so there was plenty of stuff in the freezer. And a nice, fresh lemon sole for tonight.

39

Benny had almost calmed down when she heard the click of the gate. She sat up sharply, alert and straight-backed. Who could it be? Not the postman on a Sunday. Footsteps rang out on the old brick path. So, no attempt at concealment. That was encouraging. Benny hurried over to the window and scrambled up to sit on the edge of the old stone sink. She twisted round, leaned sideways and pressed her plump, cushiony cheek hard against the glass lozenges. At this angle, with one eye closed and the other squinting, it was just possible to make out, through the openwork trellis of the porch, who the visitor might be.

It was a friend. Probably her closest and dearest friend now that Carey had gone. Comforted, a little excited even, Benny hurried to open the door.

The village of Forbes Abbot had long ago given up trying to agree on what exactly went on between dippy old Miss Frayle and the outwardly respectable Dennis Brinkley. Frankly unable to imagine any sort of sexual liaison, it was at a loss to understand what else they could possibly be up to. So it simply labelled the dry and dusty duo 'a likely pair' and let them get on with it. This the couple did with dignified reticence, hardly even aware they were the subject of speculation: Benny because it would never have occurred to her that she was clever or attractive enough to be talked about; Dennis because he always assumed his complete lack of interest in the lives of his neighbours would naturally be reciprocated.

Forbes Abbot had not always been so sanguine. Admitted, Benny Frayle had been a write-off virtually from day one as far as making any sensible contribution to village life was concerned. But there had been high hopes of Dennis. It was quickly discovered that he was a professional man, partner in a successful consultancy and also the owner of a large, if strangely transformed property at the posh end of the village. As such he could have taken his place in the community and been well respected. The Parish Council would have welcomed him with open arms; ditto the Homemade Wine Club. However, it didn't take Forbes Abbot long to decide that first appearances could be very deceptive and that there was rather more to the newcomer than met the eye.

First, though he was as attractive as any middle-aged man shut in an office all day handling other people's money had any right to be, he remained unmarried. Then there was the absence of visitors, of either sex, to the house. And everyone knew what the word 'loner' stood for. But what caused the most unease throughout the local rank and file was Dennis Brinkley's hobby.

That every man should have one was agreed. It kept them out of mischief and from under their wives' feet. A nice bit of DIY, gardening, bowls or snooker, mysterious activities in the potting shed – fine. Killing machines – something else.

Not that killing *per se* was frowned on. This was the country, after all. Several families in the village and surrounding farms had a properly licensed shotgun, as many a rabbit or pheasant had discovered to their cost. One or two people who were more serious about the sport were members of a gun club at Causton and thought fine fellows for it. Boys will be boys, after all.

But the problem here was a matter of scale. One man, one gun, one target – what reasonable person could argue with that? But weapons of mass destruction within the confines of the home . . . And it wasn't as if they were the sort of thing your average man in the street could recognise.

War memorabilia, fair enough. Badges and medals, ration books, the odd German helmet, shells and gas masks – such sentimental souvenirs could bring back lovely memories to those of a certain age. But you'd have to be a six-hundred-year-old pile of dust, as one historical mastermind explained in the Horse and Hounds, happily to recall Brinkley's monstrosities.

One of the first things Dennis had done before moving into the old primary school was knock the place about. This was to be expected – a school was not a domestic dwelling. But instead of a nice conversion, all the interior walls and ceilings had been taken out, leaving a huge, empty shell reinforced with iron girders. Modest living quarters were then built taking up barely a third of the space. All this caused plenty of talk and speculation, which the removal van's contents – a few tea chests and some ordinary, old-fashioned furniture – did much to defuse. Then, barely a week later, the machines arrived.

Not that they were recognised as such. Disassembled, their various parts, massive and sometimes strangely shaped, had been transported in specially, constructed crates. Four men had carried these into the house and had left several hours later carrying the crates, now dismantled and roped together.

A short while after this, more men arrived with ladders and scaffolding and were in and out for three days, knocking and hammering. The minute they left, the village was in there, starting with the chairman of Neighbourhood Watch and his consort. Others followed in order of seniority. Alas, all were disappointed. They were courteously received, shown into the rather small living room but not encouraged to browse. And so it continued for the next ten years.

This meant few of the locals were destined to see the constructions assembled in all their glory, for the windows in the machine room were tall, extremely narrow and very high up. Even by jumping in the air one still only got the barest glimpse of a dangling loop of rope. Or a massive iron claw.

But Mrs Crudge, who was allowed to wax the floorboards on which the machines were precisely placed, relayed sensational descriptions as to their extraordinary appearance. Apparently there were large cards printed and set in glass boxes next to each exhibit, giving a detailed history as to their fearsome capabilities. Some of the boxes had illustrations that Mrs Crudge said fair turned her stomach. Worse than the Chamber of Horrors at Madame Tussauds. Not what you'd call a nice sort of hobby at all. And she was quite right. For the war machines were not a hobby for Dennis, but an all-consuming passion.

He remembered vividly the moment this sprang into being. He was fourteen and until then had shown no genuine interest in anything at all. He played no sports and had no friends – at least none he brought home. Eventually, somewhat shamefaced, his parents admitted to each other that their only child was as dull as ditchwater.

There was only one TV set in the house and Dennis's father kept a firm eye on the control knob. So Dennis read, simply because he could and it was something to do. As her son seemed indifferent to subject matter his mother changed his library books when she changed her own. She tried to select an interesting mixture: teenage fiction, true adventure – sailing, mountaineering and so on – biology and the natural world, or history. It was in this section she had come across a work entitled *The Soldier's Armoury: Twelfth to Sixteenth Century.*

Dennis opened it, sucked in his breath and cried, 'Wow! Just look at this!'

The page in question showed a contraption for breaking knees, elbows and neck, then screwing the captive's head round till his spine snapped. Mrs Brinkley had barely drawn a protesting breath before her son, tightly hugging the book, rushed to his bedroom and, unlike the unfortunate man in the illustration, never looked back.

Over the next twenty years Dennis rooted out every scrap of information extant on the period in question. His shelves were crammed with relevant books. Holidays were spent in museums all over the world poring over manuscripts describing battles and photographing weaponry, armour and all the cumbersome but lethal machinery of early war-making. The artefacts were very fragile and only once, in a library in Verona, had he obtained permission to trace a document. This was a map showing the Battle of Montichiari (one thousand lances, seven hundred archers). As Dennis touched the faded, ivory parchment he felt the warm golden earth, running with the blood of warriors, incarnate beneath his fingertips.

Gradually he built up a small collection: a sheaf of exquisitely balanced longbows; a gun carriage supporting a vast crossbow so heavy that two men were needed merely to handle the bolt; a rusted helmet with a horsehair crest and hinged side pieces.

He was almost forty before it occurred to him that there was nothing to stop him owning a facsimile of one of the great early war machines themselves. He drew up precisely detailed plans, even though they would never be put to any practical use. He started with the trebuchet, a giant leather catapult on a winch mechanism in a frame thirty feet tall, used for hurling rocks and boiling liquids over castle walls. Dennis followed this with a belfry, a movable tower capable of holding over a hundred men, and began the search for a craftsman with the necessary skills to build them. As this was being done he began looking for a suitable property to house his new treasures.

Dennis had been delighted with the purchase and eventual transformation of Kinders. Now never an evening passed but that he did not enter the vast space holding the war machines. He especially liked to be there at dusk, when their grotesque shadows met and mingled, spreading like grey mist beneath his slippered feet.

As he moved about he would hear, in fancy, the whistling rush of a thousand arrows. Or the strain and creak of a cable as the trebuchet's vast leather sling was winched into a hurling position. Gradually, over the years, these scenes became more and more vivid, incorporating not only an increasingly large amount of grisly detail but also the sound and lately even the smell of carnage.

For a long time these extraordinary historical recreations occurred only when Dennis was confined within the parameters of the war room. When he closed the door to go about his business the sound and fury immediately vanished. But lately his mind had been breached at other times. Once, to his great alarm, this happened in the office during a discussion with two of his staff. Sometimes, even when asleep, the groans of wounded men and screams of terrified women and children disturbed his dreams.

Naturally Dennis kept these frightening experiences to himself. Eventually, however, the daily memories of night-time horrors began to wear him down and he decided to seek help. Loath to visit a psychiatrist – he was neither unhappy nor inadequate in the matter of conscious day-to-day-living – Dennis finally settled on a dream therapist. Embarrassedly he told his tale. The woman listened, then suggested various interpretations that all seemed pretty daft to him. As was the suggestion that, every day for a month, he should write the dreams and visions down. But Dennis decided to give this a go and, to his surprise, it worked so well he never had cause to visit her again.

Mallory remembered speaking to his aunt once about the friendship between her companion and Dennis Brinkley. Like most people he found it surprising, even faintly humorous, and was unwise enough to say so. Carey had been angry at this implication that the unattractive and socially inept did not deserve friends. Or, in the unlikely event that they made one, that this friend should be as plain and clumsy as they were themselves.

After he had said he was sorry Carey had unbent enough to discuss Benny's situation a little. As she saw it the relationship was grounded not only in liking, though there was that, of course, but in a tender stability arising from the mutual understanding that neither would ever do the other harm. Benny's anguished shyness, hidden behind her blundering and rushing and general overeagerness to help was perfectly balanced and gentled into quietude by Dennis's patient manner and genuine interest in her wellbeing. They were comfortable with each other. Once, Carey explained, she had needed to talk to Benny when Dennis was visiting and had discovered them sitting in wing chairs on opposite sides of Benny's fireplace with all the calm and gravitas of an old married couple.

Benny knew nothing of this conversation but now, as she hurried to the front door of Appleby House, the expression on her face completely bore it out.

'Come in, Dennis. It's so good to see you.'

'I did hesitate . . . a bit soon after the funeral. But I saw Kate's car drive away and thought you might be in need of a little company.'

'You're right, as always.'

'Are we in the kitchen?'

In no time they were settled at the scarred deal table. Benny threw away her stewed Earl Grey and made what Dennis always called 'some proper char'. She set out the big Mason's ironstone cups and saucers, yellow and blue with lovely flowers. Really they were breakfast coffee cups but Carey had believed in using anything and everything in whatever way suited you. She would cut ice cream with a fish knife if it was to hand and had once served oysters, complete with lemon slices, shaved ice and seaweed, on a three-tier cake stand. Why, Carey wouldn't give a fig if . . .

'Oh, Benny. My dear.' Her tears were falling like rain. Dennis produced a large, white linen handkerchief, shook out the immaculate folds and laid it close to Benny's saucer. 'I'm so very sorry.'

'Hnuhh . . . hnuhh . . .' Snorting and sobbing Benny wrapped her arms across her chest as if in a strait-jacket, clamping them fast. She gripped her shoulders against the pain. 'I was all right . . . when everyone was here . . .'

Dennis waited. He didn't speak again and Benny was grateful. So many people had said so many things to her during the last few days. Their intentions were sympathetic but the pious generalities meant nothing. Worse, they were an irritation. What did they know of the real, true Carey? Of her relish for jokes and occasional crossness, her raucous laugh and sharp mimicry of various village worthies once their unsuspecting backs were turned. Her love of gossip, good wine and rich tobacco. Recalling all these things aloud and adding to them took so much time the tea got cold.

'Shall I make some fresh,' said Dennis. A statement rather than a question. He filled the kettle and by the time it started to whistle and shriek again Benny had stopped crying.

'Is there any cake?' Dennis asked. Not out of greed, though he did have a sweet tooth, but to distract her.

'Oh, yes, yes.' Benny started bustling about, pulling tins out of the cupboard. One fell and rolled across the floor. Then she remembered that Polly had taken home all the leftover cake from the funeral. 'There's only Battenburg.'

'My mother's favourite.' Dennis got out some clean cups. 'Though she didn't like marzipan.'

'It isn't home-made.' As Benny put slices of the cake on an almost translucent plate with a worn golden rim the anomaly sank in. 'Didn't like . . .?'

'She'd take it all off and just eat the other bits. I used to say to her, why not buy angel cake instead? That was pink and yellow if you remember, Benny?'

'Oh, yes. Stuck together with sugary grit.'

Dennis talked on. He moved from his mother's idiosyncratic eating habits through other family stories, with one or two of which Benny was comfortably familiar, then introduced some strange neighbours who had lived next door to the Brinkleys at Pinner.

'They had a stuffed armadillo. After dark, when no one was about, they used to take it for walks.'

'How wonderful!' Benny clapped her hands with pleasure. 'Was it on wheels?'

'They carried it.'

'You can't take something for a walk by carrying it!'

As Dennis extended and embellished this entirely imaginary family, Croydon jumped on to Benny's lap and started to purr, the first occasion for a long time. She sank her fingers into his cream and orange ruff and massaged his neck. The cat stretched out his chin to facilitate these caresses. Gradually, soothed by the gently meandering conversation, its restful pauses and the rumbling vibration beneath her fingertips, Benny's heart became less troubled. Her earlier anxieties now seemed fanciful in the extreme. She really must try and put some sort of brake on her morbid imagination.

It was unfortunate that Dennis was preparing to deliver some information calculated to banish all this hard-won tranquillity. Gossip and the local paper made it inevitable that Benny would hear this awful news one way or the other. Knowing her so well, understanding her wildly nervous temperament, Dennis wanted to be sure it came from him.

The facts were these. At the village of Badger's Drift, just a few miles away, an elderly man had been found battered to death in his council bungalow. His seventeen-year-old grandson, who had been living with him for the past five years, had disappeared. Neighbours testified as to ongoing rows, and the youth had already been in trouble for vandalism and fighting. The police were asking for any information as to his whereabouts, and a poster with an up-to-date photograph was already in circulation.

Benny listened, her face gradually draining of colour. When she could finally speak she cried, 'What if he comes here?'

'There's no chance of that,' said Dennis firmly. 'A crime like this is what the police call a domestic. That means only the family of the mur— perpetrator is at any sort of risk. And in any case, the police seem to think the lad's already in London.' This last sentence was pure inspiration.

'I'm all by myself.' Benny had jumped to her feet and looked ready to fly away.

'Benny, look – where do you want to stay tonight? Over here or in the flat?'

'At home. This place is so big.'

'So what we'll do is go and check it out right now for security, all right? And then we can go and buy anything we need – window locks or whatever – and I'll fit them straight away.'

'Oh, Dennis.' Benny sat down again. 'What would I do without you?'

CHAPTER FOUR

A long time ago, nearly eight years to be exact, though it seemed several lifetimes to him, Mallory Lawson had been a stable, healthy and contented man. He had always wanted to teach and, after leaving Cambridge with a 2:1 in Biological Sciences from Downing College, had obtained a Post Graduate Certificate in Education at Homerton and promptly set about it. He applied first for a junior teaching post in a comprehensive school in Hertford but, to his surprise, did not even get an interview, so took a position at an excellent middle school in the Fens, near Ely. He had already fallen in love with a beautiful girl, Kate Allen, then reading English at Girton, and by the end of his first term in the new school they were married. Kate managed to get her foot in the door of a major London publishing house – the first step towards her ambition to become an editor – and commuted to London every day.

Young, childless and with only themselves to please, instead of getting lumbered with a mortgage the Lawsons rented a small flat in Cambridge. They entertained friends, went to concerts and theatres, took long, expensive holidays and generally had a wonderful time. While Mallory was at Little Felling he continued to write and research, publishing several papers including 'The Transmigration of Whooper Swans' in *Nature* magazine, which was especially well received. It was at a conference that he met the head of a direct grant upper school at Cheltenham, who suggested he apply for the position of Head of Science there when the vacancy arose at the end of the current term. Mallory did so and, after a nail-biting two weeks on a short list of three and a second interview, was successful.

At this point in their lives Kate was pregnant. Both of them, tremendously happy at the news, became suddenly and seriously aware that it was time to settle down. Time to do all the responsible things. Buy a sensible family car (Mallory sold the Morgan quickly, even at small profit) and, of course, a house. Three bedrooms and probably just a semi to begin with. Leaving their Cambridge address with estate agents, they were astonished at details of the local property that started arriving through the post. In Cambridge they knew prices had tripled over the past ten years but that was a university town. Oxford was the same, if not worse. But this was the country, for heaven's sake.

In the end, as both wanted to live in Cheltenham itself, they chose a Victorian terraced house, took out a hundred per cent mortgage and used their combined savings to decorate, rewire the place and buy more furniture. Kate gave up her job to freelance and, first-class copy-editors being extremely rare birds, continued to find work. She eased off somewhat after Polly was born and began reading as well as editing manuscripts. This was much less demanding, and easier to pick up and put down when a fractious child needed attention. Not so well paid but you couldn't have everything.

And so the Lawsons lived and modestly prospered. Kate fed the family. Mallory paid the heavy mortgage, all the other bills and kept the car on the road. Polly, intelligent, self-willed, secretive even then, thrived. She proved to be good at science, outstanding at maths and very good indeed at games, both on and off the pitch. Everyone wanted Polly on their side.

When Mallory had been at the Willoughby-Hart School for almost ten years the deputy headship became available and it was discreetly suggested that an application from himself would not be unfavourably received. And so it proved to be. But then, barely a year later, something happened that changed all their lives, and immeasurably for the worst.

Not too long after this catastrophe occurred, when they were already edging towards what proved to be a bottomless pit of despair, Kate looked back at their happy days in Cheltenham and wondered at her own complacency. But wasn't everyone like that until something dreadful happened to them? Tutting and sighing and shaking their heads at someone else's tragedy on the news; enjoying *Crimewatch* as if it were a drama series but with the added spice that the enactments had once happened for real. Voyeurs one and all, comfortable with the knowledge it would never happen to them.

This downward spiral started with a television programme caught late at night and quite by accident. Mallory was on the point of switching off after *Newsnight* and going to bed when his attention was fatally caught by the opening credits of a documentary. The programme itself would show a secondary modern school in a desolate and deprived area in the North-East of England. Scarred buildings in a scarred landscape struggling somehow to contain and even attempt to teach scarred children. What the media called a 'sink school'.

Mallory recalled that, only the other day in the senior master's common room, frivolous attempts had been made to define this term. The overall favourite, 'the rubbish that's left behind when the plug's been pulled', got several laughs and a round of unironic applause.

Mallory sat for a long time, through the night in fact, after the programme had finished. He could not put the pinched, bitter, hopeless faces out of his mind. A sense of guilt, of shame even, began to pervade his thoughts. He remembered his youthful idealism, recalled the ferocious arguments with fellow students who had thought him mad wanting to teach at the rough end of the market. A waste of a Cambridge degree. Angrily he had demanded to know how it could ever be a waste to open windows in the minds of disadvantaged children, admitting light and hope, transforming their lives. This provoked both tears and jeers and the sincere hope that, when the film was made, Tom Hanks would get to play Mallory.

How would his life have gone, Mallory wondered now, if he had got the very first job he had applied for? The one in the comprehensive. From the beginning Kate had understood and sympathised with his ambitions; they would have been just as happy. There would still have been Polly. And he would have been of some real use in the world.

It was this observation that truly struck home. For Mallory was aware that, if he left his present job, no child would lose out by one iota. The school's reputation was such that he would be quickly and easily replaced by someone at least as good, if not better. But there were places where his presence could make a huge difference.

Understanding this Mallory immediately saw himself embroiled in situations of high drama where not only his teaching skills but his heart, soul and every scrap of his considerable energy would be tested to the limit. Suddenly, at three o'clock in the morning in an empty, totally silent room, he felt the reawakening of a faith that he had almost forgotten had ever existed. Once more fizzing with ambition and feeling incredibly alive, his mind became crammed with exciting possibilities.

Later, cooking breakfast before the others were properly awake, Mallory started to think things through. It would be a hell of an upheaval, an awful lot to ask of his family. In fact, looking back at the ease of their life so far, he recognised that this would be the first time really serious demands had been made on any of them, including himself.

The Ewan Sedgewick School in South-East London was always advertising in the *Times Educational Supplement* and the *Guardian* for staff. Presently they were not only seeking teachers in nearly every department but also a headmaster. Mallory sent away for an application form. After all, it committed him to nothing. When he had filled it in and sent it back he tried to feel detached. In any case, such brief experience that he had as a deputy head would hardly qualify him to take over and run a large inner-city comprehensive. But within a fortnight of his application he was invited for an interview at which the board politely attempted to conceal their bafflement at his application in the first place. Barely a week later he was offered the job.

Kate, previously a source of support and encouragement for anything her husband and daughter undertook, struggled to conceal the depths of her dismay at the seriousness of this new situation.

Polly surprisingly, given the friendships she had made and her enjoyment of several aspects of country life, was immediately enthusiastic. Everyone knew London was cool and where it was all at. With the confidence bordering on rashness that was to lead her into so much trouble in later life she could not wait to get down there and start hanging out.

Money was going to be the real problem. Their current mortgage was by no means paid off and they knew that prices in the capital were horrendous. A pathetic London weighting allowance of just under three thousand pounds showed as nothing more than a blip on the Abbey National screen. To make matters worse, Kate insisted that Polly would not pay the price of her father's sudden resurgence of idealism by attending a bottom-of-the-league school. This meant the few comparatively cheaper areas were out of bounds. Mallory, ashamed of cutting his cloth before even starting his new job, brought up the time-worn argument that poor schools would never improve if the middle classes abandoned them. Kate would not budge. For the first and last time in their marriage the Lawsons came close to out-and-out war.

In the end Kate won. They found an excellent all-girls school, the Lady Margaret, at Parsons Green, and bought a two-bedroomed terraced house in the area by putting down the modest profit made from the sale of the Cheltenham house, borrowing double Mallory's annual salary and an extra fifty thousand against Kate's earnings, which left them with a combined mortgage of a hundred and seventy thousand pounds. Kate returned to work full time and, early in September, Mallory took up his post at the Ewan Sedgewick.

His appointment coincided with a modest lottery grant. Repairs had been carried out, buildings were painted, new desks arrived. The gym was refitted and some musical instruments had been bought. Five new teachers were appointed to join the weary cynics on the permanent staff. Many of these, due to their rackety state of physical and/or mental health, were frequently absent. Not infrequently, supply staff outnumbered the regulars.

Gradually Mallory came to understand what he had taken on. Bullying, present to some degree wherever he had worked, had at the Ewan Sedgewick an organised savagery that was truly frightening. Drugs were everywhere: bought, sold or swapped with a defiant lack of concealment. The previous term a teacher had tried to interfere. The next night her teenage daughter had arrived home covered in bruises, her clothes ripped apart. Shortly after, petrol was poured through their letter box followed by some matches with the words 'Next Time' scrawled on the box.

All of this Mallory gradually discovered. He discovered violent children, children who were mentally ill, children who sold themselves, pregnant children, children who were not children at all – who perhaps never had been. Frequently he confronted one or the other of the parents and marvelled that their offspring were still alive. He talked to more police officers during his first month at the Ewan Sedgewick than in the rest of his life put together.

Other pupils – the majority, though it often didn't feel like it – struggled on, taught by worn-out, disenchanted teachers or visitors who knew nothing about them, didn't wish to and disappeared almost as soon as their faces became vaguely familiar.

Mallory got himself dug in. For the next four years, although the hope took a tremendous battering, he somehow found the willpower and energy to continue. Not to succeed, not even to cope, but to go in day after day and wrestle with the job. Overwhelmed by floods of nit-picking paperwork, quarrelling teachers, incompetent administration and inadequate finance, he somehow held at bay the great flood of despair that constantly threatened to overwhelm him. And struggled to remain open to the troubled children in his care, even the one who had plunged a screwdriver into the back of his hand. But then something truly dreadful happened.

Two men, one describing himself as the uncle of a twelve-year-old boy at the school, had turned up saying the child's mother had had an accident. The uncle explained they had come to take him to the hospital. The Office let the boy go. When he did not arrive home his mother contacted the school. Mallory rang the police. Later that night the child was found wandering at the side of the road several miles away, traumatised, naked and bleeding.

Mallory took full responsibility for this appalling incident even though he was not on the school premises at the time. It was right that he should but the effect on him was profound. He felt he could not bear to continue in his post yet knew he must. He had uprooted his wife and child, dragged them halfway across the country and plunged the family into heavy debt on the strength of what seemed to him now a maudlin, sentimental dream. Bitterly he recalled how, buoyed up by waves of naïve vanity, he had seen himself fighting for and transforming a school supposedly beyond hope of reclamation. Had even pictured himself addressing conferences at home and abroad. Becoming famous as the man who . . .

Sickened now by this former posturing Mallory started to apply for other posts: headships, for he could not afford even the smallest decrease in salary. His applications were acknowledged but that was usually the end of it. The two interviews he did obtain were fairly quickly concluded, for the truth was by then he stank of failure and neuroticism. And so Mallory was forced to stay on at the Ewan Sedgewick. To keep sane he withdrew from all but the minimum contact necessary to do the job, hardening his heart against any emotional involvement with either staff or children.

But the cost of maintaining this stance was high. Aware always of what was pressing against the prison walls Mallory could never relax. Soon he was unable to sleep without medication. For the first time in his life he had violent headaches and intense back pain. Sometimes he felt unable to breathe. He was prescribed tranquillisers, drank too much and his libido sank without trace. Recently, in the middle of the night, his whole body had gone into spasm and he was unable to move. Unaware then he was merely days away from delivery Mallory had wept with fear.

*   *   *

51

Though he had always known he would inherit Appleby House, Mallory had never thought to rely on this or take it into any of his calculations. It was his aunt's home, not a counter to play with in the property game. In any case, he loved her far too much to anticipate her death. But when she did eventually pass away Mallory, even while still in shock, could not help being aware of the difference this would make to him and marvelled that a window had opened at last in the hellhole that was his life, admitting light and hope.

In the middle of the week after the funeral he and Kate were sitting in the walled space behind their terraced house drinking Meursault and watching the sun go down. Kate had painted the walls a soft, washed-out blue. Some Greek pots holding honeysuckle and clematis and a tiny lion's head wall fountain prettified the area somewhat, but failed to disguise the fact that it was basically a very small brick and concrete back yard. She still found it hard to believe their property was on the market for four hundred thousand pounds.

Rock music thudded away next door, big Lucy was belting out 'Nessun dorma' on the other side and planes roared overhead. To Mallory, chaos permanently raging both inside and outside his head, neighbourhood noise had barely registered. But Kate, especially when Polly had still been living at home, found it hard to handle and frequently resorted to foam earplugs. She used to long for the time when they would visit Forbes Abbot again. Sometimes she dreamed about the place. Bathed in sunlight she would be walking in the still, calm air through cornfields or avenues of May blossom. Once, in a vision, she had seen herself crossing Sawyer's Lake on foot. The water had felt cool and slightly springy, like soft grass. That she would be going to live there always now, growing old with Mallory, filled Kate with happiness. Of course it wouldn't be tomorrow or even next week. Lots of things were still to be sorted and it would all take time, but soon . . .

They had spent the last three hours talking about money. Mallory was retiring early so could not expect to receive a full pension. Even so he had worked for twenty-six years, the last seven at the top of his profession, and could expect to pull in around twenty-three thousand per annum. Hardly untold wealth but it would cover their basic expenses. The money from his aunt's estate would remain sensibly invested. The rent from the apple orchard would be put towards Polly's maintenance in her final year. After that she would be on her own and, fortunately, far from penniless.

As for the house, if they got the asking price, and Kate had been assured that they would, the mortgage would be cleared and they would have made a profit of almost a hundred thousand pounds.

'So with that,' she was presently explaining, 'and my savings, such as they are, we're in business.'

'And on rent-free premises!' exclaimed Mallory. 'The experts would be impressed.'

He referred to the authors of a pile of glossy packages crammed with advice from assorted banks and financial advisors: 'How to Start Your Own Business', 'You and Your Future', 'Be Your Own Boss', all stacked up on the computer table. Though assured of Dennis's help and advice, Kate wanted to show that she had made at least some effort on her own behalf.

Alas, though all the banks and advisors seemed keen to lend her money, the brochures harped boringly on about the necessity of being sure to find a gap in the market for her product first. She was only too aware that it was thought, and by people who knew the business inside out, that there was no gap for the type of literary novel she hoped to bring out.

This was not to say they were never published. There were always a few in every successful firm's catalogue. And, very occasionally, one would astonish the trade by making money. The whole world now knew about Captain Corelli and his mandolin. But this was extremely rare. Most were published for the kudos and invariably made a loss, though this would be more than recouped by sales of the latest Tom Clancy or Danielle Steel.

Kate did not doubt that good stuff was out there. She had read three manuscripts over the previous year that seemed to her absolutely outstanding. She had fought for them all but, with one exception, they had been turned down as hopelessly uncommercial. The one that did get through was already winning prizes. Now she recalled her first shock of pleasure when scanning the first pages and her excitement when told it would definitely be published.

'You're not listening.'

'What?'

'You're not listening, Kate.'

'Yes, I am.'

'What did I just say?'

'You're not listening, Kate.'

'Before that?'

'Don't know.'

'This is important.'

'Sorry.'

'I said, don't forget that the first viewing is eleven thirty tomorrow.' Mallory nodded at the telephone message from the estate agents that lay between them on the round zinc table. 'So don't wander off.'

'As if.' Kate picked up the notes. There were three appointments and she had only taken the details in a couple of hours ago. 'I can't believe what they're asking. These used to be workmen's cottages.'

'Now the chap who reads the news on ITV lives round the corner.'

'Does he?'

Kate hardly knew a soul. People came and went, bought and sold. The idea that London was actually made up of lots of little villages had not proved to be the case in her experience. Or perhaps she had just not made the effort to mix.

She said, 'Do you think I should get some of that stuff you can spray about?'

'What stuff?'

'Smells like fresh-baked bread or bacon sandwiches. Supposed to make people long to move in.'

'What if they're vegetarians?'

'We want to sell it, Mal.'

'It'll sell. And then we shall move down to Forbes Abbot and live in the peace and quiet of the English countryside, eating apples and publishing wonderful books – what could be nicer?'

He poured some more wine. Kate took up her glass and drank deeply of the greeny-gold liquid. Then she rested her head against the striped cushion of her chair, closed her eyes and slipped back into lazy daydreaming. The words, peace and quiet . . . English countryside . . . eating apples . . . wonderful books . . . running through her mind, twisting and twining, a golden thread of pure delight.

'Don't say no.' Mrs Crudge, having rinsed through the final tea towel, was draping it on the airer. 'Say maybe.'

'Mmm.' Benny was constantly recognising habits and rituals of half a lifetime that could now be honourably broken. The other day she had thrown away the screaming kettle. Now it would be all right just to put tea towels in the washing machine instead of soaking them overnight and simmering them for hours in the little zinc boiler. This understanding gave her no pleasure.

'Woof . . .' Mrs Crudge heaved on the nylon rope, hand over hand like a sailor doing a hornpipe. The airer creaked up to the ceiling. She wound the cord tightly around a peg on the wall, calling over her shoulder, 'All done and dusted.' Then, 'How about a cuppa, Ben?'

Five minutes later the two women sat facing each other, stirring freshly made tea. Mrs Crudge returned to the attack as Benny had known she would. But attack was the wrong word. She genuinely wanted to help. It was just unfortunate that her suggestion was outrageous. Quite impossible. And not only impossible but rather frightening.

Benny said: 'But I'm C. of E., Doris.'

'A person's religion is immaterial,' insisted Mrs Crudge. No pun intended.

'Not if we're talking about heaven, surely?'

'We're talking about the world of spirit.'

'Carey said it was all in the mind.'

'Mrs Fawcett in the Gardening Club, what does that meditation,' Doris sniffed the final word with great scorn, 'she reckons the mind's a void.'

'That can't be right,' said Benny. 'There must be some backing. Otherwise how would you see all the pictures?'

Mrs Grudge poured Twining's Breakfast into her mouth. She didn't seem to swallow like other people. Just opened her mouth and tipped the stuff in. Apart from a very occasional gulp it could have been water disappearing down a drain. Even after twenty years Benny was still impressed by the strangeness of it. Doris seemed quite unaware of this unnatural proclivity. She put her empty cup down and leaned forward. Benny held her ground.

'You'll meet some lovely people, Ben. Very sincere.'

'I'm sure they are.'

'And children come. You like children.'

That was true. Benny was very drawn to children.

'One of the mediums always brings her little girl.'

'It's not that I'm not grateful—'

'I've got a very soft spot for Karen. She's a lovely kiddie. Very quiet and shy.'

'I don't know . . .'

'After the service there's a slap-up spread: fruit buns, gingerbread. Roulade sarnies.'

Benny looked bewildered.

'Like a Swiss Roll but with a toothpick.'

'I see.'

'And when we've all had a lovely set-to there's the laying on of hands.'

'Oh dear.'

'Healing's not compulsory. Although . . .' Her own rough hand slipped over the check tablecloth, covered Benny's and gave it a gentle squeeze. 'Couldn't you do with a bit of help in that department at the moment, love?'

Not that sort of help, thought Benny. Not supernatural help, thanks very much. She had known as soon as Carey died that this moment would be forthcoming and was only grateful for Doris's restraint in letting a whole fortnight elapse. What a pity she had chosen Friday the thirteenth to speak out.

Over the past twenty-odd years Benny had got to know a great deal about her friend's religion, which she herself described as 'down to earth but spirit-based'. Benny had picked up the information in dribs and drabs. The subject would be dropped, sometimes for weeks on end. Then a further astounding revelation from beyond the grave would lead to more excitable whispering. Mrs Crudge, after fervently praising the medium in question at great length, always concluded with the same unanswerable and triumphant cry: 'Now, how could she possibly have known *that*!'

These tête-à-têtes only took place in their employer's absence. Quite early on, when Doris Cotterby, as she was then, had first come clean as to her secret leanings, Carey had jumped fair and square on what she called 'such barmy burbling'. So Benny now felt quite justified in saying, 'I'm sure Carey wouldn't like it.'

'Of course she'll like it! I bet she's dying for the chance to talk to you.'

'She always said the dead had nothing to do with us.'

'That was in earth space. Now Carey lives in the light. And knows the truth.'

'Mmm.'

'Seize the moment, Ben. While she's still on the first etheric level.'

Benny was not convinced. In the unlikely event that Carey was still on the first etheric level Benny was sure she would not relish being ordered back to earth space. She would probably be swigging a cocktail, drawing deep on one of her cigars and trying to set up a rubber of bridge. Any interruption would turn the ether blue.

'I don't think one should meddle with these things.' She hesitated. It was Benny's nature never to offend. She took this trait to extremes, even attempting conciliation with Croydon should he become sulky, or just mildly reticent.

'Also, I've heard such creepy stories. About weegy boards and crystal balls. People sitting in the dark holding hands. Things tapping on the table . . . ghosts . . .'

'Nobody holds anyone's hand. Not unless you want them to.'

Benny noticed she hadn't said anything about the ghosts.

'And we certainly don't sit in the dark. The Church of the Near at Hand is the cheerfullest place you could possibly imagine.'

Benny had walked past the building many times and one word she would never have used to describe it was cheerful. However, even as she told herself she was being utterly foolish, she couldn't help thinking what a wonderful comfort a message from Carey would really be. Perhaps in her very own voice.

She took a deep breath, said, 'I'll think about it,' and quickly changed the subject.

'Mallory rang up last night. He wanted to talk about the new business.'

'What's that then?'

'Book publishing. They're anxious for me to be involved. We'll be talking about it when they come down next weekend.'

'You'd be good at that. Being a reader, like.'

'I think I'd be most useful in reception. Meeting people, putting them at their ease. Carey used to say I had a real gift for it. I could give the authors tea. Maybe even some of my special twists.'

'That should hit the spot,' said Mrs Crudge.

Dennis had listened to Kate and Mallory expounding on their new business subject in his office with judicious calm. But underneath this professional exterior he was, in fact, pretty excited. Forbes Abbot, which had always thought there was more to that Mr Brinkley than met the eye, was absolutely right. By day successful financial strategist, by inclination collector of alarmingly strange machinery; the third string to Dennis's bow had so far been revealed to no one. Not even Benny.

When transcribing his dreams, as the therapist suggested, Dennis had been surprised to find this occupation extremely pleasurable. Exciting even. He began to get up an hour earlier than usual while the dreams were still fresh in his mind. Far from resenting this he looked forward to it, occasionally beginning to write even before he had had his tea.

Sometimes there was nothing to record but Dennis sat down anyway, reading through his previous notes and trying to see if there was any connecting thread. Sometimes there appeared to be a link but mainly not. If this was the case Dennis would forge one of his own in an attempt to make some sort of sense of the night-time chaos. Although he had never been good at English as a child, he found this creative process came quite easily.

Also, at this time, his nightly perambulations around the war machines would become slower and more reflective. Dennis would pause frequently to study the framed notes that detailed their fearful capabilities. The notes that had so alarmed Mrs Crudge. These were illustrated by drawings of human beings, mainly for the purpose of scale. Now, his imagination well and truly stirred, Dennis began to examine the figures more closely. Fleshing out their images in his mind he started to name them, making a note of their age and probable occupation. Inevitably they became increasingly real. Dennis placed them more precisely in an imaginary landscape of soft green hills and waterfalls and white turreted castles, backgrounds familiar from early religious paintings he had seen in Florence and Rome. He blessed them with wives and children and adventures. Cursed them with enemies. Gradually one man, more vivid and passionate than the rest, came to the fore.

It was at this point that he abandoned the simple notebook and Biro previously used to take his dream notes. Shy to acknowledge, even to himself, what was actually going on, he nevertheless began to take the whole business very seriously. He went out and obtained several reams of best-quality cream vellum and some black ink. Even as he bought a Mont Blanc pen he found himself regretting there was no feather to sharpen. A swan or goose quill, perhaps, or, best of all, one from a crow as was the way of the master mapmakers. The vague notion of himself as a writer persisted, becoming clearer and eventually inescapable as the piles of carefully inscribed paper grew. He would hurry home from work in the evening, sometimes barely pausing to eat before reimmersing himself in the medieval world.

He named his protagonist Jean de Mares and brought him to life in the year 1340 in the village of Cocheral in Normandy. Jean became apprenticed to the local blacksmith and grew up to be a superb swordsmith and designer of shields. As his reputation grew, noblemen and their knights spoke of him in such terms as eventually to attract the attention of the great mercenary, Sir John Hawkwood. Summoned to Paris, de Mares and his wife, a simple country girl, struggled to adapt to the world of mystery, betrayal and intrigue surrounding the court of Charles the Fifth. But almost immediately the honest smith fell foul of treacherous Pierre d'Orgement, head of the King's judiciary. This powerful antagonist used his mistress, a beautiful sorceress, to cast a spell on Jean, temporarily capturing his heart. Enmeshed in plot and counterplot, not knowing who was friend or foe, he became trapped into seeming to betray the King. His punishment? To charge and tilt in open combat against Bertrand du Guesclin, a thuggish, unscrupulous guerrilla fighter, brilliant at strategy, indifferent to the rules of tournament.

This was the great set piece and conclusion of the novel. When Dennis had, after nearly a year, finally reached this scene, he wrote it at great speed, his brain spinning with excitement and emotion. When it was all over (three o'clock in the morning) he raised his head and gazed about him in bewilderment. The orderly, homely surroundings of his sitting room seemed insubstantial, part of another world. It was the jousting tournament that was real to him. The fluttering pennants and swaying silken tents under a copper sky. The clash of steel and thunder of smoking hoofs. Creaking leather, horse muck and horse sweat. Humans screaming hatred and shouting encouragement. Blood everywhere.

When he was calmer, over the next two evenings, he rewrote this final scene, pacing it more effectively while struggling to keep the blazing colour and fierce energy, the power that drove the novel inexorably to its dark conclusion.

By now Dennis's right hand felt as if it were dropping off. Quite early on he had recognised the preciousness of his earlier affectation but had not been able to bring himself to change methods in mid-flow. Now he transferred *The King's Armourer* to a computer, polishing as he went. He still remembered the thrilling sensation of authority when typing the first line, the sheer strangeness of creating a human being out of thin air.

The completed manuscript ran to nearly five hundred pages, and once it was completed Dennis was rather at a loss. He felt exhausted but in a satisfied way. And his dreams were different. Infrequent, muted, without danger. Even though he now had a novel living and breathing in his army officer's trunk in the sitting room, its creation was still a mystery to him. How could a man possibly be a writer and live for over fifty years without knowing? Unbelievable. He wouldn't tell anyone, of course. It would be too embarrassing. It was enough simply to have written it.

CHAPTER FIVE

Barely a week after 13 Cordwainer Road was put on the market the house was sold. They got five thousand over their first offer and Mallory said, 'I told you so.'

Kate felt only slightly guilty about this, for the man who was gazumped had been awful. A stout city porker, he had strolled around hardly bothering to conceal his contempt for the Lawsons' shabby furnishings and well-worn carpets. Kate's suggestion that there might be fixtures or fittings he'd like them to leave behind was greeted with a barely concealed snigger.

The people who bought the house had a young daughter and wanted to move into the area, as the Lawsons had, because of the schools. Fortunately they were not part of a buyer/seller chain and so a contract could be drawn up straight away. They were an amiable couple, chatting, asking questions about the area, talking a little about their life, recently lived in Hong Kong. They were still there when Mallory came home. He opened a bottle and they all had a drink and shook hands over the deal.

All this happened on Monday evening, the beginning of his final week at the Ewan Sedgewick. Later, while devouring Marks and Spencer battered haddock and potato croquettes and broccoli washed down with Tavel rosé, they started to plan the move.

Kate had finished editing her last manuscript the previous month. All her publishing contacts knew of the grand plan. All offered masses of encouragement, while indicating their doors would remain open should, well, things not quite work out. Consequently, unencumbered by any other pressures, Kate was free to start sorting, packing, getting removal estimates and generally clearing out stuff. She looked forward to all this tremendously, having always experienced the most intense satisfaction from throwing things away. Even a single empty jar or can hurled into the bin made her feel good. Momentarily in her life there seemed to be less muddle. She sometimes felt that if she could throw everything in the world away – except her family, a few close friends, books and music – she would finally enter a serene and balanced world full of fresh air and clear light and loving kindness. Ha!

'What d'you mean – "ha"?'

'Oh – dreaming of Utopia.'

'I'm dreaming of bread-and-butter pudding.'

'Won't be long.' Kate went to the kitchen and checked the oven. She called over her shoulder: 'We'll have to get Polly over to sort her stuff out. And decide what furniture to take.'

'I think,' said Mallory, 'we should offer Benny anything she wants from Appleby House.'

'Of course, we must.' Kate came in with the pudding. 'It's a sad lot of stuff in that flat.'

'But it's her stuff. We'll have to be very tactful. She's quite capable of parting with things she's really fond of, then accepting all sorts of things she doesn't want just to please us.'

As they were musing on the impossibility of ever getting a simple, direct, uncomplicated response from Benny, the telephone rang. Mallory was nearest.

'Poll!' Mallory beamed. His eyes screwed up with pleasure as if blinking against the sun. 'Hey – the house is sold.'

'We haven't exchanged contracts yet,' called Kate.

'Take no notice of your mother.' Mallory waved his hand back and forth against Kate's objection. 'It's in the bag.' He listened. 'I *am* happy . . . How kind . . . Very thoughtful, darling . . . Don't forget to give her our love. Ring when you get back.'

Kate heard the phone click. As Mallory sat down again she said, 'What was all that about?'

'Polly thought she'd go down to Appleby House for a little while.'

'Is anything wrong?'

'No. She's a bit worried about Benny being on her own. You know how Ben panics over the smallest thing.'

'That's why I tried to persuade her to come back with us.'

'She'll be more comfortable with someone there.' Then, when Kate remained silent, Mallory added defensively, 'I think it's very sweet of Poll.'

Kate did not believe a word of it. Whatever the reason for her daughter's sudden return to Appleby House she was sure it would have naught to do with anyone's comfort but Polly's own.

That girl was down again. The one who walked around with almost nothing on. Someone had seen her getting out of a taxi in the drive of Carey Lawson's house, wearing a frock no bigger than a dishcloth, held up by a thread of ribbon. Also, added the perspiring observer (Mr Lattice from Mon Repos) as far as he could see, just from a quick glance you understand, there seemed to be no back or front to it.

Polly had not thought to telephone and tell Benny she was coming. The first Benny knew of her arrival was the clicking of anonymous heels across the hall's worn flagstones. Then there was a thud as something was dropped and the heels continued clicking across the wooden parquet of the living room.

Benny, invisible, huddled in a tall chair by the empty fireplace. Her face was pale with fright. She couldn't help recalling the creepy exchange with Doris just the other day. Would simply talking about ghosts be regarded as an invitation to one to materialise? Did they do it in the daytime? Surely they didn't make a noise – what would they have to make a noise with? And then there was that awful crime at Badger's Drift. No one had been caught so far. What if that youth the police suspected had not gone to London after all, as the police thought? What if he had come to Forbes Abbot instead? Benny held her breath and peered timidly round a corner of the chair. Then cried out, 'Oohhh . . .'

Polly nearly jumped out of her triple wedges. 'For heaven's sake!'

'I'm sorry. I didn't mean to—'

'My fault, just walking in.' Stupid woman. If she's that hysterical why not lock the front door?

Benny thought, but I locked the door, didn't I? And it would soon be getting dark. If she could forget something as important as that . . . Scrambling to her feet she began, in her clumsy way, to look after Polly.

'Have you eaten, dear? I could do an omelette. Perhaps you'd like a wash first?'

'No, thanks. Wouldn't mind a bath, though, before turning in.'

'It shouldn't take long to heat the water.'

'What?'

'But it can be temperamental.'

'Forget it. I'll just have a shower.'

'I'm afraid we never got round to putting in a shower.'

Polly sighed, then, with an air of great fortitude: 'Is there any form of running water at all here, Benny?'

Polly retired then, taking Benny's radio which she played, quite loudly, till the small hours.

Benny woke very early and immediately started worrying about Polly's breakfast. She had taken some sausages and bacon out of the freezer the night before but now realised this was not at all the kind of food a slim and glamorous young woman would want to start the day. She would probably ask for fruit. Fresh orange juice and the stuff Kate and Mallory liked – all grains and nuts and gritty bits. But Kate had taken the nearly full box back with her. All Benny had were porridge oats. Would raw porridge be acceptable? It didn't sound very nice.

But Polly didn't want any of those things. She finally appeared at noon looking, to Benny's unsophisticated gaze, like a princess in a fairy tale. She lit a cigarette, asked for coffee then said, 'Christ, instant,' though it was Sainsbury's best. All the shiny oranges, the speckle-free bananas even a ripe mango, Benny had managed to find in Forbes Abbot's tiny Spar lay unwanted on the table.

'I always think missing breakfast,' she said, 'gives you a wonderful appetite for lunch. Do you fancy anything special, Polly?'

'I'll get something in Causton. I've an appointment there this afternoon.'

'What about tonight?'

'Oh, do stop fussing, Ben.' With a bit of luck she would be on a Green Line going home by then. 'There's bound to be something in the cupboard.'

The cab put Polly down outside the Magpie Inn. Determined to be punctual for her meeting she had allowed so much time she was now twenty minutes early. Entering the pub, Polly immediately wished she hadn't. There was a stuffy, postprandial atmosphere. A smell of fried food, stale spices and cigarette smoke wafted out from the empty dining room. Polly glanced in as she wandered by. A penguin motif held sway. They were everywhere: posing in niches, perched on ashtrays, running wild over curtains and upholstery, jammed into high chairs. A tall wooden one wearing a real bow tie, held a 'Welcome' board inscribed with the menu.

Polly ordered a Campari and soda with ice. The fortyish barmaid took her money and pushed the ice-bucket over with a sour attempt at a smile. Polly ignored this. She was used to sourness from middle-aged women. And middle-aged men too, once they realised they were being sent about their business. There were half a dozen or so propping up the bar. Polly picked up a crumpled copy of *The Times*, sat as far away from them as possible and drank her Campari, enjoying the tart, herby fragrance. As she put the glass down the ice cubes clinked and chimed, an exquisite sound on a hot day.

Sensing one of the figures at the bar starting to walk towards her, Polly opened the newspaper, turning to the financial pages. He drew a stool up to her table. She smelled beer, monosodium glutamate and something else best not gone into. Polly wrinkled her nose and held the paper in front of her face.

'Like another?'

Polly closed *The Times*, folded it. Stared at the man. Bumpkin turnip head, sprouts of coarse skimpy hair, unspeakable teeth. Grandpa Simpson to the life.

'Another what?'

'One of them.' He nodded at her empty glass.

'No.'

'No, *thank you.*'

Polly sighed, threw the paper down, reached for her bag.

'Ay, ay.' An elbow nudge. 'Something tells me you're not from these parts.'

'What do you want?'

'Just making conversation.' A warty eyelid trembled into a wink. 'No objections, I presume.'

'Let's put it this way. How would you feel if you were happily having a quiet drink and a deeply unattractive, foul-smelling old woman came over, sat practically in your lap and started chatting you up?'

Polly watched with interest as the man's mouth dropped open, giving an unwantedly intimate view of several stained, snaggle teeth. Gross.

Eventually he said: 'Can't take a joke then?'

'It's your wife that has to take the joke,' replied Polly. 'Not me.'

Deeply refreshed both by the cold drink and this sharp little exchange, she swept from the bar, pushed hard on a blue door displaying a penguin in a pinny and found herself in the ladies. A satisfactory five minutes then drifted by as Polly considered her appearance.

She was wearing a plain blue dress with a calf-length skirt made of soft cotton. This had been filched from her mother's wardrobe during a recent visit to the house. With it Polly wore some flat white espadrilles, high-laced around golden, burnished legs. Her cloud of dark hair was confined at the nape of her neck within a black, petersham bow. She could not help looking beautiful – her cheeks glowed like peaches – but she had managed to look neither louche nor blatantly sexy. She applied Lancome's Brilliant Beige, the most subdued shade she had ever worn, to her lips. For the first time in her life she wished she wore glasses. Horn rims would have been the finishing touch. They would have given her face focus and added a responsible, intelligent, trustworthy look. The look of a woman who could sensibly handle sixty thousand pounds.

As this cool assessment of her appearance continued, Polly's mind, just as cool, was busy anticipating the coming meeting. Funny things, meetings. They might be with people you knew or perfect strangers; you could have planned your strategy in advance or decided to think on your feet but the outcome was nearly always uncertain. In the fierce mock meetings on her course Polly had played things as they came. She found this exhilarating, like jumping into a river with unknown depths and strong currents. Careful planning was for wimps. But today was not a mock meeting. Today was for real. She must not be reckless: too much hung on the result. Softly, softly . . .

At this point in Polly's reflections the mean-faced barmaid came in with some rolls of cheap toilet paper, a canister of Vim and a J-cloth.

She said, with bitter satisfaction, 'The toilet's closed for cleaning.'

'Would you like to try this?' Polly, who had been spraying her hair with Rive Gauche till it ran out, handed over the empty container with a smile of ineffable sweetness. 'It's really awfully nice.'

Walking down the High Street in the sunshine, crossing the market square and checking her watch, Polly found she was on time to the second. As she approached the office she saw an Asian man, holding the hand of a small boy, opening the street door. The boy had a boat and was chattering excitedly as they climbed the stairs, Polly following. Then the man opened a second door and she glimpsed a further set of steps. So, there was a flat over the office. She wondered if this too belonged to Brinkley and Latham. Dennis must be pretty well off. Mallory had said once that one of his clients owned half Bucks county. Polly now found herself standing exactly where she had stood just a few days earlier but blessedly unencumbered of either parent.

'Miss . . .' the receptionist referred to her diary, 'um . . . Layton?'

'Lawson.' Obviously Gail Fuller had decided to pretend not to remember her. Today was plainly the day for jealous women. This one was really knocking on. There was a silky moustache on her top lip, which Ms Fuller had attempted to conceal by bleaching. Fine until it caught the light, as it did now, when it positively sparkled. A naturally coarse-grained complexion had been likewise disguised with a solid layer of rosy foundation. She looked, decided Polly, like a hairy raspberry ripple.

'I'm afraid Mr Brinkley's running late.' A vague wave at a hard, narrow chair with wooden arms. 'Do sit down.'

Polly sank instead on to a small settee, adjusted the cushions to her satisfaction and studied the reading matter: today's broadsheets, fairly recent numbers of the *Economist*, the *Spectator* and a couple of *Private Eyes*. She picked up the *Independent* and tried to immerse herself in an article about street theatre in the Gorbals. It failed to hold her attention and, as the minutes passed, she felt herself getting crosser and crosser. When she thought of all the trouble she'd taken to arrive punctually. She picked up *Private Eye* and flicked through the pages. As asinine as ever. Polly only just stopped herself flinging it down with some vigour.

The door to reception opened and Polly looked up eagerly. It was Andrew Latham. He had a stack of letters which he dropped into a wire tray marked 'Post' on Ms Fuller's desk. He grinned and winked at Polly before disappearing again. She didn't like him any more this time than she had at the funeral.

How different all this was from her imaginings. Polly had seen herself arriving and Dennis waiting to greet her in the outer office with a warm, friendly smile. He would usher her inside, fuss a little, making sure she was quite comfortable, then sit down for a long, understanding heart-to-heart. In reality it was another half an hour before she even clapped eyes on him.

'My dear child . . .'

Child? Don't like the sound of that.

'Gail been keeping you entertained?'

I've had more fun under anaesthetic. 'Absolutely, Dennis.'

'Would you like a drink?' asked Dennis when they were settled in his office.

'It's a little early for me,' blushed Polly. She saw Dennis's nostrils twitch and wondered if he could smell the Campari.

'I meant a cup of tea.'

'Oh, yes. Lovely.'

Dennis rang through to the outer office then embarked on a round of courteous questions. How were Polly's parents? Had they got any further forward in their plans for the new business? Was Polly staying long? It must be so nice for Benny to have company.

Polly could not begin to say how kind and welcoming Benny had been. And her parents sent their regards. It was such a load off both their minds that she had someone like Dennis to turn to for advice. An old family friend.

A girl brought in a tray holding cups of red-brown liquid strong enough to dissolve not only any sugar that went into it but the spoon as well. There was also a plate of squashed-fly biscuits. Dennis drank deep and tucked in with every appearance of relish. Polly took a single disbelieving swallow and prayed the residue on her teeth would brush off.

Eventually, pushing his cup, saucer and the few remaining Garibaldis aside, Dennis said, 'So, Polly – what exactly can I do for you?'

'Well . . .' Now that the time had come Polly found herself uncertain how to begin. She had rehearsed various opening gambits. The one she chose would depend on an accurate reading of the situation when the moment to speak arrived. Now it was here and the reading was much harder to take than she had expected.

On the surface Dennis appeared his usual, slightly avuncular self. But his eyes were as sharp as tacks. And he had not apologised for keeping her waiting. What if this had not been a flustered oversight but a deliberate example of the sort of power play she loved to indulge in herself? One thing was plain – this was not going to be a friendly get-together with business arising almost as an afterthought. Polly decided the only sensible approach was to be completely open and straightforward.

'It's about my—' She broke off remembering that the word 'money' had not been mentioned once during the reading of the will. This ridiculous delicacy it seemed prudent to uphold. 'My legacy.'

'I see,' replied Dennis, who had never thought otherwise. 'Well, as you can't collect for another eleven—'

'Ten.'

'—months there's little point in my offering investment advice at the moment. The market's a volatile animal. What promises high returns today can wipe you out tomorrow.'

'I realise that.' He was talking to her as if she was six. 'I don't know if Dad told you, but I shall soon be in my final year at the LSE.'

'He did. Well done.'

Polly's cheeks flushed. She swallowed hard. This patronising pat on the head was the final straw. Dennis took up a pad of headed paper and unscrewed his fountain pen.

'If you have any savings to invest I can recommend—'

'Thank you, Dennis. I wasn't looking for free tips.' Savings! If only . . . She had nothing. Just this monstrous debt waxing fatter every day. 'I was simply trying to demonstrate that I'm pretty capable when it comes to handling money. Even . . . quite large amounts.'

'Polly, I can't help you on this one.'

He had known all along why she had come. Of course he had. And what the outcome would be. In which case, surely even agreeing to see her was no more than a tease. Indignation swelled in Polly. Swelled and burst forth.

'It's pretty ridiculous, don't you think? I can vote, have a child, get myself killed in the armed forces, marry, win the lottery, become a criminal, get tried with the grown-ups and go to prison and still not be thought capable of handling a measly sixty thousand pounds!'

'It must seem very unfair—'

'You wouldn't have to tell my parents.' Oh God! What was she saying? As if he would ever dream of colluding with her against them. This was all going so wrong. 'Sorry. I didn't mean that.'

'I do understand your frustration, my dear. And I sympathise. But it's simply not within my power to release the money.'

This statement, though true, was not for the reasons of professional probity that Polly immediately assumed. The fact was that the bequest, as part of Carey Lawson's general estate, was already technically in the Lawsons' hands. Dennis hoped Mallory would be wise enough to keep this to himself.

Polly, angry, disappointed and feeling furious tears about to spring, got up and began awkwardly to make her way to the door.

'Polly?' She stopped but barely turned. Dennis could see a pulse at her throat flutter. 'Are you in some sort of trouble?'

'Trouble?' She gave a thin, incredulous laugh. 'Honestly, Dennis . . .'

'Why not talk to me about it? I might be able to help.' He saw her fingers grip the doorknob, turn it. There was a brief hesitation. He went on: 'All meetings with clients are confidential. No one will know you've been here.'

Oh right, thought Polly. That's no one as in only Andrew Latham and Miss Hirsute in reception. Only the entire staff in the outer office. And anyone else in the building who happened to have seen her climbing the stairs. She slammed the door and walked away.

Latham saw her leave. Noticed the tightened lips and flushed cheekbones as she wove a path between the desks, towards the door. He was not the only one. As Polly disappeared Andrew put in an instructive moment watching everyone else watching her go.

Two out of the three females – one was pretending indifference – looked respectively envious and wistful. The men's expressions ranged from uncomplicated lust through simple yearning to light-hearted pleasure that the day could offer up such a treat for sore eyes. But no one cracked a mucky joke or described what they'd like to give Polly to make her life complete. No one clenched a fist and thrust their forearm into the air. The moment passed and they turned back to their machines, looking dazed and somewhat at a loss.

Andrew strode over to his window to see where Polly went. Crossing the market square, she stopped suddenly by the statue of Reuben Cozens,

66

a third-rate sculptor and Causton's only claim to fame. She sat down on some steps by his great bronzed boots, drummed her knuckles fiercely on her knees then suddenly swung her head round, staring hard up at the office of Brinkley and Latham.

Andrew stayed where he was. It would have been foolish to do otherwise. It was too late to pretend he wasn't there and jumping back would have made him look furtive and guilty. As if he was indeed spying on her. The girl's anger was clear even from this distance. The set of her neck, the rigid shoulders. He felt that at any moment she might shake both fists at him.

Andrew shifted his gaze, as if taking in the rest of the busy High Street, then turned slowly from the window. He would give a lot to know what had happened in Dennis's office to put her in such a paddy. Pointless asking – the po-faced old bastard was tight as a drum when it came to discussing clients. Still, no harm in having a word. Just the normal day-to-day exchange.

'Ah – Dennis.'

Everything about Andrew Latham irritated Dennis. The habit of always sounding surprised when he opened the door marked 'Dennis Brinkley' to find a man called Dennis Brinkley sitting behind it was only the beginning.

Latham had been wished upon him seven years earlier when George Fallon, the original owner of the business, had become convinced that the firm was top heavy and foundering. This was not true, as Dennis repeatedly tried to explain. Yes, it had grown over the years and they had taken on more staff but the work was there for them. The old man, unconvinced, thought they should start sacking people. They had reached an impasse when one evening, at a dinner at his wife's golf club, Fallon had found himself sitting next to Charlie Berryman.

Barely a fortnight later Berryman's daughter and her husband visited Fallon and Brinkley's offices. And just a few weeks after that, following an enormous injection of his father-in-law's cash, Latham took over George's half of the business and Fallon retired.

Dennis, who always thought taking against anyone on sight was extremely unfair, struggled to like the man. When it became plain that that was out of the question he struggled to be civil. Nearly always he succeeded, though Latham's coarsely robust sense of humour and crass insensitivity to the feelings of others made it extremely hard.

Three-quarters of George Fallon's clients had transferred their allegiance to Dennis or Leo Fortune, his most senior subordinate. The rest simply left. Sometimes Dennis wondered what Latham did all day. He turned up on a fairly regular basis and sat around fiddling with papers but his visitors were few. What there were seemed to be pretty much of his own stamp: all loud voices and back-slapping braggadocio. The sort of person that used to be described as 'hail fellow well met', though it seemed to Dennis that anyone with half an ounce of common sense who saw them coming would run a mile.

'Did you want something specific, Andrew?'

'Nope.' He picked up the remaining few biscuits and started cramming them into his mouth. Then he pushed the plate back on to the desk, sneering to himself as Dennis lined it up precisely with the cup and saucer. 'Just popped in for a chat.'

Dennis loathed that phrase. They were always using it on the television, which was why he hardly ever switched it on. Chefs would be 'popping' things into the oven, characters in plays would be 'popping out to post a letter' or 'popping round for a drink'. Once, in a crime story, a pathologist had suggested 'popping' a cadaver on a slab to 'open him up and have a looksee'. This brief recollection combined with concern over Polly's visit made Dennis as near to bad-tempered as he ever came.

'I'm rather snowed under at the moment, I'm afraid.'

'You should take a breather, Den. Come back refreshed.' Andrew smiled as he watched the skin above his companion's collar redden. Dennis hated being called Den. 'Did you have a holiday this year?'

'Why ask a question to which you know the answer perfectly well?'

'Just making conversation.'

'Well, you may have the time. I haven't.'

Dennis turned to his screen, tapped a few keys, frowned. Andrew stopped perching on the edge of the desk and flung himself into the chair that Polly had so recently abandoned.

'Mmm,' he said, insinuating his bottom deeper and deeper into the cushions, 'this is still warm.'

Dennis went even redder, clenched his teeth and tapped on.

'Beautiful girl. Why don't I ever get clients that look like that?' Pause. 'Didn't I see her at old Carey Lawson's funeral?' Pause. 'Don't tell me she's come in for some of the swag?'

Dennis clamped his lips together, pressed his buzzer with savage precision and told the girl who responded that he had some correspondence and would she come in straight away.

'Listen . . .' Drew Latham took his time getting out of the chair. 'You must come and eat with us. Gil was saying only the other day, "We haven't seen that Denny for ages." You know how fond she is of you.'

Dennis did not reply. He could count the times he had met Gilda Latham on one hand. Once when she had come into the office with her father at the time of the merger, at Carey Lawson's funeral, and also when he had given a talk on his machines to the Causton Library Users Association. She had gushed all over him afterwards and insisted on helping to put his slides away. It had taken him hours to get them straight.

Now he wondered at which moment during these brief encounters Gilda could possibly have become 'very fond' of him. He presumed it was a figure of speech used as carelessly as the word 'love' seemed to be these days. This had turned up last year on nearly all his Christmas cards, even from people he hardly knew, only the milkman showing decent restraint.

When home time came and people were packing up to go, Dennis decided to have another look at the Lawsons' account. As financial advisor to the new publishing business he should have up-to-date figures to put on the table at their inaugural meeting. He typed in the password, which was 'Parmain'.

Dennis was rather chuffed with his compilation of passwords, which were all medieval French. They had been chosen very carefully to complement the business or personality of the relevant client. So a drunken landowner gambling away his estate had 'Soteral'. A dress manufacturer 'Asure'. The owner of a prep school 'Enfancegnon'. A judge who rode with the local hunt, 'Esmochior'. A greedy banker, 'Termoint'. Aubain, fauconcel, dringuet, lorain – who would guess to what these words referred?

Only Leo Fortune had been told. And Dennis had been so delighted with this clever conceit that Leo hesitated to mention that labelling the disk on which the words were kept 'ENTR'OVRIR' might be a bit of a giveaway. But he agreed that the words themselves were pretty impenetrable. Having little knowledge of apples and their infinite variety, neither man noticed how near 'Parmain' was to Pearmain – as in Worcester.

On the bus going back to Forbes Abbot Polly sat and seethed. Seethed primarily because she didn't see herself as the sort of person who travelled on buses, ever. But also because she had been humiliated by some stuffy, dried-up old boot of a man purely for the pleasure of seeing her squirm. And he would tell Mallory. Of course he would. He was the sort. She could just hear him, pompously describing the scene in his office with mock regret. I felt as her father you should know . . . Yeah, right.

There were two stops in the village. The first was by the duck pond at the bend in Hospital Lane and almost directly opposite Dennis's house. Several passengers prepared to get off. It took a little while. They were loaded down with shopping and one woman with a toddler had a pushchair, which the driver got out of his cab to help her with.

As all this was going on Polly sat staring out of her window directly into the garage of Kinders. No sign of a car – presumably Dennis drove to work. No sign of that odious cleaner either. In fact, no sign of life at all. As the driver got back into his seat Polly jumped up, calling, 'Just a minute,' and got off the bus.

In the lane most of the disembarking passengers had wandered off but a couple remained, heads close together, talking in low voices. Polly crossed over to the pond and felt their glances follow. She sat on a little bench and observed the ducks. Uptailing, skimming, fighting. Then there was a sudden outburst of fierce quacks and by the time they died down the two women had gone.

Polly looked about her. A man in a cheese-cutter cap was walking his Labrador further up the lane, moving away in the opposite direction. Quickly she crossed the road, opened the gate of Kinders and entered the garage. There was the large pegboard and keys, just as she remembered it. What a fool the man was. Even though she could see no main house keys he was still asking for trouble. You could almost say she was doing him a favour, drawing attention to the risk he was taking before anything serious took place. A man should always be on his guard. Polly unhooked the bunch marked 'Office' and slipped them into her pocket.

She made her way down the lane, the weight of the three keys pulling on the skirt of her soft cotton dress. So, there it was. She had them. No one else knew she had them. She was safe. Yet Polly still felt uneasy. Having taken them on impulse she now had to think about how soon she could safely put them back. In an hour or so Dennis would be returning from work. Of course he might not check out the board. And he'd hardly be leaving the keys of the beautiful dark blue Lexus Polly had spotted on the day of the funeral hanging there. But he was bound to lock the garage at some point. How late might that be?

Slowly it dawned on Polly that if she was going to make use of the keys – and having stolen them she certainly intended to – she simply could not risk trying to put them back at all. Even if Dennis hadn't noticed their disappearance, finding a safe opportunity could prove extremely difficult. And if he had, and they then turned up on the board again, he'd get seriously worried. An impression could have been taken. He might even contact the police. But if she left things as they were Dennis would probably just think he'd mislaid them. Old people were like that. Always losing stuff.

In the kitchen, having wisely picked up a few Diet Cokes in the post office that morning, Polly took one out of the fridge, rolled the cool metal against her burning cheek, listened with pleasure to the soft hiss of escaping gas and drank deep. She removed the severe black ribbon and shook her hair out, running her hands through the glowing mass, lifting it away from her face. Then she eased her dress away from her sweating skin and splashed cold water over her neck and face, leaving the pearls of moisture to dry naturally.

The house appeared to be empty, which suited Polly fine. The last thing she wanted was non-stop wittering. Perhaps Benny was in the church. She had mentioned that morning being on the flower rota. Polly was incredulous. If God had made her that ugly and that stupid she would not have been playing the handmaiden at his altar. She would have been pissing on him from a great height. If not worse.

Now that she felt cooler Polly decided to sit outside. She thought first of the banks of a stream, which ran under a little bridge just a few yards from St Anselm's. The thought of resting her feet in the clear running water was most appealing, but in fact Polly got no further than the front door. A heavenly scent of lavender, mixed with rich perfume from a huge swag of honeysuckle smothering the porch, changed her mind. She sat on one of the wooden seats – just a shelf really – put her feet upon the shelf opposite and, for a brief moment, felt almost sorry that first thing tomorrow she would be returning to London.

But back to business. There were two things she had to work out and the first was how soon she could safely return to Causton and let herself into the offices of Brinkley and Latham. What time had it got dark last night? Half-nine? Tennish? What time did the pubs turn out? And did it matter if the odd drunk noticed someone slip a key into a door through which they had no right to enter?

Secondly, although she could come and go as she chose while at Appleby House, Polly decided it would be prudent, bearing in mind possible future conversations between Benny and her parents, to have a reason for her nocturnal rambling. She planned to ring her mobile using the house phone and mock up a conversation with a friend who, briefly in the area, wanted to take her out for a drink. No – he wouldn't be coming to the house. She would be meeting him at the village pub. This invention caused Polly to laugh aloud at her own cleverness. She drained her Coke, tossed the can into a clump of honesty, looked at her watch and sighed. Another three hours to get through. Polly was already dissing her earlier notion that peace, quiet and assorted herby fragrances held any sort of appeal. They were, in fact, excessively boring. The country sucked.

She thought about getting Benny's radio from her room – there was still some Emma B to go – but decided she couldn't be arsed. What she really wanted was a nice line of charlie, a Vodka Zhenya and the latest figures from the floor click-clicking, tackata tackata, through her hungry fingers.

But then something happened that wiped this irritation completely. Judith Parnell came out of the house opposite, got into an old grey Mazda and drove off, turning right, presumably aiming for the Causton road. Polly watched open-mouthed. The town was at least ten miles away. Even if she had only a couple of errands to do and came straight back it should take around an hour. And in an hour . . . why, the whole world could change.

Polly walked slowly towards the house called Trevelyan, the tarmac spongy beneath her feet. She made her way slowly down the side of the house, past a cloud of delphiniums and summer stock, fragrant in the blinding heat.

The back door was heavy and quite solid enough to be at the front. It had a letter box too and a brass knocker in the form of a lion's paw. Polly lifted it and rapped very gently – far too gently to be heard by anyone inside. Then she lifted the latch and walked in.

The sunlight vanished as the door closed behind her. She was in a tiny hall in which three white-painted doors stood open. Polly waited, motionless, for a long moment, almost holding her breath, then quietly called, 'Hello?'

But there was only silence. Perhaps he hadn't heard? In spite of her intense pleasure at the thought of the coming meeting, Polly was not entirely averse to extending this second-by-second delay. She had dreamed and dreamed of being with Ashley again. She didn't count their brief exchange of closely monitored smiles the last time she saw him.

Inevitably she had pictured their meeting. Played a few emotional variations, tried out some dialogue for style and content, wondered how soon they would touch and what the excuse – if any was felt to be necessary – would be. But of one thing she was quite sure: Ashley would be pleased, very pleased indeed to see her.

And if there should be any awkwardness – though no way could Polly imagine any such thing – she planned to say she was there purely to ask himself and Judith over to Appleby House for a glass of wine before supper. A simple transparency. She knew Judith would refuse and guessed that Ashley would recognise the invitation for the cover story that it was and have the nous not to pass it on. Indeed, with a bit of luck, by the time she left they would have reached the sort of understanding that would render any such subterfuge quite unnecessary in the future.

Polly pushed open the door on the left and found herself in a kitchen. She didn't linger – what would be the point? A kitchen was a kitchen. But she did notice that everything looked pretty shabby. The cupboards had been recently painted, rather clumsily. All this was a bit depressing and Polly frowned as she stepped back into the hall. Seediness seemed to her even more unattractive than outright poverty. At least poverty was in your face and minus that awful creeping pseudo-gentility that came with keeping up appearances. That was simply pathetic. In fact, Polly decided, given the right circumstances, poverty could be quite an advantage. After all, didn't everyone crave simplicity these days? You couldn't open a magazine without seeing some C-list celeb clad in artfully tattered rags, squatting on an African birthing stool in a stripped-down loft in Clerkenwell.

Momentarily diverted from just how near she herself presently was to out-and-out poverty, Polly pushed open the second door and, this time, entered a small, extremely cluttered sitting room.

Though there were masses of books on sagging shelves there were also several wide empty spaces.. Once-beautiful wallpaper (yellow and ivory toile de Jouy) was now faded, even slightly torn in one or two places. There was a darker rectangle in one corner, from the floor almost to the ceiling where for years something must have been standing. Polly, guessing at a grandfather clock, then noticed other different sized patches on the walls where presumably paintings had once hung. In the centre of the ceiling, from which depended a single light with a plain linen shade, were several holes, the Rawlplugs still inside. Polly wondered what sort of light had been replaced and guessed at a chandelier. Finally a large glass and walnut cabinet held just three pieces – a silver salt dish lined with dark blue glass and an exquisite shepherd and shepherdess in Watteauesque costumes.

On the top of the cabinet was a large coloured photograph of Ashley and Judith. They were on a boat, leaning over the side, laughing into the wind. Their hair was all blown about and Judith's cardigan, its sleeves knotted loosely around her neck, was flying up and out behind her like a sail. She was staring fixedly, devouringly even, at Ashley who was gazing out of the picture at the far horizon.

Polly, not easily impressed, caught her breath at the sight of him. At the vivid brilliance of his smile; at the golden brown glowing skin and muscular shoulders. What a contrast to his companion. Coarse black hair, a thick neck and a complexion so dark and muddy Polly felt she could, in all honesty, describe it as swarthy. Plus the woman was extremely short, barely up to Ashley's chest. Dwarfish, to be precise. So engrossed was Polly in enjoyable contemplation of Judith Parnell's squat sturdiness that her heart almost stopped at a sudden clatter directly behind her. Jumping round, she all but fell over. No one was there.

Then she realised the sound came from a fax machine in the final room, only fractionally bigger than a dog kennel, underneath the stairs. Polly took a step or two inside – three would really have been stretching it – and gazed about her. A small-screen monitor, a computer, disk drive and keyboard on what looked like a card table. An elderly Epson printer, a mug of pens and the *Financial Times*. The phone, answering and fax machines were on a broad window ledge.

She wondered if Ashley might be in bed. Asleep presumably or he would surely have responded when she had called out. So that was that. There was no way Polly was going upstairs. That would be clumsy in the extreme. Positively crass. The game here was flirtation, casual and light-hearted. She was wooing Ashley, not hunting him down.

But then, stepping back out on to a cinder path, she saw him at the far end of the garden, inside a fruit cage. He had a white china bowl in the crook of his arm and was picking raspberries.

The force of Polly's immediate reaction truly shocked her. Dry throat, quickened heartbeat, nausea. These were not familiar sensations and she was deeply uneasy when they occurred. Almost afraid. She hesitated. Nothing had happened so far. She could walk away now – walk down the path, through the wrought-iron gates, across the road to Appleby House and never look back. Ending something before it began and still in control. That would be the sensible thing to do.

But Polly, who had always had everything she ever wanted, was ill-equipped for sensibleness, let alone self-sacrifice. The nausea passed, an

73

upsurge of excitement took its place and she was just about to make her way towards the vegetable garden when she noticed a movement. Near the ground, between the first two rows of canes, there was a large circle of blue and white stripes, which suddenly shifted, revealing itself to be the rear end of Benny Frayle.

Back at Appleby House Polly felt no gratitude that what might well prove to be an acutely wise decision had been taken by the Fates on her behalf. Instead she felt furious with Benny. What on earth had the woman been doing over there, monopolising Ashley? It wasn't as if they could have anything in common. Benny had nothing in common with anyone as far as Polly could see, except perhaps one of those stumbling stammering overweight losers who turned up regularly on television quiz shows, barely able to answer the simplest question and present only as an object of ridicule.

But by the time Benny returned with a huge amount of delicious raspberries Polly's mood had softened. After all, there was no special hurry. Wasn't hope deferred supposed to make the heart glad? The recollection was admittedly vague. Her mother had given her a diary one year with a quotation on every page from Shakespeare or the Bible or some famous novel or other. Tried to explain the beauty of the words and their context, hoping to lead Polly towards literature, to broaden her mind. Had even suggested she give figures a rest for a while. Fat chance. What had literature ever done for Polly's mother? Twenty-five years in the business and still only picking up peanuts. Polly had met jobbers and brokers, some hardly older than herself, earning as much in a month.

But then, not too long after this, when Benny was cutting some white bread and butter to go with the kippers (kippers!) for supper, Polly, previously fretting at the slowness of time passing, realised what an excellent opportunity had suddenly presented itself. No point in questioning her mother about the Parnells. Look how suspicious and snappy she'd been when Polly had merely suggested asking them around for a drink. But Benny, who had known the couple for as long as they'd lived in Forbes Abbot, Benny would not be suspicious. And she loved to talk. All Polly would have to say was something along the lines of: 'How kind of Ashley to give you all these lovely raspberries, Ben. I must say they do seem to be awfully nice people.' So Polly tried exactly this, with immediate success.

'Oh – but he's always bringing salads and vegetables over for us, dear,' replied Benny. 'Judith too. They are so kind.'

As the evening wore on Polly discovered more and more about the kindness and niceness of Benny's nearest neighbours. About how they always looked after Croydon and took in post and watched out for burglars when Ben and Carey had gone away. How, when Carey became seriously ill, Judith had driven into Causton to collect her prescriptions even though she had her own work and Ashley to care for. Poor Ashley, ill for months now and no one seemed able to find out what it was. Judith had tried everything under the sun, such expense. And she worked so hard.

When there was a bit too much of Judith, which honestly meant any mention longer than a couple of seconds, Polly skilfully directed the babbling stream back towards Ashley.

Benny chattered happily on. She welcomed the opportunity. It was the evenings when she felt most lonely – daytime could be easily filled – and she was really enjoying herself. And one of the nicest things about the conversation was how interested Polly seemed to be in everything she had to say. It was really heart-warming.

Benny branched out a little, touching on Dennis. Had Polly seen his war machines? They were really amazing, though rather frightening too. Benny had only seen them once and nothing in the world would induce her to go into the room again. Then, sensing Polly's interest waning, she began to describe various village worthies, all seemingly just as nice and kind and interesting as the Parnells.

Polly listened, hardly able to disguise her amazement. She had never heard a conversation like it. This woman seemed to think ill of absolutely no one. How could anyone remain so innocent in this day and age? And how on earth did she cope with life? You'd hardly trust her to post a letter.

Eventually dusk fell. Polly excused herself and went upstairs to use the phone in her great-aunt's bedroom to dial her mobile. It worked a treat. Running back downstairs, rootling about in her rucksack on the kitchen table she talked excitedly to a friend who'd come especially down. The call concluded, Polly cut short Benny's interested but slightly anxious questions, saying the first thing that came into her head.

'Someone I'm going on holiday with, Ben. To Crete, actually. They just want to sort out the final arrangements.'

CHAPTER SIX

Nearly all the buildings on Causton market square had been there since the nineteenth century and most from the eighteenth or even earlier. The local preservation society, which had strong moral if not financial support from British Heritage, was very hot on parity of historical detail. There had been several heated discussions when Fallon and Brinkley had applied to put up a simple brass plate next to the, by now, half-fake Tudor frontage of the Nat West Bank. It was gravely pointed out to Mr Brinkley that the said offices were, in fact, over rather than adjacent to the bank and thus the plate would be rather misleading. Dennis, with admirable restraint, asked if his clients were supposed to leap twenty feet in the air to check that they had arrived at the correct address for their appointment. Despite such levity he had finally received permission, though it had been touch and go. Of course that had been years ago. Now the rot had well and truly set in.

One of the shops had been converted to a private dwelling and the new owners had painted the outside walls lime green. Furious, frothing correspondence ensued but the couple were adamant about cheering the old place up a bit. They were breaking no laws and were blithely indifferent to emotional blackmail along the lines of sceptred isles, thrones of kings and silver seas. When told by the rector's wife that if they remained firm no one of any standing would speak to them, hysterical cackles followed her all way back to St Hubert's Close.

Then there had been Lovage and Cardoon, wide-ranging haberdashers, also selling fine linens and dusty-pink restraining garments to the middle classes since the 1950s. The remaining partner having finally retired, the business was taken over by a rather common cake shop. The new owners ripped out all the beautiful stained-oak fittings and narrow, glass-fronted drawers, put in cheap chairs with tartan seats and plastic tray attachments, then had the cheek to christen themselves Patisserie Française. An offence under the Trades Description Act, sniffed the preservation committee, the pastries being about as French as Colman's mustard, and the '*café crème*' indistinguishable from gravy browning.

But Mr Allibone, the fresh fish and game merchant, was a shining jewel in this crown of struggling conservation. The facia of his lovely shop had been installed by his grandfather, Albert Allibone, in the 1930s and remained unimproved to the present day. Heavy black calligraphic script impressed on a background resembling crumpled silver paper described the business. In the front windows crabs and shining mackerel, mussels, orange-speckled dabs, fresh monkfish and undyed smoked haddock circled a huge turbot. All this lay on great slabs of ice garlanded with real seaweed. The game was kept in cold storage.

Dennis enjoyed a nice piece of fresh fish, and it was fresh at Allibones. Bright-eyed with sparkling scales and smelling of the sea. Rather pricey, but his customers never minded that. Were inclined to boast of it, in fact; make remarks along the lines of: 'You'd be lucky to find quality like this at Tesco's. Or service either.'

There was a queue, three women clutching old-fashioned wicker shopping baskets. Dennis patiently tacked himself on the end, exchanging greetings.

'So what's your fancy today, Mr Brinkley?' asked Brian Allibone, winking at nothing in particular and tipping back his boater. 'A nice pair of herrings? Wing of skate?'

'To tell the truth – though I hate to spoil such perfection – I really fancy a bit of that turbot.'

'Then turbot it shall be, sir.'

The fishmonger heaved the huge creature off the slab, wiped his hands on his blue-and-white-striped apron and picked up a sharp knife. The saucily tipped straw hat, rosy cheeks and glossy black moustaches gave a first impression of jovial warmth and humour. But the twinkling eyes were cold and his nose was white with a pointy, pinched tip. All the better for poking into other people's business, folk said. And they were not far wrong.

'Working late again the other night, Mr Brinkley?'

'Late?' Dennis looked puzzled.

'Tuesday, I believe. I only took a casual glance but your little snake lamp was on well past midnight.'

Mr and Mrs Allibone lived above the shop that faced Dennis's office across the cobbled square. It was rumoured that his casual glances were reinforced by a set of powerful field glasses kept on the sitting-room window seat for just that purpose.

'It couldn't have been.' Dennis knew what Mr Allibone meant by 'again'. A couple of weeks ago he had been kind enough to point out a similar occurrence, though the hour was somewhat earlier. And once last week too.

Dennis had assumed a light left on and had made sure every evening after that to switch off before leaving. He had even written a little stick-on note, 'Remember Switch', and attached it to the outer doorframe.

'Oo-er,' shuddered Mr Allibone, adding fresh parsley to the turbot and wrapping the lot in thick white paper. 'Dirty work at the crossroads.'

Dennis watched the man's nostrils flex and twitch, sniffing a mystery. All this was most distasteful.

'I've ... er ... got one of those time things,' he said, handing over a

77

five-pound note and receiving a few pence in exchange. 'Can't be too careful these days.'

'Ah, that explains it.' Mr Allibone put the parcel into a plastic carrier showing a plaice dancing on its tail. It wore a top hat and a bow tie and was twirling a cane. 'Shan't need to tell you next time it happens then?'

'That's right,' said Dennis. What else could he say? He left the shop realising the momentary satisfaction gained from squashing Mr Allibone's prurient curiosity had been dearly bought. Now he had no way of finding out if the light was ever switched on again after the business was closed. Not unless he sat in his car night after night and watched on the off chance, which was plainly ridiculous.

Instead of getting into the car and driving home, Dennis put the fish in the boot and returned to his office. He walked over to the window and watched Mr Allibone winding back his dark green awning in preparation for closing. Then he flung himself into the comfortable armchair facing his desk and prepared to think.

First – and most important – no one had broken in. Second – someone had been in this unviolated office late at night and more than once. When it first happened, or rather when it was first reported, for Mr Allibone could hardly be at his post every second after sunset, Dennis had been quite disturbed. Only himself and Latham had keys and, after checking that his own spare was safely on its hook in his garage, he asked Andrew if perhaps he had returned to the office for some reason. But even as he mentioned the actual dates Dennis realised how unlikely this would be. It was hard enough getting the man to put in a few daylight hours, let alone turn up after dark.

Andrew had been quite indignant. Explained that he and Gilda had been at a Lions' charity dinner for multiple sclerosis in the first instance, where he had become so tired and emotional that the Lathams' solicitor, a fellow Lion, had driven them home. He'd stayed on for a bit to make some black coffee and help Andrew to bed. Why on earth, Andrew asked surlily, would he then go out again purely for the pleasure of sitting in an empty office? In fact, if you asked him, this whole conversation was beginning to sound bloody insulting. Six days later when the same thing was supposed to have happened again the Lathams had gone with another couple to the theatre.

There was no cash in the office worth mentioning. It was possible someone could be so desperate to know the details of another's financial affairs that they would break into his money man's office and look them up. Possible but extremely unlikely, not to mention difficult. The passwords to all the accounts except his own were on a separate disk that was kept in the combination safe. And at least half of Dennis's clients were private, which removed any suspicion of industrial jiggery-pokery. Private but pretty substantial – two of them were millionaires several times over.

Dennis sighed and tried not to think of his turbot sweating away in the

Lexus instead of at home in the Neff, along with some white wine, cream and a fine sprinkling of minced shallots. He supposed what he should really do was examine each account in detail to see if anything was amiss. Given the impenetrability of the passwords he felt this to be rather pointless, though it seemed irresponsible not to check.

He switched on his Apple, brought up John Scott-Abercrombie and got stuck in.

Two hours later Dennis was scrutinising Harris-Tonkin (Light Aircraft) when an alarming thought exploded in his mind. Directly beneath his feet were the rear premises of the bank. The strongroom, to be precise. Could it be that a gang of robbers was even now engaged in early reconnaissance?

'Don't be ridiculous,' muttered Dennis to himself. Then: 'This is what comes of writing fiction.' All the same, it momentarily entered his mind to give the police a ring. Then he started to anticipate the interview.

A disturbance at your place of business, sir? Not a disturbance, as such. A break-in? No – that is, someone did *get* in . . . Was much taken? Nothing's really been taken, no. So what actually is the problem? An . . . er . . . acquaintance saw my office lights on late at night when I know I'd switched them off. More than once, actually. I see. Could we have this person's name, sir?

And, of course, Dennis couldn't give it. First, because he'd stupidly told Mr Allibone that the light only came on because of a time switch. Second, because he couldn't bear to see the man salivating with pleasure at the thought of being part of a drama involving his, Dennis's, discomfiture.

Damn and blow and blast and bother! Dennis put his head in his hands and groaned. He hated, *hated*, mess and muddle. Why did the nosy blighter have to pass on such anxiety-causing information? But even as he thought this Dennis recognised how unreasonable he was being. He was thankful enough for his own Neighbourhood Watch back in Forbes Abbot.

This recollection of the village, quiet in the evening twilight, soothed him. Home, that was the ticket. Things would look different from his favourite armchair with a glass of Laphroaig, some walnut bread and a nice piece of Double Gloucester. He could lose himself pleasantly in Xenophon. The *Economics*, for choice. All was in wonderful order there. A place for everything and everything in its place. A few words with dear Benny as well, perhaps, if it wasn't too late. The turbot could go on ice for a weekend treat. She might like to come and share it with him.

Sitting behind his car's padded steering wheel, glancing up at the unillumined windows of his office, Dennis realised how close other windows were. Those of the flats on either side, for instance. Chances were old Allibone had simply made a mistake. On the other hand, he had seemed pretty definite . . .

Enough was enough, decided Dennis. And there wouldn't be any more. First thing Monday he would organise a man to come and change the locks.

* * *

Earlier that same day Judith was seated at the kitchen table bagging up runner beans as quickly as Ashley could top and tail. She thought how wonderful it was that he was still able to work in the garden and had said so, unfortunately referring to it as pottering. He'd been quite sharp with her. Making him sound like an old man with nothing better to do. He always said sorry after he snapped but he didn't this time so she said it for both of them.

Scribbling the date any-old-how over a large sheet of labels Judith recalled their first harvest. Redcurrants from bushes already established, carrots, perpetual spinach and a few courgettes. A small yield but she had been determined to freeze some. After transcribing the labels she had bought some coloured pens and decorated them carefully with fruits and berries. Making chutney had been another pleasure. She'd snipped at circles of gingham cloth with pinking shears, then tied the caps over the lids with ribbons. Ashley had laughed, called it her Trianon period and produced a Laura Ashley poke bonnet as a joke. Ten years ago. Now it was all just one long chore. Judith would be glad when summer came to an end.

'When's my next hospital appointment?'

'Three weeks. You're not worried, are you, Ash?'

'No. I'd like to be worried. It'd bring hope into the equation.'

'Oh – don't say that. I'm sure things will—'

Judith stopped herself. She was doing that more and more these days: chiding him for not being more positive or jollying him along with helpings of pie in the sky. I'm sounding, she thought, like one of those inane self-help books: *You Too Can Dance Like Darcey Bussell*; *Look Like Michelle Pfeiffer*; *Write Like Woody Allen*; *Rule the World*.

How long it seemed now since this whole sad frightening business started. It had been so gradual. General tiredness. Limbs aching slightly for no reason that Ashley could discern. Mild skin irritation. Gradual loss of appetite. First, meals not finished. Then smaller meals, which soon were also left unfinished. His teeth had begun to ache, though a visit to the dentist found nothing wrong. He would feel cold in any temperature under twenty-five degrees. His heartbeat quietened.

Investigation at the hospital had been ongoing and thorough. First were blood tests, all showing no disorder. His immune system had not broken down. He was not anaemic. His liver and kidneys were functioning properly. He also had a stomach endoscopy. A colonoscopy. A CT scan (very unpleasant). An MRI scan (worse). A few days ago he'd had yet another blood test. Poor Ash.

In tandem with all this had run every alternative therapy under the sun. They had worked through the lot with only Ayurvedic medicine still untried. Nothing helped physically but sometimes Ashley seemed a bit brighter, a little more confident afterwards. The money spent was astronomical, and didn't include the hours, days and weeks surfing the Net, for there were hundreds of rare diseases, or the sending and receiving of e-mails.

'I was wondering . . . Jude?'

'Sorry. Drifted off.'

'Could we go out, d'you think?'

'Out? Um . . . I suppose . . .'

'Just to have tea, perhaps. A change of scene would be really nice.'

'Of course we could.' He must be sick to death of these four walls. Why on earth hadn't she thought of it? 'Anywhere special?'

'There's that new hotel on the way to Beaconsfield. I think it's called the Peacock—'

'No. I . . . wouldn't want to go there.'

'OK.' Ashley, frowning, put the colander of beans aside. He waited, curious and concerned.

'They're . . . um . . . surly.' Judith calmed her unsteady breath. 'I found them surly.'

'Then we'll go somewhere else. The Soft Shoe Café?'

'I love that name.'

'So Fred and Ginger.'

Judith sang: ' "Isn't this a lovely day to be caught in the rain?" '

Suddenly she was happy. It would be an event to go out together even if it was just to an ordinary caff in boring old Causton. She smiled in anticipation. This was the second nice thing to happen in so many days, the first being the disappearance of the Lawson girl.

Judith assumed she had gone back to London. She had last seen Polly a couple of nights ago, running through the gates of Appleby House into the soft grey evening light. Swinging her bag over her shoulder, lifting her head towards the early stars, smiling. Where was she going, without wheels, at this time of night? Meeting someone presumably. Someone who didn't want to drive up to the house. Then, just a few yards along the lane, she used her mobile. Talked briefly, checked her watch and wandered off into the village.

So vivid was this recall that Judith gave quite a jump when their own phone rang. She got up but Ashley, who was nearer, stretched across the back of his chair and picked up the receiver. He said: 'Kate!' the exclamation warm with surprise and pleasure.

Judith's contentment dissolved like mist on the sea. She longed to snatch the thing from him. It would be for her anyway, wouldn't it? Something domestic. She reached out a hand. Ashley waved her away.

'How are you? More important, when are you coming back?' He laughed then said, 'Too long, too long.'

'What does she want?' Even to her own ears Judith sounded shrill. 'Ashley?'

'Really? We saw her only this morning . . . Of course we will. You

81

should have rung before . . . Try not to worry. I'm sure everything's OK. Do you want a word with Jude? . . . Fine. We'll check it out. Bye.'

'What did she want?'

'I wish you wouldn't do that.'

'What?'

'Interrupt, try and take over. I may be ill but I'm still capable of handling a phone call.'

'Sorry.' I should have a record made.

'They've been trying to ring Appleby House for two days. The operator said the phone was off the hook.'

'Right.' Judith got up, glad to leave the beans. 'I'll go and sort it.'

Benny was amazed at Judith's news. They checked both the downstairs telephones, which were securely on their rests. The only other set, explained Benny, was in Carey's room and it couldn't be that because no one had gone in since she died. Well, herself once, but only because she'd absolutely had to.

Seeing Benny becoming increasingly anxious and distressed Judith suggested the operator could have made a mistake and there was actually a fault on the line. However, before they reported it shouldn't they make absolutely sure . . .?

'I must come with you,' cried Benny, and immediately regretted it. She had spoken impulsively, feeling somehow that no one but herself should enter Carey's room. Yet, as they both climbed the stairs, Benny made herself acknowledge how foolish this attitude was. Pretty soon Kate and Mallory would be living here and then not just Carey's room but the whole house would probably change beyond recognition.

'This is the one.' Benny paused only long enough to take a single deep breath, then turned the white ceramic knob and went in. She saw the telephone receiver straight away. It was lying on its side on the bedside table.

Judith moved quickly, putting her arm round Benny's waist. Taking the full weight.

'Benny – look, it's all right. Come and sit down. You must have made a call and forgotten to—'

'I didn't! *I didn't* . . .' Benny let herself be supported towards the bed. 'I haven't been in here . . .'

She sat, pale as paper, lips trembling, hands jiggling. Further denying the possibility, she shook her head back and forth with such ferocity Judith feared she would hurt herself.

'Oh, dear . . .' Judith attempted to hold Benny and calm this terrible agitation. She tried to remain patient but it wasn't easy. Surely this was a reaction too far? Next time, she thought, I'll send Ash. 'Would you like me to make you some tea?'

Benny did not reply but her eyes kept sliding sideways to the telephone and she became very still. When Judith picked up the receiver to replace it she gave a little whinny of fear. Judith sighed, struggled not to show her vexation and went downstairs to put the kettle on. The minute the tea was made she would ring the Lawsons. The sooner they came down the better. Benny was not Judith's responsibility. She had more than enough on her plate without having to cope with hysterical old maids.

The following morning Mrs Crudge, having spent at least half an hour attempting to comfort, console and counsel was on the point of giving up. As she was to say to her Ernest that very evening, 'I was wrung to a wither.'

'Benny, my love – you don't know how lucky you are.' She drained her coffee cup. 'Some folks'd give their right arm to have a direct sign from the paralogical.'

'I thought it was that murderer. From Badger's Drift.'

'He's miles away by now.'

'Or a burglar.' Benny started crying and snuffling again.

'Burglars burgle things. They don't just take a phone off the hook then run off.'

'I suppose not.'

'I mean – it wouldn't be worth their while, what with prison and everything. Just going around taking phones off hooks.'

'Judith said I must have made a call but I didn't, Doris. I haven't been in that room since just before the funeral.'

'Of course you haven't. No living hand touched that apparatus. It's a pity you didn't get on to me straight away. There might have been etheric traces lingering.'

'What could you have done, Doris?'

Doris hesitated. Her solid cheeks took on an almost clover-like hue and Benny realised that her friend was actually blushing.

'Well, I am actually what is known in psychic circles as a sensitive.'

Benny wanted to ask, a sensitive what? but it seemed a bit rude. 'What does that mean exactly?'

'We see things.' A definite note of superiority had crept into Mrs Crudge's voice. 'Things that other people can't see.'

'You mean things that aren't there?'

'I shouldn't fret about technical details, my love. What matters is – the sign's been given. Miss Lawson's in touch. All you have to do is come along next Sunday afternoon to receive the message.'

This time Benny didn't immediately reject the idea. She sat quietly, thinking about it. She thought, what if, in the face of all modern knowledge and intelligence and science and common sense and everything, Doris was right? Could it be true that Carey was making huge efforts to connect, leaving signs and wisps of stuff and suchlike? Imagine the strain, the sheer energy involved in heaving that receiver off its stand. She would not be very pleased if Benny could not even be bothered to go along and collect any messages. It didn't bear thinking of. Even a disembodied Carey was a force to be reckoned with. What if she came to the house and started haunting?

'Would other people be aware of a ... presence, Doris?' Even mentioning the word made Benny feel all spooky. 'Kate and Mallory, for instance?'

Doris hesitated before replying. She had known Mallory all her grown-up life. He had been seven years old when she had first started working for Carey Lawson. A regular visitor to Appleby House and a bright little chap always helping himself to cakes and biscuits the minute her back was turned. Or hiding her bag and outdoor shoes, then finding them just as she was about to explode with frustration. But Doris, having no children of her own, had grown quite fond, for there wasn't a spark of malice in him. Which was more than you could say of that brazen trollop, his daughter. She had been a spiteful, manipulating child and Doris was glad when she got old enough to be left at home.

She liked Kate, though. Unlike some of Carey's visitors Mallory's wife was really thoughtful. You'd never arrive first thing to find a sinkful of dirty dishes with food caked on when the Lawsons were staying. Or unmade beds and the bathroom floor swimming and soaking towels thrown all over ...

'Sorry, Ben?' Doris'd drifted off for a second there. That was the strange thing about the past: you always remembered it as being much more interesting than the present yet at the time it was happening it had actually been rather dull.

'They're coming today, you see ...' Benny had been overwhelmed with emotion when Judith, having rung the Lawsons, had returned to say that Kate would be with her as soon as possible the next day. And that Mallory would drive down after school had closed. She had wept tears of gratitude, much to Judith's embarrassment. '... so I was wondering if I should tell them. About Carey ... um ...'

'Coming through?'

'Yes.'

'Best not.'

In discouraging Benny Mrs Crudge was not prompted by any notion of exclusivity. She had no wish to shut the Lawsons out – quite the contrary. Nothing would have made her happier than all four of them going along to the Church of the Near at Hand and partaking of spiritual sustenance. But experience had taught her that such an excursion would never happen. That there would always be a barrier dividing the likes of the Lawsons and the church's congregation. And Mrs Crudge, over the years, had come to the reluctant conclusion that the barrier was education.

Or rather overeducation. Doris had left school at fifteen and started work straight away. She had never seen the point of exams and did not regret her inability to pass any. Intelligence, it seemed to Doris, could be quite a handicap for a simple person. Obviously everyone needed to read and write. They needed to understand figures, though that wasn't as important as it used to be what with calculators and everything. But then a line should be drawn. Going on and on and on led to nothing but trouble. Scientists who made bombs, doctors who chopped all the wrong bits off, judges who let criminals go scot-free, all so-called educated people.

As for education opening the mind . . . That was not what Mrs Crudge and fellow strivers after a new order of cosmic being had found. The minds of the sneering cynics – which seemed to include practically everyone you met these days – were closed tighter than sprung traps. Oh, the workers for the high meridian knew what it was to be a persecuted minority all right! And yet these know-alls, these eggheads, were the real losers for they had lost the ability to believe in miracles. They had lost their way.

'I think, Ben – if you're worried about telling Mallory, say you're going round mine for tea come Sunday.'

'Oh, I couldn't do that,' said Benny, deeply embarrassed. 'It would be a lie.'

'No, it wouldn't.' Doris was getting up now, reaching for her outdoor coat, a light wool in spite of the warmth of the day. 'That's exactly what we'll be doing after the service – having tea together.'

'I suppose you're right.'

Though sounding subdued and even a little fearful, in fact Benny had already decided she would go. If anything dramatic happened she would be with a friend and surrounded by people so could come to no harm. And if nothing happened she would regard the whole thing as a bit of an adventure and enjoy the slap-up spread.

Benny sighed and wished she felt what Doris would doubtless call 'a bit more smart'. She had slept thoroughly, if not very well, waking with nothing worse than a dry mouth, a bit of a headache and a general feeling of stupefaction. Judith had offered her some of Ashley's sleeping pills, which Benny had refused to take on the grounds that they could be dangerous, being someone else's prescription.

Judith got really terse then, saying that she couldn't possibly leave Benny in the state she was and that she, Judith, had a job to do the next day and a sick husband to look after and needed her sleep just as much if not more than Benny did. So Benny had meekly swallowed two pills and was now wishing she hadn't.

When Doris had left, Benny got slowly to her feet, washed up the coffee cups then made the bed in Kate and Mallory's room with clean linen and lavender bags underneath the pillows. She had no notion of when Kate would actually arrive but, in case it was before lunch, decided to buy some fresh crusty bread from the Spar shop.

It took almost twenty minutes to cover the quarter-mile walk for Benny had to stop and chat to anything on two legs and pat or stroke anything on four. The store had some really nice York ham on the bone. Benny bought half a pound for sandwiches, some peaches and a quilted paper towel roll decorated with apple blossom. She picked up a *Times* then, making her way to the till, spotted the jolliest little item imaginable. A Highland terrier carved from a huge cake of soap, coloured and scented lilac. It came with a bone-shaped sponge, also coloured lilac. The bone was encircled by a tiny collar made of real leather holding a disc marked 'To:' and 'From:', all ready to write on.

Benny felt she owed Judith an apology for being such a nuisance last night as well as a thank you for all her kind help. She would call in on the way home – they would have finished breakfast by now – and what's more she would take the terrier as a present!

Judith appeared somewhat taken aback by the soap and sponge. She handed it straight to Ashley saying, 'Just look what Benny's brought us.'

'How lovely.' He smiled, taking the box. 'Do stay and have some tea, Ben. It must get a bit lonely over there.'

'If you're sure . . .' Such a welcome. Benny, beaming at both the Parnells in turn, settled happily by the window. She had just started to tell them of Croydon's latest adventure – overtaken by greed and confidence he had fallen into the fish pond – when Judith leaped up crying: 'My fax! Excuse me . . .'

'I think being underwater is really frightening,' said Ashley 'I've always been afraid of drowning.'

'*I'm* afraid of drowning too.' Benny spoke as if it was the most joyful coincidence ever. She was also afraid of being kidnapped, falling through the sky, and being bitten by tarantulas, which she knew turned up on a regular basis in crates of bananas. 'Which is why I never eat one. Or sail.'

Ashley offered Benny a croissant. 'There's plenty left. And some black cherry jam.'

'You've made a real friend over at Appleby House,' said Benny, taking a croissant and smothering it with butter. 'Polly was talking about you for ages the other night. Asking all sorts of questions.'

'Really?'

'She's such a kind person. So sympathetic.'

'I've only met her once but she seemed . . . charming.' Ashley adjusted the blanket around his legs then, with a sudden impatient movement, threw it off altogether. 'I suppose I should return the compliment. Do you know when she'll be coming down again? Will she be living here when her parents move? And what about boyfriends – she must have lots – is there anyone special?'

'Someone rang up very late the other night and she went rushing out. Young people . . .' Benny sighed and shook her head looking so bewildered she might have been talking about young dinosaurs. Then she said, 'I know it's rude to make personal remarks so I hope you'll forgive me but you're looking so much better today, Ashley.'

Benny was not just being polite. There was colour in Ashley's lips, his eyes were bright and his cheeks flushed.

'D'you think so?' Though he hadn't noticed looking better – Ashley looked in the mirror as little as possible these days – he suddenly felt it might well be true. Actually he had felt pretty well the other day too, talking to Kate in her kitchen. He should be with people more. It wasn't good for him and Jude to be cooped up here twenty-four hours a day. He wondered for the first time if his illness might be psychosomatic.

'Look, I've had an idea. Next time Polly comes down we must have a little supper – just the four of us – so Judith and I can get to know her better.'

'Gosh – that sounds lovely.'

'Maybe you could give me her London address? And we can sort dates out.'

'I'll bring it over right away.' Life, thought Benny, was getting more interesting by the minute.

'It's Judith's birthday soon. We could make it a celebration.'

'What a wonderful idea,' cried Benny.

'Only . . .' Ashley put a finger to his lips and spoke very quietly, 'I'd like it to be a surprise.'

'I understand.' Benny became equally hushed. 'Mum's the word.'

Judith sat in her dark cubbyhole, listening. Wondering at the sudden shift from clear audibility into whispering murmurs. There had been no fax, of course. She just had to get away. One more minute of Benny's bouncing, indiscriminate enthusiasm and she felt she would scream. As for that ghastly soap . . .

Now they were laughing. She couldn't remember when Ashley had last laughed out loud. It was a strong sound, reminding her of the old days. How could this stupid woman make Ashley laugh when she herself so often failed? Well, they would not shut her out. Judith closed down her computer and was about to return to the kitchen when the telephone rang. She snatched up the receiver and all her mental grumbling ceased. It was the clerk at their doctor's surgery. Could Mr Parnell manage a 4.30 appointment next Tuesday? She was irritatingly vague about the reason. Judith expected nothing else. People who worked in Appointments always pretended they didn't know anything. It must be the results of his recent blood test. Her mouth suddenly dry she hurried away to tell Ashley.

CHAPTER SEVEN

Halfway through the afternoon of 20 July, the last day in his final week at the Ewan Sedgewick Comprehensive, Mallory was trying not to let his euphoria show. It would not be kind. He knew there was not a teacher in the school who did not envy him. Or who was not keenly aware that he had not earned his retirement fair and square. Like winning the bloody lottery he had overheard his secretary muttering and, in essence, Mallory had to agree. Except that he had won something far more important than money – he had won his freedom.

He was in his office, stripping the walls of posters, timetables, lists of sports fixtures home and away. Once, dates to remember and now to forget for ever. He picked up his heavy desk diary, sprayed the page edges fiercely against the ball of his thumb and seven months of inscribed misery spun by. Parents' meetings, staff meetings, union meetings, governors' meetings; meetings with the police, probation officers, janitors, ground staff, schools inspectors, caterers, admin. Old Uncle Dave Blunkett and all.

About to toss the hated book into the bin Mallory was suddenly seized by a gleeful, childish will to destroy. He wrenched the spine apart, then ripped out the pages a fistful at a time, ripping them up, tearing them again and again, then hurling the bits into the air like so much confetti. Halfway through this ridiculous display he stopped, the pointlessness of the whole business overwhelming him, making him sad.

Only forty minutes to go. He didn't have to stick it out, of course. Indeed, he need not have come in at all, and actually got the impression that the Office was surprised to see him. But, by some strange reversal of feeling, now that Mallory could choose he chose to be present at the Ewan Sedgewick to the no longer bitter end.

He was trying not to regret too much that the celebration he had planned with Kate for tonight had had to be cancelled. Of course they must go down to Forbes Abbot if Benny was ill. But he had been so looking forward to it.

They hadn't eaten at Riva's, their favourite restaurant, for almost three years. The last time was Mallory's birthday but he had been so tired and strung out that even the delicious food, discreet service and lovely surroundings could not make the evening a success. How different this time would have been.

At this point in his reminiscence the phone rang. He was disinclined to answer. What could it have to do with him? He had cut free of all duties, said goodbye to the handful of people he would be sorry not to see again and for sure there was no surprise party waiting in the wings. So why pick it up?

Afterwards he wondered what difference it would have made if he had gone then. Just put on his coat and left with it ringing in his ears. Possibly, in the long run, not a lot. Things would have been delayed, is all. The outcome would have been the same.

'Hello?'

The receiver made a strange, strangled noise.

'Who is this?'

'Aahh . . .' Crying, sobbing. 'Dad . . .'

'Polly? *Polly . . .*'

'I'm in such . . . such . . . trouble.'

'Where are you?'

'Home. Oh, Daddy . . . please come . . .'

'What is it?'

'*Just come.*'

'OK, OK! I'm leaving now. Listen – don't— I mean – stay where you are, all right? I might be— The traffic . . .'

'Don't tell anyone, please! *Nobody.*'

'I won't.'

'Promise!'

Of course he had promised before racing out like a mad thing and throwing himself into the car. Driving off, scraping the metal gatepost, he suddenly realised he had not asked which home she meant. Perhaps she'd been ringing from her flat, which was in Dalston, miles from Parsons Green. What if she was waiting there now, distraught, watching for him through the window?

'Oh God.' Already in a solid jam he dialled home on his Nokia. When there was no reply he rang the number of her flat. Nothing. Mallory cursed himself for racing off in such a state. If he'd stopped even for a couple of minutes to think things through he might have dialled 1471. But then, if she wasn't picking the phone up . . .

He reran the few brief sentences over and over in his mind. She'd been terribly upset, yes. Crying, yes. Frightened? He wasn't sure, perhaps because he had never seen Polly frightened in her whole life. It occurred to him then for the first time that she might not have been alone. That perhaps someone was forcing her to make the call. Standing over her. She might have discovered a burglar trashing the place . . . The very thought drove Mallory mad. He started putting his terror into words, mouthing threats, muttering obscenities. Then he punched the dashboard, hurting his hand.

Two women paused on the pavement and bent to stare in through the car window at him. One of them mouthed what could have been, 'Are you all right?' The other started laughing. The queue dragged itself slowly forwards.

Mallory inhaled deeply and struggled to keep his mind on the traffic. He was a rational man, he must think rationally. Try and separate what he actually knew to be true from the seething mass of frightening images now threatening to burst his brain. Concentrate on the facts. His daughter was distressed and in some sort of trouble. She was at home and almost certainly by herself. He would be with her soon and between them they would work it out. More deep breaths.

By the time he turned into the home stretch he was feeling slightly calmer. A feeling that vanished, giving ground to a great swoosh of alarm the moment he saw parked cars, nose to tail, both sides and the whole length of Cordwainer Road. He hesitated but was driven forwards by angry hooting from behind. At the corner was a red-and-white-striped hut used by workmen drilling the road and narrowing it to single traffic only. No space there then. He turned into Elmstone Road – hopeless. Harbiedown Road the same, plus skips. Desperate he finally left the car blocking a garage heavily inscribed 'Positively No Parking'.

Polly opened the door and stared at her father in amazement. Sweating, panting, holding his side against an agonising stitch, Mallory could hardly speak.

'Dad?' She reached out and helped him inside. 'What on earth have you been doing?'

'Run . . . Running.'

'What for?'

'I'm all right.' She was struggling to support the full weight of him. 'Honestly.'

'Why were you running?'

'Worried.' Mallory leaned against the stair banisters, feeling weak at the knees with anxiety. He released a single, rasping exhalation that really hurt. His breathing gradually became less laboured. 'You sounded so . . .'

'Oh, Dad.' She put her arms around him again. They swayed clumsily for a moment and almost overbalanced. 'Here, come and sit down.'

The sitting room, which he had been wildly seeing as half destroyed or at least intensely chaotic, looked just as usual. Weak rays from the afternoon sun spilled over the furniture, showing up the dust. Touching a vase of dying roses. Mallory made for the settee and Polly helped him as though he was an invalid.

'I'll make you a drink—'

'No, no! Tell me Polly, for God's sake.'

Mallory gazed at her intently. There was no trace of tears. He was touched that she'd washed and dried her face and made an effort to overcome her distress. Now she appeared calmer than he was. But even as he watched her eyes darkened, her lips drooped and began to tremble. She clamped them together so forcefully they all but vanished. Mallory reached out and took her hand.

'Just tell me, Poll.'

So she told him. About how she had got drawn into playing the market with a group of sharky people who she thought were friends. And how she won and won and then lost and lost. And how she had a chance to recoup everything and make lots more because there was a whisper everywhere that this new dot.com company were going to be the next big thing. Anguished at being excluded from this marvellous opportunity, when she was offered a loan by the group's banker she jumped at it. He was sure the whisper was true and he was always right.

'Honestly, Dad, this guy's not even thirty and he's so *rich* and he started with *nothing*. He drew up a contract. I signed and things were OK for a few weeks – not great but the shares seemed pretty stable – then everything just collapsed overnight and I lost the lot.

'That was when I read the small print. Twenty-five per cent compound interest because I had no collateral. That was three months ago and the interest's already nearly as high as the debt. He . . . um . . . did suggest another way out but I just couldn't do it. He's like a slug – so slimily foul, so greasy—'

'Of course you mustn't do anything like that!' Black rage welled up in Mallory. Hatred for the unknown man, a longing to grab him by the throat and squeeze and shake and throttle and choke. Christ! What a bastard.

'Daddy, you're hurting.'

'Sorry.' He released her hand. 'Sorry, love.'

'So it's just piling up and up and up. He's like those vicious sharks on housing estates. Borrow five quid, turn around three times, you owe five hundred.'

'How much did you borrow, Polly?'

'Ten.'

'Ten *thousand*?' Polly hung her head. Her hair fell forward, a thick mat of dark curls.

'And how much does this debt stand at now?'

'Nearly sixteen.'

'This is unbelievable.' Mallory carefully drew in his breath and exhaled a long despairing sigh. 'Have you talked to anyone about this?'

'Like who?'

'Doesn't the LSE have an advice—'

'I don't need advice,' screamed Polly. 'I need fucking money!' She burst into tears, covered her face with her hands and rocked slowly backwards and forwards.

'Oh God.'

'I thought you'd understand.' Her voice was muffled. Flat and dull as if the argument had been wrestled with for hours already and they had already worn it out. 'I thought you'd help me.'

'I do – I will. I only wish you'd come to me before.'

'Couldn't. Not with what you were going through.'

'The thought of you carrying a burden like this all by yourself . . .'

Mallory suddenly remembered the argument, weeks ago now, about Polly's flat. The row that had been interrupted by Benny's telephone call and the news of Carey's death. This must have been what the money was for. He remembered Kate's caution; her wary scepticism. And she had been right. Even just acknowledging this made him feel disloyal to Polly.

'So that's why, when Aunt Carey left me all those shares I went wild with relief. But you do see, Dad, waiting another ten months'll be just crippling. Hardly any of it will be left.' Polly gazed directly at her father, eyes swimming with unshed tears. 'You've known Dennis all your life. If you asked him, as a special favour, to bend the rules just this once, I'm sure he would.'

'Polly—'

'I wouldn't expect it all – just enough to cover the debt.'

'There's no need to ask Dennis.'

'I don't understand.' Polly spoke with simple bewilderment. She held Mallory's gaze, her own, clear and shining. She had been preparing for this moment ever since discovering, in Dennis's office, who actually had control of her legacy.

'Your bequest is part of the Lawson estate. Which has all been transferred to me.'

'I can't . . . what?' Polly looked incredulous, her pretty mouth wide open. Then she was laughing and crying all at once. Flinging her arms around his neck, soaking his jacket with tears. 'Then everything's all right.'

Mallory awkwardly patted her hair. After a while Polly sat back, wiped her face on her shirt and stared at him with great seriousness. She frowned, then squared her shoulders as if coming to a decision.

'I did it for you, Dad.'

'What?'

'You were locked up in that hideous place like someone in a madhouse. It was so cruel. I watched it killing you. And all because there was no money.'

'It's over now.'

'Once when I came round you looked so manic. You stared at me as if you didn't know who I was. Do you remember that?'

Dumbly Mallory shook his head.

'I was afraid you'd do something desperate. And I couldn't have borne that. I just couldn't.' She clenched her fists, banging them hard on the arms of the chair. 'They make obscene money, those arseholes. On the turn of a card. And I thought, why shouldn't my dad have some of it?'

'Oh, Polly.' Choked with emotion Mallory could hardly get his words out. So much was tumbling through his mind. Admiration for his daughter, for her courage in carrying all this in silence. Sick loathing for the unknown man who had dared, *dared* to try to blackmail Polly into having sex with him. But, most overwhelmingly of all, joy and gratitude at this demonstration of how much his daughter loved him. Of course he had always loved her. Most parents love their children, it comes with the territory. And they, thought Mallory, love us when they're small. They must, for we are their lifelines. But when they are grown up and have no sensible reason to love you yet love you still then, my God, then aren't we the lucky ones?

'Dad?'

'Sorry – yes, Poll.'

'How long . . . I mean, when could you—'

'Quickly. A couple of days.'

'And could I have it in cash, please?'

'Cash?'

'A cheque he might just hold on to. Not bank it, I mean. Christ knows, he doesn't need the money. Then, in a way, he's still controlling the situation.'

This was not the real reason. The truth was that Polly couldn't wait to fling the money into Slaughter's astonished face. Shove a giant fistful past those wet, slobbering chops. Ram some up his hairy nostrils. Stuff it into the waistband of his obscenely large trousers. Panting slightly now with triumphant expectation, she began to laugh. The vignette had been so vividly realised it was as if it had happened already. What he would do didn't enter into it. Divorced from his power suddenly Billy Slaughter was nothing.

Mallory had got up, was walking towards the window. 'I'd better ring your mother—'

'No!' Polly jumped up. Suddenly frantic she ran across the room and grabbed the phone. 'You mustn't.'

'She's expecting me.'

'OK, but— I mean, don't tell her about this, will you, Dad? Promise?'

'I can't do that.'

'It's none of her business.'

'She's your mother, Polly.'

'She won't understand – she doesn't care.'

'That's nonsense.'

'She hates me.'

'Of course she doesn't hate you.'

'Now you're getting angry,' cried Polly, swinging on her father's arm like a child, trying to grab the phone. 'You see – already she's coming between us.'

'You're making all this up.'

'Am I? Look how pleased she was when I left home.'

Mallory said, 'That's nonsense' again but, even as he spoke, couldn't help remembering the change in Kate once Polly had gone. Drowning as he had been in misery of his own making he had still been aware of the gradual lightening of her face and manner. She moved slowly, would spend time sitting about doing nothing special but smiling a lot. She was at home more and even gave up a couple of evening classes, which she had always said she couldn't bear to miss. Yes, she had been happier after Polly left home.

Polly watched her father, not without affection. He was so transparent. She said, with sorrowful gravity, 'You see?'

'I don't "see" anything.'

'I shall never hear the end of it. How can I possibly come and visit under those circumstances?'

'What do you mean?'

'Oh, don't look so stricken, Dad.' She released her tight grip on the telephone and replaced it on the table. She gave him a reassuring smile. 'We shall still see each other. Meet up in town for lunch and stuff . . .'

Mallory, cold to his stomach, said, 'This is unworthy of you, Polly.'

'It's how it has to be. I'm sick of family rows. And this one'll run and run.'

Perhaps she was right. Mallory had never thought of Kate as naturally censorious but there was no doubt she would not just listen to the story and let it rest. There would be questions; she'd be as angry as he was. She'd demand the man's name, perhaps try to see him. Which meant another person entangled in the mess. Two more really, for Mallory would not be able to stand aside if Kate got involved. Slowly he dialled the number of Appleby House.

'Hello, darling . . . yes, everything's fine. I'm just running a bit late . . . Oh, there was more to do at the last minute than I expected. People kept coming in to . . . er . . . say goodbye, you know? Wish me well . . .'

'Are you ringing from home, Mal?'

'Um. Sorry?' Mallory remembered now that he had packed everything into the car that morning so that he could drive down to Forbes Abbot straight from work. Kate had helped him. 'Home . . .?'

'I can hear the drilling.'

'Ah, yes. Home, yes. I forgot something.'

'What?'

'. . . Some books. Look – you and Benny eat. I'll be down as soon as I can.'

He hung up and looked across the room at Polly. She was standing very still, her head drooping. He noticed her toes were very slightly turned in and felt a keen pang of memory. Exactly so had she used to stand as a child when, after some lengthy argument or discussion she had finally got her own way. A less subtle child would rejoice; be triumphant even. Not Polly. She never crowed. Just smiled, shrugged, murmured something more or less unintelligible and slipped quietly away.

'Thanks, Dad. I'll never forget this.'

'It'll take a few days to get the money transferred.'

94

'OK, fine.'

'And it's just to cover what you owe, Polly. Don't ask for any more.'

'I won't, I won't,' cried Polly, recognising immediately what a fool she had been to name the correct amount.

Kate had emptied the food cupboards and the freezer before driving down to Forbes Abbot. Quite unnecessary, really. She would pass plenty of supermarkets on the way and the sensible thing would have been to get there first, see what was actually needed, then go out and buy it. However, Kate was not feeling sensible. To her stripping the freezer, packing all the stuff into padded bags and polystyrene cartons then stuffing them into the car boot was moving house in miniature. A tiny step but something to be going on with till the real thing.

Kate asked what Benny would like for supper, emptying all her bags on to the kitchen table. Benny had no preference. She said everything looked lovely and she would have what Kate had. So they decided on Sainsbury's Goa Fish Curry with fragrant Thai rice and some mangetout from the garden.

In spite of Mallory's suggestion that they go ahead and eat, Kate delayed cooking for an hour or so, just in case. She opened a bottle of Vouvray demi-sec. Benny, after only one glass, started giggling so much she couldn't swallow. Consequently Kate drank rather more than she intended. And, as she poured a third glass, felt her mood beginning to change. *In vino veritas* and all that. She started to feel aggrieved and inclined to defiant behaviour. A bit silly as there was no one present to be defiant to.

The truth was she had been tremendously looking forward to going out with Mallory tonight. To drawing a line under the past and celebrating the beginning of their new life together.

When Judith had rung describing Benny's distress Kate, genuinely alarmed, did not hesitate. Mallory would have come with her if he'd been able. Both agreed it was sad about Riva's but they could go another time. Anyway, their dinner that evening could still be a celebration but this time for three, which would be quite right, said Kate, because Benny would also be working in the new business. But, as eight o'clock slowly came around, there were still only two of them.

By now extremely hungry, she and Benny started to eat. They took it slowly and even had some pudding, apricot panacotta. Kate realised that in another hour or so this day, that was going to be so special, would be over.

So where was Mallory? The journey, even during the worst the Friday evening London exodus could muster, had never taken longer than three hours. They had spoken on the phone at around 5.30 and it was now nearly half-past ten.

Benny, aware that Kate was somewhat on edge, tried to express sympathy and concern without talking too much. Experience had taught her that this could be very annoying when a person was all wound up. She cleared the table, washed up quietly and put things away.

In herself, Benny was feeling much better. The muddle over the phone, while not exactly cleared up, now seemed pretty childish. Kate had actually laughed about it and said weird things were always happening to her as well. It was lovely, Benny thought, that they would both be down here now for the whole weekend. She pictured them sitting at the kitchen table, planning all sorts of things to do with books, and herself making tea and producing sandwiches and biscuits to sustain them all. Busy, useful, contented.

Suddenly headlights swept the faded walls, bathing them briefly in a flood of amber light. A car drew up outside and Benny hurried to open the door. It was Mallory.

He said, 'Hello,' in a forced, hearty manner.

'Mallory,' said Benny. 'We've been so worried.' Mallory frowned and Benny thought that had been the wrong thing to say. 'What I mean is, I have.' That wasn't right either. It sounded as if Kate hadn't been worried at all. 'That is . . .'

But he wasn't listening.

'Well,' concluded Benny feeling suddenly awkward, though she couldn't have said why. 'I'm off to sunny Bedford. Would you say good night to Kate for me, please?' She pulled the heavy front door closed behind her and made her way across the stable yard. Climbing the wooden steps to the flat over the horse's mews, Benny found herself even more than usual looking forward to being at home. Truly, as the poet said, there was no place like it. First she would have a warm bath, then make a nice cup of cocoa, pile up the pillows on her bed and settle down with the latest edition of the parish magazine.

Kate, having spent the previous two hours struggling to disperse a huge knot of rancorous ill feeling, felt it regather with energetic force the moment she heard Mallory's voice in the hall. To restrain a terrible impulse to stand up and start shouting, Kate struggled to play devil's advocate. At least find out why he's so late. It's probably not his fault. What if he'd had an accident – think how you'd be feeling then. Be grateful he's here at last, alive and well. She wished she hadn't drunk so much.

'Kate – I'm terribly—'

'Where the hell have you been?'

'I'm sorry.'

'Sorry? What use is sorry? This was going to be our evening – remember?'

'Of course I—'

'A special day.'

'I know that.'

'The first day of the rest of our lives as *The Little Book of Psychobabble* would doubtless have it.'

96

'What on earth's got into you?'

'Well, let's see. Disappointment. Escalating boredom. Irritation. Mounting resentment—'

'And quite a bit of alcohol from the look of it.'

'Yes, that too. Shock, horror.'

'I can explain.'

'So explain.'

'The car wouldn't start.'

'Mallory, Mallory. Five hours and that's the best you can come up with?'

On the contrary Mallory had come up with many alternatives driving down but he knew that, from him, they would all sound unbelievable. This was not because they were in any way extraordinary. It was enough that they were not true. Even at the age when children fib as easily as they breathe and with as little concern, he could never do it. He would turn scarlet and shuffle and wriggle and cry. Naturally now he did none of these things but the lie still lay, sharp as a bee sting, on his tongue.

The truth was that he and Polly had sat for a while drinking tea. Then she had suggested they grab a quick bite at Orlando's just round the corner. It would be empty so early in the evening. They'd be served straight away; just a plate of pasta. In and out, twenty minutes tops.

It took Mallory barely five seconds to see the reasonableness of this. Even if he set off now they would probably have already eaten at Appleby House by the time he arrived. It would be pretty selfish to expect them to start cooking all over again.

Sitting in Orlando's, which was nearly full, Mallory realised that this was the first time he and his daughter had been out and about on their own since she was quite small. He noticed people staring at her and was not surprised. She had on a tight, short-sleeved jumper of some gauzy black stuff. It was scrawled all over with silver pen markings and, even to Mallory's inexpert eye, looked very expensive. She had done something to her hair, which showed rich, red glints where it took the light. The soft, curly mass was piled on top of her head and secured by a bronze comb studded with pearls and turquoises and tiny shards of coral. That looked expensive too.

They waited nearly half an hour for their tonnarelle alla paesana, nibbling bread sticks and drinking Rosso de Verona with Polly making up cruel and funny stories about the other diners' private lives. Then, halfway through the pasta, she started to talk, quietly and seriously, about her own. Mainly about her course at the LSE and problems with her tutor in Business Statistics. Mallory, who, like Kate, had been subsisting on a crumb of information tossed occasionally his way for years, soaked up every word.

Polly had just got on to the other students, who seemed to fall into two categories: those who wanted desperately to be her friend and wouldn't

97

leave her alone, and the rest who were simply jealous, when Mallory noticed the time. Polly begged for a zabaglione because, 'They are my utterly absolute favourite, Dad and they're all on the trolley look, it won't take a second and I can eat it while you're paying the bill.'

It didn't work out quite like that because she ordered a cappuccino at the same time, then disappeared into the ladies for what seemed like hours but was actually only ten minutes.

The lights were against Mallory at almost every stop in London and once he got on to the M40 and was able briefly to put his foot down the dreaded cones appeared, leading directly into a one-mile tailback.

'What?'

'Why didn't you ring?'

'The mobile was down.'

'How convenient.'

'I'm tired.' Now Mallory was becoming resentful. Hell, it wasn't just his daughter he was saving from financial ruin.

'It was only serviced last week.'

'What was?'

'The bloody car!' Kate sat down suddenly. She felt as if someone had taken a chisel to her skull. 'Did you ring the AA? Or the garage?'

'. . . Um . . . no . . . Turned out to be damp plugs.'

'Damp . . .? It's been twenty-two degrees all day.'

'Oh – for Christ's sake, leave me alone!'

They stared at each other, suddenly aghast. Two strangers in a strange room. Aghast and afraid.

If only I hadn't promised Polly, thought Mallory. I was wrong to promise not to tell. And wrong to go out and eat when I knew Kate would be waiting. Now she's angry and suspicious and I'm standing here full of mysteries and lies.

If only I hadn't been drinking, thought Kate. Her mind replayed Mallory's arrival differently now. She saw herself going up to him, relieved at his safe arrival, hugging him. Producing food kept warm or making something fresh. They would laugh and talk and drink some wine then go to bed and make love on this, the first day of the rest of their lives. Instead he stood there, exhausted and bad-tempered while she struggled not to give way and start crying. But perhaps it was not too late.

Kate forced a smile and said: 'You must be starving, Mal. Let me get you something.'

'That's OK. I've already—'

'Have you, really?'

'I mean, it's too late . . .'

'Got it in one,' said Kate. And walked out.

The next morning Mallory, who had spent the night on the library sofa, made some tea as soon as the hour seemed civilised. He took the tray to

Kate's room. She was deeply asleep. Soft light, gradually spreading into the room through semi-transparent curtains showed clearly where tears had dried, imprinted on her cheeks. Tenderness for her mingled with shame over his own behaviour consumed Mallory. He put the tea down on the bedside table very gently, but Kate opened her eyes and was immediately awake. She struggled to sit, pushing herself up against the headboard.

'Darling Kate – I'm so sorry about last night.' Mallory sat on the side of the bed. 'I really, truly am.'

'No, no.' She was talking over him. 'I shouldn't have said what I did. I'd been drinking . . . worrying if you were—'

'Listen. I want to tell you—'

'It doesn't matter.'

'Yes, it does.' He took her hand in both of his own. 'I was with someone who is in real trouble. They asked for help and I couldn't refuse. It took longer than I expected.'

'Was it someone at school?' Already Kate's warm heart was drawn to this unhappy soul. 'Is there anything I can do?'

'I promised not to discuss it with anyone.'

Then Kate understood. And Mallory knew that she did. He reached out and took her other hand. Gripped them both. And hung on.

Here we go again, thought Kate. Two against one. In spades, this time. In bloody spades. At least up until now everything that happened between the three of them – discussions, rows, jokes, arguments had been just that – between the three of them. Or had it? That was the whole point of secrets. Those outside never knew there was something they didn't know. How could they?

Kate had always considered herself a pragmatist. Someone in the family had to be. Clear-eyed, she understood how things really were, though accepting things as they really were had never been easy. She remembered Polly as a tiny child climbing on her daddy's knee. Playing with his tie, putting her arms around his neck, whispering in his ear. Winding her silky hair around his fingers.

And now she was in 'real trouble', her mother was not allowed to help. Was not even allowed to know what the trouble was. To Kate's surprise – for had she not found herself only the other day wondering if she still loved her daughter? – this hurt a lot. She went with the pain, bowing over slightly, one hand against her breast. Mallory put his arms around her and they rocked gently for a while back and forth.

Eventually he said, 'I thought I'd get breakfast today.'

'Brilliant,' said Kate. She took a deep calming breath. And then another. 'I'll have a shower and come right down.'

'And afterwards we'll have our first business meeting.'

CHAPTER EIGHT

Benny had been invited to dine at Kinders. She was looking forward to it immensely, and not just for the pleasure of Dennis's company, for he was also a wonderful cook.

She arrived about seven, carrying a bottle of Carey's apple wine and a stephanotis she had been bringing on in the greenhouse. She balanced the pot awkwardly in the crook of her arm to open the gate. Dennis's strip of garden, running around the base of the house and full of agapanthus and marguerites, looked bone dry and Benny itched to get her hands on a watering can. She knocked quietly on the blue front door and waited. No one came so she did it again, as loudly as her shyness would allow, but with the same result.

Then she made her way through the garage, squeezing past the car and up the double steps to the kitchen door. It was unlocked. Stepping inside she was filled with apprehension. If Dennis was in and had not heard her knocking there was only one place he could be. The kitchen was full of warm, delicious smells. Benny put her plant and wine on the spotless draining board, then stepped into the carpeted passage that led to the rest of the flat.

'Cooee?'

Pointlessly she peeped into the sitting room. Evening sunshine illuminated the lovely Chinese rugs and gilded the ornate picture frames. There were some yellow roses and lots of books and newspapers. A quiet, sad wailing came from the hi-fi speakers and she recognised Dennis's Saracen songs from the crusades.

Benny hurried past the bathroom and paused briefly outside the single, monkish room where Dennis slept. The door was ajar. She coughed hoarsely into the aperture and called again. Silence. Now all that was left was the war room.

The flat had lightweight walls, which were about ten feet high, and artificial ceilings. Once inside, as with any other building, the surrounding landscape was invisible and consequently unthreatening. But observed through one of the arrow-slit windows under Kinders' high roof it must have looked extremely fragile. Vulnerable too, like a climber's hut crouching between steep and silent cliffs of white plaster and menaced by the great dinosaurs of iron and steel and wood that stalked the shining floors.

Benny, standing by the door that led to this great space, already had her strategy planned. She would sweep the room with a single glance, swift

100

but thorough. This would show her whether Dennis was there and, if he was, where he was. Then she would go directly across to him, walking carefully and looking only at the ground. Having done this once it would inevitably be less frightening the next time. Even less the next. And so on . . .

'And after all,' murmured Benny, her hand already trembling the latch upwards, 'it's not as if they're alive.'

She saw him straight away. He was standing in front of the giant slingy one looking up at the high rack of heavy wooden balls and the fearsome ropes and ratchets. He stood motionless like a statue, his hands clasped loosely behind his back. Though full of trepidation Benny walked quickly to his side.

'Dennis?' She waited, hesitating. 'My dear, are you all right?'

There was a short silence, then Dennis shook his head and sighed.

'What is it?' urged Benny. 'What's wrong?'

'I'm not sure. Nothing, probably.' He smiled but his expression remained uneasy. Then turning away he added in an absent-minded manner, almost as if talking to himself, 'Or perhaps . . . a ghost in the machine.'

'Oh!' Benny gasped as if cold water had been thrown in her face. 'How awful! Ghosts, oh!'

Dennis linked arms. Something he had never done before. He must be *really* worried, thought Benny. Gladly she turned with him away from the death-dealing mechanism and they walked away, soon to be out of the fearful place.

'It's good to see you, Benny. I'm sorry I wasn't present when you came.' Dennis poured a glass of Madeira to which Benny had become extremely partial. She sat at the kitchen table while he took a small blue iron casserole out of the oven. 'It's turbot in a white wine sauce.'

'Lovely. D'you think it's true that fish is good for the brain?'

'Not so good,' said Dennis, adding tiny carrots and new potatoes to warm plates, 'as reading and music and paintings.'

They ate in the dining room, sitting in soft, springy armchairs with trays on their laps. The sort that were really comfortable, with big bags underneath, full of granules, so the tray didn't slip and slither and upset your food. Benny confidently accepted another drink, this time white wine. She knew she could handle it. It wouldn't be like it was the other night with Kate. She didn't get all giggly or silly or stupid with Dennis. He brought out the best in her. His grave attention to everything she said made what she said more considered. She was never compelled to rush into speech to cover gaps in conversation as she did with strangers. Instead the pauses felt more like little comfort stops along a delightful walk.

'This turbot is just beautiful.'

'That's a relief. I bought it on Thursday, then got home too late to cook it.'

'Was that pressure of work, Dennis?'

'In a way.'

Benny was the last person he could unburden himself to. An incident merely out of the ordinary would worry her. A genuine mystery and she'd be consumed with anxiety on his behalf. But Dennis did want to discuss his concern. He hoped that another point of view might put the business of the lights in some sort of perspective. Show it up for the trivial bit of nonsense it might well prove to be. He had been thinking about this all morning and had almost decided to talk to Mallory.

'We had our first meeting today.'

'Really?' Dennis felt rather disappointed. As the new company's financial advisor he had hoped to be present at this. 'How did it go?'

'It was so exciting! We didn't talk about money, of course, because you weren't there, but Kate's worked out a brief advertisement that should be in *The Times* on Monday. And we decided on the company's name. Excuse me.'

Benny took a break to finish her turbot and drink the rest of her wine. Dennis, entertained by all the 'we's' waited, smiling.

'Obviously we had quite a list and, l must admit, some were a bit out of the way. But eventually we got them down to three. The Pierrot Press, which was Kate's suggestion, Fireproof Books from Mallory—'

'I like that,' interrupted Dennis. He recalled newsreels showing towers of flaming books in countries under the rape of tyranny. 'That's good. Fireproof Books.'

'It is,' agreed Benny, 'but Kate thought not everyone would understand the sym— Um . . . symbols . . .'

'You mean they might take the title literally?'

'Exactly. So anyway, what happened was . . .' Benny squirmed with embarrassment and delight. She could hardly speak and her next words seemed to be squeezed out against their will. 'They chose mine.'

'*Benny!*'

'Yes, they did.' Her face shone, radiant with success. She nodded her head. 'Mine.'

They sat beaming at each other, equally thrilled. Dennis said, 'Well?'

'I thought of it because they're all over the orchard in the spring and Carey was very fond of them. Also there's a lovely watercolour in the library that Kate thinks we could use as our trademark. So we're going to be called . . . the Celandine Press!'

'This should be champagne.' Dennis poured them both some more wine. 'How clever you are, Benny.'

Benny felt her face go all hot and prickly. As far as she could remember no one in all her life had ever told her she was clever. 'Tomorrow we're going to start looking at equipment. Computers, printers and suchlike.'

'On Sunday?' Dennis was disappointed. Tomorrow would have been the ideal time to have a talk with Mallory.

'Places are open every day now,' said Benny. 'They'll bring me back, then they're going home for a couple of days to start packing up.'

'I see.' A couple of days wasn't long. He would try to ring Mallory before they left. Set a definite time. 'Would you like some chocolate tart?'

'Yes, please.'

After Dennis had served the tart and Jersey clotted cream in glass bowls shaped like waterlilies he put his own dish down on a little side table.

'The thing is . . . erm . . . I have this friend.'

'Oh, yes?' Benny, tucking carelessly in, now had a little brown and cream moustache on her top lip. 'This is truly scrumptious.'

'Written a novel.'

'What sort of a novel?'

'Historical, I believe. Does that sound like the sort of thing the Celandine Press would be looking for?'

'Anything that has literary merit, Kate said.'

'As to that . . .' Dennis seemed uncertain.

'Don't worry,' said Benny. 'You know what they say, nothing ventured, nothing gained. What's your friend's name?'

Dennis stared at her.

'So I shall know who to look out for.'

'Walker.'

'Get him to send it in,' said Benny, 'and I shall give it my personal attention.'

In the end Polly did not change the money she owed Billy Slaughter into cash to ram down his trousers and up his nose. She recognised this impulse now for what it was – a childish 'sucks boo' born of rage at her previous impotence. Also, if she tried it he might hit her.

There was, too, the question of prudence. Polly remembered sitting at a shared table in the LSE Brunch Bowl a while ago when an anthropology student read out a news item from his paper. Apparently someone was being mugged every three minutes night and day in London. They all laughed when he added: 'You'd think the stupid sod would move to Brum.' But it wouldn't be funny, Polly thought now, if it happened to you. Especially if you had several thousand in cash about your person. So she decided to pay her debt with a banker's draft.

Of course she had not been able to wait, as her father had suggested. She had rung the only number she had the very next day, only to be told that Mr Slaughter was in the country and would return after lunch on Monday. The person speaking sounded just like some crusty old retainer in a crusty English play.

Polly had been surprised at Billy's address. She had imagined him hanging out somewhere really flash. At the top of a high tower in Canary

Wharf with a Porsche in the garage or over the water in a converted Docklands warehouse. Maybe even at Montevetro, the gorgeous Richard Rogers building, shaped like a gigantic slice of glass cake, sparkling and glittering on the river at Battersea. But he lived at Whitehall Court, Whitehall Place. A few minutes from the Cenotaph. Central, sure, but how dull.

Polly asked around to see if anyone had heard of the place. She drew a blank with one exception. An old Etonian reading Philosophy and Economics. Apparently his uncle, a retired admiral, had a flat there. Handy for his club in the Mall, and the House of Lords. Always grumbling about the service charge, which he swore was higher than his daughter's mortgage.

Polly walked there from Embankment Tube station. The vestibule to the apartments was richly carpeted in pale rose and full of flowers. Polly, about to go straight through, was stopped by a porter who enquired about her business. A telephone call was made to confirm that she was expected and she was directed to the lift.

Making her way down the long, thickly carpeted corridors past cream and grey marble pillars and panels of beautiful stained glass Polly, in spite of herself, began to feel impressed. And it was so quiet. Minutes from Trafalgar Square and you couldn't hear a mouse squeak.

Then, way above her head, Polly heard the lift door clash to and the mechanism start whirring. Waiting, she recalled the novels of John le Carré. Surely this was exactly the sort of discreet, anonymous place that civil servants and their masters, their moles and droppers of notes into hollow trees would gather to trade and betray. Somewhere a stone's throw from the nation's seat of power. A place where no one knows your name. And suddenly it didn't seem so strange that Billy Slaughter should be living here.

She came out of the lift into another long, dimly lit corridor running into deep shade at the very end. Then a heavy door was opened, flooding the space with light. Into this illuminated area stepped a man in evening dress. He raised a hand and called something that Polly didn't quite hear.

She stepped out, walking the walk. He watched her coming on. She wore a soft dress, tiny navy dots on cream with a flirty skirt that swished and swirled above her dimpled knees. She stepped out swinging her hips, her long tanned legs making confident strides. Her pretty, pink-toed feet nonchalantly balanced on four-inch heels tied around her ankles by narrow strips of glittery stuff.

How do women do it? mused Slaughter, admiring Polly's swagger. How do they stay up there? As she got nearer he went back into the flat. Polly, who had been afraid there might be some form of physical *rapprochement*, was relieved. She wouldn't put it past him to try to kiss her. Or sneak a crafty arm around her waist. He'd got enough cheek.

The interior of the flat was a further surprise. The room into which she followed Billy was furnished like the sitting room of a country house. The dark green Knole sofa was well worn, as were several armchairs. Diamond-paned bookcases were crammed with what appeared to be much-handled books. There were several small oil paintings, mainly landscapes, but two showed fine, elegant horses standing in formal gardens in front of playing fountains. Some framed pencil sketches of dancers hung on the opposite wall. A clarinet lay on a low table beside a stack of scientific journals and next to a glazed blue dish holding ripe apricots.

'Well, Polly?'

Slaughter was standing behind a desk, honeyed mahogany and green leather, which also looked pretty old. There was nothing on it but a computer and a copy of the *Evening Standard*.

Polly, impressed and surprised by her surroundings, did not immediately reply. She was also slightly surprised by Slaughter's appearance. It had been some weeks since they met but, in her constant and angry remembrances, he had been fat. Gross even. Now, though plainly a big man, he was not a fat one. Polly wondered if he had lost weight. Or if she had blown him up (so to speak) in her imagination.

He wasn't quite as ugly either. His flat almond-shaped eyes were as cold as she recalled but his lips were full rather than thick. They weren't smiling. Now she came to think of it she had never seen him smile.

'Won't you sit down?'

'No, thanks.' Polly opened her bag and took out the banker's draft. It was in an envelope. 'I just came to deliver this.'

'Hang on.' He disappeared into what was presumably the kitchen and came back with two glasses and an ice bucket with a bottle in it. 'We must celebrate.'

About to be very grand and refuse, Polly changed her mind on recognising the dark green bottle held in a metal casing of delicate pale blue leaves. Slaughter filled two glasses to the brim, gracefully without spilling a drop. Polly accepted one with a great show of reluctance, took a sip and wandered over to the window. It looked down on two stone figures, Epstein or very much like, squatting atop an archway.

About to ask, she was anticipated by Slaughter.

'Ministry of Defence.'

Polly remembered her earlier thoughts on John le Carré while drinking deep of the Perrier-Jouët, which was quite wonderful.

'You're running out.' He added to her glass, standing quite close but not so close she could legitimately take offence. Even so, Polly moved away.

'I didn't know you played the clarinet.'

'I play all sorts of things.'

'Billy, suppose . . . that is – if I hadn't been able to get the money, would you have . . .?'

'Yes.'

'To the bitter end?'

'Wouldn't you?' He refilled his own glass.

'Of course.' But there had been a minimal hesitation.

'What if it was a friend?'

'I don't believe in friends.'

'What would you have instead?'

'People who can be of use.' Polly hesitated. 'Isn't that your philosophy?'

'My philosophy, like that of all successful businessmen, is to see with absolute clarity what is really happening.'

'And the failed businessmen?'

'They see what they'd like to think is happening.'

'I'll remember that.'

'It will serve you well, Polly.'

He held out his hand. Polly produced the envelope and gave it to him. He slipped it, unread into his pocket and sat down at the desk. He wrote a few lines on a sheet of headed paper, folded it and handed it over. Not to be outdone on the count of cool, Polly slipped the receipt unread, into her bag.

'Some more fizz?'

Polly didn't reply. She was already feeling rather light-headed. Being nervous, she had not been able to swallow a morsel before she came. She took the glass, conscious of standing there like a dummy and blurted out the first thing that came into her head. It could not have been more banal.

'You're looking very smart.'

'I'm going to the opera.'

'The *opera*?'

'Where did you think I'd be going? The dogs?'

'I'm . . .' Polly blushed. 'I didn't think anything.'

'*Fidelio*. Love, death and betrayal.'

'Sounds like a day on the market floor.'

'Apart from the love.' He had moved back behind the desk and sat down to face the computer. 'I want to give you something, Polly. A present.' He started tapping the keys. 'Have you got any money?'

'Doesn't sound much like a present.'

'If you have or if you can get some I can put you in the way of buying at 1.04 and selling, possibly at as much as 1.50 within hours.'

'Buying what?' Polly tried to keep her voice even but the shock showed. A swift kick of excitement and fear. She walked slowly across the room to stand behind his chair, to read over his shoulder.

'Gillans and Hart? For heaven's sake – they're rubbish. Worthless.'

'Not quite.'

'What are you *doing*?' She stared at the screen. At the figures; the noughts. 'You're not buying?'

'As you see.'

When Polly could speak she said, 'What's going on?'

'There's been a takeover by Channing Voight.'

106

Polly leaned on the desk edge to keep herself steady. She felt slightly sick. 'How do you know?'

'A banker with Channing. He's in my debt.'

'Must be some debt.'

'Indeed.'

'So it will break first thing tomorrow?'

'The rumour's already out. They're two points up in the *Standard*.'

Polly took up the paper and checked, and it was true. 'You're buying with a market maker?'

'Smart girl. Do you know of someone you can use?'

'Of course. But, why me?'

'Let's say . . .' He turned and smiled at her. The smile didn't reach his eyes but at least this time it just touched his mouth. 'I still have hopes that one day you'll look kindly on me.'

Polly parted lips as sweetly pink as her toes and smiled back. Where was the harm? It was not as if she would ever have to see him again. She leaned a little closer to Billy Slaughter's shoulder to watch the transfer of this truly massive amount of money and he smelled her subtle but distinctive scent. One click on Commit and it was done.

Now Polly wanted to get away. He could feel it – the feverishness of her. He stood up and she stepped quickly backwards, disconcerted. But he merely held out his hand. The grip was dry and firm, the handshake brief. Then he walked her to the door and said, 'Goodbye.'

Polly ran down the corridor, heading for the stairs. Her spirit, elated and freewheeling now, could not have borne enclosure in a lift. She looked wild and beautiful. Billy Slaughter watched her go, his face a mask of bland, steely calm.

107

CHAPTER NINE

Dennis was preparing to leave the office. He had contacted a security firm earlier that day and someone was coming to change the locks on Wednesday morning. Obviously Andrew Latham, as the only other key holder, had to be informed. Dennis had put this off all day but now he could see Andrew, already wearing his flashy white trench coat, helping Gail Fuller on with her jacket.

'Oh, I say?' called Dennis, across the deserted outer office. 'Could I have a moment?'

Latham turned round and then straight back to the receptionist. His expression showed amusement and irritation as if Dennis had been some precocious child that was outstaying its welcome. He said something too quiet to be overheard and Gail Fuller left, sniggering.

'I was just off, actually.' He met Dennis halfway and perched on one of the desks. 'Can't it wait?'

'I've . . . er,' Dennis cleared his throat. Stupid to be nervous. 'I'm having the lock on my door changed, Andrew. And the one to the main office.'

'Lock?'

'Wednesday morning.'

'What the fuck for?'

Dennis went scarlet. He found coarse language deeply offensive. Latham would never have spoken in such a way when he first joined the firm. The man's attitude was becoming more and more openly contemptuous.

'I'm sure you recall the incidents a short while ago when the lights were inexplicably—'

'God, you're not harking back to that again. You're losing it, Brinkers. It'll be voices in the radiators next.' He gave a fractious whinny, baring his teeth. Dennis, unaware it was supposed to be a laugh, jumped. 'Get a grip, man.'

'Also, as you never seem to surface before ten at the earliest, I intend giving the spare keys to Fortune. He's the most reliable—'

'Do what you like. I'm away. I've something cooking in a wine bar. Don't want her going off the boil.'

Dennis sat down behind his desk. He never drank in the office but kept some sherry, dry and sweet, for certain clients who seemed to expect it. He got out the Lustau Amontillado and poured out a glass, measuring it judiciously.

His mind was running all over the place and he didn't like that. Dennis preferred to do one thing at once and give it all his attention before moving on to the next. He drew a notepad towards him, uncapped his fountain pen and wrote, '1: Locks changed.' Then drew a neat tick. On the following line he wrote, '2: Dispatch parcel.' The parcel was *The King's Armourer*, which he planned to send in the morning, second-class post. He had already checked that Kate's advertisement had made today's *Times* and sorted out an accommodation address in Slough over the telephone.

Then Dennis remembered his phone call to Mallory the previous morning, asking if they could meet. An arrangement had been made for tomorrow evening and he wrote down, '3: Dinner at Appleby House/ Meeting of the Celandine Press.' He was looking forward to being involved in the new venture enormously and felt quite excited about the possible future reaction to the novel by E.M. Walker (his mother's initials and maiden name).

Dennis sucked his pen and tapped the heel of his left foot rapidly on the floor, a habit when he got what Mrs Crudge had been known to call 'all aereated'. To calm himself he drank the rest of the sherry and went to look out of the window.

This was not at all calming. Mr Allibone was shutting the shop, rolling up his awning as he had been just four days ago. He saw Dennis watching, tipped his boater backwards with his thumb and waved. Dennis lifted a hand awkwardly and nodded back. At his desk he wrote, '4: Ask Mrs C about keys.'

Dennis had checked his garage board on arriving home last Thursday evening and noticed that the spare keys for the office and street door were missing. The thought that they had been deliberately taken occurred to him, of course, especially after his earlier conversation with the fish-monger, but he couldn't help thinking it was not very likely. The garage was locked at night and, as the house fronted the High Street, whoever was responsible would have to take them in broad daylight with the chance that someone could walk by and catch them at it. What had probably happened, Dennis decided, was that he himself had picked them up for some reason and left them lying about.

Connecting again with Mr Allibone reminded Dennis of the aftermath of their conversation last Thursday. Of how he had come back to the office determined to check out his accounts and given up after Harris-Tonkin (Light Aircraft). And how he had had the idea of waiting in the market square just in case he might see someone, some stranger, letting themselves into the building. Switching on his brass snake lamp. Poking their nose, as Mr Allibone would no doubt put it, into his affairs.

Dennis had abandoned the plan simply because of its impracticality, well aware that he could have sat there night after night, maybe for months, without a nibble. But now things were different. Now whoever it was had little more opportunity. Of course they wouldn't know that so it would still be very much an 'on the off chance' sentry-go. But worth a try none the less.

It was light now until quite late. Assuming the intruder had no legitimate right to enter the building, he or she would presumably wait until dusk at least, and possibly even later. On the other hand, what if they did have a right? What if one of his staff had somehow got hold of the keys, had a wax impression made and was bent on mischief?

Dennis had a stern word with his imagination. Lately it seemed to be getting both wilder in conception and completely out of control. Once more he blamed writing fiction, wondering this time if locking oneself in alternative worlds for long periods of time could seriously damage a person's grip on reality.

He thought a moment longer, then gravely concluded that yes, he would carry out this experiment. He would return to Causton fairly early, just in case. He decided to wait in the first instance in the Magpie, on the other side of the square. This gave a good view of the NatWest Bank and, when darkness fell, he could watch from his car.

Having planned his strategy Dennis felt better. At least he was doing something, even if it was all rather cloak-and-dagger. On reflection the thought was not unpleasant. Though contented with his lot there was no denying his life lacked excitement. An adventure, even one so modest it might never happen, would definitely add a little spice.

The Lawsons were packing up. Tea chests stood about, half full of wrapped china and pictures and kitchen equipment. Kate was happily stuffing handfuls of wood shavings between bubble-wrapped glasses, Mallory added yet more books to a large stack by the kitchen door. Two boxes full of clothes stood in the hall, awaiting collection.

'Anything else for the hospice shop?'

'Don't think so.' Kate had been ruthless with her wardrobe. It was amazing how much stuff fell into the if-not-worn-for-one-year-dump category. 'Although . . .' She hesitated, then ran upstairs and quickly down again, carrying a hat, which she placed on top of the pile.

'Not your beekeeper's hat!'

The hat was made of natural straw, modelled directly after that of a real beekeeper, the crown rising directly upwards from the brim and coming to a half-point, like a soft little acorn. The wide upturned brim was thickly swathed in black mesh veiling, studded with dozens of tiny jewelled bees.

Kate loved the hat. Had spent a huge amount of money on it for a wedding instead of sensibly hiring one, and had never put it on since. Well, occasionally on a sunny day in the back yard. She associated it with balmy weather and good luck.

'Sorry.' Mallory took it from the box. 'The bees stay in the picture.'

'But I never wear it.'

'I'll get some hives; put them in the orchard.'

'Don't be ridiculous.' Kate started to laugh. 'We can't take up beekeeping just because I've got the right hat.'

But Mallory could see she was pleased. He placed the hat carefully on her head, tilting it so her eyes were half concealed by the veil. 'You look very mysterious.' He kissed her. 'And lovely.' The room was filled with a shrill, loud ringing.

'Why do telephones always sound angry?' Kate answered it. Said, 'Fine . . . Yes, thank you . . . in about ten minutes . . . It's the charity shop,' she explained to Mal, hanging up. 'Someone's coming round.'

'There'll be more stuff, I suppose, once we manage to get hold of Polly.'

They'd been trying on and off all day yesterday, plus a couple of attempts that morning. At least, Mallory had been trying. As the actual move wouldn't be for another fortnight Kate didn't regard it as all that urgent. But she could see that he was getting worried. She wondered if this was because of the trouble Polly was in that she, Kate, dare not ask about. Now Mallory was dialling again. Listening, frowning, putting the receiver back.

'I can't understand it. Where could she be?'

Kate tried to look concerned but, in truth, was merely bewildered. They had not known where Polly was at any given time for the past two years and it had never seemed to bother Mallory before. Children grow up and fly away. Life is like that.

As the pause lengthened and Mallory appeared more and more distressed she tried to think of a way to change the subject. Some way that wouldn't appear gratingly contrived.

'Shouldn't we ring Benny, Mal? Remind her we're bringing food for the dinner tomorrow? As there'll be four of us she's probably getting into a tizz already.'

'Of course. What a good idea.' But before he could pick up the phone the doorbell went. So Kate got to make the call and Mallory helped the charity people move the boxes. He put his head round the sitting-room door when they'd been loaded and said, 'I'm going to give them a hand at the other end.'

'Fine.' And pigs'll dance the polka. 'See you later, then.'

Mallory got stuck in the worst of the school run. The road was full of Volvos, Golfs and four-wheel drives, the latter unsullied by any trace of mud. Screaming infants ran about swinging rucksacks that looked like furry animals. Whole bundles of children climbed into assorted vehicles and in one case straight out again. Car doors swung open at random, not always on the pavement side. Cries of 'Fiona!' and 'Tarquin!' rent the air.

Mallory sat and cursed. It had not occurred to him that a private school might still be up and running or he would have taken another route. He couldn't go back and he couldn't move forward. A taxi behind him started hooting.

And, of course, he was wasting his time anyway, because Polly wasn't in. If she was in she would answer the phone. And if she was in and couldn't answer the phone then there was also nothing Mallory could do because he didn't have a key so wouldn't know whether she was there or not. Still, he had to try.

The truth was he was worried sick over this obscene, disgusting man – this Billy Slaughter. Surely Polly couldn't be with him? There'd be no reason other than settling her debt and she had promised to forward the banker's draft by registered post.

She couldn't have forgotten. Or deliberately broken her promise. He couldn't believe that. Kate would easily believe it and the thought made Mallory sad. Sometimes, discussing their daughter, they seemed to be talking about two different people.

The school run dispersed, the taxi driver took his finger off the horn, stuck it through the open window then thrust it violently into the air against the departure of the final Volvo. Mallory moved off.

The place that Polly shared was just off Queensbridge Road. She was on her own at the moment, Mallory knew, since the departure of one flatmate, post exams, to the Lebanon and the other more recently for a lengthy yoga and meditation retreat in Majorca.

Mallory climbed the steps, worn to a scoop in the centre by age. The shabby Edwardian house was on five levels and the bell board listed twelve names. Mallory read through them quickly. Polly's wasn't there. He wasn't altogether surprised – she had always guarded her privacy fiercely. The trouble was he didn't know the names of the other girls either. He pressed all the bells in turn on the off chance, but without any response. Presumably everyone was out at work. Then, turning away, he noticed some narrow steps leading to a basement. They were very steep but there was a metal rail to hold. A door at the bottom, glass-panelled with iron bars protecting the glass had a printed card pinned to it. 'Fforbes-Snaithe. Hartogensis. Lawson.' There was no bell.

Mallory banged the knocker fiercely. He kneeled down and tried to peer through the letter box but some sort of felt hanging blocked the view. Curtains, none too clean, at the large bay window, were closely drawn. Mallory, treading over old newspapers, orange peel and takeaway cartons, tried to peer through a tiny gap at the furthest end. He squinted but could see only darkness.

He rapped on the glass and called, 'Polly?'

A man walking his Jack Russell stopped while it took a wee against the basement railings. He looked suspiciously at Mallory, who said, 'I'm trying to find my daughter.'

The man, a picture of disbelief, carried on staring. Mallory didn't blame him. He would have done the same. He climbed back up to the street just as an elderly woman laden with Safeway shopping bags was entering the house. He called: 'Excuse me,' and moved quickly towards her. She turned a frightened face towards him and rushed inside, almost dropping the bags in her anxiety to close the door. Mallory, just close enough to put his foot in it, couldn't bring himself to do so.

Cursing softly, he hurried back to the car. He shouldn't have come and wished he hadn't seen where Polly lived. And to really put the lid on it, he'd been gone well over an hour, leaving Kate to cope on her own with the packing. He checked his watch – half-past three. And they had planned to leave before four to escape the worst of the traffic.

Seconds after Mallory had driven away Polly came swinging round the corner. Carrying a bottle of champagne, she was dancing on air and laughing to herself. Bursting with *joie de vivre*, she looked very beautiful in a floaty dress and sparkly high-heeled shoes.

By 7.30 Dennis was back in Causton. There were a lot of cars parked on the square, presumably customers of the Magpie, for Causton, like most small market towns once the shops and offices had closed, was dead as mutton. Dennis tucked in the Lexus as far away from the bank building as possible and went into the pub.

This was such a rare occurrence that he didn't know what to ask for. The whisky was cheap blended stuff and he wasn't keen on any other spirits. He ordered a glass of white wine, was offered sweet or medium dry and took the second. It wasn't very nice but, on the positive side, he nabbed an excellent observation post from the window seat.

Dennis had brought his *Telegraph* to act as a sort of screen while watching. He had seen people doing this in television dramas: plain-clothes chaps in cars, though they were usually hiding behind the *Mirror* or the *Sun*. He also thought that, should the guilty party walk past the Magpie, or worse, into it, they might recognise him.

The atmosphere was really most unpleasant – overheated, smoke-filled and very noisy. Any pub *habitué* could have told Dennis that the noise level in fact was pretty reasonable, but to him it was like being shut in a tin box, the outside then being hammered by hobnail boots. At the far end of the room a group of women were screeching with satisfaction at a joke well told. Men grouped at the bar argued, their voices raised and raised and raised again to make their point or shout down someone else's. A machine with a lot of lights was being manhandled by a youth who kept banging the sides and whooping. And there was music, if you could call it that. Why did people come to such dreadful places, wondered Dennis. And – the women let out more mirth-filled shrieks – what on earth did they find to laugh at?

'Anything else for you?' The bar manager had picked up the empty wineglass.

'Oh – thank you.' Dennis looked at his watch and realised he had been there half an hour. Though unfamiliar with ale house etiquette he was pretty sure he couldn't continue to occupy a seat without buying something more. 'The same, please.'

When the drink was brought the man bent down and whispered, 'Doing a bit of surveillance, sir?'

'Um . . .' Dennis produced a note to pay. 'Well . . .'

'Say no more.' He tapped the side of his nose, pocketing the ten pounds. 'I can keep as schtum as the next man.'

Dennis moved his head from side to side and up and down. His neck had got quite stiff by staring at a fixed angle through the window for so long. He drank some of the wine, which was different from the first, being at once more fruity and considerably warmer.

He needed the lavatory. No way round that. He was tempted to go to the office so as not to miss a moment but was terrified of colliding coming out with the very person he was watching out for coming in. So the Magpie it was. In and out – spit spot – and back to his post.

Another half-hour dragged by. Dennis, deciding not to drink any more so as to stay alert, thought it best to leave. Resigning himself to no change – he just could not seem to catch the barman's eye – he went outside and got in the car.

More time passed. There was an exciting moment when some people opened the street door leading to Brinkley and Latham but it was just the family from the top-floor flat.

Dennis switched on the radio, sticking to music so he didn't get involved in some gripping narrative and lose concentration. It started to get dark. He began to feel not only tired but extremely self-conscious. What on earth was he doing playing detective at his time of life? How undignified. How foolish. Colouring up now, recalling his earlier enthusiasm, Dennis decided enough was enough and slipped his key into the ignition.

A cab drew up outside the bank. Holding his breath, Dennis also cursed under it for the cab was blocking all sight of whoever had got out. What's more, if it didn't drive away sharpish they'd be through the street door and safely inside. Dennis scrambled from his seat and eased his way between the cars, ready at any second to duck. He craned his neck slightly – all discomfort gone now – so that he could see better.

Mr Allibone did not need to crane his neck. Having just taken one of his casual glances from the sitting-room window he had both Dennis and the passenger from the taxi clearly in his sights. She turned round, Dennis dodged down, she put a key in the door and went inside. Very interesting.

Dennis climbed back stiffly into the Lexus. He gripped the steering wheel to stop his hands from shaking and sat very still for a while, wishing with all his heart he had never embarked on this enterprise. He felt an intense desire for sleep, for oblivion. For the simple happiness he had once known as a child. He put the car into gear and drove away.

CHAPTER TEN

Kate was stuffing a large duck with apricots and hazelnuts. She'd brought her food processor down and Benny had produced soft white breadcrumbs and ground the nuts. She was as delighted with the machine as a child with a new toy and questioned Kate eagerly about its exact capabilities. 'It's a miracle!' she exclaimed. The kitchen at Appleby House was totally gadget free. Carey thought two or three good sharp knives could cope with anything and had been deeply puzzled when Benny once requested a potato peeler for her birthday.

Kate, still nursing a certain amount of resentment over the journey down last night, was filling up the bird more forcefully than was strictly necessary. Mallory had disappeared for nearly two hours, then made things worse by lying clumsily about being dragged into helping at the charity shop. Kate had finally driven away from Parsons Green into the worst traffic imaginable. The misery of their row the previous week still fresh in her mind and determined not to go down that road again she could not even give vent to her feelings, so the duck was for it. A final fistful of stuffing, a savage shove up the bottom, pricked all over and into the oven it went.

'There's lots of potatoes ready to lift,' Benny was saying. 'Shall I get some in?'

'I'll do that. And we'll need vegetables, courgettes maybe?'

'Dennis is very partial to broad beans.'

'And what about you, Benny. What do you like?'

'Oh, I don't mind. It's just so lovely for us all to be having dinner together.'

Benny's happiness was palpable. Kate, looking at her open, radiant face, thought how marvellous to be so uncomplicated. All that joy simply because two or three friends were gathering to sit down and eat. Impulsively she moved around the table and gave Benny a hug.

'It just wouldn't be the same, coming down, if you weren't here.'

'Oh,' cried Benny, trembling with pleasure. She wasn't used to being hugged.

'And that is the most gorgeous outfit.'

Benny had on a peacock-blue silky jacket and matching skirt. She was even wearing earrings and had abandoned her usual T-bar sandals for shiny court shoes.

She had taken great trouble with the dining arrangements too. Kate had decided to use the oval Sheraton table with a beautiful inlaid key design around the edge, and Benny had arranged summer-flowering jasmine and tea roses in the centre and put out Carey's most beautiful Venetian glasses. There were tall ivory candles in the candelabrum, which she had spent all morning cleaning, along with the cutlery, polishing so hard she could see her face in the spoons. The reflections were elongated, as in a fairground mirror.

'Perhaps, Kate, after dinner, we could look at the manuscripts?' Benny had already learned not to call them books. 'Maybe read bits out?'

'That's an idea.'

Kate had been astonished when the postman delivered a heavy canvas bag, drawstrung and stencilled with black letters, early that morning. Astonished and then depressed, for there was something ominous about the rapidity of this influx. Instinctively she felt the contents of the bag were not new books. Not freshly written, hot from a gifted author's fingertips but tired and grey, exhausted from doing the rounds, maybe stained by the occasional tea ring. She had come across plenty of those in her time and they were nearly always unreadable.

'I'd better get moving.' Kate picked up her sunglasses from the dresser. 'Courgettes and beans, right?'

'Broad beans.'

'Keep an eye on the duck, would you? You might need to pour off some fat.'

Left alone Benny remembered she had promised Mallory to make some Pimm's. Carey had always loved a glass at lunchtime in the summer so Benny started to feel quite sad as she sliced up a cucumber. For distraction she turned her thoughts around to the previous Sunday when she had attended the Church of the Near at Hand with Doris.

Message-wise the visit had not been a success. In spite of Doris's enthusiastic decoding of the telephone receiver's strange behaviour Carey did not come through. Doris suggested the reason could be she was in a queue. Benny doubted that. Carey had never queued for anything in her life, even when there were things worth queuing for, so she certainly wouldn't be starting now. Perhaps she just didn't fancy the medium, who had been a great disappointment, striding about all in black and looking like the wicked queen in *Snow White*. Benny had been hoping for someone more ethereal, perhaps in gauzy garments and with a delicate, uplifting voice. This woman had sounded quite common.

But, as promised, the tea was delicious and the congregation friendly. Benny had met the medium's little girl, though met was perhaps too precise a word. A plain, shrinking little soul, she had been timidly talking to Doris, accepting cakes and a drink of squash. But when Benny said 'hello' she ran away. Doris explained later that it taken her months to get Karen to take as much as a biscuit. Her mother disapproved of too much mingling.

In spite of her disappointment Benny decided, after talking it over with the man in charge of the service, to give it another go. Fortunately the times didn't clash with St Anselm's so, with a bit of luck, the vicar would never know.

In the vegetable garden Kate found an old wicker basket lying on its side by a wigwam of runner beans. She picked some courgettes, warm and shiny in her hands, half hidden behind glowing yellow flowers. There was summer savory to go with the beans and mint for the potatoes. The earth was pale in the heat and bone dry. She traced the hose, snaking between rows of newly planted broccoli, to its source and turned on the tap.

Moderating the flow, Kate watered dreamily in a silence broken only by the heady thrumming from the orchard of hundreds of wasps and bees. The gentle splash as the water soaked the ground and the rich vanilla fragrance of bean flowers combined to effect a trance-like involvement in the moment that wiped all else from her mind.

When Mallory touched her hair she jumped. He said, 'Sorry. Were you miles away?'

'Yes – well, no. I was absolutely here. But in a way I can't quite describe.' At the sight of him the final shreds of Kate's resentment vanished. Mallory's shoulders were stooped, weariness lay upon him. He looked as he had coming home at night from the Ewan Sedgewick.

'Is there anything I can do?'

'We need some spuds.' She smiled, taking his hand. 'I'll show you where they are.'

Mallory found a fork in the shed and started to dig, putting the Nicola potatoes in an old bucket. As Kate began to pick the broad beans she suddenly remembered what day it was. At four o'clock this afternoon Ashley had been due to see his GP. Had been called in specially. They must be home by now. She hoped the news was good but couldn't help feeling that if it had been they would have rung to say so.

When Mallory's bucket was full he took it and the beans to the kitchen, returning almost straight away looking slightly more cheerful.

'Benny's made us some Pimm's.'

'*Pimm's* . . .'

'My aunt's favourite.'

'What's it like?'

'Floating salad. Come and try.'

There were several fraying Lloyd Loom chairs on the flagstones outside the french windows. And a great stone table on worn-away lion paws. Kate poured the drinks and went to find Benny so they could all sit down together.

Mallory picked the borage and cucumber out of his glass, drained it and filled it up again. He leaned back, faking relaxation. The croquet lawn, half the size of a playing field and still studded with rusty hoops, stretched widely before him. Perhaps they could have a game soon? A croquet party – ask some friends down from London. Heaven knew, there was enough room to put people up. He would invite the Parnells and maybe some members of his aunt's bridge club. He dwelled on this attractive prospect for a while, seeing small groups of people strolling across the grass: girls in summer dresses, men in crumpled linen jackets and straw Panamas. Occasionally there would be a burst of laughter. Or a cry of 'Hoopla!' when someone's mallet thwacked a precisely angled ball.

Mallory, trying to fill up every corner of his mind with pleasant things, struggled to add yet more verisimilitude to this pastoral idyll. Some huge sunshades materialised, a swing in the cedar tree, a brightly coloured gazebo. For a moment he was really there amongst them. Taken out of himself, as the saying goes. But then a real sound broke across his consciousness and the dazzling picture vanished.

'It's all right for some,' said Kate. She sat down and splashed the Pimm's into two glasses, adding ice from the portable ice box, smelling the orange mint. 'Would you like another one, darling?'

'I've had another one.'

'These things are a bit creaky.' Kate tipped the chair back, resting her heels on a stone trough of Madonna lilies and tiny green ferns, tightly curled, like shepherds' crooks. She took a deep swallow of the drink then slowly exhaled, letting everything go.

'I told Dennis,' continued Kate, 'half-seven for eight. It's now seven thirty-five and Benny's already fretting.'

Dennis. Mallory, about to drain his glass, put it down. He had quite forgotten that Dennis wanted to have a talk with him directly after dinner. Something personal, he had said. And afterwards there would be the inaugural meeting of the Celandine Press. At this rate he'd be drunk before they'd even started eating. Angry and ashamed at how little it had taken to hurl him back into self-indulgent misery, Mallory smiled across at Kate.

'I'm sorry, sweetheart.'

'About what?'

'Ohh . . . being me.'

'I'm not sorry you're you. If I woke up one morning next to someone who wasn't you I'd be livid.'

'I wouldn't be best pleased, myself.'

'That's all right then.'

Benny, rosy from attending to the duck, appeared on the terrace steps. 'This Pimm's is delicious, Ben,' said Kate. 'I've poured some out for you.'

'Thank you.' Benny took the glass and perched on the terrace wall. She agitated the ice cubes gently but didn't drink. 'The thing is – I'm getting worried about Dennis. He's never late, you see.'

'He's not late now.' Mallory found it difficult to sound reassuring when he could see no reason for anxiety. 'It's only ten to eight.'

'Even so . . .' Benny, though sensing his impatience, stood her ground.

'Look,' Kate got up, 'I'll walk over, if you like.'

'We'll all go,' said Mallory, leaning back with his eyes closed.

'No,' said Benny. 'You stay here; it's such a lovely evening.' She disappeared back into the dining room, calling over her shoulder. 'I'll probably meet him halfway.'

It was not generally known that, to balance the unhappy condition of spending her entire life riddled with anxiety, Benny had been given a protective talisman against disaster. All she had to do was remember to call upon it in any situation that looked like being even remotely hazardous.

She had her father to thank for this device, which he drew to her attention when she was barely thirteen. Benny remembered exactly the moment this occurred. The family had been watching the local news on television. Sally, their Cairn terrier, was curled up in Benny's lap. A woman, whose husband and son had just been pulverised when their car had been squashed under the wheels of an articulated lorry, was being asked by a sparky young reporter how she felt.

'Shattered,' had been her reply. Then, choking between sobs, 'I never thought this could happen to me.'

'Did you hear that, Mother?' asked Mr Frayle. 'Doesn't that bear out what I've always said *vis-à-vis* the human psyche.'

'What's that, dear?' replied Mrs Frayle.

'Time and time again my point is proved.'

'What point, Daddy?'

'Hush, Berenice,' said Mrs Frayle. 'Your father's listening to the news.'

'The only people disaster ever strikes are the people who think it could never happen to them.'

Unaware of the devastating effect of these words on his teenage daughter Mr Frayle folded his *Daily Express* and turned his attention once more to the tiny blue screen flickering in its cabinet of light oak.

Forty years on and Berenice was still conscious of her extreme good fortune in having such a perceptive and intelligent father. What devastating stroke of ill fortune might have shattered her whole world any day at any time had she not taken this warning sincerely to heart?

Every morning, from then on, Benny would write down a list of incidents that the following twenty-four hours might reasonably be expected to hold. Then she would imagine every single thing that could possibly go wrong during each occasion and, when the time came round, expected them all to happen. And it worked! Not a single catastrophe had ever occurred.

Of course, she couldn't quite hold each and every imagined possibility simultaneously in her mind while its companion event was occurring but she did her best. Naturally all this was a terrible strain and meant that only half her attention – if that – was on what she was supposed to be doing at any given time.

119

Obviously some happenings were easier to classify as potentially disastrous than others. For instance a check on carrot root fly (catching foot in garden hose, falling, breaking leg) was not nearly as complex or alarming as a visit to the zoo (mauled by escaping tiger, trampled by rhino, catching psittacosis from parrot bite). Or a trip on the underground (pushed under wheels in rush hour by maddened claustrophobe). And there were a few rare occasions when Benny did not feel the need to use her talisman at all. Visits to Dennis fell into this category. However disorderly or unharmonious the real world, once in his presence Benny always felt nothing could go ill.

These reflections had brought her to the gate of Kinders. It stood wide open, which was strange. Dennis was meticulous, not just in closing but also in fastening gates. Gates, doors, cupboards even. And lining up edges, straightening cutlery; even drawers were closed with hairline precision.

Just as she had three evenings ago Benny made her way into the house via the garage. No warmth from the cooker tonight, no fragrant smells of turbot in white wine. Benny reprised her 'Cooee?' but without much confidence. For no reason she could name she felt sure the flat was empty. But she checked the other rooms, just in case. Finally she approached the war room. The door was shut but Benny, emboldened by her previous successful sortie, opened it and stepped briskly inside.

When Benny came back Kate and Mallory were still on the terrace, relaxing in the amber haze of the setting sun. They had been drifting idly in and out of conversation, talking of nothing special while shadows from the giant cedar slowly spread across the lawn, finally disappearing into the long grass.

Mallory said, 'Here she is.'

Benny had appeared at the corner of the house and was making her way towards the terrace. She was walking slowly in an odd sort of shuffle. Then, as she came closer, Kate saw that her whole body was stiff and unnaturally straight, the arms held up at a sharp angle before her, poised to return an embrace. Like a bad actor playing a zombie.

Kate sprang up, knocking over her glass of Pimm's. Her welcoming smile vanished as she cried out Benny's name and ran towards her.

'Benny – what is it? What's wrong?' She took Benny in her arms and embraced a column of stone. 'Tell me. *Tell me.*'

Benny made an unintelligible sound.

'Oh God – Mallory—' He was already by her side. 'What shall we do? *Benny. . .*'

'She must have had some sort of stroke.'

'Let's get her inside.'

'Rook.'

'What?' Now, in the glow from the terrace lamps, Kate experienced fully the stamp of horror on Benny's ghastly countenance, the disturbed violent agony in her eyes. 'What do you mean?'

'I'll find a doctor.'

'At this hour?'

'There's always someone for emergencies.'

'It'll take too long. Ring for an ambulance.' Kate put her arm around Benny and tried to persuade her into the house. 'And then,' she called after Mallory, 'go round to Kinders.'

'*Aahhhhh* . . .'

'All right, Ben. It's all right.' Kate, knocked off balance by the scream blasting directly into her face, could hardly get the words out. 'Come . . . come and lie down, darling.'

'. . . rook . . . rook . . .'

'That's right – lean on me. Lean on Kate . . .'

Mallory ran, first to the telephone and then from the house. He passed a little knot of people at the gate, their faces avid with the happy curiosity of the uninvolved. No doubt Benny had been spotted by someone making her blind journey, her dreadful sleepwalk back along the High Street. Pushing past them, sensing them snuffling and sniffing behind him like hounds, Mallory wondered if he was, after all, cut out for life in a small village.

At Appleby House Kate was trying to make Benny comfortable. An impossible task, which anyway didn't signify, for whatever she did or said seemed not to be understood in any recognisable way.

When the ambulance arrived the paramedics very gently, even tenderly, carried out the necessary checks. Benny spoke once more – 'Just like the rook' – but the words were addressed to the night air and her eyes stared blankly through them all.

Kate found a nightdress and toothbrush, took the duck, black and shiny now, from the oven, threw it in the bin and put her coat on. Just before she left, the telephone rang. It was Mallory to say that something terrible had happened at Kinders and that he had notified the police.

By the time the patrol car arrived a group of forty or so people had gathered outside Dennis's house. Most were on the little green by the pond opposite, but a few crowded round the gate. As the uniformed officers pushed by they were questioned, unsuccessfully, as to what was going on. Denied any solid description of events, people felt obliged to make up a free-wheeling scenario of their own.

'They'll be putting that blue and white tape round next.'

'What for?'

'Protect the scene of crime.'

'How do you know there's been a crime?'

'Yeah – maybe he's just had an accident.'

'You don't call the old Bill out for an accident.'

'True. Could be a burglary?'

'Look who's letting them in.'

'Him from Appleby House.'

'One thing I do know – it'll be something to do with them machines.'

'Terrible things.'

'Doris Crudge – she reckons there's an iron cage in there. For roasting people.'

A concerted gasp of horrified satisfaction.

'Sounds like he got what he deserved then,' said the man with the hot tip about the tape.

Mallory closed the front door behind the two officers and leaned back on it, legs trembling. His face was salt white, clammy and beaded with sweat. He had been very sick and still felt extremely nauseous.

'Are you all right, sir?' asked the younger policeman. 'I think you'd better sit—'

'What we've been given,' cut in the other, a Sergeant Gresham, 'is a fatal accident which you – Mr Lawson? – discovered this evening. You then made a call to the emergency services at eight seventeen. Is that correct?'

'Yes . . . that is, no.' Mallory stumbled, somehow groped his way into the sitting room and fell into a chair. 'I made the call but I didn't discover it – him.'

'So who did?'

'Her name's Benny Frayle. But she's in deep shock. They've taken her to hospital.'

'That Stoke Mandeville?'

'No idea.'

'Right. Now – if you'll just show me—'

'I'm not going in there again.' Memory brought more drowning waves of nausea. The sergeant loomed suddenly closer, then swam out of Mallory's vision. A hand on the back of his neck eased his head down between his knees.

'Don't overdo it, Palmer. You'll be running him a bath next.'

'Sergeant.'

'And try and get hold of the dead bloke's doctor.'

Gresham disappeared. He checked out the kitchen and tiny bedroom. Then opened the door at the end of the hall and stood on the threshold of the vast awful space, his jaws agape with sheer astonishment.

The sergeant had not the slightest interest in history. He had never been to a museum in his life and so, confronted with these astonishing weapons of destruction, had no idea what they were. At first he thought they might be some wonky form of modern art, sculptures or suchlike. Then he noticed the huge crossbow. A weapons freak, then. A weirdo. They were up to all sorts, these survivalists.

The body lay face downwards, huddled against the apparatus that looked like a giant's catapult. It was wearing men's clothes, very light tweed but still heavy going, the sergeant would have thought, in this weather. Even then you'd have to take them off to prove he was a man 'cause there was not much left of his head. Spread all over the place, it was. Red stuff both runny and jellified, grey stuff, white stuff and pounded bits of bone.

None of this fazed Sergeant Gresham. He was a veteran. Thirty years of examining evidence following the discovery of murder victims. Or suicides. Not to mention trying to sort out the unspeakable carnage resulting from the worst traffic accidents. Gresham had been there. And he had done all that.

Now he noticed a large slick of vomit just a few feet from the corpse and was glad he hadn't brought young Palmer into the room with him. One person chucking up was more than ample.

He walked round the area of the big machine carefully. It was easy to see what had happened. There was a wooden rack set up on a frame around twelve feet square standing directly alongside the catapult. Six huge wooden balls were secured there. A seventh, heavily stained, was lying a short distance from the dead man's head.

Gresham called into the station to ask for a photographer. This looked to him like an accidental but it was always advisable to have a record of the scene. Then he went back to the sitting room to find the guy who had called them out, looking slightly less green and drinking a cup of tea. Palmer had already produced his notebook.

'Got the medic sorted, Palmer?'

'Yes, Sergeant. Dr Cornwell. He's been notified.'

'My aunt's doctor,' offered Mallory. 'He'll be so—'

'Could you tell me how Miss Frayle came to find the body, Mr Lawson?'

'He – Dennis – was expected for dinner at Appleby House – which is where I live – and Benny too. But he didn't turn up.'

'You were on social terms then?'

'He was a family friend,' replied Mallory quietly. 'I'd known him all my life.'

'Surname?'

'Brinkley.'

'Did he live here alone?'

'Yes.'

'Any idea who his next of kin might be?'

'I'm afraid not. His parents are both dead – thank heavens. I believe he had a cousin somewhere in Wales but I don't think they've been in touch for years.'

'Right,' said Sergeant Gresham. 'Now, this person you reckon found the body . . .'

'Benny Frayle,' supplied Palmer.

'She seems to have been sick, by the way—'

'That was me. Sorry.'

123

'I presume she rang you from here?'

'No. She made her way back . . . somehow . . . to Appleby House.'

'Somehow?'

How was Mallory to describe Benny's terrible perambulation? Her blind stare and lumbering mechanical stride. The screwed-up blinking eyes and gaping mouth.

'Do you remember what Miss Frayle actually said when she arrived?'

'No.' He saw no point in mentioning Benny's strange repetition of the word 'rook'. 'She was . . . well, she seemed to have no grasp at all of what was going on.'

'Understandable,' said Gresham. 'And you came straight round here?'

'Yes.'

'How did you get in?'

'The kitchen door was unlocked.'

Here the volume of sound outside the house became suddenly louder. There was knocking at the front door and Palmer disappeared to return almost immediately murmuring, 'Photographer.'

'How did you let him in?'

'Key in the lock, Sarge.'

Gresham's questions continued, all entirely off the beam as far as Mallory could comprehend. At one point he was asked why he had called the police in the first place.

'I don't understand.'

'Most people under such circumstances, having dialled nine, nine, nine, would have asked for an ambulance.'

'What on earth for?'

'There are procedures to be followed, Mr Lawson. The body has to be pronounced dead. It has to be removed.'

'You don't think of . . . I was all over the place. Christ – you've been in that room. How would you have felt?'

Cool as a Cornetto, thought Palmer, giving his note-taking wrist a break. That's how the sarge would've felt. Palmer thought he'd like to be as detached, as laid-back as Gresham one day. That is, sometimes he thought he would. Other times he wasn't so sure.

'So you didn't feel there was anything . . . out of order?'

'Out of order?' Mallory frowned at the sergeant, puzzled. Then the puzzlement became incredulity. 'You can't mean—'

'Suspicious, sir, yes.'

'Of course not. That's . . . ridiculous. Unbelievable.'

That was the sergeant's opinion too but it didn't hurt to stir the pot. All sorts of things had been known to float to the surface on these occasions. Not necessarily relevant to the case in point but often very interesting.

At this stage in his reflections the doorbell rang again. Once more Palmer jumped to it and shortly afterwards Jimmy Cornwell came into the room. He went straight across to Mallory.

'God, Mallory. This is just appalling. Dennis. What actually happened?'

Mallory described what had happened. Cornwell listened, occasionally compelled to interrupt. He said, 'Christ! Not Benny,' and, 'That terrible place.' Then he went with Gresham to identify the body. Cornwell rolled Dennis over, glanced briefly at what was left of his face, nodded and walked quickly away. In the kitchen he filled a glass with tap water and, once more in the sitting room, opened his case.

'Look, Mallory – I'm going to give you these tablets. And I want you—'

'I'm all right.'

'Believe me, you are not all right.' He turned to Sergeant Gresham. 'How soon can he leave?'

'Presumably Mr Lawson will want to wait until the body has been removed. And the house secured.'

'Of course, yes,' blurted out Mallory. The thought had never occurred to him, though he hoped it would have done when the time came.

'What would be helpful is for us to talk to the last person to see Mr Brinkley alive. Do you have any ideas in that direction at all, sir?'

'Not really. It could have been someone in his office. Or maybe a neighbour saw him coming home.'

Palmer noted Dennis Brinkley's business address. Dr Cornwell stood over Mallory until he had taken two of the tablets. Then he scribbled on the bottle and placed it next to Mallory's nearly full tumbler before leaving. Meanwhile Sergeant Gresham, after having checked over the sitting room, could be heard moving about in the rest of the house.

'What's he doing?' Mallory asked Constable Palmer.

'Checking for a note, Mr Lawson.'

'A note!' It took Mallory a moment to work out the connection. Then a manic desire to laugh seized him. The idea that Dennis, *Dennis* of all people, would decide to end his life at all, let alone by releasing a cannon ball, then laying his head in its path, was utter lunacy. Surreal, in fact. Uncontrollable like hiccups, the laughter forced its way out of Mallory's mouth in little moaning shouts.

Palmer watched helplessly. The usual method of dealing with hysterics was out of the question here. There was no way he was going to risk being up on an assault charge with only six months' probation under his belt. Sergeant Gresham came in, summed up the situation, threw the remaining water at Mallory and sent Palmer for a towel.

'Sorry about that, Mr Lawson.'

'No, no.' Mallory mopped his face. 'You were . . . I mean, it's all right.'

The ambulance arrived and left a bare ten minutes later, bearing Dennis away. The small crowd, satisfied at being present at the final curtain, slowly dispersed. And not long after the police prepared to do the same.

Mallory was left then in sole possession of Kinders. His first act was to ring Appleby House but there was no response. Presumably Kate was still at the hospital. He would find out which one, but first there was the clearing up to do. Mallory's stomach heaved at the thought but there was no way he could decently leave it for anyone else.

He took a large paper towel roll and a black bin liner and went back into the war room, putting all the lights on and leaving the door wide open. He scooped up most of the vomit and other mess, filled the bag with stained towels, knotted it tightly and threw it in the dustbin. He wiped the ball as well as he could, then washed it clean in the kitchen sink. Then he filled a bowl with hot water, mixed in some Dettol and washing-up liquid, found a scrubbing brush and some old dusters and went back to finish the job. When he had finished he scoured his hands at the kitchen sink until they looked like newly boiled lobsters.

Securing the house was relatively uncomplicated. He pulled the garage door down from the inside and locked it, then locked the entrance to the kitchen and pocketed both the keys. The main door had an extremely solid double Yale. Mallory removed its key and stepped outside, slamming the door behind him.

Having seen Benny properly admitted and put safely to bed, Kate had to find her own way back. Fortunately there was a cash machine at the hospital. She drew out fifty pounds and hoped it would cover a taxi home.

She found Mallory deeply asleep on a couch in Carey's sewing room. A small lamp threw a soft light on his face, which was grey with exhaustion. She bent closer and could see he had been crying. His breath smelled sour. His shirt was filthy. Tempted to let him sleep on, oblivious to the dreadful happenings of the night for a little longer, she could not bear to think of him waking alone. So she took his hand and shook it gently. Waking, he smiled. Then she saw recollection flooding his mind.

'Come and rest, darling,' said Kate. 'Come to bed.'

CHAPTER ELEVEN

The death of Dennis Brinkley made the local breakfast news. Though sparse, the information 'Found dead at his home in the village of Forbes Abbot' was still pretty shocking. Yet the very words concealed as much as they revealed. How, dead? everyone was asking. An overdose, a fall, a stroke, a heart attack, food poisoning, an accident? Was an intruder perhaps involved? Being ignorant of the details was utter anguish, especially as far as the village itself was concerned. It felt, as Dennis's very own community, it had a right to know. And before anyone else too.

The Parnells, who listened with half an ear only to Radio 4 in the morning, remained ignorant of the news until Judith went out with her bundle of letters to catch the postman. Although neither she nor Ashley had known Dennis, except by sight, the proximity of sudden death was most distressing. Judith seemed especially upset and Ashley had the pleasantly satisfying experience of looking after her. He even made the breakfast, grinding coffee beans, buttering toast and boiling some eggs.

At her semi-detached bungalow in Glebe Road, Doris Crudge was lying down. Ernest made three phone calls on his wife's behalf, apologising for her inability to come to work that day. He explained that she was not very well, which seemed the simplest and most straightforward thing to say. In truth, Doris was flat out on their best recliner. There was a bag of ice cubes on her forehead, a bottle of her nearest neighbour's tranquillisers to hand and a mug of sweet tea so strong it was nearly black. She was moaning gently.

Ernest regarded her with sympathy but not undue concern. Doris had always been one to give of her emotional best in situations that called for a dramatic response, and today was plainly no exception. But he was doing her an injustice in assuming this was all display. Doris had grown quite fond of her Mr Brinkley. Apart from his weird hobby he was an ideal employer. Always courteous and kindly, asking after her relatives from time to time. A nice Christmas box and, on the very rare occasion when she had been unable to work, still paying her wages.

Ernest decided not to pass on the information from Mrs Lawson that poor Benny Frayle had discovered the body and was now in hospital suffering from shock. He reckoned Doris had enough to be going on with for a while.

At the Lathams', Andrew was in the shower when a piercing shriek from downstairs caused him to slip on the soap, grab the sequinned curtain and only just save himself from a nasty crack on the head against the tiled floor.

Pausing only to shroud himself shoulder to heel in a thick towelling robe – even at seven in the morning Gilda was not averse to a jump or two – and belt up, he raced downstairs.

'What is it, moon of my delight?'

'Dennis is dead,' said Gilda.

'What?'

'It was on the telly.'

'Our Dennis?'

'Who else's?' She watched him for a moment, then started to laugh. 'Your face.'

'But . . .' He fell into the chair facing her. The one with the back like a huge seashell and wooden mermaids supporting the arms. 'How? I mean . . . what did they say?'

'Nothing. Just found at his home. There's bound to be an inquest – there always is in these cases. We must go.' She made it sound like a nice day out. 'Hadn't you better give thingy a buzz?'

'Who?'

'That chap who's in charge when Denny's not there.'

'Fortune.' Andrew was still staring at her, dazed. 'I can't believe it.'

'I don't see why. Happens all the time. Middle-aged bloke, fit as a fiddle, always at the gym, out jogging, keels over at the side of the road—'

'Dennis was *jogging*?'

'I'm giving you an example, stupid. Catch me near a gym.' She shifted her huge bulk from side to side; tried in vain to ease her bolstery legs apart. 'I suppose that means another funeral outfit.'

'But you've already—'

'More greedy rip-offs for some hideous hat. People seem to think I'm a walking gold mine.'

'I'm sure he didn't die on purpose,' murmured Andrew, paying for it over and over again during the next half-hour.

For the first and only time in his life Andrew Latham was first at the office. Only just, though. As he unlocked the street door Leo Fortune appeared at his side. Politely attempting to conceal his surprise, Fortune murmured: 'Good morning.'

Andrew responded with a curt nod. He had no interest in forming any sort of relationships with the male contingent at Brinkley and Latham. Female staff were something else.

Entering the main office, he retreated to his cubbyhole and watched through the glass as the rest of the crew arrived. He saw those who had heard the news about Dennis pass it on to those who hadn't. Noted their expressions of shock and disbelief. Then, in total silence, each of them turned and stared in his direction. Andrew felt quite uncomfortable. It was like being under observation by a group of the living dead. He gave it five, adjusted his features and walked out to join them.

'I see you've all heard the bad news.' A pause, giving it ten, this time, to emphasise the solemnity of the occasion. 'I'm afraid I don't have much information for you about what happened. But I believe there's to be an inquest and I expect more details will be available then.'

'I'm not sure I want any more details,' said one of the clerks.

To Andrew's surprise he sounded almost angry. There were several murmurs of agreement. One of the girls started to cry. A definite air of sadness pervaded the group and gradually seemed to spread outwards, filling the room.

Andrew remained totally puzzled. Whoever would have thought it? All over a dry old stick like Dennis Brinkley. Wonders would never cease.

'I suggest we continue as usual today.' He noticed one or two cynical smirks at this, no doubt directed at his own indolence. 'But if anyone feels they really aren't up to it, by all means feel free to take a break.'

Silence, then Leo Fortune said, 'I think Dennis would have wanted us to carry on.'

God, Mr Sanctimonious. Pass the sick bag, Edna.

'By the way, Latham, the locksmith is due at ten o'clock. I presume we honour Dennis's wishes and have the work done?'

'Suit yourself.'

'Also I shall need to make use of his office. I presume you've no objection?'

'Why should I have?' said Andrew. 'You're his "second in command" after all.' He made it sound like lickspittle to some reptilian trader in living flesh. 'No doubt you can't wait to get started.'

He returned to his cubicle with a satisfied smile, watching as two of the girls hovered comfortingly round Fortune, who was plainly extremely upset. Brenda, Dennis's secretary, glared across at him. Andrew smiled broadly back. What an excellent day it was turning out to be. And still barely ten o'clock.

At Appleby House Kate and Mallory moved slowly and carefully about, saying very little. Mallory still seemed devastated and withdrawn. Kate got on with necessary tasks. She made their bed – the discovery of Benny's lavender bags carefully placed beneath the pillows was most upsetting – and prepared a breakfast that neither of them ate.

At mid-morning she rang the hospital and was told Miss Frayle had spent a comfortable night and would be seen by a doctor quite soon. It was suggested she rang back at lunchtime. Asking how soon she could visit, Kate was told between two and four that afternoon.

Though the sky was overclouded, Kate returned to the walled garden. She wandered aimlessly about, marvelling now at her innocent pleasure the previous evening. Even as she had watered the parched ground and turned her face happily to the evening sun, Dennis was lying dead. She still didn't know how and, at least for now, didn't want to know.

Disturbed by voices, then shocked by a sudden burst of laughter Kate hurried down the brick path to the blue door that led to the orchard. She opened it and stepped through. At first glance, the place seemed full of people. Then she looked again and realised there were barely a dozen.

A few were up on ladders, attending to the growing apples. Others were picking up early thinnings – wizened tiny fruit, falling to give space so the rest might grow. Kate had noticed the knobbly bumps under her feet when she had explored the orchard shortly after Carey's funeral.

Watching them in their bright shirts and jeans, listening to their unselfconscious chatter, Kate's indignation quickly subsided. Why shouldn't they laugh? The passing of a local middle-aged man meant nothing to them. They had probably never even heard of Dennis Brinkley.

She vowed then to try to keep the tragedy that had overtaken them all at some sort of distance. She would have neither the time nor energy to get caught up in grieving or constant emotional speculation. There would be Benny to comfort and support – Mallory too. And sooner or later, no matter how much later, no matter what obstacles fate threw in her path, Kate would be overseeing the launch of the Celandine Press. Because it was her turn now and no way was the dream going to be lost in the shuffle.

Almost time to check with the hospital. Kate made her way back to the house, only to find that Mallory had already made the call. It seemed Miss Frayle had been seen by a doctor and was now able to be collected and go home. Relief that there was nothing seriously physically wrong was tempered with anxiety as to Benny's mental state. The memory of the figure stumbling, bolt upright and blind with fear and shock, was still startlingly fresh in Kate's mind. She wondered just how much difference a few hours' sleep – and that almost certainly drugged – could have made

Mallory cried off driving to the hospital but promised to pick some peas and mint and make soup for lunch. Also to buy fresh bread and a newspaper from the village store. He kissed Kate goodbye somewhat absently and wandered off across the croquet lawn.

I'm on my own with this one, thought Kate. Again. Then chided herself for meanness. God knows what Mallory had found at Kinders last night. Found and somehow handled in whatever awful way it had to be handled. Just be grateful, Lawson, she muttered as she swung the Golf round, that you got the better half.

Returning to the house with a colander of bursting pea pods and a bunch of pineapple mint, hardly ideal for soup, Mallory made directly for the telephone.

From the moment he set off for Dennis's house the previous night until he was running his bath this morning the sensational and shocking nature of the discovery he made had driven all thoughts of his daughter from his mind. Now they returned, energised by their absence, tormenting him anew.

He recalled his earlier convincement that Polly had been inside the Dalston flat when he rang the bell. Though this idea was without any logical foundation Mallory couldn't let it go. He regretted bitterly now that he had not, in fact, pushed past the elderly woman on the front step and got into the house. There might have been an alternative way down to the basement. Or he could have slid a note under the door of whoever lived over it. They would know if anyone was still in there. However quiet a person might be, you could always hear some sounds of occupation – taps running, a lavatory flushing, a window being opened or closed.

Mallory recognised there was no way he could return to London at the present. Apart from his wishing to support Kate – and Benny too, of course – the police had indicated that he might well be called at the inquest. So all he could do was keep phoning. Over and over again.

Kate had been annoyed by the suggestion that Benny could now be collected. It made her sound like a parcel. A thing, inanimate. Dumped somewhere until whoever could be bothered came along and took it away. She knew this was unreasonable. They must answer hundreds of enquiries every day and it was only a word, for heaven's sake. She did this when nervous – latch on to something completely trivial and worry away at it to distract herself from the heavy stuff.

Entering reception, Kate looked around, then realised she was foolish to expect Benny to be just sitting there. There was bound to be some sort of procedure to go through. A friendly middle-aged woman behind the counter directed her to the ward. A busy staff nurse spoke to her briefly and gave a prescription for strong sedatives to be filled at the hospital pharmacy.

Driving over, Kate had several times imagined the coming meeting and how it would go, what Benny would look like, what state she would be in. What state would I be in, wondered Kate, if, within the space of a single month, I lost the two people dearest in the world to me? My husband and my child. How would I carry on? Would I want to carry on? What would be the point?

So, when she saw Benny, Kate's first feeling was of relief. Benny looked as she always looked, neat and ordinary except for her rather striking clothes. She was sitting beside her bed, feet side by side together, hands folded quietly in her lap like a child being good. It was only as she got closer that Kate saw the difference.

Benny's cheeks were blanched; her lips ashen. And she seemed to have shrunk in some indefinable way. She certainly wasn't any thinner. Or any shorter. But she was definitely smaller. And her wig was crooked.

'Hello, Ben.' Kate kneeled down by the chair, took a soft, boneless hand in her own and squeezed it gently. 'I've come to take you home.'

131

Benny's pale lips moved. She whispered something that Kate couldn't quite hear and got obediently to her feet. She seemed to be holding herself together with thoughtful care. And watchfully, as if bits might start falling off any minute.

What to do about the wig? Kate had no intention of leading Benny through the hospital and car park with it slipping over one ear, thus risking unkind remarks and perhaps even laughter. On the other hand it seemed disrespectful in the extreme to simply reach out and adjust it. In the end she gave Benny a hug, murmured, 'Now look what I've done – I'm so sorry – do you mind, Benny?' and put it straight that way.

During the journey home the one or two remarks that Kate offered were met with a vacant stare and almost inaudible mutterings. Kate was disturbed by the stare, which was without either light or intelligence.

But the worst moment was when they actually arrived at Appleby House, and she tried to help Benny from the car. Benny struggled on her own for a moment, then took Kate's arm and tried to smile. It was a heartbreaker, that mockery of a smile, and it really did for Kate. She started to cry. Benny didn't cry. Not then or for a long while to come.

Later that afternoon the Parnells called round to offer their condolences. Judith brought a large bunch of sweet peas and Ashley a bowl of glowing, nearly black cherries. They sat down in the kitchen, taking a cup of coffee. Ashley spoke first, awkward but with obvious sincerity.

'We were both very sorry to hear the news. He was an old friend, I believe.'

'Yes,' said Mallory. 'A kind man. Very . . . decent.'

'Benny must be extremely distressed.'

'But she'll have you, won't she?' put in Judith quickly. 'I mean – you won't be going back straight away?'

'No. Not until the inquest is over.'

'When you do she must come over,' suggested Ashley. 'For meals or just to spend time. She shouldn't be on her own.'

Judith shifted uncomfortably in her seat and stared out of the window through which beams of sunlight poured.

'One of us will stay,' said Kate. She didn't add that Benny hardly seemed to notice whether other people were present or not. 'Apart from removal day, that is.'

'And when is that?' asked Ashley.

The conversation moved on. Mallory was grateful for Ashley's lack of prurience. He had been braced for questions along the lines of: what actually *happened*? How come it was you who found him? What did the police say? Was it anything to do with those machines?

Mallory had had the first of these quasi-concerned exchanges that morning while out buying some milk. A man he vaguely recognised from Carey's funeral stopped him on his way back to Appleby House.

After the opener: 'How awful for you what a shock my deepest sympathy I understand it was an accidental hanging one of those big ropes in his museum,' the man, eyes shining, put his hand on Mallory's arm. 'Talking things through can be a great help. I live at Mon Repos and was a close friend of your aunt, name of Lattice. Please feel you can come at any time. Day or night you'll be most welcome.'

An unpleasant experience. All very well for Kate to say it was just human nature. There were certain aspects of human nature Mallory felt he could well do without, especially in his present state. He tuned back into the conversation.

'So I feel a bit embarrassed,' Ashley was saying, 'introducing such news at a sad time but you've always been so kind . . .' He was speaking to everyone but looking mainly at Kate.

'It is a sad time,' repeated Judith firmly. 'So I think we should be—'

'Sorry,' interrupted Mallory. 'I missed that last bit.'

'They've found out what's wrong with Ashley,' said Kate.

'That's marvellous,' said Mallory. 'At least, I hope.'

'It's pericardial disease.'

'Pericarditis,' corrected Judith.

'They think it might be from when I was working in Africa—'

'Over ten years ago.'

'And the chances are it can be treated.'

'Oh – I'm so glad,' said Kate. 'Let's hope the waiting list—'

'We're going private,' said Judith. 'Seeing a Harley Street specialist the week after next.'

'Jumping the queue.' Ashley laughed.

'We are not jumping the queue. We're joining a different, shorter queue. Thus leaving a space, incidentally, for a National Health patient.'

Kate filled an awkward pause by getting up from the table, saying, 'I must find a vase for your flowers. They smell wonderful.'

While Kate was running water at the sink someone knocked loudly at the outside door. Ashley, being nearest, opened it, and with such an absent-minded, comfortable air Judith couldn't help wondering if he'd done it more than once before. The postman stood fair and square, mail bags lapping at his ankles.

'Any empties?'

''Fraid not,' said Kate. 'Maybe tomorrow.'

'How many's that so far?' asked Ashley.

Mallory started bringing them in. 'Thirteen.'

'You must be overwhelmed,' said Judith. 'And here we are holding you up—'

'Perhaps I could read some for you, Kate,' said Ashley.

Kate turned, scissors in one hand, a chopped-off bunch of sweet pea stems in the other. She was about to accept with gratitude when she noticed Judith squinting against the sun, her face a mask of malign intensity. She looked angry and jealous and afraid.

Kate said, 'That's kind of you, Ash. But, to be honest, most of them won't be worth it.'

There were a few letters in the post as well. Some were for the Celandine Press but there were also a couple of bills. Mallory was just putting them under his coffee cup when Mrs Crudge put her head round the door.

Judith hurried over to Ashley then and dragged him off, saying they had a million things to do. Mallory thought Ashley looked as if he had very little to do and would much rather have stayed behind. Through the open kitchen window Kate could hear them in the porch. Judith was saying, 'Since when has she been calling you Ash?'

Mrs Crudge came in a little further. 'Just popped round to say I'm sorry about earlier, Mrs Lawson. But I'll be in ten sharp tomorrow as usual, all right?'

'Of course it is,' said Kate. 'Stay and have some tea as you're here.'

'That's all right. I expect Ben'll be making a pot.'

Kate was glad Benny had a visitor. Especially one who was an old friend. Perhaps she would feel able to talk to Doris. So far she had hardly spoken, either to Kate herself or to Mallory. Of course, these were very early days. Kate put the flowers on the table and went off to attack the bags. Mallory, expertly concealing his enthusiasm, trailed behind.

But they had no sooner turned the nearest one upside down than Mrs Crudge came in carrying a large plastic carrier.

'That was quick,' said Mallory.

'How was she?' asked Kate, nearly adding, 'and how are you?' for Mrs Crudge appeared pale and quite disturbed.

'I don't know what to say,' replied Mrs Crudge, sitting on the sofa. 'It's not Benny – I know that much.'

Mallory said, 'She's had a severe shock.'

'She looked straight through me as if I wasn't there. Just put this in my hand and started shouting: "Take them away! Take them away!" Then I was outside again.'

'What's in it?' asked Kate.

Doris turned the bag upside down and out fell Benny's beautiful peacock-blue jacket and long skirt, underclothes, stockings and shoes. Also her wig with the curls like brass sausages. Even the watch and earrings she had been wearing the night before.

'What shall I do?' asked Mrs Crudge. 'Take them to a charity shop?'

'Not down here,' said Kate. She started putting the clothes back. The chances of Benny ever seeing anyone wearing them must be a million to one. Even so. 'I'll do it in London.'

Later, after Mrs Crudge had had some tea after all and a bit of a cry, Kate and Mallory planned a desultory early dinner – the rest of Mallory's pea soup and bread and cheese. Benny did not share the meal, explaining, when Kate rang through, that she had stuff in her fridge that might spoil if it wasn't eaten up.

Kate had no way of knowing if this was true and suspected it wasn't. However, there was not much she could do. The fact that Benny had refused to eat with them and done her own thing was so extraordinary in itself as to cause slight concern. But she plainly did not wish to talk to anyone and that wish must be respected.

As they were sitting down to eat the telephone rang. Mallory leaped to answer it and Kate saw his expression change from hope to disappointment. He said, 'Yes, fine . . . That might not be possible . . . All right. Thanks for letting me know.' Then hung up.

'The inquest,' he explained. 'Ten thirty, Friday. The coroner's court. There's a proper letter in the post. I won't necessarily be called but I should be there.'

'What "might not be possible"?'

'They say Benny—'

'Oh, no!' cried Kate. 'She can't . . . she's in no state to answer questions. She can't even talk to us.'

'Don't get upset—'

'It's just not on, Mal. If she was still in hospital they couldn't call her.'

'I'll get hold of Cornwell. He'll have a word with them, explain the situation.'

But to both Kate and Mallory's surprise when Jim Cornwell called around after a visit to Benny's flat he said she was determined to go to the inquest. She was, in fact, quite fierce about this.

Both the Lawsons were disturbed at the news. Convinced that Benny had not really grasped what an inquest involved, they hoped, by the time Friday arrived, to have persuaded her against it.

135

CHAPTER TWELVE

The next thirty-six hours passed in a sort of limbo. Things that had to be done were done. Benny pulled up a lot of weeds and watered tomatoes and peppers in the greenhouse. Doris came, cleaned, gossiped in a generalised, harmless way, and went. Kate and Mallory worked through nearly all the mail bags. Just a couple, the very first to arrive and consequently at the bottom of the pile, remained.

The submissions were almost as dire as Kate had feared. A few had the saving grace of being funny, albeit unintentionally. Mallory dipped into one, gushingly overwritten and starry-eyed, all about putting on a school musical. He had sat in on enough rehearsals of such mind-numbing entertainments to last him several lifetimes. All the performers wanted to be pop stars and the show was invariably misdirected by a completely talentless English teacher flinging himself excitedly about the stage like Warner Baxter in *42nd Street*.

'Look at this,' Kate was exclaiming now. She had emptied the first of the remaining bags and was holding a long, narrow parcel wrapped in heavy watermarked parchment and sealed with red wax. It had an air of tremendous self-importance. Inside there were folds within folds of stiff brown paper tied with curtain cord and also sealed. There was a covering letter.

'It's from a Mr Matlock.' She opened the letter. 'Sidney. Who is "the sole surviving member of a post-war observation team and whose work, scrupulously annotated, herewith comprises this noble document".'

Mallory laughed out loud. 'You're kidding.'

'Maybe we've found another *Spycatcher*. It's certainly in some sort of code.'

'Let's have a look.'

Kate passed some sheets of foolscap over. They were set out in columns. Engine capacity and numbers. Fuel load. Departure and destination times. Locomotive base shed. Name and number of driver and fireman. It was proudly described *The Precise History of Locomotives Departing and Returning from Euston Station to Nuneaton Trent Valley During the Years 1948–1957.*

'Trainspotting!'

'Don't laugh,' said Kate. 'It's his life. Poor old man.' She replaced the book in its envelope and decided to use registered mail when sending it back. That was another thing she had thought of too late: return postage. She would make sure it was mentioned in any future advertisements.

They checked out the remaining manuscripts. One, described as the writer's 'hilairos adventures in Morroco', was called: *Thongs Aint What They Used To Be*. It had beer stains and lots of strangely placed quotation marks. Kate liked 'fish "and" chips' best. There was a thriller calling itself fast-paced, with a plot that started on page 160 and finished three paragraphs later. A comedy – *Lord of the Flies* – about a randy window cleaner, and a sad ecological tome about a tribe of frogs who caught a virus from polluted lily leaves and were making their way to the promised sea led by a philosophical windbag, Old Croaker. The others were mainly dreary diaries styled after the manner of Bridget Jones, but without the jokes and decent prose style.

'No good?'

'Makes Tom Clancy look like Homer.'

'I thought Homer had a beard.'

'Let's open a bottle.'

The three of them ate together that night. Mallory and Kate, walking on eggshells, made innocuous conversation. They touched on the garden, the hopeful news about Ashley's illness, the warm beauty of the day. Benny said very little but ate most of what was on her plate before laying her knife and fork edge to edge together. Kate recalled a phrase her mother frequently used about people recovering from an illness or unexpected disaster. 'Going gently along.'

Earlier, before Benny arrived, Kate and Mallory had discussed whether or not to mention the inquest. They decided, if Benny herself did not bring the matter up, they would not. Both still hoped she had changed her mind. But then, toying with a bowl of raspberries still warm from the sun, Benny began to talk about it.

First she asked a few questions and was reassured. Yes, they would be taking her and bringing her home. Yes, Mallory was certain they would all be able to sit together. No, there wouldn't be a witness box and judge and people in wigs. And he was sure there was still time to get some sort of dispensation if Benny was worried.

But Benny was not worried. Something – she had assumed it was the drugs, though they must have worn off by now – was holding the terrible events of the present and immediate past at bay. It was as if she viewed them through the wrong end of a telescope. Far distant and shrunken, they had lost the power to harm. But Benny also understood that this situation was temporary. That the pain – and she knew it was there, crouching, biding its time – was merely on hold.

She didn't have the time or energy, though, to grieve right now. Things had to be put right, procedures followed, starting with the inquest tomorrow. That was the first step. Then the investigation. Then the capture and punishment of whoever had committed this wicked, wicked crime.

* * *

137

The coroner's court was packed. Everyone from Forbes Abbot who was not housebound or working was present, and several, it was noted, who should have been at work and who appeared to have taken the day off.

As cleaner of the premises that had housed the lethal machinery Mrs Crudge had half expected to be called and had had many serious conversations with Ernest as to how best to present her evidence and what hat to wear. Now, uncalled but still feeling entitled to a certain status, she seated herself in a prominent position next to the Lawsons and Benny Frayle.

The proceedings opened with evidence from Mallory Lawson of Appleby House, Forbes Abbot. On the evening of Tuesday the twenty-fourth of July he was expecting a friend Dennis Brinkley for dinner. When Mr Brinkley did not arrive he called at his house in Hospital Lane, Forbes Abbot. Here he found the body of a man, later identified as Mr Brinkley. He did not touch or handle the remains in anyway but notified the police.

Sergeant Roy Gresham of the Causton Constabulary gave the time of his arrival at Kinders as 8.23 p.m. and continued: 'After viewing the body I called for an ambulance and a police photographer. I obtained the name of the dead man's doctor from Mr Lawson and contacted him. I examined the scene and could see no outward sign of foul play or that any other person had been present there.'

At this there was a cry from the court and Doris saw Benny's auburn wig turning urgently to Kate, who was sitting next to her. Everyone was straining to see who had called out and murmuring among themselves. The coroner appealed for quiet and Benny subsided, Kate's arm around her shoulder.

'I also,' concluded Sergeant Gresham, 'failed to discover a note or message of any kind from Mr Brinkley.'

'You wouldn't,' cried Benny, not bothering to lower her voice.

'We have a lot of business to get through this morning,' said the coroner. 'If you can't keep quiet, madam, you'll be asked to leave.'

Written evidence from the ambulance staff was then read out by the clerk, as was a letter from Dr Jim Cornwell, who had identified the body.

Finally Leo Fortune of Brinkley and Latham, thought by the police probably to have been the last person to talk to the deceased, was called.

Asked about the dead man's state of mind at this point, around five thirty on the evening that he died, Fortune replied: 'Dennis seemed his usual self, calm and quiet. We'd just finished discussing a new account and were about to leave the office. This was about five thirty. It was a beautiful evening. I asked if he was doing anything special and he said having dinner with some friends. I got the impression he was very much looking forward to it.'

Fortune was thanked and stood down. He was the last witness. An air of disappointment possessed the assembly. The whole business had taken no more than fifteen minutes from start to finish. The coroner expressed his sympathy for the friends and relatives of the deceased before bringing in a verdict of Accidental Death.

That night Kate and Mallory sat companiably together in their big four-poster drinking real hot chocolate – dark squares of Valrhona melted in water and whipped up with cream.

Kate said, 'What are we going to do?'

'God knows. I give up.'

'Mal . . .'

'What do you expect me to say? She's immovable.'

'There must be something.'

'There's nothing. You heard Cornwell's opinion.'

'But where has it all come from?'

'She's had an absolutely appalling experience.' The green fuse, its contents squeezed out into a grey and white and scarlet puddle seared his memory. 'A terrible shock. And it's left her very . . . unbalanced.'

It had taken them ten minutes to get Benny out of the coroner's court and ten more to persuade her into the car. The moment the verdict had been announced she had got to her feet, pushed her way to the coroner's table and begun to harangue him with great urgency. Her face was flushed and angry and there was lightning in her eyes.

'You have made a terrible mistake. Dennis's death was not an accident. He was deliberately killed.'

Immediately Kate clambered out of her seat. Attempting comfort, she took Benny's arm but was shaken off.

'It's not too late to change your mind,' cried Benny.

'The verdict was justly arrived at—'

'Justice! I'm telling you the truth. Why are you believing everyone else?'

The ushers were trying to clear the room with little success. At last people had got what they came for and they were not going quietly. Some were even sitting down again.

Mallory said, 'Stop shouting, Ben, please.'

'He won't listen.' She was struggling for breath.

'Let's find somewhere to talk about this on our own.'

'Then it'll be too late.'

'Not at all.' The coroner's voice was low and insincerely serene. He sounded like an undertaker. 'Inquests can always be reconvened should any reasonable doubt arise.' He caught Mallory's eye, making it clear what he thought of the chances in this case while also blaming him for introducing a rogue element into the court. He nodded his head in the direction of the ushers and one of them moved firmly forward.

'You see?' said Kate, gently persuading Benny away from the table. 'We can always come back.'

'Can we, Kate?' urged Benny. 'Can we *really and truly*?'

In no time at all Kate was sorry she had said that. In the car Benny started asking how soon coming back could possibly be arranged. And what had to be done to bring about this happy state of affairs. How quickly could they start? Where did they start? What could she, personally, contribute? What was the legal situation? Should they have a solicitor? Would any solicitor do or must they engage a specialist in criminal law? Should they perhaps use Dennis's own solicitor?

After two or three hours of this Kate felt she wanted to run and hide. She kept going to the lavatory just to shut the sound out. At one point she pretended to go to the Spar and took a book and hid in the orchard, only to find, coming back, that Mallory had become worried and gone all over the village looking for her. At least they then had a short break. Left alone, Benny had returned to her flat.

In despair Mallory had rung Jimmy Cornwell and the doctor promised to make yet another visit to Appleby House on his way home from afternoon surgery. Prepared to comfort and tranquillise a grief-stricken woman suffering from post-traumatic stress, his expectations were immediately confounded. He found himself confronting blazing determination and a barrage of accusing questions.

How was it he had not grasped the real situation at the time of Dennis's death? Did he understand that his evidence helped to bring in a shamefully wrong verdict? A re-examination was urgent. There was no time to be lost. Could a police doctor be used next time – someone more experienced in matters of unnatural death?

'She's thrown her tablets from the hospital away,' said Mallory, walking Cornwell to his car. 'Says she can't afford to be only half awake when there's so much work to be done.'

'Oh dear.'

'We simply can't get through.'

'You won't. Obsessives don't respond to reason. Or common sense.'

'So – what happens now?'

'I can arrange for some counselling. Bit of a wait on the NHS—'

'We'll pay, of course.'

'But as things are at present I doubt if she'd agree.'

'You don't think she'll just . . . give up?'

'From Benny's point of view there's nothing to give up. It's everyone else who's wrong.' Cornwell got into his car. 'I've left another prescription with Kate. You might be able to slip her something by stealth.'

'I hate that idea.'

'Sorry, but that's about it.'

Now, recalled to a miserable present, Mallory put his empty chocolate mug down and knew he wouldn't be able to sleep. Through the window moonshine poured, washing the walls and furniture with pale light. All this tranquillity, which should have been soothing, seemed somehow an affront, totally inappropriate to the turmoil that was presently containing them all. He could see Benny's flat through the window. All the lights were on. Mallory checked his luminous clock. Half-past two.

Kate, heavy against his chest, had drifted off. He couldn't move without disturbing her. So he sat on, worrying about Benny, worrying about Polly, worrying about moving house, worrying about the new business. He remembered the day, now seemingly years ago, when he and Kate and Polly had sat in the offices of Brinkley and Latham for the reading of his aunt's will. How excited and happy they had all been.

Dennis too, for entirely selfless reasons. Mallory remembered how spontaneously he had offered to help. How thrilled he was by the very idea of the Celandine Press. Mallory's thoughts slid even further back. He recalled times when he was quite young and Dennis had come to his aunt's house. And how he, Mallory, was always politely included in any nonbusiness conversations. Mostly, of course, he wasn't interested and ran off to play. But he never forgot the kindness, the serious attention paid by Dennis when he did attempt to join in.

There had been so much drama over the past three days, so many practical things that had to be done after Dennis's death, that the process of mourning had passed Mallory by. Now he felt it, a slow paralysis of grief, gradually stealing across his heart.

Naturally Benny Frayle's outburst in the coroner's court was all over the village. Most people were sympathetic, especially those who had witnessed her terrible, stumbling progress from Kinders towards Appleby House the evening Dennis Brinkley died. Others were more heartless, pointing out that she'd always been several cards short of a full deck so what was new?

Only Doris Crudge had reacted with genuine distress. The next day she brought Benny over some special chocolates. Really expensive ones that she'd been keeping for her sister's birthday.

Benny was in the kitchen with Kate and Mallory. She took the box, put it aside and carried on talking. Doris was gobsmacked. Though familiar with the saying that someone or other had suddenly become 'a completely different person' she had always thought it meant they'd had a sort of makeover, like on the telly. How else could a human being become completely different? Yet here it was happening before her very eyes.

Benny – shy, hesitant, anxious-to-please Benny – was actually arguing with Mallory over Dennis's funeral.

'Honestly, Ben,' he was saying, 'does it really matter?'

'Matter? Of course it matters.'

'The vicar thought . . . space . . . you know?'

'Dennis *hated* the idea of cremation.' Here Benny actually thumped one of her clenched fists on the table. 'He had this terrible dream about being trapped in his coffin and coming round in the furnace.'

Mallory thought that sounded like a typical Benny Frayle dream. Then understood – of course! This is about having a body to exhume and re-examine when the non-existent murderer was finally caught.

But she was so very distressed and had been through a terrible ordeal. What did the way Dennis's mortal remains were disposed of really matter? On the other hand, if a cremation was carried out it might help to put a stop to all these terrible imaginings.

'I'll see what I can sort out, Ben.'

'Thank you,' said Benny. She got up, briskly abandoning the breakfast table. 'I'm going over to the flat now to start on my campaign. I think the London papers first, don't you?'

'I'm not sure,' said Kate. 'More notice would be taken should your letter be published. On the other hand, they do get a huge amount so the chances of it happening are much less.'

'I hadn't thought of that,' said Benny. 'Better start locally. And then after lunch I must talk to the police.'

Kate and Mallory exchanged wary glances. Doris, equally on edge, sat down at the table and poured herself some dregs of coffee.

She said, 'I'm not really up to date on things here, Ben. What's actually happening?'

'Kate will explain. We're all working together on this.'

The police proved to be a tough option. No difficulty in dropping into Causton station at any time to have a chat. But great difficulty in speaking directly, face to face, with a senior officer in the Criminal Investigation Department. But surely, argued Benny, with the very pleasant-sounding woman on the other end of the telephone, as they were the people who would be dealing with the subsequent inquiry there was little point in her talking to anyone else.

Benny listened to the response for a moment, then switched off for it was plainly negative. Odd phrases filtered through. '. . . in the first instance . . . usual procedure . . . then your statement would be . . . an interview with . . .' She hung up. Now, what?

Benny, though normally hesitant, fluttery and somewhat gullible, was not a fool. She knew how she was regarded by those who did not know her well, which would certainly include anyone she spoke to at the police station. The chances were that if she simply turned up prepared to argue and stand her ground they wouldn't take her seriously. They might ask – even force – her to leave.

What she needed was someone to vouch for her. A person who was on her side, obviously. And with some standing in the community. She thought of Dr Cornwell. He had had a practice in Causton for over twenty years. The chances were high that some of his patients were police personnel. Perhaps one or two might be from the higher echelons.

Benny reached for her address book, then hesitated. She remembered the doctor's last visit to Appleby House when she had practically accused him of incompetence, of misdiagnosing Dennis's cause of death. He had not seemed to take offence but such an incident would hardly prejudice him in her favour. It might be safer to look elsewhere.

What about Hargreaves, Carey's solicitors, an extremely respected and long-established firm in Great Missenden? The senior partner, Horace de Witt, had looked after her legal affairs for over thirty years and knew Benny well. He would be even better than Dr Cornwell, being familiar to the police from appearances in court.

Pleased at her own cleverness Benny dialled the number, only to find that Horace had just left for a holiday in Guadeloupe and would be back in two weeks, just in time for his retirement party.

Benny sighed, made some tea and sat down to drink it. Who else could there possibly be? There was the vicar, of course. Heaven knew, he was respectable, but he was also new to the parish and so not really knowledgeable as to Benny's finer character traits. She decided it would be kinder not to ask him to vouch for her.

More to give her mind a break than out of a wish to read, she picked up the *Causton Echo*. The murder of that poor old pensioner over at Badger's Drift had still not been solved. The police were urgently seeking the public's help. Two men had been seen getting into a G reg. green Sierra on the outskirts of the village shortly after six on the evening of . . .

Benny read on. At the end was an emergency phone number. She was about to put the paper down when, with a tremble of excitement, she recognised that she was now looking at a perfect means to an end. She found a Biro, drew a circle round the number and reached for the telephone.

Detective Sergeant Gavin Troy was entertaining himself by imagining his chief's response when he showed in the middle-aged woman now trailing along behind him on the third floor of Causton police station. Responding to their appeal for information she had refused to speak to anyone but the officer in charge of the Badger's Drift investigation.

How old she was was anybody's guess. The almost fluorescent pinky orange hair was plainly not her own. It looked like the spun, varnished stuff glued to the heads of little girls' dolls. Her dress was a muddy brown-green colour, swarming with black wriggly things. There was an awful lot of it and it was tied up in the middle with a length of shiny, pink ribbed plastic. She looked like a camouflaged bundle of washing. Troy opened a door inscribed 'Detective Chief Inspector Tom Barnaby' and followed her in. This was one interview he was not prepared to miss.

Benny regarded the man getting to his feet behind the large desk. She was not nervous. Her cause was just. But if it had not been she would certainly have been nervous. He was a very large man. Not fat but bulky. Solid in his build and in the way he looked at you. Very straight and direct from beneath thick, heavy brows.

'Miss Frayle, sir.'

The man introduced himself and shook Benny's outstretched hand. 'Thank you for coming in. Please sit down. I understand you have some information for us.'

'Yes I do,' replied Benny. She wished the thin, younger man had left them alone. She hadn't taken at all to his weaselly profile and high-standing brush of stiff, red hair. Although he had been perfectly polite she had sensed hidden laughter. Unkindness too.

'Do you have any objection if we tape what you have to say?'

'Of course not,' replied Benny, thinking how encouraging such efficiency was. 'But I'm afraid I don't have any information regarding that terrible business at Badger's Drift.'

'But I understood—'

'Yes,' replied Benny. 'I do have information about a murder. But it is not that murder.'

'Is it something presently under investigation?'

'Not yet,' replied Benny. 'Which is why I'm here.'

'This sounds a bit complicated, Miss Frayle.' Barnaby looked at his watch. 'And I'm extremely busy. But if you go along with Sergeant Troy—'

'*Please* hear me out,' cried Benny. 'I know it was wrong to get in here under false pretences but this is very, very urgent. No one will listen, you see.'

The chief inspector tried not to let his impatience show, for she was plainly extremely distressed. Out of Benny's sightline Troy was screwing his index finger into the side of his forehead and winking.

This contemptuous display prompted the DCI to say: 'Tell me about it then, Miss Frayle. But be brief, if you would.'

So Benny told him about it and tried to be brief, although it wasn't easy. Mainly she looked into her lap but whenever she did glance up Barnaby appeared to be attending closely. Troy had also tuned in but almost immediately tuned out again, recognising the inquest story that Gresham had been circulating round the canteen. He was also somewhat distracted by Benny's belt, which was more and more reminding him of a length of human intestine.

'And he knew something bad was going on,' concluded Benny. 'A day or so before he died I found him in the war room in front of that dreadful trebbyshay thing. He looked so worried. I asked what was wrong and then . . . the most frightening thing. "Benny," he said, "there's a ghost in the machine." '

'I can't make out why you're, doing this, Chief.' Sergeant Troy returned from his errand and laid the Dennis Brinkley file on Barnaby's desk.

Barnaby was not sure why either except that she had been quite despairing and on the verge of tears and had begged him to look into it, and he had said that he would. If her description of the incident was correct the whole business sounded fairly uncomplicated and shouldn't take more than half an hour, if that.

And so it proved. Sergeant Gresham had been scrupulous as to procedure. The correct forms dealing with continuity of the body's state and position and circumstances of death had been written up. Several photographs had been taken from all angles, showing details of the machinery's disfunction as well as different aspects of the corpse's sorry state. No evidence could be found that any other person had been present in the room during or immediately prior to the incident and a thorough search revealed no suicide note. The death certificate was as straight-forward as the paramedics' statement The last person to see Brinkley alive had reported his state of mind as calm and quiet. He was looking forward to a dinner that evening with friends.

And so Barnaby dictated a brief note to Benny Frayle stating that the inquest verdict seemed to him perfectly correct and he saw no reason for further investigation into the matter or manner of Dennis Brinkley's death.

On the Monday following her visit to the police, Benny was watching eagerly for the postman. Not only for their response – though this, of course, was paramount – but also from the editors of the various newspapers to which she had written. None of her earlier correspondence describing a grave miscarriage of justice had been printed and Benny wanted to know why. The reason was simple. Kate, offering to post the letters, had disposed of them. She had not done this without considerable soul searching and consultation with Mallory. At first thought it had seemed an outrageous, shameful thing to do. Benny had handed the letters over so trustingly. And surely, as a capable adult, it was her own business who she chose to write to. But Kate feared not that the letters would be ignored but that they might be printed. She saw Benny encouraged in her hopeless quest, perhaps even interviewed by some local hack anxious to get his or her byline noticed. A feature that could be discreetly slanted to make the journalist look clever and Benny a fool. Even so, the words 'it's for her own good' sat uncomfortably at the back of Kate's mind and she had already decided that, were more letters to be written, she would not interfere.

Neither of the Lawsons knew about Benny's visit to Causton CID. Aware that she had cheated her way in, Benny felt it better to keep quiet. When the admirable chief inspector, in whom she had the greatest confidence, vindicated her visit by ordering a new inquiry, then everyone could be told. Not boastfully, of course. That would be extremely ill-mannered.

When the post came, Benny was in the kitchen having tea with Doris. As the letter box flapped she rushed out and rushed straight back, dropping everything on the hall table but for one letter.

'You're in a bit of a state, Ben.' Doris spoke with genuine concern. Benny's cheeks glowed a hectic crimson and her gaze was wild as she ripped at the envelope. It didn't open easily and she tore it practically in half to get the single sheet of paper out. Her face changed as she read it. So quickly it was almost comic, thought Doris. Like when children wipe an expression off their face with their hand. Benny's mouth was a round O and her eyes bolted from her head.

'What on earth's the matter?' asked Doris. 'Benny?'

'They're not going to do anything.'

'Who aren't?' Passionately interested, Doris reached out and picked up the letter. 'You've been to the police?'

'I haven't told the others,' said Benny. 'It was going to be a surprise.'

'Well, they won't hear it from me,' said Doris.

'This is devastating news. He seemed such a nice man. And so intelligent.'

'Then perhaps, now's the time—'

'A chief inspector in the CID.' Benny, profoundly sick at heart, could hardly take in the written words. She read them again. 'How could he possibly not have understood?'

This level of wilful battling against the tide of truth was hard to handle. At a loss as to what to say, Doris decided to have one last attempt at getting through to what she wistfully thought of as the old Benny.

'Would you consider, love, him being so high up and all, that this inspector might actually have got it right?'

'Now I don't know where to turn,' replied Benny.

'It's a problem,' agreed Doris, jumping with one bound into the opposite camp and feeling, what the hell, if you can't beat 'em. 'Let's have a think, shall we?'

They stirred their tea and thought. After a little while Doris suggested, eyes cast down and cautiously, for she knew her friend's opinion on such matters, a second visit to the Church of the Near at Hand. She was thinking how wonderful it would be if Dennis came through. If he described what actually happened on the day he died and so laid to rest Benny's terrible obsession.

Benny was silent for a moment, then lifted her head and smiled at Doris. Her expression showed an awesome awareness as if she had just received news of great significance. She reached out and seized both of Doris's hands.

'Yes – you've got it! Oh, Doris, why didn't I think of that?'

Doris felt uneasy at this sudden burst of confidence. Benny seemed to think all she had to do was go along and a hot line to Dennis was a certainty. It seemed wise to point out this might not be so. The poor soul had had more than enough to cope with already. Doris tried to put it gently.

'Spirits don't always turn up just when you want, Ben.'

'No, no,' cried Benny. 'You mustn't worry about that. In fact, Doris, you mustn't worry about anything. I'm on the right lines now, thanks to you. From now on, everything is going to be just fine.'

THE CHURCH

OF THE

NEAR AT HAND

CHAPTER THIRTEEN

There was a depressing little queue outside the Church of the Near at Hand. The building itself was hardly less depressing. About the size of a village hall, it was made of overlapping clapboard shingles once coloured a rather sickly clover. Now little of the paint remained. Just a few loosely attached shavings curled up in the August sun. The corrugated iron roof, heavily stained, was scabbed with moss. Its rusty extremities had crumbled away leaving a rather pretty scalloped edge, like a lace doily. One of the rear windows was cracked.

Sentinel along each side of the church and dwarfing it even further were six yew trees. These were immensely tall and so dark as to be almost black. Even on a bright, summer's day the church seemed threatened by their long, pointed shadows. They made it appear both isolated and sinister, like a house in a fairy story, suddenly and mysteriously present in a woodland clearing.

A board had been hammered into the grass just behind the scruffy railings. On it, a white square of card in a plastic cover read: 'The Spirit Is Willing: Matthew 26, 41.' This reassurance was garlanded by tiny moth-like creatures with human faces and patterned wings drawn with a felt-tipped pen. They were smiling in a dreamy sort of way and holding hands. Beneath their twinkling feet another notice. 'Key with Mrs Alma Gobbett, Paradise Bungalow, 17 Midgely Road.'

The queue was plainly, even poorly, dressed. It was mainly female and some of the women had bags of shopping. A pinched-looking girl wore a sling holding a tiny baby. She was smoking, blowing the smoke carefully away from the baby's face, not seeming to notice when it drifted back. Two stout elderly reeking men were supporting each other back to back, like a pair of bibulous bookends.

Near the opposite pavement a new primrose-yellow Beetle was parked close to the kerb. Inside, Cully Barnaby and her husband, Nicolas, watched as the little line began to shuffle forward.

'They're opening the doors.' Cully took the keys from the ignition. Nicolas stretched over to the back seat and picked up his jacket. 'You're not coming.'

'Try and stop me,' cried Nicolas.

'Nico, you promised to wait outside.'

'Would I promise such a thing? With Mother begging me on her death bed—'

'Your mother's fine. I saw her in Sainsbury's on Wednesday.'

'So you say. Anyway, the principle's the same. "See if you can contact your Aunty Ethel," she cried. "Ask her where that Victorian tantalus—" '

'That's exactly the sort of attitude . . . ' As she spoke Cully sprang out of the car and targeted the locks. A fraction of a second too late.

Nicolas beamed at her over the gleaming roof. 'What do you mean "attitude"?'

'Snorting derision. Look what happened last time.'

The last time was a week previously. They had both gone to a spiritualist meeting in Causton. The medium, poised delicately on four-inch rhinestone heels, had begun fervently to roll her thumb and index finger together. Conjuring the gradual formation of a crumb of invisible dough she enquired if someone had recently lost a baker. Nicolas stood up and asked earnestly if the crumb could possibly be clay as he had recently lost a sculptor.

Cully struck out firmly across the road. Nicolas kept alongside, mocking her with principal-boy strides. He produced an exercise book, slapped his thigh with it, then waved it under his wife's nose.

'Look – look! See what a help I shall be.'

'What's that for?'

'To take notes – discreet notes,' he added quickly as she turned to glare at him. 'You can't be expected to remember everything.'

Nico offered one of his best audition smiles – sincere but with a hint of irony to show he was intelligent. Cool but not overly detached. Humorous while appreciating that something really serious was happening right here, right now. A hundred per cent engaged yet a free man, able to walk calmly away should the situation not work out while still remaining overwhelmingly aware of the powerful inner radiance of his talent.

'Don't do that, Nico. I've just had lunch.'

'Sorry.'

To Cully's surprise in the short space of time that they had been arguing the queue had grown much longer. Cars were being parked and quite a lot of people were making their way towards the church. By the time she and Nicolas entered, the rows of narrow, unvarnished hard-backed chairs were almost full.

This was the fourth meeting they had attended in as many weeks and the interior of all the churches proved to be remarkably similar. The Church of the Near at Hand was different only in that it was crowded with shadows. The few patches of sunlight admitted through the dense yew trees shimmered on cream walls. A dais, shabbily carpeted, was backed by dusty black velvet drapes. These had been drawn back to reveal a poorly designed and crudely coloured stained-glass window. A man with golden curls and doll-like crimson cheeks and lips stood in a rackety rowing boat. He wore a long white robe and a long white wing sprouted clumsily from his nearest shoulder. About his head was a rainbow made in several sections and clumsily conjoined.

150

A card table on the platform held a carafe of water with a glass turned upside down on the neck. A sunburst of vivid plastic flowers balanced on a mock marble column. A portable gas heater at the back of the stage was unlit and some rather old-fashioned sound equipment played 'You'll Never Walk Alone'.

Nicolas came to rest beside Cully, who gave him such a savage nudge he almost fell off the seat. Muttering, he got up and settled himself further down the hall. Looking round, he thought what a washed-out, colourless lot they were. And curiously similar. Not in feature perhaps, but in the vacant stolidity of their expressions. No frisson of suppressed excitement at the thought of soon getting in touch with the dear departed. No expectant glow lightened their tired, parched skins. What a bunch of losers. Nicolas risked glancing over his shoulder at his gorgeous wife in her vivid patchwork jacket, saffron silk shirt and dark green velvet trousers. She looked like an orchid on a dung heap.

The woman next to Nicolas pulled some knitting from an Iceland carrier bag. He entertained himself by wondering what had happened to the angel's second wing. Was its absence laziness on the artist's part? Or an unwillingness to wrestle with the problems of scale and perspective? Maybe the money had just run out.

In the front row an elderly man who had been welcoming people at the church door now stood up from his seat, clambered the few steps to the dais and turned to address the gathering. He smiled broadly, his false teeth glittering, raising his voice above the swelling strings.

'Friends, welcome. Welcome to another afternoon of love, light and laughter. I hope everyone will be able to stay on afterwards for tea. There will be a collection as usual, which this Sunday is in aid of the Animal Healing Centre. Our cosmic inspirer today is Ava . . .' He paused, nodding in response to the smiles, murmurs of satisfaction and even some hand-clapping. 'Ava Garret – known and I'm sure I can say loved – by you all.'

Nicholas positioned himself directly behind the person in front so as to be invisible from the platform. His crafty scribblings had never yet been remarked upon and he'd prefer things to stay that way. But if comments did arise he had his story ready. They were simply questions from his mum on the off chance that today might be the lucky day that her late sister decided to come through.

He had expected the woman beside him to abandon her knitting at this stage but she clicked on regardless. It was like sitting next to a lively deathwatch beetle. An immense tan-coloured sausage depended from her four steel needles and he could see a teddy bear's head with one vast ear poking out of the bag. Nicolas tried to picture the bear's eventual dimensions and did not envy the toddler squaring up to it on Christmas morning.

A youth with long greasy hair and rings though every visible orifice attended to the sound equipment. He wore a leather jacket with flying witches painted on, and army combat trousers. As the music faded Cully leaned forwards slightly, emptied her mind of all but the present moment and concentrated on the stage. The previous sessions had been remarkably similar and, should this follow the same pattern, Cully had already decided it would be the last.

The signs were not encouraging. The setting had been exactly as she expected. As for the performance, Cully was afraid that by now she could write the script. The medium would be fat and dressed in flowing garments stiff with tacky but bombastic decoration. She would be wearing quite a lot of flashy jewellery, even more highly coloured make-up and her coiffure would never, ever move. Her patter would mix sickly endearments with sentimental messages from the dear departed and deeply unfunny humour. Psychomancy as showbiz.

So when Ava Garret stepped on to the stage Cully had quite a shock. The first idea that came into her head was Aubrey Beardsley, for the woman closely resembled one of his illustrations. Then a quick and less charitable thought – Morticia Addams. Tall, sinuous and robed simply in black, she leaned on the plastic column and threw back her dark flowing hair. She began to drift back and forth across the stage, stretching out her hands in a most peculiar way. The left, palm out in front of her face as if warding off a rush of seekers after truth. The right, vaguely groping upwards as if to seize any shy, celestial beings before they changed their minds and dissolved once more into etheric vapour. At every turn she kicked the long train of her dress neatly behind her before setting off again. Cully, acting in her cradle, acting before she could even lisp the word, recognised a trick of the trade when she saw one.

'Someone is coming through now . . .' Estuary English overlaid by Received Pronunciation in a nice reversal of the current mode. 'I'm getting a Graham – no, tell a lie – Grace. Does Grace connect with anyone here?'

'Very much so.' A woman on the end of the row opposite Nicolas stood up. She had bright ginger hair cowled in net veiling scattered with red and black beads. They looked like tiny insects.

Nicolas wrote down: 'Could do with a good spray.'

'Grace wants you to have your legs looked at, my darling. Because you've only got one pair and I believe there's been trouble in that department already, am I right?'

Nicolas stretched his neck and looked across at the woman's legs. They were thin and straight, fragile sticks with tiny, bony bulges, like little basins, sticking out at knee level.

'My GP says it's cramp, Ava.'

'Earth doctors.' She laughed, shaking her head at the naïve conclusions of these simple inadequates. The audience joined in. Someone at the back started clapping. 'Grace suggests a pendulum.'

'Oh! Thank you—'

'Plus a fenugreek massage.'

'Could you ask her—'

'I'm sorry but someone else is calling now, a gallant gentleman holding a red rose. I'm getting the letter T . . . Yes? A lady towards the back . . .'

'My son . . .' A shabbily dressed figure got up. 'Trevor – he . . . was on his motorbike . . .'

'Now, my love, this is going to sound a little bit hard but Trevor has seen you on your tod having a weep over his picture and it makes him very sad. And we don't want that, do we?'

The woman, unable to speak, covered her mouth with a scarf and shook her head.

'Because he liked a bit of jollity – didn't he, young Trev? A little glass of something . . . I'm getting quite a lot of bubbles here . . .'

Trevor's mother struggled with unintelligable sounds. Eventually a strangled resemblance to the word 'snorkelling' emerged.

As she subsided the next communication arrived. This was Tom with apologies to Mavis for passing to spirit before he'd had time to finish limeing her outhouse.

After Tom messages came thick and fast. Nicolas wondered if everyone was supposed to receive one before they went in for tea, the way all children at a party expect a present. He was longing to look around at Cully but knew, if she caught him, he'd never hear the end of it.

'I'm being wafted shades of green now – overalls and masks. Bright lights and a definite scent of ether. A dear one recently lost in the theatre, perhaps?'

Nicolas wrote down, 'Gielgud?'

'And here's someone – a bit of a Charlie, he tells me. And an Albert. Do these names connect at all?'

What a question, thought Cully, yawning. The miracle would be if two of the most common names of the last century did not connect with such an elderly audience. Where were the Crispins and Algernons, that's what she wanted to know. Why didn't Rollo and Georgiana, Araminta and Pauncefoot 'come through'?

And why were there no really helpful or exciting messages? Like a recipe for low-calorie chocolate fudge. Or a new sonnet from William S. Something that would give pith and moment to the whole tedious procedure.

'I hear a baby chuckling now in the world of spirit . . .'

'My grandson, little Darren.' A man in the front row burst into floods of tears.

'You wouldn't know him, my darling. He's getting to be a lovely boy, because they do grow up, you know, in the higher realms.'

The man, amazed, started to dry his eyes.

'And he has his very own guardian angel – Brother Thundercloud – so rest assured no harm can ever come to him.'

'Thank you, thank you. Oh! Darren, we think of you all the time. Nana sends her love . . .'

It was at this stage that Nicolas stopped sneering to himself at the audience's credulity and started to feel angry on their behalf. Angry at the easy promises and consoling images tossed to rows of hungry faces like crumbs from the table to starving birds. The words 'bread' and 'stones' came to mind.

Then, as the medium tilted back her head, the light fell fully on to the right side of her face and Nicholas noticed for the first time a pinkish, plastic shell tucked neatly inside her ear. Deaf – oh, brilliant. Able to talk to the deceased a trillion, zillion light years away but unable to hack it with the living at spitting distance. After this observation all his light good humour returned.

There was a silence from the platform. The pause lengthened. Nicolas's neighbour nudged him and whispered kindly, 'Nothing for you today then, dear?'

'No.' Nicolas glanced down at the tan sausage, which had grown alarmingly. It now looked more like a chair leg. 'I'm here on my mum's behalf. Hoping for contact from my Aunty Ethel.'

'Her sister?'

'They got very close towards the end.'

'Aah – peaceful was it?'

'Lovely.'

Nicolas was beginning to feel worried at the ease with which he was slipping into this by now familiar scenario. I'll be believing it myself next, he thought, and vowed, if Cully's research went on, to invent a more colourful departed relative to talk about. A mad axe murdering uncle perhaps, now chuckling in the world of spirit as he laid about him with a sawn off, double-barrelled harp.

The meeting was getting somewhat restless when Ava Garret, now positioned dead centre, front of stage, lifted both of her hands and held them, palms facing out towards the audience. A strange expression had transformed her face. It was marked now with a deep frown of concentration. Apprehension too. It seemed that easy access to the higher spheres had suddenly deserted her. However, all was not lost.

'I'm getting . . . a D . . . and an E . . . The name's becoming clearer . . . It's definitely Dennis.'

Two women in the front row turned to each other. One built, as far as Nicolas could make out, along the lines of his formidable father-in-law, appeared very excited. The second woman raised her arm, high and straight in the air like a child at school.

'There is a message for you, my dear. It is . . . a distressing one . . .'

A feeling of unease pervaded the hall. Messages were never distressing. The congregation started to shift around, rustle bags. Began to crave refreshment.

154

'I'm aware of some strange shapes . . .' She opened her arms wide, then leaned back slightly. Her eyes widened as if seeing a frightful vision. 'Huge constructions like nothing I have ever seen . . . They throw great shadows . . . white walls are all around with windows high in the air. A man, small with red hair, clad in green, approaches them. But he is not alone . . . Someone else is hiding in the shadows . . . someone who means him dreadful harm. I see them handling one of the machines . . . causing damage . . . Now it is no longer safe. The merest touch could bring it crashing down . . .'

A concerted gasp swept the church. Even the lady with the chair leg stopped knitting.

'As the man draws nearer the watcher in the shadows creeps forward too . . . coming as close as they dare to gloat . . . to watch a terrible plan succeed. The mist around this figure is clearing now . . . I can almost see an outline . . . even perhaps a face . . .'

A baby cried – the tiny baby held in a sling against his mother's breast. He was wet and he was hungry. His cries became yells and screams.

The tense atmosphere ruptured beyond repair. People started to relax, a few laughed, marvelling aloud at the amount of noise coming from such a minute scrap. Someone held him while the mother got her things together. For a moment the medium hesitated. Then she caught the eye of the man in the grey suit, made a negative movement with her head then swept slowly from the stage, gazing ahead as if tugged by some magnetic force.

As the service finished the youth who had switched on the hi-fi at the beginning worked the rows with a velvet drawstring collecting bag. Nicolas dropped in a jingle of drachmas he had brought back from Corfu. The music began again and the congregation filed out to Dean Martin's liquid gargling: 'Everybody Loves Somebody Sometime'.

Cully and Nico had been the last to move. She pretended to search for something in her bag as the others streamed by. But the Master of Ceremonies was walking up the centre aisle, sweeping and shooing with both hands, as fussy as an old woman rounding up hens. He bared his teeth in a fearsome grimace of synthetic friendliness.

'Get that smile,' muttered Nico, allowing himself to be eased into the general stream. 'Like a mouthful of Chiclets.'

About ten minutes later everyone was in a large room off the hall, enjoying their tea. Cully was taking dainty bites out of a fragile cucumber sandwich. Nico gnawed on a huge chunk of bread pudding. Smiling, nibbling and gnawing, responding politely when spoken to, they waited for an opportunity to slip backstage.

The MC had accepted a plate of food composed by the lady with the teddy bear knitting. There were a lot more teddies on a large table under an Oxfam poster, amended to read: 'Teddies For Tragedy'. They were hand-knitted too and all wearing different clothes. There was a teddy

155

surgeon, a policeman and a gardening teddy with a little hoe. They were all for sale at different prices.

'I rather like the idea of teddies for tragedy,' said Nico, helping himself to a cream horn. 'Why shouldn't they have a rotten time like the rest of us? Want one of these?'

'I think I'd rather have one of those.' Cully nudged her husband round to face another smaller table behind them.

'Aaarrgghhh!' cried Nicolas, *sotto voce.*

He was looking at the most extraordinary display of candelabra. They seemed to be made of string, knotted and tangled then glued into twisty Gothic shapes. From time to time the glue had dripped a little, hardening into tiny orange beads.

'Look,' whispered Cully. She pointed out a card which read: 'Geo. Footscray. Candelabra & Pot Holders. Chandeliers to order.' 'We could have a chandelier.'

'But they're only to order.' Nicolas too spoke with quiet reverence. 'You said we wouldn't be coming back.'

'Damn.'

'How's he doing – Mr Sparkle?'

They both stared across at the MC. He was in earnest, not to say excited, conversation with the woman who had responded so positively to the advent of the final visitant. Cully gulped down the remains of her cucumber sandwich. No one noticed them slip away.

'I don't know why we're bothering,' said Nico, following Cully down the deserted aisle. 'She won't be any different from the other two.'

'She's already different.'

'How?'

'That last connection was pretty strange. And what's with the "we"?'

'I'm here to help.'

'So wait in the car.'

Cully climbed on to the platform, her hand stretching out to the velvet drapes.

Nico, a step behind, whispered 'Shall I take notes?'

The two people already behind the curtains had very little room to move. Ava Garret was sitting on a fold-up chair by a small table, staring into a mirror on a stand. Her hands were raised, the fingers loosening gauze that secured a wig. The only other piece of furniture was a moth-eaten old chaise longue. A child was drying glasses by a small stone sink. She saw the intruders first. Flinging her tea towel down over the table she gave a sharp cry.

'What do you want?' Ava Garret jumped to her feet. 'No one's allowed back here.'

'I'm sorry, Miss Garret. I didn't realise—'

'If it's healing, George will be in the Salamander Suite at five.'

'I was hoping to talk to you.'

'Then you'll have to take your chance in the vestibule with the others. And I'm quite exhausted so I shan't stay long.'

Pompous cow, decided Nicolas. Who did these people think they were? Take your chance indeed. She'd be giving them her autograph next.

'Do you see people privately?'

'No.'

'Not even on special—'

'Not never,' said the child.

Cully responded with an apologetic smile. She studied the little girl without seeming to, taking mental notes as she always did, storing stuff away. The most utterly colourless creature she had ever seen. Totally washed out. Long straight hair, blonde as far as one could tell – it looked pretty filthy. Skin, fine as paper. An almost perfectly heart-shaped face, which was not nearly as appealing as it sounded in fairy stories. The chin came to a very sharp point indeed. You could have eased the lid off a jam jar with it.

'It was all just so . . . amazing.' Cully gave Ava Garret a deeply admiring smile. 'I'm longing . . . that is, if you could possibly explain how—'

'I'm just a channel through which departed souls contact the living.' She rattled it off, plainly bored.

'Do they come to you one at a time?'

'They throng, dear, and that's the truth. Once one's through they're all at it.'

'I see. Any special ord—'

'Mother's family on the left. Father's on the right.'

'And do you see them clearly?'

'Not always. There's a lot of murk around the openings to the dromeda stratosphere.'

'What's she asking all these questions for?' said the girl to Nicolas. 'What d'you want?'

'That final . . . connection was rather—'

'I don't encourage common curiosity. Now I have to change. Go away.'

'But it isn't common curiosity.' Nicolas spoke hastily, having noticed a certain stubborn persistence tightening Cully's lovely profile. 'My wife is an actor. She's playing a medium, you see—'

'You're in the business?' Ava Garret stared at them, an expression of longing softening her hard, heavily painted face. A wistful smile completed the transformation. She looked at Nicolas. 'The theatre?'

'Yes.' Eagerly Cully seized this stroke of luck and ran with it. 'I'm rehearsing *Blithe Spirit* at the moment. For the Almeida.'

'Aahh . . .' sighed Ava, 'the Almeida. I used to dance there as a little girl. I was in all their shows.'

Cully and Nicolas remained silent, carefully avoiding each other's gaze. The Almeida, one of London's most exciting theatrical companies, was presently performing at an old bus depot at King's Cross. Before then it was in the shell of the Gainsborough film studios. Soon they would be back at their real home in Islington. A movable feast.

'I sensed there was something.' Cully smiled warmly, linking herself and Ava in starry complicity. 'You can always tell.'

'I'm afraid I didn't quite . . .?'

'Cully. Cully Barnaby. And this is my husband, Nicolas.'

'I'm an actor too,' cried Nicolas, thinking to build on the goodwill so suddenly and surprisingly present.

'I don't know if you know the play,' said Cully, 'But Madame Arcati—'

'Aaah, poor Margaret Rutherford. She used to come to me with all her troubles.'

'I do like to research my character. And you are plainly outstanding in your field.'

'Say no more.' Ava waved at the chaise longue. 'Please, make yourselves comfortable.'

Nicolas and Cully sat down on what felt like thistle stuffing. Cully did not care. She had got what she wanted. Nico wondered if it would be safe to take notes, risked asking and was given permission.

Then Ava leaned forward with a gesture of confiding grace. The wise sibyl about to reveal the secrets of the universe. The storyteller with a million legends up her sleeve. Once upon a time, in the little market town of Causton . . .

Ava Bunton had always wanted to be somebody. As a child she thought of being a dancer or a singer and danced and sang at home while constantly pleading for lessons. Eventually, driven half mad by this theatrical posturing, her father boxed her ears and threatened to tie her ankles together. And, when she cried, started unravelling the Sellotape. That soon shut her up.

But the dreams continued. She did errands and delivered papers to buy tap and ballet shoes and pay her subscription to Causton Amateur Society's Junior Club. Every Saturday morning she improvised becoming a tree or a kettle or a hedgehog. She exercised her voice, did pliés at the barre and acted her little socks off. She was in all the pantomimes to which no one in the family came, not even when she played the cat in *Dick Whittington*.

In her last term at school she ran away to London, got a room through a flatshare agency and started office temping to keep herself and pay for more tuition and glamour photographs. She grabbed *The Stage* the second it was on the newsstand, went to any open auditions, tried to get an agent. Ava was never defeated. A fatal mixture of rock-hard confidence and a blinding lack of intelligence protected her from the unhappy understanding that she was completely untalented. Not even good enough to be called mediocre.

Eventually she got a job dancing on a second-rate cruise liner and spent the next seven years more or less afloat, occasionally winging it in nightclubs in Turkey and Beirut. It was in the Lebanon that she met Lionel Wainwright Garret, a once-handsome ex-public schoolboy, now living seedily on what little he could earn giving English lessons. Impressed by his accent and thrilled with the idea of going up in the world, Ava moved in with Garret, parting with nearly all her savings in the process. For a short while he took some sort of interest in her – enough to make her pregnant at any rate – before reverting to his previous passion for young boys. Ava returned to England, sadder though no wiser, for she was the sort of person who blamed her troubles on everyone but herself. But then, something wonderful happened.

Ava was not looking forward to having a baby. She was in her late thirties and, had she not returned from the Far East too late for a National Health Service abortion, would certainly never have had the child. And that would have been a real mistake because, not too long after the baby was born, Ava became aware of a strange new presence, an intelligence at work which she had not experienced before. She put this down to some mysterious genetic intermingling between herself and Lionel Garret. What else could it be?

However, the assurance which had seen her through so many years of rejection and sordid show business wrangles unaccountably absented itself when the question of how to make the best use of this new opportunity arose. It was so strange, for a start, so outside all her previous experience. In fact, it was quite a long time before she worked out how best to handle things. Bringing up the little girl took a great deal of her time, and struggling to make ends meet took a hefty chunk out of what was left. But eventually a way, an opening, presented itself almost out of the blue. And what an appropriate phrase that was, Ava had thought, even back then.

At the time she had joined a friendship club for the divorced and separated, passing herself off as a widow. Refusing to admit to loneliness, she referred to this move only as extending her circle of friends. But her devoted self-interest made friendship impossible and she was on the point of abandoning these meetings, where everyone talked endlessly about themselves, when she met George Footscray.

George, a middle-aged man living with his mother and into one or two deeply unadventurous hobbies, showed the keenest interest when she told him about the messages from other realms that were now transmitting almost daily. He said excitedly they should be shared with the world and described her as a born medium. Another Doris Stokes. Ava had never heard of Doris Stokes and was somewhat uneasy with the word 'share', but her longing to be someone burned as strongly as ever. If anything, years of disappointment had fanned the flame to an even fiercer strength.

George explained that she would not necessarily have to be a platform medium. There were those who did only private sittings or group seances. But Ava loved the idea of rows and rows of faces looking longingly up at her, hanging on her every word. And in respectful silence too, not laughing and drinking or making obscene gestures and rude jokes as they had in nightclubs and aboard ship.

She was not so keen on George's suggestion that a certain amount of training was important. That, for example, she must learn how to prepare before working from the platform. How to handle a congregation. What to do when a spirit manifested only to be met with indifference or blank incomprehension. Never mind how to cover when no one came through at all. Ava assured George that would never happen as her connection was absolutely genuine. And anyway, she'd practically been born on a stage. Improvise was her middle name. It was not until she realised that without a certain degree of training she would not be allowed to tread the boards at all that she grudgingly gave way.

George took her to several church meetings to illustrate the way of things and one or two established mediums kindly attempted to take her under their wings. Ava listened. She gritted her teeth at what she saw as patronising condescension but she listened. Her confidence disturbed them. She seemed to have no nerves at all.

From the very beginning, like an old-style travelling magician, Ava was always supported by an assistant, her daughter, Karen. She would carry Ava's long black velvet cloak, set up her mirror and cosmetic tray, check that everything on the platform was in its correct place, brew her special herbal tea. She had also, in the early days, presented Ava with a bouquet 'from a grateful client' at the conclusion of each meeting; flowers which Ava herself had purchased earlier. However, this was abandoned after complaints from other psychics that a precedent was being set. A precedent that not everyone could afford.

From the first all went well. The voices never let her down and Ava revelled in the attention; in the silent waves of intense longing that poured over what she still thought of as the footlights the moment she began to speak; the gratitude of the gathering afterwards, thanking her, shaking her hand, telling her she was marvellous. That she had changed their lives; brought sunshine out of sorrow. All very nice.

The trouble was that three years later, though everything was still going well, she found herself trapped, journeying round and round the same restrictive circuit. Occasionally she was invited to 'guest', as they put it, in a few churches somewhat further afield, which she was happy to do, and also to take part in various 'evenings of clairvoyance', which she always refused. But fame, as experienced by Doris Stokes, who Ava now knew all about, remained elusive. Like most of the other mediums she came across, outside the limited world of spiritual and psychic practice Ava Garret was still a nobody. And the money was no great shakes either.

At this point, perhaps recognising she had drifted somewhat from her glowing representation of an outstanding oracle to her visitors, Ava suddenly stopped speaking. Then, with an artificial start of Eureka-type astonishment she clapped her hands and cried, 'How fortunate that we have met. You'll need advice, of course. Practical, artistic, psychic. I will sit in on your *Blithe Spirit* rehearsals. No – but me no buts. I won't hear a word against it. The matter's settled.'

'Notice how she veered off when you brought up the question of that last visitation?'

'Of course I noticed!'

'No need to be snippy. If it wasn't for me telling her you were in the business you'd have got zilch.'

'As far as any helpful research is concerned I did get zilch. We heard her life story—'

'Boy,' said Nicolas, chewing on a frangipane, 'did we hear her life story.'

'But I couldn't pin her down as to how the actual experience of transmission felt.'

'Probably indescribable.' He pushed his plate aside. 'Like these tarts.'

'Mine's all right.'

They were in the Secret Garden Tea Rooms, having decided that all that listening had left them in dire need of more refreshment. Sitting at a little window table they watched the world go by. There wasn't much going on at half-past five on a warm Sunday afternoon. A few people wandered past. Some backpackers sat on the kerb licking ice lollies.

'Let's walk round a bit before we go and see the folks,' said Cully. 'It's such a lovely day.'

Nicolas went to pay the bill. The proprietess was behind the cash desk. She didn't put herself out on the charm front. Experience had taught her to recognise those who might become regular customers from the passing trade.

Nicolas, recalling the terraced houses on either side and spotting a brick wall through the café's rear window asked, *faux naïf:* 'Where is the actual garden, then?'

'That's the secret, smarty pants.'

Nicolas gave her one of his warmest smiles. 'My mother made cakes just like yours.'

'Really?' The sour lemon pucker of her lips loosened slightly.

'Mm.' He retrieved the pound coin he had left under the saucer and slipped it into his pocket. 'They were actually cited in the divorce petition.'

As they emerged, hand in hand, into the sunshine Nicolas said, 'Whatever happened to have a nice day?'

'Don't be pathetic. You surely don't think they mean it?'

'I've no problem with people who are insincerely pleasant. It's the sincerely unpleasant that get up my nose.'

They wandered round the village, unwilling wholeheartedly to admire what Nico described as yucky, picture-postcard kitsch, yet drawn into the quiet, apparent serenity of the place in spite of themselves.

161

'Take that, for instance.' Nicolas scornfully faced an exquisite, tiny thatched cottage with mullioned windows. 'Half a dozen peasants used to live in that six-figure biscuit box. Mud floors, chickens scratching about, water coming through the roof, children in rags . . .'

'That was then, darling.' Cully took her husband's hand and led him across the lane, past a vast orchard of apple trees and towards the parish church of St Anselm's. 'And since when have you cared tuppence for the peasants?'

'True, true.' Nicolas laughed. 'Mind, to be fair, I don't expect they ever cared tuppence for me.'

They wandered around the churchyard, looking for interesting gravestones. Some were quite new and shining, addressing rectangles of sparkling white or green gravel. Others were so old the inscriptions were almost worn away. A few of these were listing dangerously and one had fallen on its back. Some graves, even more ancient, were just gentle bumps in the ground. They were so numerous it was difficult not to walk on them.

'Careful, Nico.'

'What?'

'Look where you're standing.'

'They won't know.' But he moved all the same. 'God, I am so incredibly glad that I'm not dead.'

'Me too.'

'So utterly overwhelmingly mind-blowingly glad. Imagine, no more first-night parties.'

'Or last-night parties.'

'No more applause.'

'No bacon and eggs at Groucho's.'

'No Margaritas at Joe Allen's.'

'Or frocks from Ghost.'

'No sunrise.'

'Or sunsets.'

'No sex.'

'Oh, Nico. Worst of all.'

'I shouldn't worry. In twenty years' time they'll have found a way to keep us immortal.' He turned, looking backwards at a splendid Norman tower. 'D'you want to look round?'

'I'd rather go.' Running from the impartial cruelty of time passing Cully was already halfway down the rose-brick path, calling over her shoulder, 'It'll be locked anyway.'

Nicolas caught up with her at the lych-gate. Saw shadows fall across her face as she slipped through. Thought they were caused by leaves in the elm trees. Then was not sure.

'You all right, Mrs Bradley?'

'Fine.' No Mum and Dad. No terrible meals and touching hints about possible grandchildren. No bear hugs and garden cuttings or surprise presents. No sensible, loving advice . . .

'Oh, shit. Sorry.'

'Here.' Nicolas offered his hanky and drew her close. 'Have a good blow.'

'Sometimes I hate loving people, don't you?'

'No. Not when you think of the alternative.' He paused. 'C'mon let's hear it for the Lion King.'

Cully trumpeted loudly into the handkerchief. Gently Nicolas wiped her tears away. Then they linked arms and walked back into the street. Just a few yards further it humped itself into a bridge with a little carved parapet. They leaned over together and listened to the fast running water rattling the pebbles. Diamond-bright water; crystal clear.

'We could bottle this,' suggested Nicolas. 'Make our fortune.'

'Those sheep are pooing in it.'

'Added minerals.' Nicolas pulled out some loose change before replacing his hanky. 'I think we should throw money in. Like people do at the Trevi Fountain.'

'That's because they want to return, silly.'

But Nicolas threw his money in anyway. He tossed a fistful high into the air and it descended in a glittering shower to lie winking and sparkling on the sandy bed of the stream.

By nightfall every coin had been removed by village children and consequently Nicolas and Cully never returned to Forbes Abbot. On the other hand Cully's father, a detective chief inspector in the Criminal Investigation Department of nearby Causton, got to know it very well indeed.

CHAPTER FOURTEEN

Like all villages Forbes Abbot had its down side. There was more to it than the bijou constellation of Barrett homes with their fake leaded windowpanes, swirls of bubble glass and electric carriage lamps. More than the few large, beautiful old houses in their own grounds, the renovated Edwardian terrace and carefully restored nineteenth-century cottages. Unfortunately there were also council houses.

The blessing was that these, of which there were around twenty in the form of a crescent, had been sensibly constructed right on the edge and so could be fairly easily ignored. Of course, they were full of people who would insist on going in and coming out, but most of them appeared to have cars and shopped in bulk at Asda or Tesco, which mainly kept them free of the local Spar. It was grudgingly admitted that nearly all the houses had well-cared-for gardens and clean curtains. Some were even privately owned with fancy front doors and lemon mock stone cladding. Even so, living there, confided the upside residents to each other, definitely constituted a stigma.

The majority of the council tenants had no idea they constituted a stigma and wouldn't have given a monkey's had anyone been brave or foolish enough to point it out. But there was one exception. Returning from the Middle East seven months pregnant, Ava Garret had been reluctantly taken in by her now elderly parents. Rows started almost immediately and, contrary to all received wisdom, nothing changed once the baby was born. Ava's mother, barely able to cope with the stairs and already on the waiting list for a council bungalow, made some increasingly urgent phone calls, and when Karen was six months old, she and her husband moved out.

Ava stayed on in sole possession of a modern, two-and-a-bit bedroomed, centrally heated home on which both the rent and council tax were paid. Far from being grateful she seethed with resentment. Removing the number of her house and renaming it Rainbow Lodge merely confused the postman. The neighbours, who laughed at her pretensions, had not always been unkind. When she was first on her own they would ask her round for a cup of tea and a chat. A surplus of allotment vegetables occasionally appeared on her doorstep. The family next door even offered to sit with Karen in an emergency. But gradually it became clear that, though Ava proved to be the world's greatest taker, giving was not her bag. Gradually people came to see that they were simply being made use of and the offers of help dried up. Ava was not surprised. It was the story of her life. Everyone all sugary smarmy till they got what they wanted, then you could be on fire and they wouldn't widdle on you to put it out.

However, no such resentments clouded her thoughts on the morning after her most recent appearance at the Church of the Near at Hand. In fact Ava sat at the kitchen table as near to happy as she had been for years. Two things had happened within the past seven days, that looked fair to turning her fortunes round. The latest was her meeting with Cully Barnaby, which reawakened in Ava all her early dreams of theatrical success. And how understanding the young actress had been. How intelligent her questions. How impressed by everything that she, Ava, had had to say. Heavens, the husband even took notes!

And to be invited to the theatre *as a consultant*. It would be the legitimate theatre too, not some sleazebag cesspit in Soho crammed with fawn raincoats jacking off under the *Evening Standard*. She wondered what the pay would be like. If they would offer a fixed sum and expect her to be available when needed or if she would be asked to attend every rehearsal. If that was the case she would insist on a taxi, door to door. Either that or a hired car. You had to make your status clear from the very beginning or no one would respect you.

Ava lit her first cigarette of the day, sorted through a stack of junk mail and pulled out a leaflet about a carpet sale in Pinner. On the back she wrote 'Almeeda', underlined it, chewed on her pen for a moment then added, '*Blithe Spirit*'. She must get hold of a script, that was the first thing. Spending money would hurt but it was in a good cause. The film, which she had seen on the box a year or so ago, was now just a memory. Anyway, the play – and it had been news to Ava that there was a play – was bound to be completely different. When people made movies out of books and such they always changed everything.

'Clothes.' Clothes were vital. If you looked the part you were home and dry, and in show business that meant glamour. She could not turn up at the theatre in the boring old things she wore to drive to church meetings – ordinary skirts or trousers, a padded jacket, her old camel coat. Fortunately she had some money. A sudden windfall had dropped into her hands a few days ago. Just in time, as it happened, to accommodate this second stroke of luck. An omen if ever there was one. Her stars had been spot on as well: 'A meeting with a stranger could expand your horizons.'

Ava decided to go up West to get the things. She saw herself making an entrance and knocking them dead, like she had at auditions in the old days. A dress some way above the knees – her legs were still good – and matching coat. Or a really stunning trouser suit in cream with a patterned shirt, possibly turquoise or aquamarine, matching earrings and her tan slingbacks from Dolcis sale, still in their box at the back of the wardrobe. She must also get a smart briefcase for her copy of *Blithe Spirit*.

Next, hair. Ava chewed on her pen for a while then wrote 'ends trimed plus rinse'. Of course the colour must be in no way frivolous. Her natural shade, faded mouse, was commonly enhanced by Strawberry Fayre highlights but wouldn't they be rather inappropriate? Partyfied rather than workmanlike? She decided to go for Autumn Leaves, a warm chestnut plus an ash-grey streak to denote competence and sincerity. Here Ava paused and reflected briefly on her mother who had recently died (thank you, God). About the only sensible bit of advice Mrs Bunton had ever passed on was: 'Get your hair right, everything else falls into place.' And in spite of the fact that her own had always resembled a supernova of rusty iron filings, Ava believed her mother, then and to this day.

She stubbed out her cigarette in a smear of marmalade and poured some more tea. Overhead Karen was clumping about in some shoes she had got off a girl at school in exchange for doing her homework. They were ridiculous, Ava thought. Hideous even. Dull black leather with ankle straps and platform soles so high they looked like surgical boots.

'That's right,' she had said as Karen had proudly staggered through the front door, 'break your bloody neck.' It never occurred to her that the child might know she looked ridiculous but still longed to wear what everyone else was wearing.

Roy, the paying guest, on nights this week, was sleeping upstairs. He had been staying at Rainbow Lodge for around eighteen months. Since, in fact, he had come to the end of his time in the children's home at Causton. Of course, the neighbours had shopped Ava. Couldn't wait. Living off the fat of the land already, wasn't she? On the social, drawing child allowance, housing allowance, family allowance, fucking ferret-keeping allowance as like as not, and now subletting and pocketing the divvy. I should cocoa, said righteous Fred Carboy (invalidity benefit/moonlighting for Cox's MiniCabs), residing dead opposite and well placed to observe chicanery in his near neighbours.

The powers that be called round. Ava swore Roy was staying temporarily, doing the garden and decorating the house in lieu of rent. Roy, desperate for a real home in a real house instead of yet more hostel accommodation, backed her up. He pretended to leave after a couple of weeks, then came back, then went again, and after a bit more of this toing and froing the neighbours gave up trying to cause trouble and Roy stayed for good.

Karen had been pleased. She liked Roy. He was going to be a comedian one day and was always trying out jokes. Also he was interested in a lot of weird things. Ancient civilisations: Egypt and the Pharaohs and King Arthur and magic and dragons. In fact his main reason for helping out at the Near at Hand was to learn how to raise the dark forces and use them to his advantage. But he wasn't at all frightening himself and often brought little treats home from Tesco where he worked mainly in the warehouse, but also filling shelves if someone was off sick.

Alas, Roy's rent, which Karen had assumed would really make a difference to their pretty constrained lives, didn't. At least not to hers. Her mother smoked more and better quality cigarettes and fresh pots of cream and stuff started appearing in the bathroom but the food didn't change and Karen still had to get all her clothes from charity shops. As Ava crossly explained when asked if there might now be some pocket money seventy-five pounds went nowhere these days. If Karen wanted money she'd have to earn it. Other kids did. What was wrong with a paper round? But you needed a bike for a paper round.

Now Karen, having safely tottered across the landing, began to descend the stairs, tightly gripping the banister. There was a pleasant smell of warm toast.

'Hello, sweetheart,' cried Ava as her daughter safely negotiated the final stair. 'Brekkies up.'

Karen paused, hesitated. She almost looked over her shoulder to check that no other person, the 'sweetheart' of the greeting, had mysteriously materialised. She wasn't hungry, but who could resist such a welcome?

'Great – thanks.' The table was full of rubbish: dirty plates and cutlery, a huge glass ashtray brimming with scarlet-tipped butts, an empty jam jar, a scraping of marge in a saucer, the *Evening Standard*. 'I'll get some cornflakes then.'

But Ava had already gone back to her writing. Karen found a waxed bag with a rubber band round it and shook out the few remaining fragments. She added some UHT milk (£1.50 for a packet of six). Unopened it kept for ever. You bought it off a lorry on the market. The side rolled down and things were stacked really high inside. Everything was past its sell-by date and some of the tins were rusty and had labels you'd never heard of but it was all incredibly cheap. Karen sat down, then got up again to move the ashtray, which smelled disgusting.

'If you're making a list we want some more cereals.'

Ava immediately put her arm around the bit of paper like a child at school. Not that she was embarrassed to reveal that she was planning to treat herself but because Karen would then know she had some money and would begin looking for it. She'd probably tell Roy too, just to start something. The pair of them were as thick as thieves.

'I'm just making some preliminary notes for when I'm called to rehearsals. Aahh – *Blithe Spirit*'s such an enchanting play.'

'Good idea.' Karen left it at that, though she had been present at the conversation with Cully Barnaby and knew that any future involvement was all in her mother's mind. It wasn't easy to keep silent. When Ava discovered her mistake all in the immediate vicinity would suffer from the fallout. Would be castigated and lectured as if caught out in some crafty misdemeanour. Her ability to shift blame was awesome. On the other hand, attempting to point out any error in advance could also bring about unpleasant repercussions. Either way you couldn't win.

Karen picked up the *Standard*, blew some ash off a picture of Phil Collins and turned to Entertainments. She started to read down the theatre column: Adelphi, Albery, Aldwych, Ambassadors, Apollo, Arts,

167

Astoria . . . Then paused and read backwards, running her nail carefully past each name lest she had missed one out.

'Ava?'

Ava made an impatient yet regal gesture, like a pasha swatting some importunate insect. Karen, having taken the risky decision to speak added boldly: 'It's not in here.'

'What?'

'The theatre.'

Ava looked up and sighed. 'What *are* you on about?'

'The Almeida.'

'Let me see.'

Ava snatched the paper, folded it, brought it up to her eyes and squinted. Karen watched as alarm flickered over her mother's face. The corner of her eye twitched.

Ava said, 'If they're rehearsing I expect it's closed.'

'But don't they put the number in anyway,' asked Karen, 'in case people want to book for shows and things.'

Ava had by now got to Wyndhams and was anxiously retracing her steps. It was true. The Almeida was not listed. That bitch of a girl – that so-called actress – must have been stringing her along. She started furiously flicking the pages, turning them back, reading around the listings.

'There!' Ava was so relieved she almost choked. Her finger stabbed the *Standard* so hard it went through the paper. 'See?'

'Oh, yes.'

'There is such a thing as fringe, darling. Though you wouldn't know – not being in the business.' She frowned at the clock, then at Karen, now lolling about in the chair opposite with all the time in the world at her disposal. And she'd be doing it for the next six weeks. Whoever invented school holidays, thought Ava bitterly, couldn't have had any kids.

'We must get on. There's a lot to do today.'

'I haven't finished my breakfast.'

'Don't whine, dear. Whining's for wimps.'

Karen scraped at her cereal bowl, licked up the last of the grey metallic-tasting milk. 'Could I have some toast?'

Ava sighed again and adopted one of her put-upon looks. The child had been like this since the day she was born. Want, want, want. Never satisfied. Hoping that silence meant yes Karen found a heel of bread in the bin and put it under the grill.

'I expect you'll be out most of the day with a friend?'

'Don't know.'

'Stay with them for lunch. And tea,' suggested Ava. 'Eat someone else out of house and home for a change. That's what friends are for.'

Karen had no idea what friends were for. She had never made one. Never come even close. Ava had taught her that. Don't trust anyone, then you won't be hurt. Karen saw the sense in this; saw indeed that it was true.

Of course she would never know how much hurt she'd been saved but tried to believe it was an awful lot as this made never having a friend easier to bear.

'Alternatively,' continued Ava, 'the lounge could do with a good going over.'

A short while later, when Karen was washing up, the telephone rang. Ava answered and in next to no time was engaged in quiet but rather frenzied conversation with George Footscray. He had called to say that her revelations at the conclusion of yesterday's meeting had struck him as so sensational that he had contacted the *Causton Echo*. They very much wanted to do an interview. Should it be convenient a reporter and photographer would come to Rainbow Lodge that very afternoon. As her representative he would naturally be present to support and advise her.

Ava put the phone down with great care. She sat still, breathing very slowly, calming her nerves. It would never do at this stage to go to pieces. Not that there was much chance of that – she could cope with Fame; had been training for it all her life. Of course, George would have to go. Setting up an interview with the local rag was one thing. The nationals, radio and television, the media as a whole was something else. Ava made a careful note of the name Max Clifford.

Kate was gradually feeling more and more at home in Appleby House. It was over a week now since Dennis had died and yesterday his ashes had been interred, at Benny's request, in the churchyard of St Anselm's. The Lawsons had been surprised at the turnout. Most of the village had been present and all the staff from Dennis's office. His partner's wife, Gilda Latham, organised everything and also put a notice in *The Times*, which probably explained the presence of quite a few mourners strange to the village. For such a private person Dennis seemed not to have been as short of friends as was generally imagined.

Of course, Kate's main concern was Benny – how she would cope with such a painful occasion so soon after her traumatic experience at Kinders. So Kate was relieved, if a little surprised, when Benny said she was not going to the funeral but would pay her respects in her own time and in her own way. Benny was continuing to hold herself together with what seemed to Kate a determination bordering on the manic. Her pursuit of 'justice for Dennis' remained both fiery and constant and she wrote more and more letters, though Kate could not help noticing there were still no replies. Perhaps Benny had given up hoping, for she no longer stood at the gate at ten o'clock looking out for the postman.

This morning, thought Kate, watching her help to clear the table, Benny appeared to be listening for something. As she handed cups and cereal bowls to Mrs Crudge at the sink her head was cocked on one side, like that of a bright bird. Something was going on between those two. Kate had noticed complicitous smiles. Lips tightening with satisfaction, raised eyebrows, whispered conversations that stopped if anyone happened by. They were like two children bursting with a secret.

The telephone rang. Still attached to a toast rack Benny shot across the room and snatched up the receiver. She listened briefly, said something barely audible and hung up. Her face was burning quite red with excitement as she stared at Doris.

Doris's eyebrows went up so high they almost disappeared into her hairline. She stuck her thumb up in the air and cried, 'What'd I tell you?'

Benny gave a choked-up little squeal and ran from the house.

Well, if they think, thought Kate, I'm going to ask what it's all about they can think again. Even at school she had never wanted to join any of the supposedly secret societies. She picked up her clipboard and pencil and went off to finish listing Aunt Carey's furniture. An antique dealer from Aylesbury was coming that afternoon to value what she and Mallory wished to sell.

To Kate's surprise this was nearly everything, for Benny, offered whatever she would like, had chosen a single picture that had always hung over Carey's bed, a small but beautiful oil painting of a pewter jug holding rich, creamy roses and a tangle of honeysuckle resting on a highly polished table. You could see reflections of the flowers, their outlines wavery and indistinct as if underwater, the colours subdued but still full of life. Benny, stammering out her gratitude, had pressed it to her heart.

Kate had worked her way through the attics, all the bedrooms and the two large rooms on the ground floor. The ones with french windows that opened on to the terrace where she and Mallory had sat drinking Pimm's and dreaming their dreams and waiting for Dennis to come to dinner. But that was all behind them now, or would be once Benny had given up this mad crusade. Kate wondered how long that would be. She hoped not too long. It was painful to watch Benny, as Kate saw it, deliberately wounding herself afresh every day. Fighting to prove something that had already been disproved beyond any shadow of a doubt.

While Kate had been checking out the furniture, Mallory had been reading the very last book in the very first bag. Kate was trying not to get disheartened about the future – heavens, the company wasn't even registered yet. But hours of wading through leaden prose, duff syntax and jokes unfunny when they were first cracked over a thousand years ago had left her feeling she never wanted to pick up a book again – hardly an ideal position for someone about to start their own publishing house. Kate was chastened to realise just how much sifting must have been done before her monthly bag of reader's manuscripts arrived. They didn't call it the slush pile for nothing.

She found Mallory stretched out on one of the old steamer chairs in the conservatory, seemingly engrossed. For a moment Kate stood quietly, watching him through the glass. Unaware, as relaxed as she had seen him for some little while, Mallory frowned, quickly turned a page and read on.

170

It was a relief to see him really involved in something, if only temporarily. Over the last few days he had sorted through his aunt's papers, visited the offices of Pippins Direct and met and talked with their workers in the orchard. He had done a fair amount of tidying in the garden and been welcoming and sociable if people called, but Kate knew that all these activities occupied him only tenuously. Always at the back of his mind she sensed a growing anxiety and assumed it was to do with Polly. Where she was, how she was, what she was doing, who she was doing it with. Kate longed to share the anxiety – indeed, had quite a bit of her own after discovering Polly had been in trouble – but her concern was mixed with considerable irritation. After all, their daughter was grown up. She'd probably just gone off somewhere for a break with some friends. Why couldn't Mallory ever let go?

'Mal,' she moved down the black and white steps, 'I was just wondering . . .'

'Mmm.'

'What you think about—'

'Hang on a sec.'

'Don't tell me you've found something worth reading.'

There was a cry from the kitchen. Then another. Two voices joined in overlapping jubilant conversation. Someone (it sounded like Doris) started to screech with excitement. Kate hurried to see what the matter was.

She discovered Benny sitting at the kitchen table with Doris leaning over her shoulder. They were reading a newspaper. Both became silent as Kate entered, staring at her with expressions she could not quite fathom. Defiance perhaps, on Benny's part. Doris seemed to be struggling to express nothing at all and succeeded in looking merely constipated.

'What is it, Ben?' asked Kate. 'What's happened?'

'This has happened,' said Doris, leaning over and tapping a black-and-white photograph. 'That's what.'

'Can I have a look?'

Benny hesitated, not passing the newspaper straight across as Kate had expected.

Kate said, 'For heaven's sake,' reached out and took it. She saw the picture of a woman excessively made up with shoulder-length black hair and heavy lidded, dark eyes. She had on a black dress with long sleeves and a lowish scoop neckline. A large jewelled cross rested on the solid shelf of her bosom. Her name was Ava Garret and she could have stepped straight out of a Dracula movie. Kate, immediately inclined to giggle, sobered as she read: 'MEDIUM MURDER SENSATION. THE TRUTH FROM BEYOND THE GRAVE.' Suddenly uneasy she pushed the *Causton Echo* back across the table.

'I think you should read it, Mrs Lawson.' Doris, vindication personified, swelled visibly. 'It's about poor Mr Brinkley.'

'Dennis?' Reluctantly Kate dragged the *Echo* back. Read the rest of the

171

article. Folded the paper so the relevant page was on the inside and crammed it into the waste bin. More disturbed than she was prepared to admit she said, 'How can people believe such nonsense?'

'Well, I'm very sorry,' said Doris, un-sorrily, 'but it's not nonsense. She described the room that the machines were in, all the details. Everything.'

'So you see, Kate,' said Benny, 'the police will have to listen to me now.'

'Benny.' Kate reached out and took Benny's hand. Little swellings, shiny knobs of incipient arthritis were developing on the knuckles. Kate stroked them gently. How could she make her affection clear without colluding in this extraordinary fantasy? 'Can't you let go of all this?'

'Oh! why won't you believe me?'

'It's not that I don't believe you,' lied Kate, 'I'm just afraid you'll make yourself ill.'

Benny stared stubbornly at the table. Doris turned to deal with the congealing dishes in the sink. Kate went away to gather early windfalls for an apple charlotte. Later on, putting the russet peelings in the bin, she noticed the newspaper had disappeared. And so had Benny.

'That mad woman's here again,' said Sergeant Troy.

'What mad woman's that?' asked Barnaby. He never seemed to meet any other sort these days. Recently he had successfully concluded a case featuring a poet who wore only latex, lived on liquorice allsorts and worshipped a horse she believed to be the reincarnation of Radclyffe Hall. And she was the straight man.

'The one who thought her friend was murdered, remember? Those weird machines?'

'I thought we'd sorted that.'

'She's now got proof.'

'So talk to her. Find out what it consists of.'

'She wants to see you.'

'Everybody wants to see me. Joyce asked what the chances were only last week. She was quite rude, actually.'

'It won't take long.' Troy paused. 'We've got an easy day.'

'The first since Christmas.'

'She's terribly excited.'

'That makes one of us.'

'Could be she's really on to something.'

'Oh God. What was her name again?'

Benny came in confidently, holding her embroidered bag, a smile all across her earnest pink face. She sat down facing the chief inspector and said, 'I knew you'd understand how important it was.'

'I believe you have some vital information for us, Miss Frayle.'

'Absolutely. Cutting the flim-flam, chief inspector, and coming straight to the point here is proof positive,' continued Benny, opening the *Causton Echo*, 'that my dear friend, Dennis Brinkley, was murdered.'

Troy perched on the wide windowsill and flipped open his notebook. He listened. Barnaby listened. Benny finished reading. The DCI turned his head and glared at his unfortunate sergeant. Troy closed his notebook and prepared to show Miss Frayle out.

'You do understand what this means, I hope?' Benny, now sounding slightly less confident, got out of her chair.

'I do, Miss Frayle,' said Barnaby and thought he spoke the truth. He understood that she had loved Dennis Brinkley and that his death had left her deeply disturbed. He wondered briefly about her family. If someone was supporting her at home and if she was seeing a doctor. Thankfully it was none of his business.

'You'll look into it now?' cried Benny over her shoulder as Troy eased her firmly through the door.

'Don't worry, Miss Frayle,' replied Barnaby. 'We'll do everything that's necessary.'

CHAPTER FIFTEEN

Andrew Latham leaned back in Dennis's office chair. His long legs were crossed at the knees, his arms crooked in the air, hands linked behind his neck. He was staff-watching through the open door and deriving much pleasure from the process. He was used to barely concealed animosity from the men. Now the women too seemed to have turned against him. Even Gail Fuller, whom he had had every which way across the photocopier after hours. But Andrew enjoyed their resentment, the quick ceasing of conversation when he came into the room. He knew what they'd been talking about for all their maudlin pretence at sorrow. What happens now? Are our jobs safe? Will we get another? That was until today. Today they were passing round the *Causton Echo*, agog with amazement, amusement, derision, distress.

Gilda appeared to take the article very seriously. At breakfast, moodily forking a lard omelette to and fro, she had announced an intention of getting in touch with the medium in question straightaway.

'What on earth for?' Andrew addressed his remark to an undercooked sausage. He had no stomach for looking directly at his wife without protective lenses, especially first thing in the morning. A blubber mountain draped in gingham, a moon face nodding and wobbling on a column of fat so soft and loose it was corrugated, like a squib. Only her coarse, beige hair, confined by several large rollers, pleased the eye, giving the charming impression of young hedgehogs at play.

'To see if Daddy comes through, of course.'

'Of course,' repeated Andrew. 'It would be interesting to see how he's getting on up there. What the scrap iron situation might be.'

Gilda looked at her husband sharply. This was not the first 'take it two ways' remark he had made lately. She hoped he was not getting above himself. Then hoped he was, because it would be such a pleasure yanking him down again.

'Anyone can be sarky, Andrew.'

'Can they, darling?'

'It's the lowest form of wit.'

He decided not to essay any higher form of wit. It might just strike her on the funny bone and Gilda had a laugh like a machine gun. He forced himself to look across the table and smile. How typical of her to home in on a really disturbing item of news and immediately translate it into something relevant only to herself. The alarming suggestion that someone they had both known well had possibly been murdered seemed to have passed her completely by. Andrew pointed this out.

'They who live by the sword shall die by the sword.'

That was the *Reader's Digest* talking. She was always writing down pithy sayings to toss into the conversational pool on the rare occasions they had guests. It made her very unpopular. No one loves a know-all.

'If you say so, dear.'

Gilda immediately contradicted herself. 'Of course, it's all made up. We're not the sort of people to know people who get themselves murdered.'

'Why go and see the medium then?'

He should have known better. The next twenty minutes was filled with a lecture on how those who depended on others for their bread and butter should know better than to keep picking those others up or putting them down all the time. And she was there to tell him that the patience of those others was not inexhaustible. But years of this had left Andrew indifferent. By the time he had backed his Punto out of the double garage Gilda's onslaught was not even a memory.

Back in the present moment he smiled again, knowing himself to be in the happy position of being about to wrong-foot a whole roomful of people who didn't like him. Any minute now Brinkley's solicitor would be arriving. He had rung asking for an appointment the previous day and the hour was nigh. It would no doubt be something to do with the disposition of Dennis's half of the business. Given their mutual antipathy Andrew did not expect to benefit in any way himself. He just hoped the benefactor would be easy-going and not the sort to yack on about the Protestant work ethic every five minutes. Should this be the case Andrew planned to say that actually he was only a sleeping partner and just came into the office from time to time to rally the troops. If he thought Gilda wouldn't find out, and if she'd given him enough money to enjoy any sort of life, this would have always been his preferred *modus operandi*. But perhaps the new partner would be a man after his own heart. One for the ladies, prepared to cover up for Andrew's lapses in return for similar favours. Pretty unlikely given that he would probably be a friend or relative of Dennis. Still, you never knew your luck.

Gail Fuller rang through to say that Mr Ormerod had arrived. Andrew strode into reception with a professional smile and outstretched hand. The solicitor looked more like a farmer: a stout man, dressed in cords and a multipocketed sleeveless jerkin over a tweed polo-necked jumper. He also wore a fly fishing hat. Andrew attempted to conceal his surprise and Mr Ormerod murmured something about meeting a client directly afterwards at the cattle market. As Andrew led the way to his inner sanctum there was a tug on his sleeve.

'A moment, Mr Latham, if you please.'

Andrew frowned. 'What is it?'

175

'It would perhaps be more relevant if I conducted our business here in the main office. Perhaps the lady in reception might also be present?'

Andrew felt a chill of apprehension. He called Gail Fuller, then walked to the nearest desk, picked up a large, extremely heavy metal tape dispenser and crashed it down, making everyone jump.

He said: 'Take a break – for a change,' followed by, 'This is Dennis's solicitor – Mr Ormerod.'

A few murmurs of greeting but most people just looked bewildered. Andrew noticed Leo Fortune didn't look bewildered, the shit-faced weasel.

'I'm sure you must all have been concerned about the situation here. About your futures.' The tone was encouraging and kindly. Mr Ormerod smiled at everyone and produced a long foolscap envelope from one of his pockets. 'I know how much Mr Brinkley valued both your work and the friendly and pleasant atmosphere that was constantly maintained here. Not always the case in a large office, I assure you.'

Oh, for Christ's sake get on with it, you maundering old windbag. Andrew swallowed sour liquid, longed to pee, tried to look as if none of this was anything to do with him. Unaware his hands were trembling.

'Certainly in my experience,' continued the solicitor, removing a single crisp sheet of paper from his envelope, 'this type of bequest is unique. Mr Brinkley has left his share of the business known as Brinkley and Latham to "all of the staff currently employed in the said business at the time of my death".' He paused as excited murmurs broke out. There was some nervous laughter and Jessica, the office junior, started to cry. Gail Fuller gave her a cuddle and said not to worry, it would be just like working in John Lewis. Andrew, white-faced, gulped down more acid. When the noise gentled somewhat Mr Ormerod spoke over it.

'This share to be divided pro rata and calculated according to the length of service of each individual represented. There is a request that Mr Fortune – who, incidentally, inherits Mr Brinkley's car – should carry out the necessary computation. Are you prepared to do this er . . .?' His glance wavered between the men present.

'That's me,' said Leo. 'And yes, I am.'

'Then I shall be hearing from you soon.' The solicitor beamed around the room again and departed, his leather top boots creaking at every step.

Andrew put on his coat, picked up his empty briefcase and followed. No way, no way in the entire motherfucking world would he remain behind. Imagine – shut up in his glass booth pretending to be busy while being forced to listen to the babbling and braying outside of the suddenly solvent. Morons popping corks, hurling party favours about, trying on funny hats.

There was silence as he passed through reception. Silence as he pulled the main door to. Then, running down the stairs, he heard ironical cheering break out. Crossing the market square he paused at the statue of Reuben

Cozens and looked back. They were all crowding around the window, waving and laughing.

At Rainbow Lodge things were proceeding apace. The local commercial station, Radio Foresight, based in Uxbridge, had picked up the news item on Ava's revelations and wanted to interview her on their afternoon chat show. The producer contacted the *Echo*, who gave them George Footscray's number. He in turn called on Ava, offering to set up the meeting and to go with her if she would like. Ava, though delighted by the speed of her rapid ascent to stardom, was not best pleased that it was still being handled by a nobody with bad breath and fallen arches. A few brisk, well-chosen words made it clear that she had already moved into another league entirely. George, who had been dreaming that his world too was about to open up and that he might be on the point of managing the next Mystic Meg, ground his unstable false teeth and sadly returned to his crack-brained mother and macramé chandeliers.

The programme ran from 3.30 for an hour. Ava was asked to be there by 3.15. She drove to the outskirts of Uxbridge, then took a taxi to the studio but could have saved the money, for no one was waiting outside to greet her. In reception a slip of a girl wearing a pink plastic skirt no wider than a hair ribbon and a T-shirt reading 'Let's Do It' took her name and asked her to wait. Soon another slightly older girl turned up, this time in a halter top and floor-length black hobble skirt.

'Hi – I'm Cambria DeLane? Corey's assistant?'

'Good after—'

But the girl, taking pinched little steps, was already disappearing. Ava followed, wondering how someone whose duties included meeting important visitors was allowed to go around with rainbow-striped hair hoicked into a bunch on the top of her head and constrained by a leopard-print bow.

Cambria opened the door of a narrow rectangular room with one glass wall through which you could see the studio. A youth with headphones, Jim by name, was sitting at a control panel and Ava was relieved to see he looked at least old enough to have left school. Another, even older, came forward to greet her. He wore shades, sprayed-on jeans and a baggy vest with 'REM' printed on it. His skin and hair were fawn and both looked as if they could do with a good detox. He said: 'He*llo*.'

'Good after—'

'Get us some tea, heart face.' As Cambria disappeared he enclosed Ava's outstretched hand in both of his own, cradling and squeezing it with careful tenderness, as if it were a ripe peach. 'I'm Corey Panting. We're just so thrilled you've agreed to come on the show, Ms Barret.'

'Garret. And it's Mrs.'

'I'm so sorry.' He frowned and wondered what other misinformation lay in wait for him. The research department was staffed by barely paid, inattentive graduates. Lightly armed with degrees in media studies, they regarded local radio as merely a stepping stone. Their eyes were always on the next big thing, which frequently proved to be the dole queue.

'I expect,' continued Corey Panting, 'you're familiar with the programme.'

'No,' said Ava.

'Ah.' This had never happened before. Even if the interviewee had never heard of *Corey's People* they had not been rude enough to say so. 'Well, briefly—'

Cambria came in with the tea. It was not even in a real cup and Ava refused it. This was not at all what she had expected.

Corey continued, 'I introduce you. Fill in a bit of background, then start the interview—'

'How on earth do you manage to see anything down here with those sunglasses on?'

'If you could just listen, please? We don't have a lot of time.' What Corey occasionally did, if the interviewee appeared lively, articulate and intelligent was ask them to stay on for the rest of the programme, contribute to any discussions or phone-ins. Not this one. 'So, if I can quickly recap on what we have on you?' He picked up his notes, rattled the information off at some speed, then asked if there were any serious errors.

'Not errors as such but you have left out a recent and extremely important development in my career.'

'What's that, then?' He glanced at his watch.

'Consultant on psychic matters to the Almeida Theatre.'

'The Almeida?' Now his voice revealed genuine interest and respect. Corey loved the theatre. 'How did that come about?'

'The actress playing Madame Arcati in their new production of *Blithe Spirit* came to see me personally. And things developed from there.'

'I see.' Somehow he found that hard to believe. Yet why lie about a thing so easily checkable? And the stuff last Sunday had apparently been witnessed by a hall full of people.

Time to go in. Determined to appear unfazed, Ava strolled up to a round table on which stood two microphones, sat down and rearranged her paisley shawl.

'Could you take your bag off the table, please?' Then, when she had, 'And say a few words into the mike?'

'That won't be necessary. I have worked in the business for many years. My voice—'

'It's purely technical, Ava. The engineer needs a sound level.'

'Of course.' Ava squared up to the mike. 'Testing. One, two. One two. Mary had—'

'That's fine.' Corey widened his eyes at the glass panel. The engineer, laughing, stuck up his thumb. And off they went.

It was not an easy interview, which was surprising, for Corey had rarely come across anyone so utterly self-obsessed and with such a need to talk about themselves. The trouble was dragging her to the point at issue. He led her forcibly from glowing accounts of her participation in West End musicals only to be blitzed by a description of cabaret performances that would have turned Ute Lemper green with envy.

'But what I'd really like to talk about,' said Corey, gamely butting in for the umpteenth time, 'are your exceptional gifts as a medium. Especially, of course, that extraordinary incident last weekend at the spiritualist church at Forbes Abbot. I understand you were visited by the spirit of a man who told you he'd been murdered?'

'That is correct,' replied Ava. 'I saw and heard him very clearly. He gave me his name and described the scene of his death in great detail. The strange machines, the towering walls. The person who killed him was present but only as a shape surrounded by mist. Unfortunately, just as it was beginning to clear there was a disturbance in what is laughingly called the real world – a child crying – and the spirit of Mr Brinkley vanished.'

'Just like that?'

'They like quiet. Human sounds put them off. I suppose it reminds them of what they're missing.'

'I can see that it would.' Fatally Corey glanced across at the control booth. Jim, his face completely covered with a white tea towel, was looming over the panel, arms wide, fingers hooked into claws.

'But he will return.'

'How . . . how can you . . . so sorry . . . excuse me . . .' Corey drank some water, carefully. 'How can you be sure?'

'Top mediums – and it's no secret we can be counted on the fingers of one hand – have special powers of clairvoyance.'

'Could you bring him up now then?'

'This isn't a game, Mr Panting.'

'It would be a first for radio. And I know our listeners would be absolutely thrilled to discover "whodunnit". Of course if you can't—'

'It is not a question of can't. It is simply not possible to speak from the angelic octave at the drop of a hat. One has to vibrate in a much higher frequency, which needs intensive preparation. Also the person the spirit wishes to contact must be present. I can't imagine anyone wanting to talk to you.'

When Corey got his wind back he said 'I know there have been cases where mediums have helped the police considerably during a murder enquiry. Are you in touch with them at all?'

'I expect to hear from them momentarily. Though we must remember that only half the story has so far been told.'

'And we shall hear the conclusion, the unmasking, as it were, this coming Sunday?'

'That is absolutely correct.'

'At the Church of the Sleight of Hand?'

'Near at Hand,' snapped Ava.

'You'll have a full house,' said Corey.

And they did too, though not for quite the reasons he expected.

Andrew Latham heard *Corey's People* almost by default. When Gilda went out she always left the radio on, having heard, via the Neighbourhood Watch committee, that it was common knowledge this deterred burglars. It seemed to Andrew that if the knowledge was all that common any burglar worth his salt would be inclined to think, on hearing a radio play, that the householder was out.

He spooned coffee into the cafetière and, waiting for the kettle to boil, studied Gilda's wall calendar. It had a square for every day and August was nearly all scrawled over, which was great. Whenever his wife was out Andrew came home, and so far she hadn't twigged. Right now Gilda would be at her art class. This meant another insipid watercolour Blu-Tacked to her study wall. God alone knew why she called it a study. The only serious academic effort made was an Open University Foundation Course a couple of years earlier. A month had been enough. After a warning from her oculist that further intensive study could seriously damage her eyes, pens, folders, set books and stacks of virgin paper were hurled into the dustbin.

Andrew made the coffee and returned to the calendar. Tomorrow night: play reading at Causton. Friday a.m.: massage, Shoshona, though how the poor girl ever found her hands again was a miracle. Friday p.m.: hair, eyebrows, manicure. No expense spared to keep madame entertained, intellectually challenged and *ravissante*. Whereas poor monsieur . . .

Andrew poured the coffee, hot and strong. He needed it. After leaving the office he'd gone into the Magpie and spent the last of this week's allowance on several large glasses of red wine and a large dish of moules marinières. Eating at Bellissima would not have been an option. Gilda would want to know why the missing food and what he'd been doing at home in the middle of the day devouring it.

She'd be back around five but that was all right. He'd explain that everyone had knocked off early for a bit of a do after hearing about their collective windfall. He wondered how she'd take the news. Torn two ways, was his guess. Hovering between delight at his discomfiture and annoyance at the sudden existence of a splinter group. He wouldn't put it past her to try buying some of them out. One sale would tip the voting balance her way. It would certainly be worth her while. The business was thriving and already worth double Berryman's original stake.

Andrew was trying not to dwell on this unpleasant example of Sod's law (to her that hath shall be given) when the Corey Panting interview began. He couldn't not listen. The whole business was connected to

Dennis, after all, as well as sounding really weird. Could this woman be genuine? Impossible. They were all fakes, necromancers. Be a funny old world if they weren't. Pretty scary, too. Andrew's spine felt suddenly tingly and cold. He shook his head and shoulders, shrugging off such a ridiculous notion. And laughed aloud, a cheery sound in the quiet kitchen. Then he drew a bentwood stool up to the worktop, took a deep swig of Lavazza's Crema e Gusto and settled down to be entertained.

Standing in the larder at Rainbow Lodge Karen was fretting about her tea. Nothing had changed since breakfast time. The same curling remnants of Kingsmill lay in the bread bin. And there was still a coating of peanut butter sticking to the otherwise empty jar. Karen scraped it on to a piece of bread, folded it over and crammed it into her mouth. Dry and stale, it almost choked her. She swallowed some water, then filled the kettle, plugged it in and wandered into the lounge.

'D'you want a drink, Ava?'

Her mother was lying on an old Put-u-up, feet draped over the arm, eyes closed. Pressing the palm of her hand to her forehead she gave an exquisite moan.

'Are you all right?' Karen hated picking up her cue so promptly but years of habit were hard to break.

'Just exhausted, darling. The press are so demanding.'

'I expect they are.' Karen's face and voice were expressionless. 'Did you do any shopping while you were out?'

'Shopping?'

'Only Roy'll want to eat when he comes in.'

The terms of their lodger's agreement supposedly covered his room, breakfast and supper. Fairly quickly his supper, which had started off in a quite hearty way with sausages or faggots or a little chicken curry in the microwave had dwindled, first to beans or an egg on toast and then to a piece of cake or a biscuit and a cup of tea. Ava calculated, rightly, that he would not complain. Where else would he find such comfortable accommodation so near London for seventy-odd pounds and no extras. And it was not as if he had fares to find. Roy travelled to and from Tesco each day on his moped.

'How did you think the broadcast went?' asked Ava.

'Brilliant,' said Karen, who had lost herself in a book and forgotten to switch on.

'They've asked me back. Want me to do a regular "slot", as they call it. Not strictly mystical.' She laughed in a light, merry way. 'I'll be talking about the theatre generally, reviewing new plays, probably interviewing stars.'

'In Uxbridge?' muttered Karen, now back in the kitchen and staring into the small, nearly empty freezer. There was a greyish-pink burger and a few frozen peas. Plus a tin of spaghetti in the cupboard under the sink.

'But if I give that to Roy,' pondered Karen, 'what'll I have?' She went back to the lounge, hovering in the doorway.

Ava gave an exaggerated wince and closed her eyes. Sometimes she found it hard to believe Karen was actually her child. Apart from the dreary plainness of her appearance she was just not intelligent. Bottom of the class in almost everything. Incredible to think her father had been to a public school. Sometimes Ava wondered if he had lied about that. God knows, he had lied about everything else. She turned her attention back to the television but was not allowed to enjoy it for long.

'Ava?'

'Look at him.' Ava shook her head, laughing. 'That Richard Whiteley.'

'Could we have some fish and chips to celebrate?'

'I must make contact. Get him on my show.'

'It's the Rumbling Tum, Wednesday.'

This mobile chippy came to Forbes Abbot once a week. It did only modest business in the village proper, where people were a bit shamefaced to be seen queuing at the counter and hurrying home with greasy parcels. But almost everyone in the Crescent would be buying. The fish and chips were excellent. Crisp and hot with little triangular boxes of tartare sauce for only twenty p extra. Roy had treated Karen one time and she thought she had never tasted anything so delicious.

'Ava?'

'Celebrate what?'

'Your new spot.'

'Slot.' But a little celebration was not a bad idea. She could afford it And it would stop Karen doing her starving waif act. Though Ava had to admit, grudgingly, that she did it very well. She was her mother's child and appeared to have inherited her remarkable acting talent. But, alas, none of her unstoppable drive. Bit of a waste really.

'What time do they come?'

'Oh, oh!' cried Karen, jumping up and down. 'Can we get some for Roy as well?'

Mallory, having had a brief respite from his paternal anxieties by immersing himself in a truly gripping historical novel discovered in the final post bag, was once more at a loose end. Kate had now started the book. He could see her at the end of the croquet lawn, lying in a hammock strung up between the catalpa trees. In the dappled light her blue and white dress was patterned with reflections from the trumpet-shaped flowers. But there was nothing dreamy about her pose. She was reading quickly, flipping the pages over, her profile alert and concentrated.

Mallory began to wander around the large, three-quarters empty house. The dealer from Aylesbury had returned that morning and most rooms were now practically empty. Everything in the kitchen stayed. Here they planned to replace stuff gradually – a decent fridge, some fitted cupboards, a dishwasher.

Mallory's continued anxiety about Polly quite blunted the sadness he had expected to feel as he watched his aunt's belongings carried away by indifferent hauliers. Beautiful things that he had been familiar with all his life. Furniture that he had slept on, hidden inside, rearranged to make forts or cars or planes or boats. Boxes of games, mirrors, pictures, ornaments, china. He ticked them all off the list with the man from Aylesbury and felt not a qualm.

As soon as the van drove away he went to the phone and rang Polly's number. Knowing how much this continual vigilance annoyed Kate he had taken to using the box in the village if she was in the house. Once or twice during the day and most evenings he would go out 'for a little stroll'. Sometimes he would manage to nip out and back before she realised he had gone.

But tomorrow – ah, tomorrow he should be able to go round to the flat in person. In the morning he and Kate planned to make a really early start, driving back to London to sort out any last-minute packing at Cordwainer Road. A final reading of the electricity meter and a telephone disconnection and they'd be all set to move out that day.

He wished they could leave now. He was sick of killing time, poodling about. He wanted to get on with life. To do something definite and practical, showing real results. Moving would definitely accomplish that. But he also believed, for no sensible reason at all, that once they were properly settled at Appleby House all manner of other things would quite suddenly be well. The Celandine Press would be properly set up and begin to function. He and Kate would get to know people and perhaps become involved in village affairs, as his aunt had been. His probably baseless worries about Polly would be resolved. Maybe she had just taken off somewhere with friends. Students do, after all. And now was the time for it. The autumn term didn't start for nearly six weeks.

He and Kate were taking Benny with them to London. They had talked this over and decided it was not wise to leave her alone in her present state. Also they were concerned as to what she might get up to. She had already boasted at lunch of one more visit to the police station and of laying new evidence as to Dennis's death before the CID. Her grip on reality seemed to be slackening by the minute. She didn't want to go. Mallory persuaded her by pretending that there was still so much to sort out at the other end that he doubted they'd be able to cope alone.

Now he wandered the desolate spaces on the ground floor of Appleby House with all these thoughts running endlessly round and round and round like a mouse in his skull. He needed to be with someone. To have a banal, pointless conversation. Benny seemed to have disappeared. Kate was reading. So Mallory came to wondering if the Parnells had got back from their mid-morning appointment at Harley Street. Earlier on they had left some spinach in the porch of Appleby House. He decided to return the basket and say 'thank you'.

No one seemed to hear his knock so Mallory just walked in. A furious tapping and clattering was coming from Judith's office as well as urgent wheezes from her fax machine. He put his head round the door and she directed a vivid strained grimace in his direction, which he decided was meant to be a smile. Then he was waved away.

Ashley was in the wicker armchair by the sitting-room window, reading *The Times*. Or rather, holding it in a listless manner while staring out at the raggle-taggle garden. Mallory wondered if the news from the specialist had not been good but hesitated to ask.

Ashley said, 'Listen to that.' There was a pause. The racket from Judith's office continued unabated. 'She's searching the Net.'

'For?'

'This Harley Street bloke gave us a list of clinics that specialise in treating my disease. France, Switzerland, America. Cuba, would you believe? So Judith's checking them out.'

'I hope it all works out.'

'Christ – so do I. I'm trying not to dwell on it, you know?'

Mallory silently thanked God he didn't know. The only pain he experienced was the dull ache of ongoing worry. Though he could feel it slowly grinding him down, at least it wouldn't finish him off. Then he remembered a book he'd read once called *More Die of Heartbreak* and couldn't help wondering.

The silence when the machines suddenly stopped, though beautiful, was brief. Judith burst in waving a piece of paper, crying: 'This is the place!' Followed by, 'Ah – Mallory.' The subtext – you still here? – was practically audible.

So Mallory found himself once again out in the fruitful, fragrant garden and easing his way through the broken wooden gate. Tired of the village street and the shop and the phone box and the duck pond he walked in the other direction, drawn by the sound of water babbling sweetly over stones.

But as he was passing the churchyard he heard a human voice, quietly murmuring to itself. He stepped up and over the low brick wall on to the soft grass, then walked towards the back of St Anselm's. Here were two new graves, both covered with wreaths. On the nearest the flowers were so fresh the colours shone. On the much smaller plot, containing Dennis's ashes, they were already half dead and turning brown.

Benny was sitting on a little fold-up stool of the type used in theatre queues. Sitting as near to the flowers as she possibly could without treading on them. She was pushing her head right down as if addressing not the dead but the merely deaf.

Concerned and anxious, Mallory moved nearer. He was not afraid of disturbing her. All her energy and concentration was focused on the square of dry brown earth. She wasn't crying, she didn't even look unhappy, just incredibly intense. Her voice, though it had an extremely urgent undertow, was muted and he could hardly make out the words, though now and again the odd one was suddenly clear. 'Promise . . .' he heard. 'Believe' and 'true'. Then 'authorities' and 'promise' again. And again.

His heart moved to pity, Mallory hesitated. He hated just to walk away. On the other hand, plainly this was something extremely private that Benny needed to do. Perhaps it was her own way of mourning. She had chosen a time in the late afternoon when the churchyard was empty and she might well become distressed at the discovery that someone had been watching. Mallory backed off silently, then turned to leave. As he did so a flock of rooks rose from the elms, cawing and croaking. Benny, scrambling to her feet and flinging both arms across her face, screamed.

'Benny . . .'

She jumped and cried out again, shrinking from him.

'It's all right, it's me. It's Mallory.' Gently he took her hand then tucked her trembling arm through his own. He kissed her cheek. It was cold as ice. 'Time for tea. We were wondering where you were.' Then, as she stood unmoving, staring at him, 'Come home, Ben.'

She came with him and not reluctantly. But as they neared the lych-gate she stopped and glanced back over her shoulder. It was a deeply worried look. 'Do you think he understood, Mallory?'

Mallory checked a sigh. What could he say? His tenderness for her sorrow was mingled with irritation that made him ashamed.

Ava was at the gate of Rainbow Lodge, wearing her floaty black and gold kaftan and ostensibly watching out for the Rumbling Tum. She had been in and out several times, to Roy and Karen's surprise, for Ava had never before shown the slightest interest in fish and chips. This was her fourth outing. So far there hadn't been a soul to notice her. No one in their garden, no one outside waiting for the chippy or gossiping over the fence. No one to hiss: 'There she is. Look – she was on the radio. You know? *Corey's People*? It was ever so good. Swayne Crescent's really going up in the world.' They nearly all listened to the local station. Ava tuned in to Radio Two but switched to Four if anyone called at the house or the phone rang.

Finally someone did emerge. The awful Mr Carboy at number seventeen, preparing to clean his Metro. Still, he was better than nothing. Ava waited until he was looking in her direction, then raised a gracious hand. He stared back for a moment, then threw a bucket of water over the car. Ava smiled ruefully and shook her head. How quickly she was being shown the underside to fame. But the resentment of little people with narrow, boring lives would soon be left behind. Her position at the Almeida would inevitably lead to other engagements. More and more people would know her name for she would insist on being listed in the programme as Spiritual Consultant. There would be other newspaper interviews but this time in the posh Sundays. 'A Life in the Day of . . .' One thing was for sure, she couldn't stay in this dump. Imagine Parkinson having to come to Rainbow Lodge. Or, even worse, Richard and Judy. Time to move on.

'Problem,' Karen was saying inside the house. 'I don't think we'll get three fish and chips for five pound. Chips are fifty p minimum and cod's really expensive.'

'Haddock's worse,' said Roy, now up, washed (well, a lick and a promise) and dressed. He had money in his pocket but this was supposed to be his supper, already paid for. Why should he chip in? Ha ha. 'Ask her for some more then.'

'She won't give me any more.'

'Yes, she will. Tell her you'll be shown up in front of the queue and they'll all be talking about how stingy she is.'

'That's a good idea.' Roy was better at this sort of thing than she was. Of course he was older and Ava wasn't his mother. 'But then she might just change her mind altogether.'

They looked gloomily at the table already set with three knives and forks, the rest of the curly bread, a tub of margarine and Sarson's vinegar.

Karen made a worried sound. She could never understand why they were so poor. She knew what her mother got from the social for the two of them because she'd seen the books. And there was Roy's contribution as well as the collection from the church. But last week, when her socks had gone into holes and she'd asked for some more, Ava had shouted, 'D'you think I'm made of money?' That same night Karen saw her mother in a dream and she really had been made of money. She was standing very still like a dummy in a shop window and was stuck all over with notes. She had a long tongue made of copper that rolled and unrolled all the time, like a frog's. And her breath was a mist of gold.

'Are you listening?'

'Sorry, Roy.'

'I said, alternatively . . .' He got up and went over to the sink. On the windowsill, cleverly concealed behind the curtain and so plainly visible to anyone walking up the garden path, was Ava's purse. He opened it and waved a second note in the air.

'We can't do that!'

'She owes me.'

'I'll get the blame. I'll be in terrible trouble.'

Roy, recognising the truth in this, replaced the note and returned to the table, digging in to his own pocket. What else could he do?

Ava, half through the door but speaking backwards loudly: 'I'm expecting a message from the theatre any minute.' Then she came inside and continued in her normal voice. 'I rang their admin number earlier to check on the *Blithe Spirit* schedule but all I got was an answerphone. You'd think a top venue like that would be a bit more on the kew veeve.'

'They'll ring back,' said Karen.

'Naturally. But, just in case I'm in the la-la, say, "Mrs Garret's on the other line," and tell them to hold.'

'What if they won't?'

'I think I'm calling the shots on this one, Roy.' Ava smiled. 'Did you hear my broadcast?'

''Course I did.' Load of crap it was, an' all. 'Took a late lunch and listened on the tranny.'

'What did George say about it?' asked Karen. She really liked George. He was always buying her sweets and crisps, which her mother had promised it was perfectly OK to accept. It had taken Ava all of five seconds accurately to sum up George's sexuality as nil and his masculinity as minus ten.

'Ah,' she sighed now. 'Poor fellow. I'm afraid he won't be representing me in future.'

'Why not?' cried Karen.

'It's a matter of savoir faire, really,' said Ava. 'That and contacts. I tried to let him down lightly.'

It hadn't been pleasant. George had done a lot of bleating about how much he had done for her and how loyal he'd been.

Ava had replied, 'Loyal doesn't cut it with me, George.' Then, when he had protested further, 'If I'd wanted loyal I'd've got a dog.' At this point in her present reflections the telephone rang.

'That's them,' cried Ava. 'I mean, they. Quick –' she seized Karen, dragged her from the table, pinching her arm – 'answer it.'

'Me?'

'Find out who it is. Say you're Ava Garret's secretary.'

'Ow – that hurts.'

'Just do it.'

Karen, her eyes watering, picked up the phone. 'Hello. This is Ava Garret's secrety. Who is calling, please?' She stared at the other two, then covered the mouthpiece with her hand. 'It's the BBC.'

Ava gave a single sharp intake of breath. She murmured, 'So soon' and began to walk with slow, fate-filled steps across the room.

'This is Ava Garret herself, in person. How may I help you? . . . I'd be happy to, though I am rather overwhelmed with . . . I see. Just a preliminary chat? Well, I'm sure I can fit that in . . .' Frantic silent mouthings: 'Paper, paper . . . pen, pen.' Roy grabbed a double-glazing leaflet and a pencil stub.

'Your name is . . . yes, got that . . . I am as it happens . . .' She glanced at the kitchen clock. 'Seven would be fine . . . And will that be at the "Beeb", as I believe you media people call it? . . . Langham Place. Near Oxford Circus . . . Reception desk . . . Oh! That is a good idea. Just in case, quite. Una momento . . .' More mouthing: 'Mobile, mobile . . . quick . . . quick . . .'

Karen passed over her phone. Ava dictated her number and said her goodbyes. She turned to the others with great solemnity. 'This must be he.'

'Who?'

'The stranger who will broaden my horizons.'

'Thought that was Corey Panting,' said Roy.

'He wants to take me out to dinner.'

'You're going to be R and F all right.'

'You know what this means, Karen?'

Karen didn't speak. She hoped it didn't mean that she was going to have to pretend to be her mother's sister's child like she had when Ava joined the divorced and separated club. 'Just in case,' Ava had explained, 'I meet somebody.' Karen often used to wonder what would happen to her if Ava, suddenly ten years lighter, actually did meet somebody. Especially as no sister ever existed. Before she could respond to her mother's question Roy shouted, 'The chippie's here!'

Karen pushed her chair back and ran out. Ava hurried after, paused briefly at the gate, then called loudly, 'None for me, darling. I'll be dining at the BBC.' She smiled graciously on her return at Roy. She could afford to smile now she would soon be seeing the back of him. 'One could hardly arrive smelling of fish and chips.'

'You could wear some scent,' suggested Roy. 'Ivy at work reckons a squirt of pong's worth a pound of soap.'

'Does she really?' said Ava. God – how had she stood it? Look at him. Spots, greasy hair, spindly arms and legs, tattoos, all those dangling rings. He even had them in his nose like a prize bull, except that Roy would never win a prize unless it was for the dimmest, most charmless male animal in the entire universe. He wasn't even properly clean.

'How're you getting there?'

'Not sure.' Ava glanced at the clock. It was 5.15. How hasty she had been. How foolish. She should have thought it through; asked for a later time.

'He'll wait,' said Roy. 'He works there.'

'As a senior producer, I expect he does.'

'Best thing is the Piccadilly Line from Uxbridge. Straight through to the Circus. Ten-minute walk up Regent Street, you're there.'

'How do you know?'

'They took a group of us from the home once. One Satday morning.'

More waste of public money, thought Ava, hurrying upstairs. What on earth was the point – she riffled through her wardrobe – of exposing the dregs of society to a fine institution like the BBC? Her mustard two-piece (a quick sniff under the arms) would just about pass. What a pity this invitation hadn't come after she'd bought all her new things. Such a thought recalled her recent windfall. She took an envelope stuffed with notes from her underwear drawer and peeled off fifty pounds. About to replace the rest she hesitated. The drawer had no lock and with the two of them on their own rootling about . . . Roy especially she wouldn't trust. She often wondered just how much of the church money made its way out of the velvet collecting bag and into his pockets. She slid the envelope under the mattress.

No time to make up. She'd have to do that when she got there. There was bound to be a ladies at the Tube station or near by. Her hair was a mess too, but that was easily solved. She would wear her auburn peruke, short and curly and quite youthifying in a gamine kind of way.

When she got downstairs they were both feeding their faces. There was a huge bottle of orange-coloured pop on the table and pickled eggs in a dish.

'I see you've not stinted yourselves.'

'I paid for those,' said Roy. 'Here's your change.'

Ava scooped it up.

Karen said, 'You look really nice.'

Roy didn't say anything. He thought she looked like a long streak of piss with a wig on.

'I don't know when I'll be back,' said Ava. 'Chris and I are bound to have heaps to talk about.' She was tempted to say, 'And no poking around in my room,' but didn't want to put the idea into their heads.

'Shouldn't you take this?' Roy held out the leaflet. 'In case you forget his name.'

'I'm hardly likely to do that.' But Ava took the paper, just in case. 'Don't stay up late, Karen. When Roy leaves for work you go straight to bed.'

'But that's only nine o'clock.'

'And don't think I shan't know.'

They sat quite still until the car drove off. Karen, her head nervously straining towards the window; Roy with a forkful of batter bits suspended halfway to his mouth. Only when the sound had died away did they carry on eating.

'That was fantastic.' Karen, her shrunken stomach bulging, finally laid her cutlery down. 'I was really hungry.'

I bet you were, you poor little sod. 'Shall we see what's on the box then?'

'You said yesterday we could rehearse your jokes.'

'No, I didn't.'

'You did, Roy. You promised.'

'Anyway, you never laugh.'

'I will today.'

'And they're not jokes. Stand-up comedy is . . .' He could never remember the word. It meant hanging around watching and listening to what people said. 'More like proper life.'

'If you get tired, can you do sit-down comedy?'

Roy was pretty confident he could succeed in the entertainment business because they were always laughing at him at work. To get the hang of it he'd been going to a pub with a room upstairs where anybody could have a go on Saturday night. He couldn't get over how easy it looked. This bloke had just stood there droning on about how hard it was to get a decent shag and they were all wetting themselves.

At the back of Roy's mind always, and at the front of his mind most of the time, was the idea that when he really made it, perhaps when he won *Stars in Their Eyes* he would find his mother again. She would be watching and she'd know him because mothers always recognised their own children, no matter how long it had been. Alone, he would rehearse their meeting, perfect the cracking brightness of his smile.

'Roy?' Karen was shaking his arm. 'Can I look at one of your magazines?'

'No.'

'Why?'

'They're too old for you.'

'No, they're not.'

'Which one d'you want then?'

'The one with men in little skirts with birds' heads walking sideways.'

'That's the Egyptians. They were dead mystic.'

'Like the Knights Templar?'

'Nobody's as mystic as the Knights Templar. They'd walk round for hours and hours in a weird sort of trance.'

'I still like the Egyptians best.' Karen poured some more orangeade and smiled. A rare sight. Indeed, a sorry sight. 'Tell me about the mystery of the Sphinx, Roy. Go on.'

'You'll only get all worked up.'

'No, I won't.'

'Last time you couldn't go to sleep.'

'Tell me about the wonderful rose crystal in its bottom. And the evil green stone of Set.'

CHAPTER SIXTEEN

It was mid-morning when Kate put her key in the door of 13 Cordwainer Road. Benny, who had not been there before, was very disappointed. As they were driving through streets of shops and terraced houses she kept looking out for a sudden change in the landscape, for the beginning of spacious semi-detached dwellings with gardens and garages; the sort of home she had always pictured Kate and Mallory living in.

Kate unpacked the fresh milk she had brought and made some tea while Mallory picked up the post in the hall. Nearly all flyers – they had already sent out change-of-address cards to family and friends – there was one personal letter, which was from the new owners. Apparently there had been some hold-up on the transportation of their furniture from Hong Kong and they wouldn't actually be moving in for another couple of weeks. As this would hardly affect the Lawsons one way or the other, Mallory dropped the note into the bin with the rest of the junk mail. Then, as the tea brewed, he and Kate looked around the sitting room in some dismay.

'Didn't we say we weren't going to take that?' He was staring at a stained oak bureau that had belonged to his parents.

'Yes,' said Kate. 'That and the zinc table and chairs outside and the big painted cupboard in the back bedroom.'

'That's right. You were going to ring house clearance.'

'We, Mallory. We were going to ring house clearance.'

'You see, Ben?' Mallory picked up the Yellow Pages. 'Can't manage without you.' He looked up the relevant section. 'Try all these people and say we've some stuff to clear. But they have to collect from this address,' he scrawled it across the page, 'by mid-afternoon.'

'What if no one can come?' worried Benny.

'Then we'll send it with the rest of the stuff and sell it down there.'

Kate, pouring the tea, stared round gloomily. 'I can't get over all these wretched pots and pans. I thought I'd packed everything.'

'There's still some space in this box.'

'Not half enough.'

'Also, there's Polly's room,' said Mallory. 'She should really be here.'

He had rung Polly's number just before they left Appleby House. Dialling carefully, waiting and waiting while Kate stood by expressionless, feeling her face might crack. And what were they talking about? Two shelves of books and enough clothes to fill a bin liner.

'Polly?' Benny had stopped dialling. 'She's on holiday.'

191

'Holiday?'

'In Crete. With friends.'

'How do you know?' The rush of relief almost knocked Mallory off balance.

'They rang when she was down at Forbes Abbot the other week. She went out to meet them. To make final arrangements.'

'There you are, Mal,' said Kate. 'Now, can we get on?'

'What?'

'We need boxes from the nearest supermarket. Then we have to pack as much as we can of the rest of the stuff before the removal men get here. The van's due at one.'

'Right.'

'Hello? Hello – is that –' Benny screwed her eyes up at the Yellow Pages – 'Mr Tallis? . . . Oh, Frank. Well, I'm Benny . . . Fine thank you, Frank. I hope you are too? Now, there's some lovely furniture here for clearing . . . Thirteen Cordwainer Road. Parsons Green, that's right. Would you be able to come and have a look, only it has to be today?'

Kate caught Mallory's eye. Both smiled over Benny's head, awkwardness and suspicion dissolving in the glance. Kate thought, this time tomorrow we'll be home with a capital H, then everything will be transformed.

Mallory thought, all that anxiety over nothing. There'll probably be a postcard any day now. Even as he pictured it arriving Mallory felt the notches in the belt of anxiety around his chest begin to slip and slide. His breathing slowed down. His heartbeat softened.

Benny replaced the receiver. 'Frank'll be round in half an hour.'

'Thanks a lot, Ben,' said Mallory. He just stopped himself saying, 'Well done.' She wasn't a child, although the look of pride in her accomplishment might lead one to wonder.

Actually Benny was already thinking of something entirely different. She was recalling her visit last night to Doris's house and pondering on what a stroke of luck it had been that her friend listened to the local radio station. Having heard an advance announcement of the Ava Garret interview Doris just had time to get her neighbour to record the programme. Listening, Benny realised that she had been right to place such confidence in the medium. How forthright Ava sounded. How vividly she described the communication between herself and the spirit of Dennis Brinkley. And how convincing her promises that their next dialogue would bring forth even more dramatic revelations as to the manner of his death. She should have been on the stage, thought Benny, nodding with satisfaction as the machine was finally switched off. You'd never have guessed that, from start to finish, the whole business was nothing but a pack of lies.

* * *

The rest of the morning went so smoothly that Kate found herself poised and waiting for the other shoe to drop. They decided to have toast and tinned soup in the garden, sitting on the grass, as the zinc chairs and table had been snapped up, along with all the other unwanted furniture, by Frank Tallis.

As they were stacking their bowls and plates, Kate spotted in the longish grass a small flowerpot decorated with a glaze of blue and yellow irises. She cried: 'Look! Look!' and seized the pot, wrapping it in newspaper and wedging it into one of the cardboard boxes they had collected from Sainsbury's.

'That is just so lucky. I would have hated to lose it.'

'It's an omen,' said Benny. 'You'll see.'

The serendipity continued. The removal van arrived a few minutes early. The men were amiable, polite and efficient. Quite quickly the house was emptied of all it contained.

The occupants did not linger. Mallory left to bring the car to the front door. Benny poured the remaining milk down the sink. Kate stood looking round the sitting room where she and Mallory had spent nearly every evening for the past nine years. She felt nothing. A box to live in, merely. Now they were going home.

'You all right, Ben?'

Benny, quiet for a moment, blew her nose on a lace hanky. 'Mmm.'

Kate linked arms, squeezing Benny closely against her side. How thoughtless she had been. Content in her own happiness, she had quite forgotten that Benny was returning to a village now bereft of her oldest and dearest friend. At once Kate vowed to love and care for Benny always, whatever the circumstances. They had heard no talk for some days about Dennis's murder and Kate hoped all that nonsense was over. But if it wasn't she would be very patient and try to understand and nurse Benny back to equanimity.

Outside Mallory hooted. As they left, Kate carrying the keys to drop off at the estate agents, the back doors of the van were being fastened and secured. The Lawsons, taking short cuts and nippy sideroads, would arrive at Appleby House first. In case of hold-ups or accident Judith and Ashley, who also had a list of what furniture went where, would let the removal men in.

But, of course, there would be no accident. It simply wasn't that sort of day. The interior of the Golf was already hot and Mallory wound the windows down. He smiled at Kate, who smiled back, then they both smiled at Benny. Kate began to feel she was in one of those uplifting Hollywood movies full of good, shining people committed to the eternal promise of the yellow brick road. Even the removal men could have stood in for the Cheeryble brothers. Then, jumping into her clear, calm, unworried mind came a vivid image of a mile-high dinosaur, flames gushing from its gaping jaws. It reared up directly in their path, blocking the way.

Of course, it wasn't true. The Fulham Road was going about its normal business. So where do they come from, these sudden visions? wondered Kate. These fearful eruptions crashing through the wall of the mind? Unlike Benny she did not believe in omens. Such superstitious nonsense could have no place in an ordered and rational life. All the same, she found herself unable to regain her previous calm and happy state of mind until they had all arrived safely at Forbes Abbot.

At seven o'clock when the Lawsons were setting off for London, Karen was waking up at Rainbow Lodge. She always did this as slowly as possible to keep the world out. During her first weeks at primary school, a teacher had read aloud *The Sleeping Beauty*. Karen was entranced. Could such a thing really be possible? To fall asleep for years and years and wake up grown up and in the arms of a handsome prince who truly loved you?

That night she had looked everywhere for a needle but no such thing was to be found. Eventually she came across a brooch with a sharp pin and pushed it so hard into her thumb it really hurt. Fairy-tale oblivion proved elusive but eventually Karen drifted off, only to wake at the usual time with blood on her pillow. Her mother had been very, very cross and Karen had to make up a story about her tooth bleeding in the night.

Now she swung her thin legs out of bed, resting none-too-clean feet on the bare lino. She scratched her head, then sniffed under her arms. It was definitely whiffy there, and down below was even more so. She knew a shower was indicated but this could be a risky business. Installed by her grandfather years ago, the system consisted of an immovable zinc shower head the size of a dinner plate and a single tap that turned both ways, producing a violent rush of either boiling or ice-cold water. Trying to catch the transforming moment meant a constant leaping in and out of the cabinet. Baths were considered an extravagance, though Ava was compelled to have one every day to refresh her aura.

Karen put on a dressing gown and crept out on to the landing. There was no sound from Ava's room. She had come to bed pretty late. Karen had heard her, stumbling on the stairs and muttering to herself. Once she had called Karen's name. Karen didn't respond. Just thought how like her mother to say, 'Get to bed early' before she went out, then deliberately wake you up in the middle of the night. No doubt she wanted to show off about what a wonderful day she'd had being famous. Well, Karen didn't want to listen. Ava had never wanted to know about her day. Never wanted to hear her read. She hadn't even come to see the Christmas play when Karen had been second page to an Orient king. So Karen had put her head under the bedclothes and pretended to snore.

The kitchen was depressing and still smelled of fish and chips. Neither she nor Roy had bothered to wash up, and greasy paper was still crumpled all over the table. A solitary pickled egg lay in a puddle of vinegar. It was gone seven. Roy would be home any minute, wanting his breakfast unless there had been some unsold sandwiches left over, as sometimes happened. Karen had gone to school one glorious morning on a Full English Breakfast baguette: sausage, bacon, egg, tomato – plus a jam doughnut and Smarties ice-cream lolly.

She stuffed the newspaper in a carrier bag, put the glasses and dirty plates in the sink, then filled the kettle to make some tea. As it came to the boil she heard Roy's moped coughing and chuffing outside. He lifted the latch and walked in.

'Wotcha.'

'Got anything nice, Roy?'

I should get the family allowance for this one, thought Roy, not that tight old cow upstairs.

'Coupla wafers.' He passed over the Jacob Clubs.

'Oohh, mint. They're my favourite.' Karen lifted the heavy kettle with both hands, filled the pot and gave it a stir. 'Um . . . are there any sandwiches?'

'Not today, love.'

'Remember those croissants you brought once? The ones with chocolate inside.'

'Do I?' He had produced a pack of four. Gut bucket had wolfed three before he'd even got his arse up to the table. He and Karen had shared the last. Now she was putting some mugs out. Roy jerked his head towards the stairs. 'Shall I give madam a call?'

Karen shrugged. She would much rather it was just her and Roy. On the other hand, Ava might come down anyway, then there'd be a lecture on how some people certainly knew how to look after themselves when others not a million miles away were lying desperate for a cuppa and parched to the bone.

Roy went to the bottom of the stairs. He shouted, 'Tea up!' Waited. Shouted again. Then said, 'I'll give her a knock.'

Karen was putting three sugars in Roy's tea when he cried out for the third time. This was a different sound. Quite panicky, as if the house was on fire. Frightened, Karen ran to the stairs and met him coming down.

'Don't go up there, Karen.'

'What is it? What's the matter?'

'Your mum's poorly.' He couldn't bring himself to say the right word. He just couldn't do it. 'We'll have to get an ambulance.'

'Wouldn't the doctor do?'

'Not this time, love.'

Ava had apparently died in her sleep. Roy met the paramedics on the doorstep, relieved to see that one of them was a woman. He told her what had happened. Asked her to break it to Karen. You could see she didn't like the idea but Roy said he couldn't bear to do it and there was no one else.

They went into the front room. Roy hovered, listening. He could see the woman putting her arms round Karen, holding her close, talking softly. They rocked, backwards and forwards for a little while. Karen started to cry and murmur, 'What'll I do without her? What'll I do?' They were huddled together on the sofa when the other paramedic, whose name was Gordon Phillips, came downstairs.

'You find her . . . erm . . .?'

'Roy.'

'Must have been a shock. You OK?'

Roy shrugged. He had seen a dead person before. More than once. Last time was a couple of years ago. He'd been out with a gang in Mumps Turvey and they'd come across the body of a tramp lying in a ditch. The others had decided to have a bit of fun setting fire to it and called Roy chicken when he ran off.

'And her name?'

'Sorry? Oh – Ava Garret.'

'Miss? Mrs?'

'Mrs, so she said.'

'You live here?'

'I'm the lodger.'

'So you'd know something about her?' He paused. 'State of health, for instance. Was she on tablets for anything? Heart, blood pressure?'

'Dunno.'

Gordon gave Roy a severe once-over. What did he think he looked like? Greasy hair standing in spikes. A T-shirt flashing a skull, slime dripping from its eye sockets over a 'Satan Rules' logo. Ears smothered in metal rings plus one in each nostril joined by a silver chain. I wouldn't like to be near that bloke when he starts sneezing, thought Gordon. They should put scum like that in the army. He had a pleasurable vision of Roy forcibly scoured, scrubbed and shiny-booted, marching in step.

'Sometimes she took vitamins.'

Roy had a pretty good idea what Gordon was thinking. He was often looked at exactly so and would have been disappointed if he hadn't been. His own pleasurable vision was of the great god Set springing through the window, seizing Gordon's round face and sparse hair in his massive jaws and biting his head off.

'Next of kin?' asked Gordon.

'Pardon?'

'Is there a dad around?'

'No.'

'Brothers or sisters.'

Roy shook his head.

'Better get in touch with the social.'

'The social.' The words were thick with disgust. Disgust and fear.

'Well, she can't stay here on her own.'

196

'Someone'll come . . . a relative . . . her aunty.'

'Tell them, not me.'

Roy followed Gordon into the sitting room. Karen was sitting up very straight, holding her knees. Roy would not have thought her milk-white skin could get any paler. But now it appeared completely colourless. On her high, bumpy forehead a twisted vein stood out, turquoise colour, like a wriggly worm.

Gordon beckoned to the other paramedic, then whispered to Roy, 'Keep this door closed till we've got her through, OK?'

'Sure.'

'You'll need to collect the death certificate. Great Missenden Hospital.'

'Will do.'

'Better ring before you go. They'll be doing a PM first.'

Roy sat with Karen and neither spoke till they heard the ambulance drive away. Roy, though relieved to see Karen was no longer crying, was still alarmed by her appearance. She seized his hand in both of hers, squeezing and mangling it.

'Look, Karen. I know this has only just happened—'

'Roy, what shall I do, Roy?'

'—but I've got to talk to you.'

'How shall I manage? Roy, my head hurts.'

'*Listen*. This is important. Before anyone comes round—'

'Who's coming? Who?'

'Bloody listen, will you?'

'All right.'

'The ambulance man might just decide to let the social know. And they won't let you stay here by yourself.'

'I'm not by myself.'

'I don't count. What'll happen – they'll get a court order and you'll be put into care.'

'Care.' Karen dwelled on the word for a moment, wonderingly and with interest. It could have been the first step in a new language. She repeated it thoughtfully. 'Care sounds good.'

'Well, it ain't. It's very bad.'

'Why is it called care, then?'

'They got a warped sense of humour, the social.'

'Oh, Roy.'

'Don't cry – I'll get it sorted. Only we got to find you an aunty.'

'I haven't got an aunty.'

'Not a real one, stupid. We just pretend one's coming, like straight away.'

'I can't pretend. I shan't know what to say.'

'Don't say anything. I'll do the talking – OK?'

'Won't they come back and check up?'

'Then we'll just have to duck and dive.'

He tried to sound confident. Fortunately there was so much trouble in the world that if the social worker thought you were properly fixed chances were you'd be left in peace while she got to grips with the next load of human misery. On the other hand, there'd been some terrible stories in the paper lately where kids had actually died and when this happened everything tightened up for a bit. So, chances were, they'd probably want to see this aunty. Talk to her. Find out if she was a suitable person and all that. Ah, shit.

'Roy . . .?' Karen's hand crept into his like a small mammal seeking shelter. 'It will be all right, won't it?'

Roy looked down at her. It'd have to be all right. Somehow he'd make it all right. The thought of her shoved in a home – skinny, frightened, small for her age, friendless. Born to be knocked about and made use of. There'd be somebody's hand in her knickers before the door slammed shut. Roy had been there. He had lived that. It shouldn't happen to a dog.

'No worries, sweetheart. Everything's going to be absolutely fine.'

A village worthy had drawn Ava's recent broadcast to the attention of Brigadier Gervase Wemyss-Moleseed and his wife Marjorie, leaders of the Parish Council. Though highly indignant on receipt of the information, they were not at all surprised. The Council had always considered the Church of the Near at Hand a blot on their exquisitely maintained landscape. They were constantly sending letters to the organisation's representatives, informing them that their rusty shingles were a disgrace and asking when the broken window would be replaced. Now, as if that wasn't enough, one of their congregation was deliberately drawing attention to herself in a most unpleasant way. Pretending to have made contact with a recently deceased inhabitant of Forbes Abbot was bad enough. But to start dispensing messages of unspeakable vulgarity via his so-called spirit . . .

Thank God, as the vicar said at a hastily convened emergency meeting, the excellent Mr Brinkley was not alive to hear it. It was agreed that the brigadier should write a strongly worded letter to the *Causton Echo* dissociating the undersigned, a disappointing eleven signatures in all, from such 'flaunting, brazen exhibitionism'. He delivered the letter personally within the hour, urging publication at once, if not sooner.

But then, the very next morning, Ava was found to have died. While this was all round Swayne Crescent in ten seconds flat, it took a while to filter through to the smart end of the village. The brigadier was proudly showing off his letter in the early edition of the *Echo* to the landlord of the Horse and Hounds, only to be informed that the mystical Mrs Garret was no more. An unpleasant silence followed him out of the pub. At St Anselm's Rectory he was also rather coolly received. The vicar who, in his role as impartial shepherd, had declined to add his name to the list of dissidents, said it was all very unfortunate. He went so far as to add that writing the letter made them all sound like heartless snobs.

Furiously the brigadier protested that he had been a heartless snob all his life and it had never seemed to trouble anyone before. Perhaps the vicar would prefer someone else read the lesson at morning service?

Doris heard the news just after breakfast from Pauline next door, whose daughter, married to Fred Carboy, had seen the ambulance. Her immediate thoughts were for Karen. Would someone be with her? Someone, that is, apart from that gormless lad who lodged there. Doris's first impulse was to go straight round to Rainbow Lodge but she was afraid how that might look. It's not as if she was a relative. Or even a family friend. She put a voice to her worries.

'I don't want people thinking I'm one of them ghouls like you see on the telly, Ernie.'

'You worried about the kiddie, you check 'em out.'

'D'you think I should?'

'I know one thing. Neither of us'll have any peace till you do.'

So Doris did. Ignoring the twitching curtains and saying a pleasant 'good morning' to anyone out and about, she went up to Rainbow Lodge and knocked firmly on the front door.

Roy, who had heard the gate go, seized Karen's hand and dragged her under the table. The cloth nearly touched the floor so they couldn't be seen from the windows. Whoever it was knocked again, waited a couple of minutes then walked away.

'D'you think it was the social, Roy?'

'Maybe. Whoever it was – they'll be back.'

When Doris arrived home she couldn't settle. Even though she now knew that Rainbow Lodge was empty and Karen presumably being looked after, the little girl was still on her mind. She was always so lost-looking. So thin and lonely. A motherless child should have very special care. And lots of love.

To take her mind off all this Doris toyed with giving Benny in London the news of Ava's death. But then, remembering Mrs Lawson's earlier scepticism and the dumping of the *Echo* in the rubbish bin, she thought she might get her friend into trouble. And, in any case, they'd probably already left to follow the removal van down.

Doris got through the rest of the day, having a good house clean. All the nets went into the washing machine. Then she polished the windows, waxed everything waxable, beat all the rugs and chivvied poor Ernest to such an extent that in the end he went off to feed the ducks and get a bit of peace.

Early evening Doris thought she'd try Appleby House and was delighted to see Benny outside on the pavement. With her hand shading her eyes against the sun Benny was scanning the far horizon like a mariner seeking land. Doris called out and Benny turned round.

'I'm watching out for the removal van.' Then, sounding very excited. 'Doris, you'll never guess. I sold some furniture. Did a ring round – you know? Yellow pages.'

'Listen, Ben.' Doris took her friend's arm and walked her a little way from the gate. To the low wall in front of the church, in fact. 'There's some bad news.'

Benny did not look nearly as alarmed or distressed as Doris expected. She did not appreciate that having recently received the worse news of her entire life, and in the most appalling manner imaginable, anything that followed for Benny must be a far lesser evil.

'Let's sit down.'

'Heavens,' said Benny. It had only been twenty-four hours since she'd last seen Doris. What on earth could have happened in such a short time to make her look so grave? 'It's not something at home?'

'No, no. Please . . .' She pulled at Benny's sleeve and they bumped down on to the low wall together. 'The thing is, Ava's died.'

Benny stared, incredulous. Seconds passed, then a whole minute and she still seemed incapable of speech.

'Ben?'

'What happened? I mean . . . how . . .?'

'No one seems to know.' Doris, genuinely regretful at the skimpiness of the detail on offer, concluded, 'Probably some sort of heart attack.'

'That's terrible,' said Benny. 'We were going to hear the second half of the prophecy on Sunday.'

'What prophecy?'

'Surely you remember?' Benny sounded really put out. 'Last week she got up to just before Dennis died.'

'Of course I remember that.'

'This week she was going to describe the actual murder.'

Here we go again, thought Doris.

'She said so on the radio.'

'That wouldn't be for sure, though, would it, love? I mean – you can't swear on these things in advance.' Doris spoke hesitantly.

Benny was looking crosser by the minute. She didn't seem at all upset that the medium had passed away. Just thwarted. Doris felt some expression of sympathy might have been in order.

Perhaps thinking to provoke one she said, 'I'm a bit concerned about her little girl.'

'What am I supposed to do now?' replied Benny, getting up and walking away.

Doris hesitated. She felt bewildered and uneasy. She wanted to continue the conversation, mainly to find out what that last remark meant. Why on earth should Benny have to do anything just because of this woman's death? It wasn't as if there was any connection between them. So far as Doris knew they hadn't even met. Consumed with curiosity, and knowing she couldn't bear to go away with it unsatisfied, Doris decided to follow Benny into Appleby House. She could say she had come to offer help. An extra pair of hands was always useful.

Journalists on the *Echo* may not have been in the same league as Fleet Street's finest but they recognised a startling coincidence when it stared them in the face. A tip-off from someone working at Great Missenden Hospital, once properly confirmed, gave them the headline: 'Mysterious Death of Local Clairvoyant'. Their own fervid imaginations supplied the following paragraphs, the gist of which was, did some human hand intervene to prevent the medium spilling the celestial beans?

It was still not a criminal story so normally would never have been brought to DCI Barnaby's attention. But his bag carrier, laying siege to a divinely pretty policewoman in reception, spotted the newspaper, recognised the link with Benny Frayle's visits and took it straight upstairs.

Barnaby sat behind his desk, glowering. His domestic life, contentment unlimited in nearly every aspect bar the culinary, had suddenly taken a turn for the worse. Joyce, the wife of his bosom and he would have no other, had suddenly taken it into her head that they should become vegetarian. It had taken a good twenty years before she had been able to produce a piece of meat that you could break up and swallow without the aid of a Black and Decker and now she wanted to give this hard-acquired talent up. Already Barnaby was looking back almost wistfully to the time when he had rejected charcoal grilled chops, convinced he had been served the charcoal by mistake because last night, last night had been the absolute end. Elephant's ears made with scooped out aubergines stuffed with semi-raw chestnuts and garlic. If they'd been from a real elephant, Barnaby had protested, they couldn't have tasted worse.

And now here was Troy, placing a paper on the desk and standing back almost quivering with pride, like a gun dog delivering a pheasant. The word 'pheasant' cut Barnaby unpleasantly to the quick.

'What is it?'

'The *Echo*, Chief.'

'I can see it's the *Echo*. Why are you giving it to me?'

'You remember the old biddy who kept coming in about this bloke and his weird machines?'

'Only as I'd remember a plague of boils.'

Blimey. Better watch your step today, Gavin. 'That medium she was on about's been found dead.'

'So?'

Troy wondered aloud if perhaps the chief hadn't heard about Ava Garret's radio interview? The sergeant only knew of it himself because Maureen and her mother had still been pulling the programme to pieces when he arrived home. Troy was furious at the sight and sound of Mrs Sproat. There had been a definite agreement between himself and Maureen that she would only visit when he was out. Mrs Sproat's novel take on personal hygiene (if it don't smell why wash it?) was only one of the reasons. Troy drank his tea to the accompaniment of his mother-in-law's screaming falsetto and thought Anthony Perkins hadn't known when he was well off.

Barnaby said that he did know about the interview. Joyce picked it up on the car radio and had talked about it after supper. They had been together in the rose arbour in the late sunshine. Joyce in the hammock with her legs up, Barnaby in a wicker chair grumbling over an article on heavy-handed policing in the *Independent* and getting up from time to time to zap greenfly with a foul-smelling spray.

'She sounded strange,' Joyce had said. 'Bragging non-stop but kind of sad as well.'

'Gotcha.'

'Do you think any of this spiritual trancey stuff is true?'

'For God's sake . . .' Barnaby was disbelieving. Almost contemptuous.

'It could be.'

'No, it couldn't.'

'She also said she'd been engaged by the Almeida – you know Cully's company – as advisor on *Blithe Spirit*.'

'Mad as well as sad then.'

Joyce went off in a huff after this, saying he had spoiled everything, what with making the roses smell of disinfectant, and sneering. Barnaby went on drenching the Ena Harkness, ending up with an irritable sinus and the beginnings of a headache. So he was hardly now in the mood to indulge in yet further discussion of such ludicrous twaddle.

'But don't you think, sir,' persisted Troy, 'that it's a mysterious coincidence? Just days before she was going to give the murderer away.'

'You been watching *Poirot* again?'

This was one of the chief's favourite gibes. Troy had only ever seen one episode and that was round at his mother's. He had been a fool to mention it. And even more stupid to follow up with a lumbering joke about having enough little grey cells in his life as it was, thank you. Being a policeman, ha ha ha. Yes, he had laughed as well but he had laughed alone.

'She died in her sleep.' Barnaby, having glanced at the story, pushed the paper aside. 'What's mysterious about that?'

To be honest Troy had always thought such a happening was incredibly mysterious. People were always going on about how terrible death was but it seemed to him that it couldn't be all that dreadful if it could happen while you were asleep without waking you up. Also, if death was such crap, why were skulls always grinning?

'They'll have done a PM by now,' continued Barnaby. 'We'll be informed if they find anything.'

Troy, recognising a lost cause, was now eager to get back downstairs. He made his way indirectly. A diagonal shuffle towards the filing cabinets.

A little sidestep to study the black-and-whites relating to the Badger's Drift case, now superfluous as the man had just been caught. A sudden nip to the coat-stand where he absently ran through his jacket pockets. One more manoeuvre and he'd be home and dry.

'Don't think you're sidling off,' said Barnaby.

'Pardon?' Troy could not have been more bewildered.

'I know what you're up to.'

Troy's puzzlement deepened. Plainly all this was beyond him.

'Chatting up that new WPC.'

'Me?' Puzzlement gave way to astonishment so profound he might have been accused of making advances to the force's mascot, a comely goat named Ermintrude.

'What's-her-name Carter.'

'Abby Rose.' Damn. But he couldn't resist saying it aloud. 'Her dad was a Beatles fan.'

'What would Maureen say?'

'We're going through a difficult time at the moment.'

'That sort of thing won't make it any better.'

'More than difficult, actually. For two pins . . .'

Troy didn't bother to develop this threat. Both men knew the emptiness of it. Both had daughters they would have given their lives for. Abandonment was not an option.

'So you can start to clear that board. Get everything sorted.'

Sullenly Troy began to remove the photographs, the maps and drawings and photostats of documents. Barnaby applied himself to clearing his desktop. Wiping obsolete files, emptying and checking folders, saving some, deleting others. For twenty minutes or so they worked in silence. Then the phone rang. Troy picked it up, listened, then mouthed, 'Talk of the devil' at the chief in clear and silent dumb show.

Barnaby, fingers idling on the keyboard, prepared to be entertained, for Troy was hopeless at concealment. Every emotion was writ not only plain but large, all over his face. Even his ears were eloquent. First his eyes widened, then the eyebrows strained into an arch. He fielded Barnaby's ironical gaze with a portentous shake of the head. He hung up, then paused, turning to face the boss, holding the moment in the interest of dramatic tension.

'Don't tell me – the butler did it.'

'Garret was poisoned.'

'How?'

'Methanol.'

Barnaby slotted the word into his memory where it vibrated gently. A recollection arose, vague and undefined. Joyce . . . Joyce with a newspaper . . . Joyce reading something out to him. A tourist in Egypt drinking a bottle of contaminated Cabernet Sauvignon. And dying.

'In red wine . . .' he murmured, half to himself.

Troy stared across the room. His mouth slowly rounded into an amazed, petrified circle. How did he do it? Just like that. Not only did he know it was wine but he knew the *colour*. No doubt if the type and year proved relevant he would know that as well. Long aware of his own shortcomings in the light of the chief's powers of deduction and analysis, Troy now had to contend with this unexpected gift of second sight. Life was unfair; only a fool would think otherwise. But there should be some sort of limit.

Barnaby sussed all his sergeant's thought processes with ease. He toyed with the notion of explaining the source of his almost by-the-way comment but decided otherwise. It never hurt to keep the infantry on their toes.

'You know what this means, Chief? She was killed to stop her talking.'

'She may not have been killed at all.'

This remark was almost certainly the forerunner to another little homily guaranteed to set Sergeant Troy's teeth on edge. He knew without being told what was coming. It was the open mind lecture.

Oh! Sergeant Troy knew all about the famous open mind. He had had the open mind right up to and beyond his own mind's gagging point. At the very next mention of the words Troy had vowed to throw himself from the office window.

'She could have drunk it in a restaurant, at a friend's house, at home.' Now Barnaby was putting on his coat. 'Don't just stand there. Get her address. And fill them in at the desk.'

'Sir.' But now it was Troy, hurriedly taking down his jacket, in whom memory flared. 'Wasn't there some antifreeze scandal about wine once? People falling over right, left and centre.'

'Which is why we have to find out where this stuff came from. It might not be just the odd contaminated bottle.'

'Blimey. You don't think it was Tesco's?'

'Why?'

'I bought some plonk there at the weekend,' Troy's arm wrestled unsuccesfully with the entry into his jacket sleeve, 'Oz Clarke recommended.'

Barnaby opened the door and stood, impassive, drumming his fingers on the glass panel.

'I think I've split the lining.'

'I'm leaving,' said the chief inspector. 'And I expect to find you in the car when I get down there. With or without that bloody jacket.'

CHAPTER SEVENTEEN

It was now nearly a whole night and day since Roy had discovered Ava's body. Karen was still in shock, given to tears and the same repetitive cries: 'What'll I do, Roy, without her? What'll I do?'

Roy tried to be understanding but couldn't really fathom the reason for all this misery, which seemed to him right over the top. A mother like that – you'd think anybody'd be glad to get shut of her. But what did he know? His own had dumped him in a phone box a few hours old and pissed off the face of the earth.

After the ambulance men had gone he made some tea and sat at the table trying to think. The sudden apprehension of all sorts of grown-up stuff needing to be handled clogged his mind, leaving him deeply disturbed. At the home everyone had told you what to do and you did it till you were old enough to give them the finger and bunk off. Same with school. At work he did his simple job as well as he could, turning up on time and keeping his nose reasonably clean, but there was nothing like what you'd call real responsibility. So – where to start?

'I think we ought to make a list.'

'Why?' Karen had found three custard creams in an old golden syrup tin. She gave him two.

'Because I can't remember everything in my head, that's why.'

'What do we have to remember?'

'We'll know that when I've made the list.'

Roy frowned and chewed his pencil. He knew there must be things you had to do when someone died but, apart from collecting a death certificate, he had no idea what they were. Probably there were places for advice but he was pretty sure they would be linked to the council, which somehow rather defeated the object. Better leave the technicalities and concentrate on the definitely dodgy present. On the fact that whoever had turned up on their doorstep yesterday morning would be coming back and sooner rather than later.

He muttered: 'We gotta think like they'd think.'

Karen said, 'The social?'

'Yeah. First . . .' He pictured them pushing in, staring round. Looking for things wrong so they could pick on him. 'We clean this place up.'

'I can do that,' cried Karen.

'And we'll have to buy some stuff to eat. If there's no food in the house we'll be in deep shit.'

'Roy? Could we have some flowers?'

'You can't eat flowers.'

'I could pick some.'

'Yeah, OK. Now, money. I've got . . .' He ferreted around the pockets of his Levis. 'Seven pounds and . . . forty-three p.' No good asking what she'd got. On the other hand, seven quid wouldn't go far. The next question was obvious. Obvious but, no matter how you put it, tricky. At the home the minute a room was unoccupied you'd naturally go through it, helping yourself to anything worth having. You'd be a fool not to. But somehow the idea of doing this now, of searching the house, made him feel uncomfortable.

'Um . . . I wonder if . . . d'you know . . .?'

'There might be some money in the toffee tin.'

'Where's that, then?'

Karen opened and closed her mouth, swallowed and tried again. 'Wardrobe. I can't.'

'No worries.'

Roy pushed his chair back and made for the stairs. But on the threshold of Ava's room he hesitated, not understanding why. After all, he was only doing a quick straightforward search. Not prying or reading personal letters or anything. And the place was empty. Wasn't it?

Roy, who had put one foot across the threshold, stepped back. A vivid recollection of just what sort of person Ava had been possessed him. A person with extremely powerful psychic gifts in constant touch with the world beyond. A person who had only just passed over. So what if her spirit was still lurking? Roy drew in a sharp breath over teeth suddenly cold and achy. What would it think, that spirit, seeing someone going through all its possessions? More important – what might it do?

Roy had heard stories about what happened to people who robbed the dead. About how tomb raiders in ancient Egypt were followed forever after by the Curse of the Pharaohs, eventually to meet terrible ends. And once he had seen an old-fashioned film where a little boy in rags stole the coins from a corpse's eyes and was straightaway run down by a horse and cart.

He heard Karen downstairs, turning the taps on. Getting ready to clean up. Putting her back into it. Disgust at his own cowardice propelled Roy into the room. He walked quickly over to the wardrobe and opened it, spotting the tin straightaway. 'Sharpe's Toffees', it said on the lid. Green letters dancing over a stout old man, cheeks bulging with sweeties and wearing tartan trousers. The tin was empty.

Roy replaced it and stood quite still, breathing quietly and carefully for some minutes before he realised none of this caution was necessary. He was completely on his own. No atmosphere, no creepy feelings, no bony fingers click-clacking along the radiator. Just him and the empty bed and a not-very-nice smell, which he recognised as Ava's hair spray. To celebrate the complete absence of any presence Roy flung open the window and let the sunshine in.

Then he went back to the wardrobe and checked out Ava's clothes, his fingers flicking in and out of every pocket, quick as lightning. Pushing the things back and forth released more smells and a puff or two of dust but no money. Roy gave the dressing table a quick once-over. Jars of pink stuff and browny liquid, powder in boxes and lipsticks, crystals, brighter colours in little pots, necklaces hanging from the mirror.

Ava's platform wig was on a stand next to a large photograph of herself wearing it. She had told Karen that this must be the first thing she saw each morning when she opened her eyes as it helped her hold the dream. Roy remembered her saying it because, straight after, she had burned every other photograph like a snake shedding its old skin. Now, sorting through a large chest of drawers (jumpers, underwear, tights) Roy thought what a good idea that was. Making yourself over, it was called. He had just started to dream of what his own makeover might involve when he spotted Ava's handbag.

It was lying on the floor on the far side of the room, halfway between the door and the bed. A black boxy thing with gilt stick-on initials. Roy thought seeing it there was pretty strange. She hadn't been the tidiest person in the world, but just to chuck it on the floor . . . Still, didn't that tie in with her not even bothering to get undressed? She must have been paralytic. Either that or already ill. Roy pushed that thought away. Stamped on the mental picture of Karen fast asleep, with her mother dying just across the landing.

He picked up the bag, sat on the side of the bed and opened it. So much stuff – why did women carry all this rubbish about? Letters, bills, hairbrush, scribbled-on bits of paper, aspirins, half a tube of Polos. No sign of her mobile. A make-up bag was unzipped and Roy got some black stick all over his fingers. He wiped them on the sheet before opening Ava's purse. Money – lots of money. Nearly fifty pounds. Roy had just finished counting it when he noticed a thin, official-looking booklet with Ava's name on the cover. A Causton District Borough Council rent book. Seemed Rainbow Lodge cost Ava Garret (Mrs) all of sixty-five quid a week. *Sixty-five quid?* Roy's jaws gaped wide. He flinched against the weight of injustice so brazenly revealed. For over a year he had been sleeping on a mattress no wider than a baby's cot in a hutch roughly eight feet square and existing on scrap's while paying a big enough screw to rent the whole house. Greedy cow. He had spoken aloud and didn't care. He didn't care and he'd do it again.

'You're a greedy fucking cow!' shouted Roy, on his toes now, dancing about and squaring up to the empty air with bunched fists. 'Come back and haunt me, right? Just try it. Try it and I'll bloody kill you.'

* * *

207

In the middle of the afternoon of that same day DS Troy parked on the far side of Swayne Crescent and the two policeman walked across to Rainbow Lodge. Barnaby looked disapprovingly at an old red Honda straddling the pavement.

'Not much of the rainbow left,' said Sergeant Troy, scraping at the painted arch on the worn garden gate. The orange and green had nearly gone and the purple was flaking fast.

'Not much of a lodge either.'

DCI Barnaby followed his sergeant up the concrete path, looking about him. His green-fingered soul winced at the scrubby, neglected garden. He ached for the parched lupins and frazzled snow-in-summer. Why plant them in the first place? Why not just pour concrete over the lot and have done with it? Knowing he was overreacting did not improve Barnaby's temper. He attempted to calm down. He was about to enter a house of sudden death and, for all he knew, genuine grief. Though in his job you'd be wise not to bet on it.

Troy, having knocked once, waited. He noticed the curtains, black velvet patterned with stars and whirling planets, give a little twitch. Encouraged, he knocked again. The door opened slowly, an inch at a time.

The sergeant's gaze met empty space.

'Hello.'

Troy looked down. A child stood there. A bony, skinny little thing with colourless squinty eyes and hair like straw. She whispered: 'Are you the social?'

'No,' said Troy. Then, gentling his tone, 'Actually we're policemen. D'you think we could come in for a minute?'

'Show her your card, Sergeant,' said the DCI, who had already produced his own. Thanks to the glories of television even toddlers seemed to have got the hang of the correct procedure in these matters. Barnaby thought that was a good thing and was only sorry people weren't as canny when it came to checking out double-glazing cowboys and tarmac touts.

They were standing in a kitchen. It was very clean but when you'd said that you'd said it all. Shabby, ugly units, one cupboard with handles missing. Hard plastic chairs round an old Formica table. A linoed floor, webbed with cracks.

Behind him Barnaby heard his sergeant making a strange noise – it sounded like 'nyuhheerr' – and turned to look. Troy had gone a whiter shade of pale. He was paler than the girl, could that be possible, and was staring, bug-eyed, at a stack of bulging carrier bags on the table. Red, white and blue carrier bags. From Tesco.

'What the hell's wrong with you?'

Troy struggled for composure and gradually common sense came to the fore. Just because they'd shopped at Tesco didn't mean they never shopped anywhere else. And he had drunk his wine nearly two days ago.

By now surely some effects would have been felt. Then he remembered how hard it had been to wake up that morning, how incredibly sleepy he had been, and experienced a lurch of nausea.

Just off the kitchen a toilet flushed. A youth came in and stared very seriously at DCI Barnaby, who stared interestedly back. A day earlier he would have been looking at a different man. Roy, recognising that his appearance was calculated more to alarm than disarm, had systematically set about improving it. Freshly showered, his hair washed free of gel and blow-dried, he now looked not only much cleaner but considerably younger. He had removed the chain and rings from his nose, a complicated, painful progress, and all but two from his ears. Jeans and a long-sleeved T-shirt, still damp from the wash, concealed most of his tattoos. The one circling his throat, an intricately dotted line under the words 'Cut Here', was harder to hide. Roy had managed it by wrapping one of Ava's scarves around his neck.

Having come into the situation blind, Barnaby was aware of the need to feel his way carefully. The dead woman could well be this girl's mother. Maybe the lad's too. She was whispering, just loud enough for Barnaby to catch the sense of it.

'It's not the social, Roy.'

'You don't have to tell me.' Roy jerked his head, indicating a sliding door: accordion-pleated plastic. 'If you wanna sit down there's more space back there.'

'That's all right,' said Barnaby. Then, hoping to reassure. 'We won't be long.'

Troy sat at the table, moved some scraggly buttercups in a milk bottle and put his notebook down. Barnaby leaned against the cooker. Karen perched on a high stool, her thin legs twining through the rungs. Roy just hovered. He looked extremely wary. The girl even more so. In fact Barnaby had the feeling she was just a breath away from out-and-out fear. He smiled and received a nervous flash of uncared-for teeth.

'Would you tell me your name, please.'

'Karen Garret.'

'And you are?'

'Roy,' said Roy. 'It's French for king.'

'Surname?' asked Troy.

'You won't find me on any of your files.'

'Just for the record,' said Troy, adding an excessively polite 'sir'. They didn't want any aggro this early in the game.

'It's Priest, if you must know.'

'And your relationship to Mrs Garret?'

'I'm the lodger. But,' Roy added hastily, 'I'm also a friend.'

'And you're her daughter, Karen?' asked Barnaby. 'Is that right?'

'Not that you'd notice,' said Roy.

'How are you both coping?'

'We're cool. We got food . . .' He nodded at piles of oranges and apples; green vegetables. Milk and fresh bread. 'Everything.'

'Are you on your own here?'

They answered together, overlapping.

'Her aunty's coming tomorrow.'

'My aunty's coming tonight.'

'We told the ambulance men,' lied Roy. 'The hospital's getting in touch with the council.'

'Fine. We'd like to ask a few questions about Mrs Garret's movements on Wednesday.'

'Like what?' asked Roy.

'Maybe we could start with the morning?'

'Just as usual really.' Karen screwed up her forehead, thinking hard. 'I got up. Ava'd had her breakfast—'

'Which was?' asked Troy.

'Toast and coffee, I think.'

'Did you have the same?'

'I had cereal first. Then a bit of toast. After that she went to the Spar for some ciggies.'

'She used to try sending her, would you believe?' said Roy. 'A kid that age.'

'Roy,' said Karen. 'Anyway, she brought two packets of Cup a Soup back, mushroom. And we had that, round one o'clock.'

'And where were you during this time, Mr Priest?' asked Troy.

'In bed.'

'You don't work then?'

'I certainly do work.' Roy's indignation filled the room. 'Pay my way, an' all.'

'So you're not able—'

'Only I'm on nights this week. 'Course, I shan't be going back till we've got the kiddie sorted. They're being very good, Tesco's.'

'So, Karen,' Barnaby eased the interview back on course, 'after lunch?'

'Then she was on the radio.'

'Was that live?' asked Sergeant Troy.

'Pardon?'

'Did she have to go into the studio?'

''Course she did,' said Roy. He slapped his forehead in amazement at such ignorance.

'And what time did Mrs Garret get back?' asked Barnaby.

'Around five.'

'She said we could have some fish and chips.'

Troy smiled at Karen. 'You got a chippie in this place?' He couldn't help sounding surprised.

'Rumbling Tum mobile,' said Roy. 'Once a week.'

'And did . . . Ava eat with you?'

'No,' replied Karen. 'She was going to but—'

'What you asking all these questions for?' asked Roy. He sounded quite belligerent. 'Did she eat this? Did she eat that?'

His annoyance at being deliberately kept in the dark was understandable. If the girl hadn't been here Barnaby would not have dreamed of pussy-footing about. Pity he had not been aware of the situation in advance. He could have brought a WPC along. The cause of death was hardly a state secret. It would be public knowledge by this time tomorrow and, even as he jibbed at putting it into words, he recognised that for her the worst had already happened. One could say the cause was almost beside the point. He tried to put it as undramatically as possible.

'Your mother died, I'm afraid, Karen, because of something she either ate or drank.'

'Which is why,' added Sergeant Troy, picking up the tone of quiet moderation, 'we need to find out what it was. In case other people might be at risk.'

'And as you're both OK,' said Barnaby, 'it's obviously something she had and you didn't. So, do you think she might have stopped somewhere after she had done her broadcast? Perhaps to have tea?'

'Definitely not,' said Karen. 'She was too excited. She couldn't wait to get home.'

'And she didn't have nothing at the radio place either,' said Roy. 'They offered her a drink in a plastic cup and she were that disgusted she wouldn't touch it.'

'I see.' Barnaby couldn't help glancing around the seedy kitchen. The phrase 'delusions of grandeur' came to mind. 'What about when she came home? A gin and tonic, maybe?'

'Ava wasn't much of a drinker,' said Roy.

'She had a vodkatini once.' Karen made it sound unbelievably glamorous.

'I reckon it was something she had with that bloke,' said Roy.

'Who was this?'

'She got a phone call from the BBC,' said Karen. 'A man wanted to interview her.'

'It was in her stars,' said Roy.

'Time?'

'A bit before half-five.'

'That's right,' agreed Karen. ''Cause the chippy came when she was upstairs getting ready.'

'Hang on a sec,' said Troy, scribbling away. 'Ready for . . .?'

'He wanted to take her out to dinner.'

For no discernible reason Barnaby felt a flicker of unease. Something perhaps about the speed of it. Barely two hours after the programme had gone out? No doubt some thrusting contender at the local station had phoned the story through, presumably with the aim of bringing his or her name to the BBC's attention. They must have talked it up a storm. Even so, Barnaby found it hard to understand such an immediate, personal response. But then, what did he know? His sole experience with the media was fielding questions at press briefings.

'Do you happen to know this man's name, Karen?'

'No. But he's a senior producer,' said Karen.

That rang with a cracked note as well. Producer, yes. Barnaby could hear someone describing himself as a producer. Senior producer? Well, possibly, if he wanted to make an impression. A bit unlikely, though. Almost naff.

'It was Chris,' offered Roy.

'Did you get his other name?' asked Sergeant Troy.

'Ava didn't say.' About to add, 'But she wrote it down,' Roy stopped himself just in time. He pictured what would happen next. Them checking her handbag for the bit of paper. Finding a purse with not a single note or coin in it. Wondering where the money could have gone. Guess who'd get fisted.

'Are we still talking radio? Or was this BBC Television?'

'Must be radio. He asked her to meet him at Broadcasting House.'

'How did she get there?' asked Sergeant Troy.

'Drove to Uxbridge – that's her car outside – then took the Tube.'

'She had to ask for him at reception,' added Karen.

Barnaby tried to visualise BBC reception. It had been a year or so since he'd been there. Cully was recording a Henry James serial and he'd called to take her out to lunch. He remembered lots of chairs and sofas scattered about a very large area. Anyone could just walk in off the street but you had to announce yourself at the visitors' desk to get into the building proper. And unless they had an appointment already listed this could prove extremely difficult. Uniformed security staff were discreetly present.

So, it appears his anxieties were groundless and Chris without a surname was a bona fide member of staff after all. Trouble was, thirty years in the force left you with a suspicious mind. Combine that with a fairly lively imagination and you saw treachery round every corner.

'Sir?'

'Sorry.'

Barnaby yanked his concentration back to the present and Troy sourly prepared to read out the last entry in his notebook. Just let his mind wander like that. One second, that's all, one second and he'd still be getting his ear bent at the end of the shift.

'Apparently Ava got back quite late. Probably around eleven.'

'Did you hear her come in?' asked Barnaby.

Karen didn't answer. Then, as they waited, some awful realisation possessed her. Her face was terribly transformed. She struggled to speak and when she did her voice splintered with emotion.

'I was in bed but I heard her on the stairs.'

Trembling hands fluttered around her mouth as if trying to trap the words. Unsay them. Roy stared at her, anxious and disturbed.

Barnaby moved to the girl, crouched down, rested his hands on her shoulders. 'Karen, what is it? What's wrong?'

'I. She. I can't. I'm sorry. I didn't know. I'm sorry. I'm sorry. I'm—'

'Stop.' He took her hand. 'It's all right. Whatever it is, it's all right.'

'No. What I've done. I'm sorry.'

'Tell me.'

'Can't. Can't.'

'Try, Karen.' Though he spoke calmly Barnaby was becoming deeply concerned at the situation. 'I'm sure we'll be able to sort it out.'

'Too late.'

Gradually she stopped shaking. The frenzy left her face, leaving dry anguish behind. Her eyes, focused now on Barnaby, were clouded with pain.

The chief inspector, gently releasing her hand, said, 'Is it about your mother?'

'Ava.' One long howl.

'Look, Karen, whatever you think you've done, unless you talk about it we can't help you.'

Yeah, thought Roy. Some help the filth'll give you. He was good at it, mind, this bloke. You had to hand it to him. Butter wouldn't melt.

Troy waited, thinking of Talisa Leanne. A couple more years and she'd be Karen's age. If he ever saw her going through something like this he'd crack up. Even the thought of it made him sick to the stomach.

'Did you talk to her that night?' Barnaby was asking now. 'Perhaps after she came home?'

This was it. She became unnaturally alert, almost rigid. And very still.

'Maybe you had an argument.' That could well be. Imagine having a row with your mother and her dying straight after. Imagine trying to live with that. 'I've a daughter myself. We're always at it.'

Karen shook her head, silvery hair flying.

'But you did talk?'

'No. She. She.' Karen started to cry. 'She called me. On the stairs.'

'Why don't you leave her alone?'

Barnaby made a quick, savage gesture in Roy's direction but Karen didn't notice. Her crying increased. Tears streamed down her stricken face.

'I heard her. But I didn't. I didn't.'

Then Barnaby understood. Understood and recognised the measure of the burden he had unwittingly placed upon this child. A burden she would carry for the rest of her life if something were not done and done quickly.

'Listen, Karen. The doctor who did the— who discovered how your mother died, said the methanol she swallowed would have begun to take effect straightaway.' He waited. 'Karen? Are you listening to me?'

213

'But . . . she came home.'

'Yes. It can take a while, sometimes several hours, before the person actually loses consciousness. But the process, once started, is irreversible.'

Karen looked bewildered.

'What I'm saying is that, even if you had got up, there's absolutely nothing you could have done.'

'Does . . . would it . . . hurt . . .?'

'No. She would simply lie down and drift off, either to sleep or into a coma. Either way your mother would have known nothing about it.'

'You see?' said Roy, as if he had been telling her this all along.

She started rubbing at her face with the sleeve of a dirty blouse. 'Oh – is it true?'

'Absolutely true.'

Shortly after this, driving back to Causton, Sergeant Troy replayed the scene over and over in his mind. He had been much impressed by the way the chief had handled things. But it was not in his nature to be impressed without being at the same time resentful. He too had been sincerely concerned about the girl. He would, in his muddled, careful way, also have tried to handle things with kindness and tact. But there was no doubt he was missing the chief's encyclopaedic knowledge. It was that stuff about the methanol that had really turned the situation round. By the time they left Karen had stopped shaking and crying. There was even a faint shading of colour on her cheeks. Where had he picked the information up? It wasn't on the PM report. Must be all that reading. He could ask, of course. No harm in asking.

'Sir?'

Grunt.

'Handy you knowing all about methanol.'

'What?'

'Really helped the kid out.'

Barnaby, who knew nothing at all about methanol, grunted again.

That was nice as well, thought Troy. He was laid-back with it, the gaffer. Not boasting or showing off like some would have done. Like he himself would certainly have done. As bosses go, Troy knew he could be a lot worse off. For instance, there was the time —

'Watch that bollard!!!'

'Whoops.' Crunch. 'Sorry, Guv.'

Around teatime that same afternoon the programme tape was delivered to the station by a courier. Barnaby was tucking into a warm maple and pecan Danish when Troy brought it into his office and slotted it into the machine.

They were in the fortunate position of being able to picture Ava as she spoke, for Barnaby had asked for a photograph before leaving Rainbow

214

Lodge. It was plainly a professional job – intensely theatrical, luridly lit and dramatically posed – but was better than nothing.

As the tape started to play Barnaby remembered Joyce's description of Ava as 'bragging but kind of sad'. Listening, he missed the sad but there was no way you could miss the bragging. It was quite funny for a while – like two point five seconds – and then just boring. But, in spite of the endless repetition, Barnaby couldn't risk pressing the fast forward.

'Poor bloke,' murmured Troy. But he still laughed at Ava's blithe insult to her interviewer's face. She couldn't imagine anyone wanting to talk to *him*.

Barnaby was equally unsympathetic. To his mind any man who allowed himself to be called Corey Panting deserved all he got.

Now she had got on to her special powers, describing how she talked to the dead at the Church of the Near at Hand. Barnaby sat up straight. Troy's attention became more serious.

'. . . we must remember that so far only half the story has been told.'

'And we shall hear the rest next Sunday?'

'That is absolutely correct.'

Troy had another chortle, this time at Panting's 'sleight of hand' joke and switched the machine off.

But Barnaby did not laugh. He was thinking what a gift Ava would be to a conman. Insecure, yearning to be noticed, lying her boastful heart out even to herself. One crumb of flattery and she'd dance to any stranger's tune, let alone one emanating from the magic portals of Broadcasting House.

'She sounded so definite,' said Troy.

'Hucksters have to be,' replied Barnaby. 'Salesmen, politicians, actors – they don't get far without the appearance of cast-iron confidence.'

'You don't reckon there's anything in this spirit stuff, then?'

'Don't you start,' said Barnaby. 'Any luck with the checks on "Chris"?'

'Some response from the BBC. Radio One has got a Chris but he's Chris Moyles, who is famous so it's not him. And they wouldn't be interested in talking to Ava anyway 'cause it's not their sort of thing. Radio Two does do docs—'

'*Does do docs?*'

'Documentaries, Chief. Features. But they're nearly always related to music or show-biz personalities. They've got three Christophers on the staff, though. One's on holiday, one's part of a graduate intake, been there a month, one's a sound engineer. I've rung their extensions and left a message. Drew a complete blank at Three. They do very few features. All high-brow stuff. Commissioned. Planned well in advance. Nothing in the pipeline relevant to our investigation. No producers called Chris.'

Barnaby put his head in his hands.

'Chief?'

'Go on, go on.'

'Radio Four should be our best bet. However, quite a few of their programmes are now made by independents. No one knew offhand if one on spiritualism had been commissioned but they're checking up. There's a guy called Christopher Laurence in Current Affairs. I've spoken to him and he's not our man.'

'No, he wouldn't be.'

'I also contacted BBC London Live, and World Service at Bush House—'

'You've been very thorough, Sergeant. Thank you.'

'Right.' Troy waited, ill at ease. 'Think we're wasting our time on all this, Chief?'

'Yes, I do. But it's time that has to be wasted. I can't go upstairs until we've checked every single thing that's checkable.'

At the words 'go upstairs' Troy struck a ridiculously exaggerated attitude of frozen horror and drew a thumbnail across his throat. The chief super was as mad as a hatter. No one entered his office without a wreath of garlic and two sticks crudely assembled in the shape of a cross. Or the twenty-first-century equivalent.

'But he did meet her at Broadcasting House, sir.'

'I've been thinking about that. Try and get hold of Roy for me, would you?'

'Roy French for king,' laughed Troy, flipping through his notebook for the number and punching it in. 'Hello, there. Sergeant Troy, Causton CID . . . Yes, it is me again.'

'Ask him if she went out with a mobile.'

Troy asked, then listened. 'She did, sir. And what's more they got the impression it was Chris's suggestion. She certainly gave him the number.'

Barnaby stretched out his hand for the telephone. 'Roy, I was wondering if there was another photograph of Ava? . . . I see . . . No one's saying it's your fault . . . In that case we may have to call on you for a more accurate description. We need to know how she looked when she went to meet this man . . . No – I'm afraid money won't be changing hands on this one . . . Also, would you mind having a look for her mobile? . . . Thank you. We'll be in touch.'

'He's a lad.' Sergeant Troy laughed again. 'What're you after, guv? An E-fit?'

'That's right.'

'D'you think it'll come to that?'

'I wouldn't be at all surprised.'

CHAPTER EIGHTEEN

'So, how's it all going at the office, darling?'

Nobody ever said 'darling' quite like Gilda. A mixture of indulgence, weariness and contempt. And the word was never spontaneous. Never tossed carelessly into the conversation but placed with great sharpness and delicacy, like a banderilla, in the recipient's shrinking hide.

'The office, darling?' replied Andrew, knowing how much she hated hearing her words repeated. Parroting, she called it. Not wishing to answer the question or even think about it, he simply sat, his face fixed in a polite smirk.

God, she'd really pushed the boat out today. Tastefully draped in a flamingo and lilac tarpaulin that would easily have covered a brace of camels, Gilda was wedged into a two-seater sofa. On the mother-of-pearl table next to her was a goldfish bowl of Maltesers. Andrew watched, mesmerised, as his wife's hand dipped into it. Watched the great white fingers scrabble, close on a dozen or so of the melting little balls and transfer them to her mouth. One vicious suck, a gulp and the whole process started all over again.

'What are you staring at?'

'I was just wondering, my angel, what the collective noun for a gathering of Maltesers might be.'

'Collective what?'

'You know, as in a murmuration of starlings. A pandemonium of porcupines.'

'A bagful.'

'A bagful!' cried Andrew, joyfully clapping his hands.

'Try not to parrot everything I say.'

'Everything you—' Andrew held it there. No point in pushing his luck. The hand that holds the purse strings writes the rules.

'Anyway, you haven't answered my question. How *is* everything going at the office?'

'Couldn't be sweeter.'

'That's not what I heard.'

Andrew refused to ask what it was she had heard. Or who she heard it from. He liked to display these tiny fragments of independence from time to time. She'd tell him anyway.

How things were actually going was bloody awful. Andrew, naturally thick-skinned, had inevitably developed an extra layer or two during the years of his present servitude. But the new situation at what was now being called, by everyone but himself, Fortune and Latham was already beginning to get him down.

Within twenty-four hours of the will being read, Leo Fortune, having come into, appropriately enough, the lion's share of the Brinkley bequest, had had his name inscribed on Dennis's door. This was kept open unless a client was present and people drifted easily in and out talking to Leo, asking questions and advice, just as they had always done. Perversely this annoyed Andrew more than if the man had become incredibly grand and started throwing his weight about.

And whereas Andrew had always enjoyed having his own office where he could look out at the worker ants from a position of idling superiority, he now found this situation becoming unbearable. Frequently, glancing up from the *Financial Times*, he would find someone staring through the glass at him. It was like living in a bloody aquarium. The last straw had been when the office junior and Gail Fuller, heads together at the coffee machine, had gazed in his direction, plainly struggling to keep straight faces. Then Gail had whispered something behind her hand and the junior had burst into shrieks of uncontrollable laughter and run off into the loo. Plainly the whisper had been about him and Andrew had the terrible feeling it had to do with his sexual prowess. This made him very angry. The unattached Ms Fuller had been glad enough of a quick shunt after hours. No doubt afraid lightning might never strike the same place twice, her knickers were off before he'd even put his fag out.

Well, this sort of thing shouldn't be difficult to put a stop to. He'd catch her before she left and make his displeasure known. By the time he'd finished she'd be so grateful to get away she'd keep her mouth shut for the duration. But when the time came someone from accounts was hanging around reception and they left together.

'It was that nice young man who has taken over Dennis's clients,' said Gilda now.

'What was?' Thank God it was Friday night. End of week.

'Who made me *au fait* with the office situation.'

'He's not young. He's forty-two.'

'Don't you have any clients *at all*?'

'I go in every day. I put the time in. I'm out from under your feet. For this you pay me a so-called salary. That was our arrangement.'

'It doesn't sound very satisfactory.'

Too fucking true, thought Andrew. The only thing that kept him going was that it could not last for ever. Because change was a condition of life, right? Also he had not been quite as supine as the little cockle of his heart supposed. From the moment the slave's collar had snapped around his neck he had been making plans. Wild plans, subtle plans, short- and long-term plans, plans so completely silly they had no hope of success but were simply designed to make him laugh. None had come to anything, but for the past few weeks he had been working on something that was beginning to look like a sure thing. Fingers crossed.

Alongside the making of plans, Andrew wrote and rewrote, then wrote again his farewell scene with Gilda. Dwelling on every tiny detail, polishing every insult, paring down the prose. She wouldn't be able to believe her eyes at first. Or ears either. Wouldn't be able to grasp that her poor, caponised fool of a husband, crushed underfoot for so many years, had put on flesh and muscle and bone and clad itself in shining garments and had taken up a spear in its bold fist and was flinging it towards her heart with all its might. Yes!

As for now, she was still droning on. Better respond. 'Sorry, darling. I was miles away.'

'If only,' said Gilda.

Yesterday, after the police had left, for no sensible reason at all, Roy suddenly became much less anxious. It was as if the first big jump had been successfully cleared. He felt capable, able to handle things. He braved the Citizens' Advice Bureau, having reasoned that asking them what to do when someone dies was less of a risk than having various people coming round wanting to know why he hadn't done those things. Of course, they tried to get his name and phone number but Roy just made something up.

Then, around teatime, the plain clothes copper who had been round earlier rang back. Would he mind having a look for Ava's mobile? Roy already knew it wasn't in her handbag but promised to do his best.

'Roy?'

'What?'

'D'you think Karen's French for queen?'

'No.'

'It's got a "kuh" sound, though.'

'That's got nothing to do with it.'

'Why?'

Roy really didn't want to get into all this. He only knew about his own name because of a teacher at school. She had found him crying, heart-broken in the cloakroom. Two girls had told him their mothers knew his mother and she'd only dumped him because he stank and was absolute garbage. Then the teacher had said how could this possibly be true when he had been given a name that was one of the grandest and highest and most important in the world. And that was how he had discovered that Roy was French for king.

Karen, bored of waiting for an answer, had gone back to peeling a big, fat Jaffa.

'Don't oranges smell lovely, Roy?'

Actually Roy noticed that everything was smelling a lot better now that the reek of stale tobacco was disappearing. Not the furniture and curtains

– they'd probably always pong a bit – but the air generally was much fresher.

'I'm glad you don't smoke, young Karen.'

'Ava wouldn't let me.'

'Quite right too.'

'She said I'd only end up pinching hers.'

Roy had not stopped worrying about Karen. He'd been watching her closely at times when he thought she wasn't looking. She'd stopped crying and now, apart from complaining about a nonstop headache, was pretending to be OK. But Roy knew she couldn't really be. Not already. He'd had first-hand experience of this sort of thing. There had been a boy in the home, only there temporary, whose mother died from a drug overdose. It had taken three care assistants to control him and his screaming had gone on for days.

'Would you like half?' She passed the orange over.

'No. We have a whole one each now, every day. And don't forget your milk'

'It tastes nice. Nice but different.'

'It's fresh. See . . .' He turned the carton round, pointing. 'Use by the nineteenth. If we don't, it'll go off.'

'Off where?'

Roy explained what 'sour' meant. He thought being with Karen was great. It was like having a kid sister. She looked up to him; asked all sort of questions. Roy hardly ever knew the answers but he always pretended he did and would give them confidently so she would know she could rely on him.

There was a lot to learn, no doubt about that. They'd already tried cooking vegetables. Last night Roy put broccoli and potatoes in a pan and boiled them till the potatoes were soft, by which time the broccoli had completely dissolved. But the fish had instructions on so that was fine.

What they planned to do next was tackle Ava's room. It seemed a bit soon to Roy but Karen had suggested it. She said it wasn't right that he should be sleeping in a cupboard when he paid all the rent. And while they were in there they could look for the mobile, which certainly wasn't anywhere else in the house.

Roy said he would start and Karen could help but only if she felt OK about it. They'd got a few boxes from the Spar shop to put things of any value in. As for the rest – Roy had promised a bonfire.

He started by emptying the wardrobe, folding the clothes in neat piles and putting them out on the landing. The chest of drawers didn't take long, crammed with fusty old jumpers and whiffy underwear. He filled a bin liner in no time. The wigs and jewellery and handbags, all empty, went into a Walker's Crisps box.

Roy left the bed till last. He really didn't want to touch it. The vivid sight of Ava lying there, eyes and mouth wide open, staring at him, was disgustingly present. Spillage from her mouth had run over the pillow-case and dried into a yellow stain. Roy wondered if he should be wearing rubber gloves but hated to seem poofy, even to himself. Anyway, they hadn't got any so that settled that.

He would burn the bedding. Duvet, sheets, pillows, mattress – the lot. He decided to throw them through the window, which faced the back garden. It'd make a grand start to the bonfire.

There was a really stupid pattern on the bedclothes. Women in funny stick-out skirts dancing on their toes and men jumping through the air, wearing sort of Robin Hood costumes. Everything was grubby. Ava had told Roy once, just after he'd moved in, that her outstanding gifts put her above housework and that anything Karen didn't do got left. This ultimately became anything Karen and Roy didn't do.

It was a job shoving the duvet through. The window, small to start with, was the old-fashioned sort that would only open in two separate halves. The mattress was going to be even worse. Roy decided the best thing to do was drag it on to the landing, down the stairs then round the side of the house. He heaved it off the bed and on to the floor. Lying underneath, on top of the box springs, was an envelope. Roy picked it up by the tips of his fingers and looked inside. It was full of money. Automatically he stuffed it into his pocket, then straightaway took it out again. He would have to start thinking differently from now on. Living life a new way. There wasn't just himself to consider.

He tried to count the money, which wasn't easy. The fifty-pound notes were damp and stuck together. He peeled them off carefully. There were nine. Four bundles of two made one hundred pounds four times. And there was one note left over.

'Karen?' He could hear her washing up. She was talking to herself as she often did. Chattering away like an old washerwoman. He called again. 'Karen?'

'What?'

'Come and see what I've found.'

That same Saturday morning Doris was having a quick whizz through the *Echo*. She thought there might be a bit more information about Ava's death but it was the usual light-weight weekend stuff. Sport, horse racing, profiles of local characters, a few recipes. Doris cut out the only one that sounded tasty – a ham and cheese sandwich fried in butter with an egg on top – and passed the rest of the paper to Ernest.

She was keeping an eye on the time. Cheated yesterday of any conversation in the muddle and rush of unpacking, Doris had decided to try to catch Benny at her flat this morning. She was aiming for 9.30, when Benny should have finished breakfast but perhaps not yet gone over to the main house. Just in case, Doris took a note to leave. But she was in luck.

Benny was at home but looking terribly upset. She was actually shaking as she opened the door. Doris was immediately concerned.

'Whatever's the matter?'

'I've been reading this book. They asked me – Kate and Mallory. I was so pleased – to be taking part, you know?'

'Yes,' said Doris, going inside. 'Is it awful?'

'Terrible. Oh! Doris – I really don't think I can bear to read any more.'

'Don't then.'

'It's about this sword . . . so amazingly sharp – like magic. It has to cut through leather and flesh and bones and muscle. It can slice a soldier in half. And there's jousting and horses and heads rolling everywhere . . .'

It sounded like a jolly good read to Doris. 'Listen, love, the last thing in the world Mallory would want is for you to get into this sort of state, right?'

'Yes, but—'

'This where it goes?' She pushed the heavy pile of paper back into a large Jiffy bag. 'Now you take that back to the house and tell him you think it's a real belter.'

'It doesn't seem a very good start,' said Benny. 'Telling lies.'

'You're in business now. Better get used to it.'

'Right!' Benny seized the package.

'Hang on,' said Doris. 'Kate's not here at the minute. I just saw her go over the road.'

'To the Parnells?' asked Benny.

She spoke quite coldly and Doris was surprised. It wasn't like Benny, who seemed to like practically everyone on sight, to be so chilly. Doris, a bit uncomfortable at asking a direct question, raised her eyebrows.

Benny ignored the hint. She would never tell anyone what had happened to turn her against the Parnells – well, only Judith really. Just days after she had given them the lovely present of the Scottie dog soap and sponge she had seen it put out with the rubbish on collection day. Judith had not even bothered to bury it under other things or put it in a bag. This absolute indifference to anyone else's feelings, for the bin was clearly visible from the gates of Appleby House, had made Benny very angry. She was glad they were going away.

'Tell you what,' Doris was saying now. 'I couldn't half do with a cuppa.'

Benny apologised, made some tea and produced almond biscuits. There was an awkward moment when she took the tray into the sitting room. Doris was sitting in Dennis's wing chair and Benny couldn't help making a little cry of distress, which she immediately smothered. But Doris heard and got up straightaway, protesting that the sun was in her eyes and she thought she'd settle better on the settee.

'You coming to the Near at Hand tomorrow, Ben?'

Benny's hand trembled so violently the lid of the teapot started to dance. 'What for?'

'Well . . . I expect there'll be a memorial service. You know, for Ava. Just thought you might be interested.'

'Ava?'

'Ava Garret. The medium who died.'

'Oh, yes.' That Ava.

'I thought there'd've been an inquest by now.'

Doris no sooner spoke than regretted it. Benny's face clouded over and Doris guessed she was remembering the inquest on Dennis. What an awful day that had been, with Benny acting so strangely and making wild accusations.

At this point Benny picked up the pot again and finished pouring the tea. As she put the milk and sugar in, Doris cautiously started to skirt around the real reason for her visit.

'I've been thinking about what you said on Thursday, Ben.'

'To do with what?'

'When I told you Ava'd died you seemed really cross. Then you said, "What am I going to do *now*?" '

'I don't remember that.'

'You definitely did, and I thought—'

'Look at the time.' Benny got up, almost tipping over her cup, such was her haste. 'I'm . . . er . . . supposed to be over there. Mallory will . . . um . . . the Celandine . . . meeting.' She snatched up the manuscript. 'No need for you to hurry, Doris. Finish your tea, have some more biscuits. Pull the door to when you go.'

Doris finished her tea and all the biscuits too. She felt she deserved some sort of compensation. For hadn't she been the one who'd urged Benny to visit the Church of the Near at Hand in the first place? Without me, thought Doris, poor Mr Brinkley would still be floating around the etheric grid desperate for a link-up. You don't expect gratitude for helping people or, these days, even thanks. But to be shut out when a new and mysterious angle on the whole business seemed to be in the offing was extremely frustrating.

Something was going on or Benny wouldn't have scarpered like that. Doris recalled the clattering cup and saucer, the grabbing of the envelope and Ben flying from the room, calling over her shoulder. She had run away, that's what she had done. Run like the wind. But from what? Doris, nibbling on the final almond thin, was determined to find out.

Kate was saying goodbye to Ashley and Judith. They had already said it once, all four of them, the previous evening at dinner. Remembering what it had been like the night before she and Mallory moved, Kate had thought asking them over for a meal would be helpful. Not that the Parnells were actually moving but they were going away for an unknown length of time.

It had all happened very quickly. Even before the Harley Street appointment Judith was surfing the Net looking for the best hospital and

223

the best-known and reputable consultant. She showed her brief list to the specialist when they met and followed his advice. Ashley told Kate all about it when Judith was in Causton, booking their flights.

The Clinique pour les Maladies Tropicales, La Fontaine, was in the *Alpes Maritimes* on the French-Italian borders. Judith would be staying in a hotel very near to the hospital. Apparently the air was wonderful. She was very excited but in a feverish, almost unbalanced way. Ashley was the calm one. When Mallory asked how he felt he just said: 'Glad something's happening at last.'

The meal had not been a success. It soon became plain that Ashley was happy to be present but Judith was only there on sufferance. And she didn't look at all pleased when Ashley urged Kate and Mallory to eat as much as they could from Trevelyan's garden as it would only run to waste.

Kate got rather fed up with this surliness – they were, after all, keeping an eye on the Parnells' house and forwarding all their post – and by the time the caramelised pears had been dished up, was a touch on the surly side herself. She was sorry afterwards, wondering how pleasant and friendly she would be to people if Mallory was frighteningly ill and might never get better. So this morning she collected some of the loveliest and ripest fruit in the orchard and took it across just moments before their cab turned up.

Ashley gave her a hug and a kiss on the cheek.

Judith said of the apples, 'What on earth are we supposed to do with those?' Then they got into the taxi and were driven away.

It was lunchtime, and Roy and Karen were dining on fresh brown rolls and soup from a carton; spicy parsnip made in Covent Garden. Karen had never heard of Covent Garden so Roy explained about it. How there were cobbled streets and lots of stalls and shops and jugglers and fire-eaters. And a man and a woman covered in silver paint who never moved, not even to blink.

'I'm thinking of doing my first stand-up in the Garden 'cause you can just start anywhere.'

'Can I come, Roy? I'd clap all the time. And laugh.'

'You don't laugh now.'

'I would then, though.'

'OK. You can take the hat round.'

Which brought them back to the subject of money. Money generally and, of course, *the* money. Roy had said that they had to be really careful but that didn't mean they couldn't treat themselves a little bit. For a start Karen had to have some clothes. The rubbish she wore you wouldn't put on a scarecrow. And shoes.

'They're not good for your feet, them big heavy things.'

'Everybody wears them.'

'It's OK sometimes. But we ought to get you some sneakers.'
'*Oohhh, Roy . . . sneakers . . .*'
'All right, don't go mad.'

Roy had spent a good hour sitting in the garden with a cup of tea before Karen woke that morning worrying about money. Just about able to add up single figures, anything else was beyond him. But he did know that after he'd given Ava his weekly rent he'd had about the same amount left. Would that be enough to keep two people? Then there was electricity and stuff. All right now, but what about when winter came?

There was no way he could draw Karen's child benefit. She couldn't draw it either, even though it was for her and belonged to her. Only Ava was authorised to sign the book and cash the counterfoil. She had always done this in Causton, believing this way no one in Forbes Abbot would know her business. But the one thing Roy had to do to get all the financial support available to someone in his position was the one thing he couldn't do. Because once the true facts about him and Karen and the house got fed into the DSS computers, all their security and happiness would vanish like smoke.

There was a tugging at his arm. 'Roy, Roy.'
'Karen, Karen.'
'Can I get my new things at Covent Garden?'
'No. We're going to Byrite.'
'When? When, Roy?'
'Today, if you like.'
'Brilliant! Do they have fire-eaters? And silver people?'
'No.'
'Now we're rich, couldn't we go to Covent Garden just to look?'
'I'll take you one day. Don't jump about like that – you're making me giddy.'
'Roy?'
'Now what?'
'Can I have a bicycle?'
'No.'
'Can I paint my room pink then?'

Roy had already been to Byrite so knew what to expect, but Karen was devastated. Mouth open, she just stood and stared at the immense space, stretching up over their heads and miles into the distance. At the thousands of shelves crammed with everything you would ever want in the entire world your whole life long.

'I thought it was a shop, Roy.'
'It is a shop. Now you hold on to this trolly, right? And don't let go. Lose you in this place I'll never find you again.'

Karen gripped the plastic handles tight. She had never seen so many people. As many as you could see if you watched a football match on television. Except here they were moving about all the time, which was much more frightening.

They started to walk around. With two bus journeys to get back to Forbes Abbot, Roy had been very firm about how much they could carry. Strictly just Karen's clothes and some paint. So it was unfortunate that the first aisle they travelled was bedding, because there was the most beautiful duvet cover telling the story of Cinderella. The fairy godmother's wand waved real sparkle and the mice had satin tails. It had a matching lacy pillowcase and a little lamp with a silver shade scattered with more sparkle. Karen offered to carry the lamp.

They had to go through food to get to the children's clothes section, which meant more exceptional offers you couldn't refuse. Though Roy drew the line at twelve cans of soup for the price of eight he couldn't resist a gingerbread house or a big box of chocolates that looked like seashells.

When they did finally get to the children's clothes section Karen chose three T-shirts, a denim skirt, some jeans and the beloved sneakers, which had a red light that sparkled in the back. Also socks, underwear and a sunshine-yellow fleece. By then their trolley was loaded, yet everything altogether came to only thirty-eight pounds.

Paying the cashier, Roy turned to Karen, proud of their double act, wanting to see her smile. She wasn't there. She had been standing next to him, now she had gone. The shock stopped Roy's breath in his throat. He could not move or speak.

She had gone. Sick with fear and trembling all over, Roy abandoned his trolly and started running round the store. Terrible pictures took over his mind. Karen getting into a car with a man who'd been following them round. A desperate woman who couldn't have kids snatching her arm, dragging her through a doorway. A couple into devil worship, young people, looking so friendly and harmless. They'd got a little girl just like Karen. Would she like to come and play?

Roy stopped running. It was hopeless, the place was so big. He must tell someone and they would put out an announcement. And call the police. He would have to describe her. Thin, small for her age. Hair? No colour really.

Roy leaned against a plaster archway, panting from his run. His heart banged painfully against his ribs. He thought he was better off without all this, sodding hell he was. Caring for somebody, letting them get to you, was absolute shite. A mug's game. He'd coped all right till now without it. It hadn't been great, but he'd survived. You could stick this love crap right up your—

And then he saw her. Standing in front of a display of dolls. Relief crashed over him like a dam bursting, almost knocking him over. Then came anger. Putting him through this. Didn't she know he was trying to look after her? The little . . . He forced himself to wait till this violence subsided, watching her every second. Then he took a deep breath, sauntered

226

casually up and said, 'I was wondering where you'd got to. Coming to help me with all the stuff?'

'Oh, Roy.' She turned a radiant face towards him, seizing his hand. 'Look, look! It's Barbie.'

So then they had to spend the next half-hour trying to decide which Barbie. Horse riding Barbie, film star Barbie, nurse or secretary Barbie, Barbie on holiday, concert pianist Barbie. Then there was all Barbie's gear. For a doll she certainly knew how to stack it up.

After Roy had paid again (for Barbie the Astronaut) they went into the cafeteria and had warm sausage rolls and chips and Coke. It was Saturday and very busy. Everywhere there were families and Roy proudly took his place among them. He listened to how the parents talked to the children. It mostly seemed to be nagging. Look at the mess you've made. Stop kicking that chair. Leave her crisps alone – you've had yours. Put that purse down. Now look what you've done.

'Karen, don't spill that drink.'

'I'm not.'

'And finish your chips before they get cold.'

'You finish *your* chips.'

'Don't be so cheeky.'

'Don't keep on at me then.'

'I'm in charge here,' said Roy. Then, 'What's so funny?'

The interior of the Church of the Near at Hand was appropriately dark on the Sunday following Ava's death. The yews seemed denser than ever. Alive, like Rackham trees in a wild wood, they pressed together, holding back the sun's rays. Inside, the lights had been switched on but were powered only by opaque sixty-watt bulbs, giving a pale, sickly glow.

George was in a strange mood. Everyone commented on it. He wore a nicely brushed black suit and looked reliably sombre but was very much on the twitchy side. It was as if, one parishioner said, underneath the expression on his face there was a different expression struggling to get out.

Mediumship was not on offer. They were here to commemorate the life of Ava Garret, now passed to spirit, though the reason and actual manner of this passing remained as yet unclear. Murmurings among the congregation had indicated an approval of this situation. Ava was so very far from being an ordinary person that it seemed only right and proper that her demise should be mysterious. The meeting opened with a rumbustious rendering of 'Amazing Grace' as George took to the platform.

'Welcome to you all. Cheerfulness breaks in, dear companions, even at a moment of great solemnity for I have just received a message from my Assyrian guide. It appears that our late friend and healer has already linked up with Zacharia, her elemental counterpart.' Scattered applause. 'Absorbed into the great firmament of light and love and abiding in

227

crystal caves the great halls of learning will now open unto them. Transfigured henceforth they will live for all time.' George paused for a moment, a thin black bird cocking its head, alert, waiting. 'Hamarchis has also been asked to send blessings to you from the Great Designer of all that was and is and ever shall be.'

Everyone sang: 'Oh, great spirit. Earth, sun, sky and sea, You are inside and all around me . . .'

George had asked earlier for a corporate eulogy, not trusting himself to handle the matter in person without breaking down. Grateful recipients of Ava's consoling ministry stood up in turn to recollect their own specific condolence and generally praise her gifts. This took quite a long time. However, an observant listener might have noticed that only Ava's psychic skills were praised. No comment was passed on her qualities as a human being, mainly because no one at the Church of the Near at Hand could stand the sight of her.

As the final musical tribute: 'Love is the reason for living', came to an end, George Footscray, by now quite overcome with some indefinable emotion, pressed a handkerchief to his face, hurried from the platform and almost ran up the centre aisle, waving away concerned gestures and crying, 'Tea . . . tea . . .'

Although no specific appeal had been made for donations, in Ava's memory a largish cardboard box covered with silver foil was prominent in the Doris Stokes suite among the sandwiches roulade and assorted cakes and pastries. A stuck-on label read: 'Funeral Expenses' and most people put something through the slit in the lid. Doris slipped in ten pounds, though what Ernest would have said if he'd known didn't bear thinking of. Really, she did it for Karen.

Then she mingled and was not surprised to find the conversation generally leaning towards speculation and disappointment. There were a lot of 'if only's' and 'I wonder who's'. Ava's amazing revelations regarding Dennis Brinkley's death the previous Sunday, though uncomfortably received at the time, had subsequently generated an atmosphere of high drama. The newspaper headlines and radio interview fanned this excitable flame. The presence of television cameras on the big day had become a foregone conclusion. People definitely had something to look forward to. No one doubted Ava's promise that the guilty would be described in such detail they would be caught bang to rights within the hour. Equally no one now put into words the thought – perhaps that's why she died.

Sharing a plate of marzipan doughnuts with Mrs Gobbett, keeper of the keys and flower rota – each week all arrangements had to be dusted – Doris put her own lesser anxiety into words.

'I didn't like the look of George, early on.'

'He thought the world of her. It's only natural.'

'Who d'you think'll take Ava's place?'

'They'll transfer somebody. Otherwise it'll be down to him.'

Both women pondered this idea in silence. George's mediumship was erratic, to say the least. Sometimes he was fine. Others he could be so uninspired you could sit through the whole service without hearing from a living soul. And he could be irresponsible. Once he'd brought up and named a man who was on holiday at the time in Cromer and had been threatened with a solicitor's letter.

'Do you know what arrangements have been made, Alma? Regarding the funeral?'

'They reckon her earthly shell's still sub judice,' explained Mrs Gobbett, 'because of the police.'

'It's just – they cost so much money. What's in that box won't come anywhere near.'

'She should've joined the SNU. We'd've looked after her.'

'George said she wouldn't pay the sub.'

'Who's sorry now?' asked Alma with regrettable satisfaction. 'I saw little Karen this morning.'

'What – in the village?'

On hearing that was indeed the case Doris gathered up her things and hurried away. As she passed the Gents' in the vestibule she heard a strange choking sound followed by some bubbling chortles. These were muffled as if strained through a sort of gag or padding. Then a single squawking cackle broke free and was quickly stifled.

Doris hesitated. Was someone ill in there? Were they telling funny stories? It seemed an inappropriate occasion. An inappropriate place too, come to that. Could they be having a fit? One thing was certain, someone else would have to deal with it. Doris had never been in a gents' toilet in her life and had no intention of starting now.

Roy was sanding the walls in Karen's bedroom when there was a knock on the front door. Immediately frightened, he knew it must be them. All that they stood for, all they had put him through, flooded his mind. He had to grip the ladder not to fall. They might be different people now but they were still the social. The ones with the power to tear everything apart. Hatred bubbled into the fear, so strong it almost made him sick. All this took only a few seconds but it was long enough for Karen to open the door. He heard her talking to someone, then she called his name up the stairs.

Roy struggled to pull himself together. He had done nothing wrong. Not only had he done nothing wrong he had done everything right. He was seventeen now, with a job where he turned up on time and behaved himself. In the present emergency he was looking after things the best way he knew how. And anyway, what could they do to him that they hadn't done already? So when Roy finally braced himself and got downstairs it was a bit of a setback to find only Mrs Crudge from the church.

229

Doris was quite set back too. In fact, she didn't realise at first that it was Roy. He certainly cleaned up well. But the house was a disappointment. She had been expecting something more exotic, Ava being so well travelled. Tiger-skin rugs and souvenirs from round the world. But everything was cheap and shoddy and dull. When Roy invited her into the lounge she couldn't help noticing how the settee was stained and the recliner covered in cigarette burns.

'Well, my loves.' Doris sat down, putting her handbag by her feet. 'How are you coping?'

'We're cool,' said Roy. 'We got all we want. Food – everything.'

'Roy's painting my room, Doris. Princess Pink. And I've got lots of new clothes. And a Barbie. She's an astronaut. She's got a helmet and silver space suit and everything.' Karen paused for breath. 'We went to Byrite. We had to come home in a taxi we had so many things.'

Doris looked slowly across at Roy. He read that look and shrank as from a savage blow. He must have been blind or stupid or something but that aspect of it had never occurred to him. He'd have his hand off before he'd touch a child that way. Any child but most of all Karen.

'I didn't buy them,' he said quickly. 'We found some money upstairs.'

'I came before.' Doris spoke gently, directly to Karen. 'When nobody answered I thought you'd gone away. Like, you were being looked after.'

'I am being looked after.'

'Hasn't anybody been round from the council?'

'Not yet,' said Roy. 'Any minute now, eh?' He gave a strained laugh. You could see her mind working. See her – oh God – perhaps taking Karen with her when she left.

'Do you know what's happening regarding the funeral, Roy?' Doris felt a bit awkward asking in front of the child but someone had to get it sorted.

'Nothing so far, Mrs Crudge. You have to register the death first and I'm still waiting for the certificate from the hospital.'

Doris glanced anxiously at Karen on the word 'death' but she seemed not at all distressed. A bit unusual after such a short time, but then Ava had never been much of a mother. At least Roy seemed to know what to do and was trying to get on with it.

'They had a collection after the service this morning. I expect George or someone'll bring it round. But it won't be nearly enough to cover the cost.'

Roy gave a helpless shrug. He didn't know what to say. Someone must pay for poor people to be buried – tramps, the homeless – otherwise there'd be bodies lying all over the place. Probably the bloody council again. One way or another he would get drawn back into the net. Be asked all sorts of questions to which he had no answers. They would take the rent book away, which meant his home as well. Then they would take Karen. Roy felt a swell of panic so strong he felt sure to drown. Now she was staring at him, old Mrs Crudge. Giving him a real funny look, actually. Sending Karen away.

'Good girl. You make us a nice cup of tea.'

As Karen ran off Doris said, 'Got a lot on your plate, son.'

'I can handle it.'

'George said it was you who found her.'

'That's right. I kept the kiddie well away. There was a woman paramedic – she told her what had happened. And Karen never saw them take Ava.'

'That was good, Roy. I can see you've been doing your best—'

'I have! I have!'

'But you can't stay here on your own . . .'

And then Roy completely lost it and what he lost Doris, devastated by the emotional onslaught, mown down by the force of violent anguished memories, unwillingly and sorrowfully found.

He'd been dumped in a phone box, he told her. Then adopted. New mum died, dad didn't want him. Fostered twice, handed back twice, dumped in a home. Tough kids, violent kids, kicked him, tried it on, laughed when he cried. Cut his clothes up, did it to him in the shower, over and over. He tried to be in a gang. If you were in a gang you'd be all right. But no one wanted him. Even the crap gangs – all the kids nobody else'd have – didn't want him. He tried to run away – sleep rough – but the police found him and took him back. Then when he was sixteen he got a real home and someone who needed him, someone to care about even if it was only a little kid. But now it was going wrong like everything else in his rotten life but he'd never let the social take Karen. She'd never go through what he'd been through. They'd run away where no one would find them . . .

Roy, his eyes bunged up with tears, snot running into his mouth, ran into despairing silence. He sobbed, knowing he was kidding himself. How far would they get, him and Karen? What chance would they have? Old Mrs Crudge had got up. Blinded, he couldn't see her but sensed her moving about. She'd take Karen now – there wouldn't be anything he could do. That would be an end to it. He could handle that. He'd been handling shit like that all his life. It was hopes and dreams that broke you. The settee gave; a weight settling beside him. It eased closer. An arm enclosed his shoulder. A hand gently stroked his hair.

When Karen came in with the tea she was shocked and a little disturbed by what she saw. Because Roy was the strong one, the grown-up who would always know what to do and never be worried or anything. So why was he being rocked in Doris's arms, howling and crying like a baby? Karen put her tray down and sat quietly, waiting. And as she waited and the tea got cold she gradually came to understand that what was happening was not a bad thing. Not something to worry or frighten. And that when it was over Roy would be himself again.

* * *

Over the following few days DCI Barnaby, having offered up all the evidence pertaining to the deaths of Dennis Brinkley and Ava Garret waited to hear from the Top Floor that permission had been granted to set up a murder investigation. On the third day he met formally with Chief Superintendent Bateman. It was an experience with which he was very familiar but one he always hoped never to have to repeat.

He was irascible at the best of times, and the worst of times brought out the beast in the Superintendent. He was a man boiling like a pudding inside his own skin. His neck bulged and rippled with purple veins. His eyes, brown marbles flecked with crimson, fastened on DCI Barnaby's tie. His fingers twitched as if eager to seize it and wrench it round and round until its wearer fell senseless to the floor. Yet his opening remarks were mild enough. Tuning up, the Station called it.

'I can't quite get the hang of this, Chief Inspector. You'll have to bear with me.'

'Sir.'

'Am I to understand that we're talking about two murders here?'

'Yes, sir.'

'*Two?*'

'That's right.'

'And the first one was written off as an accident?'

'There was no reason—'

'Is there a body?'

'No. Mr Brinkley was cremated.'

'Not many prints from ashes, Chief Inspector.'

'No, sir.' And none from a cadaver weeks in the grave either.

'And this happened . . .?'

Barnaby had more sense than to even murmur during the deliberately contrived hiatus. Just watched the sinewy, powerful hands rustling the papers. They were like wolf paws, the backs felted with blackish grey hair. The nails curved and yellow.

'On the twenty-fourth of July? Crime scene pretty much lost to us, I should think.'

'Not necessarily. I believe—'

'*I* believe we're looking at some monumental cockup. I believe I'm surrounded by fuckwits who couldn't spot a murder if it was happening in their own backyard. And for why?'

'Sir?'

'Because they'd be lying in their hammocks, guzzling Canadian Club, wanking off and singing. And what might they be singing, do you suppose?'

Barnaby decided to risk it. ' "Coming through the Rye"?'

'I do the badinage, Chief Inspector.'

'Sir.'

Barnaby risked a glance at the clock. Ten minutes so far and the old man was barely getting into his stride. The DCI waited, unfazed, knowing the attack to be in no way personal. Spleen had to be vented daily, like bad blood.

'So no one has actually talked to anyone who knew this sad bastard. What's his name, Brinkley?'

'No, sir.'

'Says Brinkley down here.'

'No one has actually talked to anyone about him, sir.'

'Not a single question put anywhere?' Each word savagely gnawed off like a chunk of raw meat. Single. Question. Put. Anywhere. 'I find that hard to believe.'

'I've already explained—'

'Then you don't have to tell me again, Chief Inspector. I've got a mind like a razor.'

'Sir.'

'And a memory like . . . a razor.'

'The coroner's verdict—'

'Coroners.' A single spit with excellent aim and range. 'They think they know it all but they are not invaluable.' He paused glaring across the desk. 'You find something amusing?'

'Amusing?' Barnaby appeared quite bewildered. 'Erm . . . no . . .'

'And this second death, this fool of a woman reading tea leaves or whatever. You reckon she's been poisoned?'

'Yes.'

'Think she was involved in the first one?'

'She described exactly how it happened and promised to reveal the murderer the following Sunday.'

'What an idiot.'

'Quite.'

'Says here she talked to spirits.' He stared suspiciously down his long nose, which had a certain boxiness at the end, giving a fair impression of a snout. 'You one of these New Age touchy-feelies, Barnaby?'

'No, sir.'

'Incense up your arse. Needles in your tickling stick.' He started laughing. Hideous barks and gleeful yaps. Joyfully he drummed his wolf paws on the edge of the desk like some lupine shaman. Then he picked up the folder and hurled it forcefully towards the chief inspector.

Barnaby moved quickly, snatching the falling papers from the air. He said, 'Are we to proceed then, sir?'

A GHOST

IN THE

MACHINE

CHAPTER NINETEEN

Before the first briefing on the Garret/Brinkley murders, Chief Inspector Barnaby made himself familiar with the little background on Dennis Brinkley that was available. He discovered the man to be a quiet, respectable financial consultant; law-abiding to the extent that he had never received as much as a parking ticket. So far the only unusual thing about his life was the bizarre way in which he left it. Of course there would be vastly more to Brinkley than this simple outline suggested. If there was one thing experience had taught Tom Barnaby it was that few things were more extraordinary than ordinary lives.

He had been given a larger team than he expected but not as large as he would have liked. But then it never was. He looked at them, the fresh-faced, eager detective constables, the hard-bitten old lags, the middle ranks, capable, experienced, not yet completely cynical. Most of them looked lively and interested and so they should. This was no run-of-the-mill domestic. This looked like being complex, unusual and, Barnaby feared, long-running.

'You've all read the background notes?' Everyone nodded or mumbled or rustled their stuff. 'As you know I always stress the importance of keeping a completely open mind . . .' An inaudible sigh possessed the room. A new DC carefully wrote down 'open mind' and never heard the last of it.

'But we have to start somewhere,' continued Barnaby. 'And in this case I'm afraid it has to be with an unproven assumption. Namely that Ava Garret was killed because she believed she could describe the murder of Dennis Brinkley. And, presumably, the murderer.'

Faces were pulled and there was a fair bit of laughter. The radio tape had entertained them all. As had the photograph of Ava in full fig, already known around the canteen as 'Rocky Horror's Favourite Fuck'.

'Hard to imagine anybody taking such a threat seriously, Chief,' said Inspector Dancey, sitting as closely as he could to WPC Abby Rose Carter without actually climbing into her lap.

'You've killed someone,' said Barnaby, 'you can't afford not to.'

'That's right,' said Sergeant Troy. 'And there have been genuine—'

'Garret and Dennis Brinkley lived in the same village. It's a small place; they may have known each other. I want to know all about both of them. Brinkley died somewhere in the early evening on Tuesday the twenty-fourth of July. Three weeks ago now, I'm afraid, but someone might remember something. Ask if any stranger was seen hanging round the house that day. Or even near the day. Talk to them in the village shop. Find out who delivered Brinkley's post. If he had domestic help or a gardener I want to know. And don't forget the pub.

'I'll be talking to the people at . . .' He squinted at the spiral notebook. 'Troy?'

'Appleby House, Chief.'

'And you can also leave out Ava Garret's immediate family. The situation there is quite fragile and involves a child.'

'Better give us—'

'The address is on the board. Audrey, I'd like your help in breaking this. We don't want Karen finding out via the telly or some nosy neighbour.'

Great. Thanks a bunch, sir. It was always the same. Always the bloody same. Any hammer blows to deliver – any painful, emotional or shocking news, a woman got lumbered. Where were all these sensitive new men when you needed one? Butching it out at nappy-folding class, no doubt.

'Also, try and persuade Roy Priest, who lives there, to come in and do an E-fit. He seemed agreeable when we talked on the telephone.'

'Even though no money will be changing hands,' added Sergeant Troy, laughing.

'Once that's done we can get them out to the staff at Uxbridge station. Issue a public appeal.'

'Shouldn't we check her car, sir?' asked WPC Carter. 'If she did leave it near the Tube someone might have clocked her coming back. This Chris character could've still been around.'

'I doubt it. He's not the careless type. Her mobile seems to have disappeared. And neither Priest nor the girl knows the number or make.'

'What about the first call he made? To the house?'

'Number withheld,' said Sergeant Troy.

'That's about it then.' DCI Barnaby stood up, dismissing them. 'Off you go. Debriefing, six o'clock.'

It was nearly two hours later before Barnaby himself was ready to depart. He passed Roy and Karen, escorted by Sergeant Brierly, about to enter the incident room and took a minute to thank them for coming in.

Karen smiled and said hello. Roy mumbled something. He could still hardly believe he was voluntarily in a police station helping the police with their enquiries, as the saying went. But once Audrey had settled them down by this seriously weird machine and the guy who worked it explained what he'd like them to do, things got really interesting.

The only photograph of Ava extant in black wig and cloak was on the screen. The idea was to change it so that she looked exactly as she had when going out last Wednesday night. By the time this was completed the only thing left from the original was the shape of Ava's face and her features. Even then the eyes, without false lashes, thick eyeliner and heavy shadow looked different. As for the wig, it was simply wiped away.

They started with the clothes. Roy described her jacket and it was drawn over and over again until they got it absolutely right. The colour proved difficult. He didn't want to use the four-letter word that was closest, what with Karen sitting there and everything. So he said, 'Sort of gold.' Then, 'Khaki-ish.' It was Karen who suggested mustard.

The curly auburn hair took ages as well, what with lightening it then darkening it. Putting more red in, then more blonde. When Roy thought they'd finally got it right Karen said it was too ginger. They were there for simply ages but the time just flew. Halfway along Sergeant Brierly brought some sandwiches and chocolate Hobnobs and orange squash. Roy was really sorry when it was all finished and they had to go home. He talked a lot about it afterwards and seriously thought about going into computers.

By 9.00 a.m. that same morning scene of crime officers had begun a scrupulous examination of Kinders. Forbes Abbot was agog. The large van, lined with shelves themselves loaded with all sorts of fascinating equipment, brought out the gawpers in ten seconds flat. Frankly inquisitive, they mostly just stared and asked questions of the officers, which were ignored.

Other villagers, just as nosy but feeling that to show it was rather infra dig, felt a sudden need to walk their dogs back and forth, visit the post office, or perhaps drop in on a friend.

The ducks had never known anything like it. Most days someone would drift down at some point with a handful or two of bread or a biscuit. This day there were hordes of feeders. And they didn't just toss a few crumbs into the water and go away. They hung around. The inexperienced ones had bought not just bread but cakes and tarts and stuff. One woman floated a whole lemon cheesecake, sending it on its way with a long stick, as if it was a boat. Another launched a large seeded bloomer. The pond became scummy, the surface crammed with bobbing confectionery. The ducks all climbed out and went to sit on the opposite bank

'They don't do all this for nothing, you know,' said an onlooker, jerking her head in the direction of the van's interior. 'A serious crime's gone on in that house.'

'They reckoned he died in an accident,' said the man next to her.

'Huh!' Another man, leaning against the van's bonnet with an air of authority. 'It'll be on *Crimewatch* – you see. A reconstruction.'

'Nick Ross'll sort it. He's ever so good.'

It was at this point that Sergeant Troy attempted to ease the DCI's car through the congestion. Restraining a natural inclination to lean on the horn and shout, which he would certainly have done had he been alone, Troy let the window down.

'Excuse me . . . Thank you . . . If you'd just . . . thank you.'

'Give them a good honk,' said Barnaby.

As the car passed through the outlying stragglers a woman, rocking a screaming toddler, stared through the windscreen. She spoke to her neighbour: 'I've seen him before – that fat bloke.'

' 'Ave you?'

'He were round the Garrets, Friday.'

Troy fixed his gaze straight ahead but couldn't help picking up the slow hiss near his left ear. The chief was very sensitive about his weight. Burly, as a description, he liked. Well built he could live with. And no one could reasonably complain on being described as 'a fine figure of a man'. But fat . . .

'I think this is it, sir.'

'Don't you know?'

'Well, according to the instructions—'

'Go and have a look. And get a move on – I'm not sitting here all day.'

Injustice plodded up the drive with Sergeant Troy. Wrongful accusation and unfairness marched alongside. He found himself muttering, as he seemed to have been doing all his life, man and boy, why is it always me? The building was Appleby House. He beckoned the DCI who, still glaring, got out of the car and slammed the door. Troy rang the bell.

Barnaby thought the man who appeared was probably about his own age. If younger, he'd been having a tough time. Perhaps he had been ill. But he smiled pleasantly enough.

'Mr Lawson?'

'What is it?'

'Detective Chief Inspector Barnaby, Causton CID.'

'Detective Sergeant Troy.'

'We need to talk to you regarding the death of Dennis Brinkley.'

'Yes – what's going on?' asked Lawson. 'Some of your people were here earlier after the keys to his house. Waving a bit of paper, which I suppose represented some sort of authority.'

'Perhaps we could come in?'

The furniture of the room they entered was strangely placed. Barnaby was reminded of a doll's house whose owner, bored, had tumbled it in any-old-how. Lawson vaguely apologised.

'Can you find somewhere to sit? We've only just moved in.'

Troy took down a dining chair from a stack of three, settled at the table and opened his briefcase to produce a notebook. Lawson remained standing. Barnaby perched on a low nursing chair. He thought the man seemed more nervous than curious, but that this probably didn't signify.

'I'm afraid I have some bad news. Recent developments have made it necessary for the police to reassess this case. It is now the subject of a murder inquiry.'

Lawson's body folded down suddenly on to the nearest piece of furniture, a coffee table. His jaw swung loose. He stared at the chief inspector, then directed his attention to Sergeant Troy as if he might there find an alternative theory.

But Troy just shrugged and said 'We have your evidence from the inquest, sir, but, given the change in circumstances, need to talk to you again.'

'What?'

'I understand Mr Brinkley was—'

'You've made a mistake. This just isn't possible.'

'Could you please help us by answering the questions, Mr Lawson?'

'No one would hurt Dennis. He was the most harmless person. Kind, friendly.'

'I understand you've known him a long time?' asked Barnaby.

'Since I was a child. He was my aunt's financial advisor.'

'How would you describe him?'

'I've just described him.'

'In business matters?'

'Scrupulous, intelligent, totally honest. Carey trusted him completely.'

'Successful?'

'I believe he was very successful.'

'Though in partnership, I understand.'

Lawson duly rattled through the history of Fallon and Brinkley now Brinkley and Latham. Asked his opinion of Dennis's partner, he said shortly, 'No idea. Never met him.'

'Would you expect Latham to – ah, inherit Brinkley's share of the business?'

'Certainly not. Dennis couldn't stand the man.'

Troy asked for Latham's first name and wrote down: 'Andrew Latham. Disliked by Brinkley. Distrusted? Reason?'

Barnaby moved to more personal matters, asking Lawson if he had any idea at all who might have had a reason for killing Dennis Brinkley.

'Of course not. The whole idea's preposterous.'

'Do you know if there was anything worrying him?'

'Actually . . . this won't be of any help to you, I'm afraid.'

'Tell us anyway, Mr Lawson,' said Sergeant Troy.

'He did want to discuss a problem that was causing some concern. We'd arranged to talk about it after dinner the night he died.'

'He gave you no idea at all what it was about?' asked Barnaby.

'I'm afraid not.'

'Not even whether it was work or something personal?'

Mallory shook his head.

'Do you know of anyone else he might have talked to? He must have had other friends.'

'Not that I know of. Quite a few people came to his funeral, though.'

'We'll need a list of their names and addresses at some point, sir,' said Sergeant Troy.

'Heavens – I don't know who they are.' He was starting to sound exasperated. 'There was a notice in *The Times*. They just turned up.'

'That's unfortunate,' said Barnaby. 'What about people in the village?'

'Dennis wasn't much of a mixer.'

'I understand that he and Miss Frayle were what one might call close.'

'Oh, yes. Poor Benny.' He looked up; a quick realisation. 'I suppose if you're right it means she was right.'

'Yes.' But Barnaby felt neither self-reproach nor guilt. No policeman would have attempted to overturn a properly obtained coroner's verdict on absolutely no evidence. 'The night Mr Brinkley died—'

'God. Do we have to?'

'Can you tell me exactly what happened from the time you arrived?'

'I . . . went into the war room.'

'The what?'

'It's a huge space where his machines were kept. He was lying on the floor close to a giant catapult thing. There's a sort of gulley overhead holding sling shot, great wooden things, heavy as cannon balls. It was hanging loose and one of them had rolled out and struck him on the head.'

'Only one?'

'One was enough.'

They must have been set to be released singly. Although Barnaby had seen photographs they had been taken purely to establish the physical details of the scene. He would have a closer look at the equipment when. SOCO were through.

'Can you tell me exactly what you did from the time you arrived at the house until the moment you left?'

Mallory went through it, sick at heart. These men didn't know what they were asking. The big one kept interrupting – which telephone did he use to call the ambulance? Did he leave the room and come back at any time? Did he touch or move the body at all? Why did he wash the wooden ball? Then the thinner, younger one asked why he cleaned up the mess.

'Christ!' At this point Mallory's ability to remain calm was lost. Provoked into anger at their insensitivity, at their persistence, at the fact that they were just damn well there, he shouted: 'What d'you expect me to do with brains and blood and vomit all over the floor? Leave it for his cleaner?'

Troy wrote down 'cleaner' and asked for her name. Barnaby continued his questioning.

'Have you been back to the house since, Mr Lawson?'

'No.'

'Does anyone else have keys?'

'Not that I'm aware.'

'What about this domestic?' asked Sergeant Troy.

'Doris? Oh, yes. I suppose she does.'

242

Mallory rested his head in his hands. His fury was evaporating as quickly as it had flared. These people had a job to do. If Dennis really had been deliberately killed he was the last person to be uncooperative.

'We shall need your fingerprints, Mr Lawson, for purposes of elimination.'

'Fine.'

'So, if you could come down to the station as soon as possible? Please bring the shoes you were wearing—'

'They were badly stained.' He gestured, pushing the memory from him. Pursing his mouth in disgust. 'I threw them away.'

Understandable, in an innocent man. Even more in a guilty one. And it was more common than was generally known for the first person on the scene, or the one who reported the crime actually to be the perpetrator.

Barnaby decided this would be a good time to imply that the interrogation was over. He struggled up from the nursing chair.

'Well, I think that's about it, Mr Lawson.' But he got nothing in the way of feedback. No sudden slackening of physical tension. Or relieved exhalation of breath. The man simply looked knackered. Maybe it really was time to call a halt. For now. 'But while I'm here I also need to talk to Mrs Lawson. And Miss Frayle.'

'They're in Causton. Benny had an appointment at Hargreaves, the solicitors.'

'D'you know what that was about, sir?' asked Sergeant Troy.

'No I don't,' retorted Mallory. 'And it's her business. Not yours.'

'Are they perhaps Mr Brinkley's solicitors?' asked Barnaby.

'So?'

'Maybe if they were that "close",' said Troy, a leer in his voice, 'she's mentioned in his will.'

'They were platonic friends who cared deeply for each other.' Mallory looked disgustedly at both men but hit on Troy for his next remark. 'No doubt that's totally beyond your comprehension.'

Barnaby decided against the Horse and Hounds for lunch. True, there was a chance of picking up some local gossip, but it was slight. Much more likely to end up trapped within earshot of someone boring for England. Or be exposed to an endless loop of musical sound bites: nothing longer than sixty seconds and guaranteed tune free. So he settled for the only alternative.

They were offered a window table at the Secret Garden. The very table, in fact, that the DCI's daughter and her husband had occupied over a week earlier. Barnaby scanned the menu. Sergeant Troy, who would much rather have gone to the pub, moodily regarded a vase of plastic freesias.

'They've got liver and bacon.'

'Right.'

'D'you want a look?'

'No. That'll do. And some chips.'

'Fried potatoes.'

'Whatever.'

There would have been a bit of life in the Horse and Hounds. A laugh and a joke. Maybe a pool table. Something on the telly. Then, having sighed over this collection of absent delights, Troy was left with the thing that was really bugging him, i.e., just who did this bloke, this Mallory Lawson, think he was? And what sort of name was Mallory anyway? Who'd ever heard of it? Troy certainly hadn't. Probably a 'family' name. A wanking public-school name going all the way back to William the bonking Conqueror. Who didn't go back to him? That's what Troy wanted to know. Everybody comes from somewhere. Just because you hadn't got your bit of paper with a seal on. Or your relatives crumbling under old church slabs.

'No doubt that's beyond your comprehension.' Troy repeated the remark, the patronising remark, in his mind for the umpteenth time. He always boasted that he didn't give a fairy's fart what anyone thought of him, a claim so transparently untrue that even Talisa Leanne saw through it. But he couldn't seem to put this insult from his mind. To a man who wanted more than anything in the world to be admired for his capabilities and intelligence to be told he was an insensitive cretin was a blow too far. And to his face as well.

'I should put that fork down.'

'What?'

'Before you snap the handle off.'

Troy flung his cutlery on to the cloth and began to shore up his defences. He recalled hearing that people who needed to put other people down were hopelessly insecure and decided it was definitely true. What other reason could they have? It was just a pity there were so many out there.

Though the woman who slapped their lunch on the table had a face like a squeezed lemon the food itself was delicious. Crisp rashers of bacon, nicely fried liver and fresh garden peas. All on station expenses too. Troy's spirits began to rise.

'So. Are we back to the Frayle woman's flat after this, Chief?'

'I want to see how SOCO are getting on first.'

'Bit of luck – no one else going in since Brinkley died.'

'We've only Lawson's word for that.'

'Think he's in the frame, then?'

'Hard to say, at this stage.'

'Have we got time for a pud?'

Thirty contented minutes later Troy followed the DCI into the village street. His heart was further gladdened by the sight of Abby Rose Carter on a house-to-house. The man she was questioning looked as if he had been struck by a thunderbolt. Troy smiled, waved, then realised he was walking on by himself. He turned back.

The chief was standing in front of a shabby building made of shingles. It had a rusty tin roof and was practically encircled by old yew trees.

'Blimey,' said Sergeant Troy. 'Talk about lowering the tone.'

'This is it.' Barnaby read the noticeboard. 'The Church of the Near at Hand.'

'Creepy.' Troy had a wander round. 'There's a window broken back here.'

Barnaby's nature was not of the type to be fascinated by the weird and the deathly but now he thought about the church and the people who came there. How lonely they must be, how desperate to be assured that the people they loved had not gone for ever. And what a comfort to be able to believe that one day they would all be together, living in paradise, time without end. Barnaby thought of his parents. Of Joyce still with him, thank God. Of his beloved daughter, just the thought of whose loss could bathe him in a cold sweat of terror. He was too honest to pretend that sometimes, in the dark watches of the night, he too did not long to deceive himself. But he couldn't, and in the bright rational light of day was not sorry. Happy ever after sounded great until you thought it through, when it began to sound like a fate worse than death. Imagine, thought Barnaby, millennia after millennia after millennia of radiant bliss. Having a nice day not only every single day but every single second of every single minute world without end, and never being able to call a halt. Enough to drive a man mad.

'It's a forest back there.' Troy came up, flicking black needles from his jacket sleeve. The two men walked on. 'Do you think Dennis Brinkley ever went?'

'Wouldn't have thought so. Not from the way Lawson described him.'

'There's gotta be a connection though, chief.'

Though hard to credit, this was undoubtedly true. Somewhere at some time something had happened to forge a link between the shy, stiffly correct financial consultant and the flamboyant, boastful necromancer Ava Garret.

'Did I tell you Cully had met her?'

'At the church?' Troy was amazed. He didn't know the chief's daughter well but she seemed to him the last person to go in for such wonky shenanigans. Cully had struck Sergeant Troy as pretty unmystical. A touch cynical, even.

'She rang last night to tell me about it. All to do with research.'

'For what?' Troy could never understand actors. He found it hard enough to be himself. Pretending to be all sorts of other people seemed quite deranged to him.

'She's playing a medium in *Blithe Spirit* and wanted to talk to some real ones.'

'But there aren't any real ones.'

'Don't try my patience, Troy.'

Oh, brilliant! When he said they didn't exist that was fine. Now I say they don't exist I'm trying his patience. Sometimes I wonder why I bother. All he really wants, all any of them really want, is a yes man. Agree with everything, praise whatever they do right or wrong, dumb your mind down, colour your nose brown. Right – I can do that. And from now on I will.

'That must be Brinkley's house.' Barnaby nodded towards SOCO's van and the strangely shaped building behind it.

'I expect it is, sir.'

As they climbed the front steps John Ferris, in charge of the SOCO unit, came out and Barnaby said: 'You through?'

'Not quite with the flat. But you're OK with the murder scene.'

'Better have a look then.'

'Be amazed.' Ferris grinned at him. 'Be very amazed.'

And they were. The twenty-five-by-twenty photographs showing the body of Dennis Brinkley and its immediate surroundings were no preparation at all for the vast expanse of space and light they now encountered. The towering structures, the great garlands of glowing waxen rope, massive crossbows, a butcher's hook on which you could have hung a brace of elephants.

Both men were disturbed by the machines, Sergeant Troy the more so. For no reason that he could have put into words, they struck him as deeply shocking. Barnaby quickly shook off this unease and turned his attention to the mechanism of the trebuchet. But Troy, who would have been completely at home at a modern armaments fair, felt his skin crawl and creep. Determined to conceal any weakness, and ignoring predatory shadows that seemed to press against the small of his back, he began to stride about, affecting an interest in the gigantic constructions. There was a hanging metal cage big enough to hold several men and next to this some stocks. Troy spent a pleasant couple of minutes picturing Mrs Sproat so constrained and himself throwing rotten cabbages, then ambled up to a three-tier wooden tower on wheels. There were long, narrow openings at regular intervals along the sides. Troy came closer and attempted to squint inside. A cool wash of air grazed his eyeball. He jumped back.

'Come and look at this.'

Sergeant Troy was glad to. He moved quickly, hurrying to where the chief was studying the apparatus that held the huge wooden balls. The rack, tilted at an extremely steep angle, was covered with grey powder.

'Blimey,' said Sergeant Troy. 'A dinosaur's bollocks. They go in this catapult thing?'

'Those or boiling oil or red-hot coals. Sometimes the heads of prisoners. They weren't fussy.'

'How d'you know all this?'

'The notes.' Barnaby indicated the illustration and paragraphs of text in a little frame on the wall nearby. 'All the machines have them.'

'So why's the sling in the wrong place for the ball to fall in?' The trebuchet had been shifted at least a couple of metres to the left of its original position. The drag marks were on the floor.

'Presumably so it would hit Brinkley instead.'

'But he wouldn't be daft enough to stand there, surely?' said Troy, already shedding his new role as yes man. 'How does the thing work, anyway?'

'Very simple.' Barnaby got out a handkerchief and pushed his shirt sleeves back. Aluminium was a sod to wash out. 'The balls are held in place by this block of wood. The rope,' he took a loose hanging cable in his hand, 'lifts the block and releases them, one at a time.'

'Only if you let it go, surely. Hold on and they'd all roll down.'

'No. There's a ridge look – halfway up. It drops down when the block moves then clicks upright again. Let's have a look at the glossies.'

Troy opened his bag and took out the photographs of Dennis Brinkley's mortal remains. Apart from the floor the only flat surface was a marble slab balanced on two columns of grey stone in the centre of the room. Troy spread the pictures out on this.

'So. He seems to have been lying exactly . . . here.' Barnaby walked back, one of the pictures in his hand. 'Would you mind, Troy?'

Yes, I bloody would mind, thought Sergeant Troy, already feeling somewhat fragile after his encounter with the spirit of the barbican.

'It would be very helpful.'

Troy got down on the floor. 'Just keep well away from that rope, Chief, OK?'

Barnaby walked slowly around the machine, studying Troy's stretched-out form from all angles.

'Can I get up now?'

'In a minute.' He got out his handkerchief. 'Lift up.' When Troy did, Barnaby spread the handkerchief precisely where his head had been. Troy got to his feet and Barnaby gave a tug on the rope. A ball rumbled down and landed almost directly on the linen square.

'That's how it was, all right.' Barnaby flourished the picture. 'See?'

'No thanks. We're having pizza tonight.'

'I think Brinkley moved the catapult himself. You can judge how far it was dragged by these marks, right?'

'Yes . . .' Here we go. First a close brush with squelching oblivion. Now an instant hernia. I shall want counselling for this.

'Drag it back, if you would. You can see the original place marks here.'

'Sir.'

But Troy had forgotten that, though skilfully aged and battered, this was but a lightweight facsimile of the real thing. He returned it quite easily to its original position. Then Barnaby again pulled on the rope. A second ball came hurtling down the ramp to fall short of the catapult's leather holding sack by about two feet.

Troy laughed. 'Measured things differently in those days, Chief.'

'No, no. Look at the finish – the precision in all of these machines. I suspect they were an obsession with Brinkley. He'd never overlook a fault like that.'

'So . . .?' Troy wandered round the trebuchet, looking upwards. 'The ramp has been messed with.'

'That's right. See if you can find some steps. Make sure they've been dusted.'

Troy found some lightweight alloy ones in the garage, brought them in and, having already sussed whose day this was for walking the plank, climbed straight up.

'How does it look?'

'Ratchet, two huge screws, a block underneath to support it. These balls must weigh a ton.'

'How's the block fixed?'

'Screws again.'

'So to alter the angle . . .?'

'Just remove the screws, rejig the ramp, put them back and retighten.'

'Taking the balls out first.'

'Blimey, yes. Otherwise the whole lot would come crashing down.'

'How long might that take?'

'Half an hour tops, I'd say.'

'The result being that the next time he reached out and tugged on the rope . . .'

'Kersplat!' Troy climbed down again.

'But why pull it at all?'

'Maybe he just played with the stuff,' said Troy. 'You know – like some blokes like trains.'

Barnaby decided to leave it there. SOCO's report should help them to a clearer understanding of the exact situation in this strange room on the day Dennis Brinkley was killed. The chief inspector collected the rest of the pictures from the stone slab, which he now saw was engraved in gold with rather beautiful calligraphic script. He read out the lines.

'Throwing first he struck the horn of the horse-haired helmet, and the bronze spearpoint fixed in his forehead and drove inward through the bone; and a mist of darkness clouded both eyes and he fell as a tower falls in the strong encounter.'

The Iliad, Book Four'

After a moment's silence Sergeant Troy spoke. 'Repressed, that's what they are, these loners. Going around that respectable and timid and law-abiding, and all the while hoarding this mad stuff. Police files are full of them.'

Barnaby said mildly, 'He didn't actually do anything.'

'Bet he did. Otherwise why knock him off?'

248

* * *

After examining Dennis Brinkley's flat Barnaby returned to Appleby House to be told that Miss Frayle was presently in her own flat above the stables.

Though the stables themselves were in a neglected state, with half the doors missing and the stonework flaky, the architect had done a grand job on the conversion. Totally in period, he had even accommodated the original clock tower, though the metal face and coach-and-horses weathercock were now heavily stained with verdigris. The hands on the clock had stopped at seven.

Benny had seen the two men climbing the stairs. A narrow veranda with wooden rails ran the length of the flat and she came along it to meet them. She was smiling and Barnaby could see the smile was not one of triumph but simply an expression of relieved satisfaction.

'Chief Inspector, it's good to see you again.' She held out her hand. 'Welcome to my home.'

And very nice too, thought Sergeant Troy, taking it all in. He was thinking of getting some work done on his loft but it was a cramped little hole and would never look anything like this.

'Nice, isn't it?' said Benny. 'It's only one living space wide, of course, so every room opens into the next – like a box puzzle. But as I live by myself that doesn't matter. They used to store all the spare tack up here. And animal feed.'

'Miss Frayle,' said Barnaby, 'I need to talk to you—'

'Would you like some tea? We're in the kitchen already, as you see. On the spot, as it were.'

'We've just had lunch, thank you,' said Sergeant Troy.

'Through here then.'

They disposed themselves about the sitting room. Troy at a satiny oval table on a spindle chair, the chief inspector on a tapestry settee and Benny in a high-backed wing chair by the old-fashioned mantelpiece. Barnaby couldn't help noticing how carefully she lowered herself into this chair, how gently she rested her fingers on the padded arms.

'I want to thank you, Inspector, for personally coming to tell me about this latest development,' said Benny, 'but Mallory has already put me in the picture. If only I'd known I could have saved you a journey.'

'There are other matters. One or two questions.'

'Oh, really?' She straightened her shoulders, setting them firmly back. 'Fire away, then.'

'I'm afraid I have to ask you to recall the night Mr Brinkley was killed.' He thought it wise to get the bad stuff over first. He was expecting fear and trembling. Perhaps a perfectly understandable refusal to confront such appalling memories.

But Benny simply said calmly, 'I understand.'

'Why were you actually there, Miss Frayle?'

'Dennis was coming to dinner at seven thirty. After waiting twenty minutes or so I went to look for him. He was never late, you see.'

'How did you get into the house?'

'Through the kitchen.'

'You didn't ring the bell?'

'I did but he didn't come. I wasn't too surprised. The front door was usually locked and bolted. Much easier, he used to say, to go in straight from the garage.'

'I see.' It must have been unbolted for the paramedics, presumably by Lawson. So where did he get the key?

'Did you notice anything out of the ordinary when you went through the flat?'

'No.'

'Please, take a moment to think. The smallest detail could be important.'

'I walked straight through the kitchen, checked the two other rooms, and then – found him.'

'Was the door to this place with the machines closed?'

'Yes.'

And then Barnaby understood how precariously her calm was maintained. He watched her open the door again. Saw the terrible image flare behind her eyes. All colour left her face. Even her lips were white.

'Can I get you something?' Troy pushed back his chair. 'A glass of water?'

Benny shook her head. Barnaby observed a tic, jumping fiercely just beneath the crescent of fat under her left eye and recognised that he had made a mistake. He should have worked up to or around this. Started with questions that would have seemed innocuous; eased her gradually into that dreadful place. Her relaxed demeanour had misled him. Too late now.

'So, did you enter the room, Miss Frayle?'

'Yes. I went in. Just enough to. Then I ran away.'

'Straight to Appleby House?'

'I don't know. I don't remember going back. Only waking up in the hospital.'

She was staring around at the furniture, at the windows and pictures as if she had never seen them before. The awkward silence lengthened. Barnaby hesitated. Troy spoke up.

'Actually – I hope it's all right – but could I change my mind about the tea?'

'Tea? Of course. Yes, yes.' Benny, propelled to her feet by convention and good manners, re-entered the present moment. 'I'll put the kettle on.'

Sergeant Troy, encouraged by a nod of approval from the DCI, followed her into the kitchen. Barnaby heard them chatting, clattering cups. The odd phrase filtered out. They seemed to be talking about cats, books,

250

someone called Ashley. Visiting Croydon. There was a crackling of paper and a cry from Troy: 'Oohh . . . I love those.' Then they came back, the sergeant carrying a heavy tray.

As Benny poured the tea she was thinking how wrong it was to make quick judgements when first meeting people. She had thought Sergeant Troy ill-mannered, even unkind, but today he couldn't have been nicer. Look at him now, passing the ginger nuts.

Barnaby, wondering how best to phrase his next question, was glancing over the contents of some bookshelves near his sofa. Most of the names meant nothing to him: Rosamund Pilcher, Josephine Cox, Mary Wesley. There was a Bible and a New Testament. Some paperbacks of a spiritual nature: *The Cloud of Unknowing*, *St John of the Cross*, *Honest to God*. Also a complete set of Jane Austen and some very old volumes that must have been prizes, for surely no child ever willingly came by *Palgrave's Golden Treasury* or *The Children of the New Forest*. *Treasure Island*, of course, was something else. Miss Frayle seemed like the sort of person who would keep a school prize all her life.

Once more Troy said exactly the right thing. 'That's a really beautiful painting, Miss Frayle.'

'Oh, do you think so? It was left to me by my . . . well, employer, I suppose you'd say. Though Carey was much more to me than that. I was her companion for thirty years.'

Barnaby knew a lead in when he saw one. 'So is that how long you've known Dennis Brinkley?'

'D' you know, I suppose it is. Heavens – where does the time go?'

'Was he a friend of the family?' asked Troy.

'He handled Carey's financial affairs.'

'And your own, perhaps?' said Barnaby.

'Gracious, no!' She nearly laughed. 'I haven't got any money.' Then her expression changed with almost comic rapidity into one of sad recollection. 'Actually, that's not true.'

Blimey, thought Troy. How can anybody be so out of it they don't even know whether they're skint or not?

'I only heard an hour or two ago but it appears Dennis has left me Kinders and all its contents in his will.'

'How do you feel about that?' Barnaby almost threw the remark away. It was barely a question at all. Just a comment, marking time until the primed one. The one where you pulled the pin.

'My immediate impulse was to reject it, though of course I won't, because it's what he wanted. But I can't imagine ever going in there again.'

'Miss Frayle,' Barnaby leaned forward but comfortably, not threatening. 'Have you any idea at all who could have killed him?'

'No. Such wickedness can have no explanation. He was a lovely man who never harmed a soul.'

251

'Then why, from the moment of the coroner's verdict to the contrary, have you persistently maintained that he was murdered?'

'I knew you'd ask me that, Inspector. And I'm afraid my answer will seem most unsatisfactory.' A curtain stirred at the window and Benny got up to close it. She didn't come back to her seat but stood fiddling with a geranium on the sill, pulling off the dead leaves.

'Dennis loved life in such a simple way. Something nice to eat. History books to read. Watching cricket on television. And his machines. Every evening he would spend an hour or so in the war room and I'm going back half a lifetime. No one else was allowed to touch them. When they needed to be cleaned or oiled he did it himself. He knew each nut and bolt and how everything worked so there is no way that what happened to him could have been an accident. Do you see?'

Barnaby saw any casualty department any weekend, full of people holding on to dripping thumbs or hopping on one foot. Do-it-yourself addicts who had also known every nut and bolt then let their minds wander. A second was all it took.

'And there's something else.'

The DCI was happy to hear it. To his mind, wishful thinking did not rate very highly as an aid to crime analysis.

'I'd been invited – just a few days before his death – for dinner. I found Dennis standing in front of that awful catapult thing. He looked so worried I asked if anything was wrong. He said, "I think there's a ghost in the machine." '

The two policemen exchanged glances. Troy had been expecting nothing useful anyway, but Barnaby was disappointed, resentful even. He recalled the scene in his office nearly two weeks ago when she had first delivered this 'information'. All that passionate insistence when all she had to go on was some daft remark about a ghost. On the other hand . . .

'Do you remember exactly when this was, Miss Frayle?'

'Yes. The weekend before he died. Saturday evening. We had some lovely turbot.'

'Might he have meant the machine wasn't . . . correctly aligned, say?'

'Oh, no. Dennis was a perfectionist. He would have noticed the slightest little thing out of order and put it right. There would have been no imbalance.' Benny faltered, then, on the verge of tears, repeated herself. 'In his life there was no imbalance.'

Useless question, anyway. Chief Inspector Barnaby, still wrestling with disappointment, chided himself for asking it. But it did confirm that the machine had not been tampered with until the day Brinkley was killed. Still irritable, his patience in short supply, Barnaby indicated that his sergeant should continue.

Troy drained his cup, murmured 'lovely tea'. Then, with a friendly smile asked Benny if she had ever attended the Church of the Near at Hand.

'Once or twice.' Benny smiled back. 'It's not really my sort of thing.'

'The reason we ask,' continued Troy, 'is because of the medium who died. Ava Garret?'

Benny nodded. She looked concerned and anxious to help.

'Did you see her at the church at all?'

'I'm not very good at putting names to faces.'

'As she seems to have a definite connection to this case—'

'If you don't mind my asking,' enquired Benny timidly, 'why are you writing all this down?'

Nothing useful happened after that. Sergeant Troy explained what a statement was. Barnaby made the fingerprint request and was assured by Miss Frayle that she would present herself at Causton police station the very next day. Then the two men left, descending the narrow wooden steps into the sunshine.

As they reached the ground Barnaby said, 'You did well back there, Sergeant.'

Troy, transformed, just stood and breathed for a moment. Then managed a mumbled, 'Sir.'

'We'll try the house again for Mrs Lawson. Save us doubling back. And we shall need the cleaner's prints. Sort it when we get to the office.'

'Right, Guv.'

'And wipe that silly smirk off your face.'

They were in luck finding Kate Lawson at home but out of luck as far as finding any fresh information was concerned. She supported everything her husband had said but had nothing new to offer.

Roy was finding it hard to believe that it was only five days since Ava had died. So many things had happened. So much had changed. Even the house looked different, mainly because of the flowers. People had started leaving them by the gate and Karen had had a lovely time arranging lupins and roses and some beautiful yellow irises in a couple of old jugs she had found under the stairs. Notes had been pushed through the letter box by neighbours offering any sort of help needed. And Fred Carboy had taken the keys of Ava's Honda, parked it neatly out of harm's way on the far side of the Crescent, and offered what he assured them was a good price should they want to get rid of it.

It was almost eleven o'clock and Roy was taking a break from painting Karen's room. The second coat of Princess Pink was drying and he was admiring the ceiling, pale blue with stick-on stars. Because of the smell Karen was sleeping in the lounge under the new Cinderella duvet. They had thrown her old curtains on the bonfire, which was still going strong in the back garden.

There was nothing left now of Ava's mattress. Or bedding. Or bed. Most of her clothes were blazing away as well. Doris had helped Roy and Karen sort through things the evening before and there was really very little that didn't smell musty, to put it politely. Some new shoes, a couple of scarves and a dress had been put in a box for jumble, cosmetics and bottles of nail stuff thrown away. And that was it. All gone.

Now, eating Mars bars at the kitchen table, Roy and Karen were going through *Loot*. Things were amazingly cheap. And barely second-hand at all, according to the sellers. Roy, having moved off his shelf and out of his hutch, was looking for a bed. Karen, quicker at reading, described what was on offer. Nearly everything said 'Buyer Collects', but there were also lots of ads for drivers with vans so that wouldn't be a problem. So Karen wrote down telephone numbers and Roy pictured good-as-new divans with sprung mattresses and stripped pine headboards, bunk beds, antique-style beds and even an inflatable one you could let down and take on holiday.

Meanwhile Doris was once more on her way to Rainbow Lodge. You could almost say she'd never left it, for she had thought of little else since Roy's heartbreaking story had left her reeling. She couldn't get it out of her mind. She had even dreamed of the newly motherless child and the never-wanted, desperate boy. As for that awful house . . .

Choosing her moment carefully, after Alan Titchmarsh but before the snooker, she shared some of this concern with Ernest. She barely told him the half of it and tried to sound casual when suggesting they might come round for a meal sometime, but Ernest was not fooled. He knew his Doris. Having no family had been the greatest disappointment of her life. When she was younger all the love she had to give was lavished on the children of her sister, who became so spoiled it had almost caused a rift between them. So now Ernest said it was fine by him if Roy and Karen came to tea. It would be nice to have some youngsters around the place for once.

Doris had packed a basket before she left. Just a few things from the larder – home-made jam and chutney, a coffee cake from the WI stall and some vegetables from her neighbour's allotment. She also picked up a bottle of children's aspirin from the Spar, having been concerned yesterday about the little girl's headaches, which hardly seemed to stop before another one began. Not that Karen complained. It was Roy who was worrying himself silly over what he called 'Karen's heads'. One aspirin every twenty-four hours, Doris had been assured, wouldn't hurt. Really she would like to take the child to a doctor but these were very early days and she planned to tread carefully.

The second she got inside the front door of Rainbow Lodge Karen ran up to her crying 'We've done this amazing drawing. On a machine!'

'What's that all about then?' said Doris. She thought how sweet Karen looked in her new jeans and a white T-shirt showing a basketful of puppies.

'And Roy's painting my room. Come and see.'

They went upstairs and Doris admired the Princess Pink colour and lovely new duvet.

Roy said, 'I'm going to paint next door all white.'

Walking back along the L-shaped landing Doris peered around the corner of the leg, finding a pile of cushions and pillows on a thin mattress and a wooden shelf holding magazines. Seeing that she was puzzled, Karen explained.

'That's Roy's room.'

'Or was,' said Roy.

Doris carried on downstairs, not trusting herself to utter a word. She believed in never speaking ill of the dead but there were no rules about thinking ill and she thought very ill of Ava indeed. Call that a room? Doris had seen roomier egg boxes. Downstairs she put the kettle on, made the tea and cut Roy an absolutely huge slice of cake.

CHAPTER TWENTY

The next morning the news that Ava Garret had been deliberately killed had made not only the local radio and television bulletins but also the *Causton Echo*. Give it twenty-four hours, thought DCI Barnaby, and the tabloids'll be swarming all over the place. The landlord of the Horse and Hounds won't know what's hit him.

The chief inspector had been in the incident room, almost empty but for the civilian telephonists, since half-past seven, working through yesterday's house-to-house reports. As he had expected, given the passage of time since Dennis Brinkley's death, they were bare of any really useful information. No one had seen any person or anything unusual in the village on the day in question, as far as they could recall. The feedback on Brinkley's general demeanour and personality bore out what little Barnaby had gathered already. His general civility stopped a little short of real friendliness. He kept himself to himself but gave generously at the door and always contributed a handsome prize to the local fête's tombola. His relationship with Benny Frayle was indulgently regarded. The landlady at the Horse and Hounds offered a kindly if slightly patronising summation: they were nice company for each other but everyone knew there was nothing really going on.

Ava Garret was something else. Only a few people admitted to knowing her but those who did had plenty to say. The way she treated that poor little kid was a crying shame. The child was afraid of her own shadow. Plus Ava's airs and graces were enough to make a cat laugh. No one believed her story about being married to a man who'd been to public school. What would he want with somebody whose dad was a navvy and mother a toilet attendant? As for her heavenly powers – the general opinion seemed to be that Ava was no more psychic than the dog's dinner. No one questioned admitted to attending the Church of the Near at Hand.

Throughout, the village opinion on any personal link between Garret and Dennis Brinkley remained firmly in the negative. As one crusty old gaffer in his retirement bungalow put it – he may have been weird but he weren't barmy.

Also on Barnaby's desk were a large stack of pictures showing Ava as she had appeared on the night she died. Quite unrecognisable when compared to the vampiric photograph pinned up on the board.

The chief inspector closed the files, pushed his swivel chair back and took a moment to savour the cool, refreshing atmosphere. Ah – the joys of air conditioning. He recalled the heat of last summer when the room had still been fitted with heavy ceiling fans. Wooden blades the size of aircraft propellors had languidly agitated banks of stale air, barely disturbing drifts of assorted insects. Progress – you couldn't whack it.

He checked his watch. Twenty minutes to the nine-thirty briefing. Just time to nip downstairs for sausage, egg and bacon. Definitely no chips. Or fried bread. And when he returned replete and in good humour there would his team be, bright-eyed, bushy-tailed and raring to go. In your dreams, Tom, as the saying went.

The briefing didn't take long. The new pictures were distributed; allocations to be covered shared out and off they went. All but DS Brierly.

'So, Audrey,' said the DCI. 'Well done, getting Priest to come in yesterday.'

'It wasn't difficult, sir. I think they both enjoyed themselves actually.'

'How were things at Rainbow Lodge?'

'I'm not really sure.' Pulling a chair up to his desk. 'She's a strange little soul.'

'Karen?' He recalled the child, frightened and wistful with her transparent skin and colourless hair. Like some manifestation in a ghost story. 'Yes, that's a good description.'

'I checked things out as well as I could without seeming to. The house is clean. There's plenty to eat. And there's someone looking after them.'

'Oh, good.'

'An Aunty Doris, by all accounts.'

Audrey had been extremely relieved that the aunt was present. She had not gone alone to Rainbow Lodge but had carefully chosen someone totally unthreatening – a young constable, barely three months into the service – who would have been pretty useless in the role of supporting adult.

But DC Cotton had not been entirely a waste of space. Admiring the newly decorated rooms, talking about football, bemoaning the lack of any decent clubs in Causton, he had got on very well with Roy while remaining blissfully unaware that Roy thought him a complete and utter wanker.

Sergeant Brierly had been terribly tempted to take Karen's aunt to one side, reveal the frightening truth about Ava Garret's death and leave Doris whatever her name was to do the dirty work. But she couldn't do that. No one forgets the deliverer of terrible news. They are remembered with revulsion: hatred even. A child especially will not forget. So Audrey sat down with Karen on the stained settee and held her hand and gently explained that someone had deliberately given her mother a poisonous drink and that was why she had died.

'Like the apple in Snow White?' asked Karen.

'Yes,' said Audrey, not knowing the story.

'But then she coughed and the apple came out and she was all right again.'

'Fairy tales are different,' said Audrey.

257

'I wonder who it was.'

'We think whoever she went out with on Wednesday night.'

'The man from the BBC?'

Audrey was spared from wrestling with an answer to that as Doris came in with a large pot of tea and some lemonade for Karen. Doris said: 'Fetch Roy, there's a good girl.' Karen ran off and Audrey repeated her announcement. Though she tried to make her voice flat and dull the words still seemed absurdly melodramatic. But Doris took it all quite calmly, saying that that possibility had been on a lot of people's minds but no one had liked to say so out loud.

'Karen hardly reacted at all,' murmured Audrey, hearing the others coming. 'But later on . . . I think she's bound to feel . . . um . . .'

'Don't you worry about Karen,' said Doris. 'I'll be looking after her. She's been sold short for too long, that little lass. She needs a lot of love.'

'Don't we all,' murmured Audrey. But silently.

Karen had obviously told Roy, who came downstairs, his eyes shining. Geoff Cotton followed, dribbling an invisible football while Karen shouted, 'Goal, goal.' Roy immediately started bombarding Audrey with questions. She fielded them patiently for a while, then brought up the matter of he and Karen coming into the station to help them sort out a recent likeness of her mother.

Roy was hesitant but Doris said he really should, out of decency's sake. And Karen, once the procedure was described, got very excited and wanted to go straightaway. She loved computers. So that was settled.

'Is she a permanent thing – this aunty?' asked Sergeant Troy. The vulnerable, fragile little girl, so near to his own daughter's age, had quite got to him.

'I think so. Mrs Crudge—'

'Crudge?' exclaimed Barnaby. 'That rings a bell.'

'It's Brinkley's cleaner, sir,' said Troy. 'She's coming in today.'

'When?' On being told one o'clock, Barnaby looked at his watch. 'We should be back by then.'

'From?'

'I want to check out Brinkley's office. See what this partner of his is really like.'

'According to Lawson he couldn't stand the bloke.'

'Hardly an impartial observer.'

'As you say, Guv.' Imparshal. One more word to look up in Talisa Leanne's dictionary. Education, there was no end to it.

The old brass plate beside the street door on Market Hill still read 'Brinkley & Latham: Financial Consultants'. Very sensible, thought DCI Barnaby. From what he had heard about Dennis Brinkley's business acumen and personal probity, the name would probably continue to inspire confidence even though the man himself was no longer present.

Leading the way upstairs, Sergeant Troy was already looking forward to checking out the talent. Alas, the receptionist proved to be a bit of a dog but, once she had led them into the main office, things began to improve. A very pretty blonde was operating the photocopier. Not as pretty as Abby Rose, but then – who was?

As Barnaby introduced himself and stated his business a man emerged from one of the enclosed cubicles. He had an air of being in charge and introduced himself as Leo Fortune.

'We've been expecting a visit. Ever since the news that Dennis had . . . um . . . since we heard . . .'

'What really happened to him,' concluded the woman from reception.

Barnaby noted Fortune's hesitation and was not surprised. It was a funny word, murder. It sold more papers and books and movies than any other. No TV drama series would risk their ratings for long without introducing one. True crime reconstructions were watched by millions. Complacently wise after the event, they would then have 'their say' by phone and e-mail. But when the victim is personally known that all changes. Then reaction is muted and euphemism sets in.

'Is anyone away today?' asked Barnaby.

'Two are on holiday.'

'One holiday, one honeymoon.' Gail Fuller nodded towards two vacant desks.

'And . . .?' Barnaby glanced towards the empty office.

'Mr Latham has not, so far, favoured us with his presence.'

'Oh, be fair, Leo,' argued a youth in a pink-striped shirt. 'It's barely twelve o'clock.'

There were a few sniggers at this but they quickly died away. Everyone became quiet and serious as befitted the gravity of the occasion. Though the staff were looking concerned, there was no feeling of unease in the room. They all met Barnaby's gaze frankly though he had been round the block enough times to realise how little that signified.

'Mr Brinkley died on Tuesday, the twenty-fourth of July. Were you all here then?'

The office junior, who turned out to be doing only work experience, was at school. And a stoutish woman with a large nose and a Snoopy telephone admitted to being absent on a Rolfing With Angels course at the Steiner Institute.

'And Mr Latham?'

'He turned up mid-morning, as usual.'

Barnaby asked the rest if they went out at all that day. Only Leo Fortune and Latham had not left the office. The others had 'nipped off' to shop, grab some lunch or go to the library. Asked to be more precise as to time, the longest anyone was absent was fifty minutes. This was down to the pink-striped man, who had spent the break in the Magpie playing bar billiards and drinking Guinness.

'And when do you close?'

'Five thirty, officially,' said Fortune, 'though Dennis and sometimes myself are often here later.'

'And that night?'

'I honestly can't remember. There was no reason to till now.'

'Quite,' said Barnaby. He came across this all the time. Unless something incredibly interesting or appalling had happened during the day under discussion who on earth was going to remember it three weeks later?

'Are any of you familiar with this Near at Hand church?' No one appeared to be. 'Did Mr Brinkley ever mention it at all?'

'He never talked about his personal life,' said Belinda, the pretty blonde.

'Isn't it to do with the other world?' asked the stout lady, whose name was Dimsie. She sounded sorrowful and just a teeny bit cross. 'I'm afraid Mr Brinkley had little time for the spiritual.'

'Did you hear this medium – Ava Garret – broadcast?'

'I shouldn't think so. We were all working.'

'Can anyone imagine why someone would wish to kill Mr Brinkley?'

The response was immediate. Fervent denials followed by warm and plainly sincere incredulity that anyone could have brought themselves to do such a wicked thing.

'It'll be a stranger.'

'That's right. No one who knew Dennis would—'

'Absolutely.'

'Wish I could meet the bastard up a dark alley.' The billiard player flexed his arm, and an incipient muscle, like a piece of thin string, upped and stretched itself.

'How come the verdict was wrong the first time?'

Barnaby spent a few moments explaining what they would soon be able to read in the papers, then asked them again to try to cast their minds back, this time to the weeks leading up to Dennis's death.

'Did any of you notice any change in Mr Brinkley? Did he seem worried about anything in particular?'

Everyone shook his or her head, though Barnaby noticed Leo Fortune frowning to himself.

'Are you permanently on reception?' he asked the middle-aged woman who had let them in. She nodded. 'Could you tell me if anyone called to visit him that you hadn't seen before? A new client, perhaps?'

'No.'

'What about phone calls? Was anyone especially persistent? Not, necessarily a business client.'

'I can assure you,' she flushed angrily, 'I've better things to do with my time than listen in to other people's conversations.'

Barnaby widened his interrogation somewhat, asking how the death of their employer might affect the staff. Would all their jobs remain secure, for example?

At this the mood changed. People looked at each other a touch mistily. Smiled and nodded. Leo Fortune spoke for them all. Barnaby offered his congratulations, noting that here were seven neat little motives and no mistake. Some doubtless stronger than others. Perhaps he had been a touch too quick to dismiss the present company. He got up from his perch on the corner of a desk and nodded at the busily scribbling figure of his assistant.

'Sergeant Troy will take your names and addresses. And those of any members of staff who are away.' He raised his eyebrows, nodding towards Fortune's glassed-off enclosure.

The man left the group, followed the chief inspector, sat down behind his desk and said, 'No, I didn't.'

'You anticipate me, Mr Fortune.'

'None of us knew about the will. We were all knocked sideways. There were a lot of tears the day the solicitor came. And they weren't just tears of gratitude.'

'You have been here . . .?'

'The longest. Twenty-four years.'

'So presumably you have taken over Mr Brinkley's clients?'

'Yes. He didn't have many but what he had were choice.'

'Which means?'

'Stonking rich.'

'Do you know any of them? Or are you going in cold, as it were?'

'I'm familiar with the accounts, of course. They were our most important, so someone other than Dennis had to be. Not that he was ever ill.'

'And the other partner?'

'Latham?' He gave a shout of what appeared quite genuine laughter. 'He's pathetic. His father-in-law bought into the business, apparently to get him from under his wife's feet. The man can hardly use a computer.'

'So what does he do all day?'

'Smokes, drinks, walks about, reads the paper. Disappears for long periods.'

'And he gets a salary for that?'

'No. Gilda – that's his wife – gives him hand-outs. When she thinks he deserves it.'

'What about clients?'

'Hasn't any. He inherited a few from old man Fallon but they all decamped. Some to myself. Others just left.'

'And his share of the company?'

'Her share. Forty-nine per cent.' He beamed with satisfaction, showing sharp white teeth. 'So we'll always have the edge.'

'I'd better take his address and phone number.'

As Leo Fortune scrawled this down he said, 'By the way, the night

Dennis died I was playing David Bliss in *Hay Fever*.' He handed the sheet of paper over. 'Amdram, you know.'

'Yes,' said Barnaby. He remembered his daughter at Cambridge. John Webster at the ADC. Amdram with a vengeance. The stage alight.

'Why did you ask us about going out during the day? The papers said Dennis died in the early evening.'

'That's true. But the apparatus that killed him was set up before he arrived home.'

Fortune looked puzzled at the word 'apparatus'. Barnaby explained in precise detail what had happened and straightaway regretted it.

'Christ . . . how absolutely . . .' Fortune then turned an interesting pale green and began to slip from his chair.

Five minutes later the two policemen were out in the street. They did not leave in good odour. Someone was pushing Leo's head between his knees while someone else, directing a deeply reproachful glance in the chief inspector's direction, rushed past with a glass of water.

The others had gathered around Belinda. The beautiful Belinda, just married, deeply in love and newly pregnant was shrilly holding forth while tossing her curls about. Of all the bloody cheek was her gist. And her with a ring on and everything. All those who weren't already giving Barnaby a hard stare went to work on Sergeant Troy.

'Anyone'd think,' he said, now sulking outside on the pavement, 'I'd asked her how much for a blow job.'

'What did you ask her?'

'Would she like a drink after work? What's so terrible about that?' Troy started savagely kicking a hamburger box in the gutter. 'I thought we were supposed to be living in the twenty-first century.'

'Only just.'

'I should have remembered my stars.' Troy, always prepared to assign to fate what he refused to concede to self-awareness, developed his theme. 'Maureen read them over breakfast. "Any desire for intimacy is way off scale this week." '

'Maybe that was just wishful thinking on her part?'

'No.' Troy, missing the point, bowed to the inevitable. 'Apparently Orion's on the cusp.'

'You'll be on the cusp any minute now if you don't stop kicking that bloody box about.'

Barnaby was halfway through an excellent steak pie and buttered carrots in the canteen when the desk let him know that Mrs Crudge had arrived.

'Off you go, Sergeant.'

'Sir?'

'Look after her, see her through the system, take her to my office. Sort some tea. The usual stuff.'

Troy watched the chief chomping away, then looked down at his own plate. At the fine piece of succulent haddock, potato croquettes and mushy peas. Not much point in asking them to put it in the oven. Once he'd left the table that was it. No wonder he was so thin. He thought, I'm fading away. They'll be sorry when I'm gone.

Barnaby finished his meal. For a shameful moment he toyed with the idea of eating Troy's fish. Excusing such a gluttonous impulse by wondering what might be waiting for him that night at Arbury Crescent and fantasising going to bed hungry, something he had never done in his life. He hurried away before greed could get the better of him.

'Look at this mess.' Mrs Crudge waggled stained fingers in the air. 'That stuff they give you to wipe it off wouldn't clean a mouse's bottom.'

'Sorry about that. Thank you for coming—'

'What d'you want my fingerprints for anyway?'

'Elimination,' explained Barnaby. 'How did the—'

'Nobody believes this. You should have heard them in the post office. Murder – in Forbes Abbot!'

People were always saying such things to the chief inspector. And with exactly that mingling of shock and indignation. It was as if their special patch had been granted divine exemption from such nastiness and the Almighty had done a runner on the deal.

Sergeant Troy opened the interview by asking if he could take one or two details from Mrs Crudge, starting with her Christian name.

'I gave all that to them what come to the house. I'm not going through it again.'

'Not to worry,' said Barnaby. 'First, could you tell me how long you've been employed by Mr Brinkley?'

'Since he moved to the village, so that's over twenty years. But the office job, nearer five. After their last cleaner retired.'

'He was easy to work for?'

'A lovely man. Straight as a die. And courtesy itself. Mind you, he was very particular.'

'In what way?'

'Things had to be just so. Take ornaments – I had to put them back precisely in their place. A fraction of an inch out and he'd know. And any bit of a ruck in a cushion or curtain he'd be there, smoothing it out.'

'Goodness, that is particular.'

'Like he was driven to it,' said Mrs Crudge.

'What about the room with the machines?' asked Sergeant Troy. 'Did you clean in there?'

'Just the floor. He wouldn't let me touch anything else. I wouldn't want to neither – horrible things.'

'The day he died—' began Barnaby.

'I never went in. My days are Wednesday and Friday.'

'And the previous Friday when you did the floor, did everything look as usual?'

'I couldn't swear to that. I just mop it over and scarper.'

'Would you have noticed,' asked Sergeant Troy, 'if there were drag marks on the floor, made perhaps by moving the apparatus about?'

'Oh, I'd've noticed that all right.'

Barnaby wondered if the murderer knew the cleaner would not be coming in on the day the machine was tampered with. If Dennis was as private a person as had been suggested, the murderer might well have been ignorant of her very existence. Unless he lived in the village. Like Lawson.

'I presume you have house keys?' Mrs Crudge nodded. 'Do you know if anyone else does?'

'Nobody. Mr Brinkley was most security-conscious.'

The DCI couldn't let that pass. 'We saw several keys hanging on a board in the garage.'

'They'd be for the garden shed and such,' said Mrs Crudge. 'Anyway, it wasn't burglars so much he was worried about as the threat of damage to his precious machines.'

Barnaby tried for the hundredth time to put himself into the shoes of Dennis Brinkley. And failed again. 'What about visitors? Did anyone come on a regular basis?'

'How would I know? When I was at Kinders he was at the office.'

'What about phone calls? Did you ever take messages?'

'No. Mr Brinkley always said to ignore the telephone.'

'Did you have keys to the office as well?'

'That's right. I do Saturday mornings, when the place is empty.'

'And now,' Barnaby smiled, 'I believe you're a shareholder?'

'Me and Ernest are already shareholders,' bridled Mrs Crudge. 'We're with BT. And British Water.'

At this point there was a knock at the door and a uniformed policewoman came in with a tray. Three plastic beakers of tea, some sugar and a plastic spoon.

'Pushing the boat out then?' suggested Mrs Crudge. Brought up never to drink tea with a hat on, she removed her black felt, placed in on the floor beside her chair and stirred in three sugars. 'Saw you coming out of Appleby House yesterday. How d'you get on?'

'You know the Lawsons?' asked Sergeant Troy.

'Worked for the old lady since I were fifteen,' said Mrs Crudge. 'I'm still there – for now, at any rate. Remember Mallory growing up. When Benny first came.'

'You must know her well, Miss Frayle.'

'I'm very fond of Ben. 'Course, it was all down to me that she got that message from Mr Brinkley in the first place.'

'The message . . .?'

264

'From the world of spirit. I was the one who persuaded her to go.'

'To the Church of the Near at Hand?'

'I'm a senior member. There's not much going on there I don't know about.'

'Really?' Barnaby put his tea aside, folded his arms and rested his elbows on the edge of his desk. He looked sympathetic, concerned and very, very interested. 'So, tell us all about it, Mrs Crudge.'

Andrew Latham rested in a vast rose-patterned hammock under a fringed awning to protect against the sun. Lying back on the puffy, goosedown cushions, he pulled on a silky cord, let it slip through his fingers, pulled on it again gently tilting the hammock to and fro. Within easy reach was a low table with a jug of sparkling water, a dish of sliced lemons and a bottle of blue label Stolichnaya. There was also a clock with a plain face and large numerals. The clock was the most important item. It told Andrew how much time he had left before he had to depart, leaving not a trace of his presence.

Today the trouble and strife was at the Malmaison Beauty Salon, being massaged and steamed and waxed and primped by Shoshona, her personal beautician. Andrew thought a more accurate description for the plucky woman who got to grips with Gilda's constantly shifting outline should be uglician. An uglician at the troll parlour.

These insights so entertained him he laughed aloud, spilling his drink, not just on his trousers but all over the cushion. It was quite a big mark. Thank God vodka was colourless and didn't smell. He was just turning the cushion over and thinking it was about time he made tracks when a car turned into the drive.

Although the car was an ordinary saloon and the two men getting out wore plain business suits Andrew knew immediately who they were. He had had near misses with them often enough. What was it about the police? A sort of wary confidence. As if whatever right you had to be where you were they claimed the same right just by waving their bloody warrant cards. They were doing it now.

'Mr Latham?'

'Yes. What can I do for you?'

'We're investigating the deaths of Dennis Brinkley and Ava Garret. You weren't at the office when we called this morning so . . .'

'Here you are, this afternoon.'

'Exactly.' The young one pulled out a chair and sat at a round table under a large umbrella. 'OK if we . . .?'

'Actually I was just—'

'This won't take long, I'm sure, sir.'

Then the big one sat down too. Bugger, thought Andrew, and looked at the clock again.

'I was given some idea as to your background with the company.'

Barnaby repeated what he had heard from Leo Fortune, leaving out the insults. 'Is that correct?'

'Roughly.'

'And how did you get on with Mr Brinkley?'

Latham shrugged. 'He did his job – I did mine. We didn't mingle.'

'Do you remember what you were doing the day he died?'

'Working, I suppose.'

'We were told—'

'Not necessarily at my desk. I'm in and out a lot. Occasionally I visit clients in their homes.'

'Is that what you've been doing this afternoon, sir?' Sergeant Troy's expression was innocent, his voice politely puzzled, his gaze extremely respectful. You felt, given the chance, he might curtsy.

'Is that relevant to your enquiries?' As he spoke Andrew gathered up the drinks bottle, jug and clock. Said, 'I have to change these trousers,' then disappeared into the house to empty the water and hide the vodka in his underwear drawer.

'That man was actually sweating.'

'It's very hot,' said Sergeant Troy.

'He wasn't sweating when we arrived.'

Within minutes Latham was back. He now had on a smart jacket, a tie, different trousers and was munching a mouthful of something green. Barnaby guessed parsley.

'I have to throw you out now, I'm afraid.'

'Just a few more questions, Mr Latham.'

'I really can't—'

'Regarding Ava Garret.'

'Who?'

'The medium who was killed just under a week ago. Connected to the Brinkley case?'

'It was all over the papers,' said Troy. 'And on the telly.'

'Yes – of course, I did hear of it. But—'

'Did you know Mrs Garret?'

'No.'

'She lived in Forbes Abbot.'

'Well, it can hardly have escaped your attention, Chief Inspector, that I don't live in Forbes Abbot. So I'm not likely to have met her.'

'Have you ever been to the Church of the Near at Hand?'

'I never go to any church. The cards I've been dealt, God's lucky I haven't razed them all to the ground.'

At this point a large BMW drew up, dwarfing the yellow Punto. A colossal woman heaved and rolled her way out. She was draped in a great deal of grey gauzy fabric with a silvery finish. The comparison with a barrage balloon was inescapable. A loud bellow crossed the distance between them.

266

'What are you doing here?'

About to explain, DCI Barnaby realised the question was not addressed to him but to Latham, who immediately launched into some rigmarole involving a Psion organiser, a client, a cancelled appointment, a stupid assistant and a lost file. Good lies always have a spice of truth and these sounded quite convincing but even Troy could see there was at least one too many of them.

In any case the woman now ignored him, introduced herself and asked if they had come about 'poor, darling Denny'. She answered all their questions, verifying what they already knew about Brinkley's character but adding little that was fresh. She had never met Ava Garret.

'One's world is hardly likely to collide, Chief Inspector. From what I read in the *Echo* it appears she lived in a council house.'

Asked to confirm her husband's presence at home on the night of Wednesday, 8 August she declined.

'All I can say is he was here when I got back from my aromatherapy training.'

'And that was?'

'Tennish.'

'And what time did you leave for this . . . um . . . training, Mrs Latham?'

'Around seven. I always arrive early. I need to sit quietly and recharge and direct my energies. It's pretty high-powered stuff.'

That was when Barnaby and Troy took their leave. Before they were in the car she had let rip. Starting at fortissimo and climbing.

'I've seen things launched smaller than that,' said Sergeant Troy, driving off.

The car paused at the great bronze gates and Barnaby regarded the happy couple in his rear-view mirror. Latham standing there, shoulders slumped, staring at the flagstones like a naughty schoolboy. Mrs L. bawling and windmilling her great windsock arms about. A clatter of rumbustious laughter ruptured the sweet summer air. He must be getting some bloody sizeable handouts to put up with all that.

'See that look she gave him, Chief?'

'What sort of look?'

'The sort Joe Pesci gives a guy that's dropped ash on his shoe.'

'Let's stick to facts,' said Barnaby. 'As far as timing goes we now know Latham could be our "Chris".'

'That wimp?' The gates swung open and Troy drove thankfully away.

'He could have rung Garret around five – sensibly, from a call box. Mrs L. leaves home at seven. He goes off to keep his appointment with Ava. Spends an hour or so dangling various promises, maybe a contract, leading her on over a nice dinner. Slips the stuff into her wine, gives some excuse as to why he can't escort her back to Uxbridge and puts her in a cab.'

'More likely the Tube, given his finances.'

'Whatever. Then back to the ghastly Dallas ranch house for a bit more grovelling.'

'It all sounds . . . I dunno, unbelievable.' Troy had thought the bungalow quite splendid. 'Like some stupid play.'

Inevitably, given his daughter's profession, Barnaby had seen a lot of plays and one or two had been pretty stupid to his way of thinking, but none had been quite as unbelievable as the case with which he was presently wrestling.

CHAPTER TWENTY-ONE

Only forty-eight hours since the first briefing on the double murder inquiry and the incident room was a very different place. A babble of voices answered busy phones. Information was recorded. Questions were being put. Maps and photographs relating to both crimes were pinned around the walls, together with large detailed drawings of the interior of Kinders.

Half an hour earlier DCI Barnaby had received and absorbed SOCO's full report on Dennis Brinkley's house. Gathering his team about him at the quieter end of the room he chose to open the briefing by describing the salient points.

'Some prints found were those of his cleaner, others of Mallory Lawson. The rest, identical to those on the Lexus and all over the flat we have to assume are Brinkley's. The prints on the trebuchet are a bit of a mess. Only his are plain, but they were made on top of some blurred smudging, which Scene of Crime say was probably left by someone wearing gloves. So far, so expected.

'Footprints give slightly more away. We know, having talked to his cleaner, that Brinkley had some special soft tweedy slippers he always wore when going to look at his machines. They were left, side by side, at the entrance. Prints from these were pretty well all over the floor but not all of them were the same.'

'How d'you mean, Chief?' asked Inspector Julie Lawrence.

'A few had been made by someone with slightly bigger feet.'

'He must have guessed what the slippers were for,' said Troy, 'and taken advantage.'

'The kitchen showed nothing, not even on the door handle. SOCO think the murderer's shoes were left on the outside step.'

'And it seems he didn't enter the flat proper.'

'Do we have SOCO's report on that?'

'Yes. Also Troy and myself went through the place.' And what an experience that had been. The word tidiness didn't even come close. Pens and pencils on his desk, shoes in the wardrobe so closely aligned you couldn't have slipped a hair between them. Ornaments equidistant each from the other to the nearest millimetre. Anally retentive wasn't in it.

'I examined his bank statements going back several months. No huge amounts either way. Some modest direct debits, probably council tax. Unfortunately his phone bills weren't itemised but the telephone company will be able to produce details of calls for us.'

'Not much of a result, is it, sir?' asked Colin Jarvis. 'Just tells us what we knew already.'

'Yes, thank you, Jarvis. So.' Barnaby gave his team a somewhat aggressive stare. 'Who's got something to tell me that I don't know already?'

A lot of stuff had come in, nearly all of it useless, but that was nothing new. Barnaby picked up one of the E-fits and waved it about.

'Any luck with these?'

'Yes, Chief,' said DC Saunders, who had covered Uxbridge station. 'The man who sold her a ticket remembered her straightaway. She asked for a single to Piccadilly.'

'Do we have a time?'

'He'd just come on shift and reckons about ten past six. I checked the next couple of departures. First out was a Metropolitan. Then a fifteen-minute wait for the Piccadilly Line.'

'Let's hope, once these are widely circulated, we'll discover which train she took. And, with a bit of luck, where she got off.'

Barnaby knew that was asking a lot. Even though the carriages would be largely empty when they left the terminus, the nearer the train got to town the fuller they would become. If she really had left it at Piccadilly Circus the chances of her being spotted were as good as nil, even on the cameras.

He said, 'What about the car?'

Quite a bit of feedback there as well. Most of the likely sounding tips had been followed up, but though the vehicles in question were all red Hondas they were not Ava's Honda. Unfortunately Barnaby's hopes that she had left it in the NCP lot near the station proved short-lived. Another two sightings had come in late last night and would be followed up this morning.

He left them all to it and set off to interview the man who had been described to him yesterday by Doris Crudge as 'knowing Ava inside out'. Apparently it was George Footscray who had started the medium off on the psychic circuit, supported her through the training and, once established, chauffeured her between various meetings. He also ran the spiritualist church in Forbes Abbot single-handed. George, explained Mrs Crudge, was also quite a sensitive himself, being born with a gift for piercing the lower ether no matter how black and dense.

All this had entertained Sergeant Troy no end. Now, driving along the A413 towards Chalfont St Peter, he was quite looking forward to meeting Footscray, whom he pictured as the sort of bloke who grew his own clothes. A mung-chewing airy-fairy ponce in beads and a raffia hat. But that didn't mean the guy couldn't pass on a few tips about ether piercing. Also Troy half hoped for an update on his stars, which were bitching him about as usual.

As if reading his sergeant's mind Barnaby said: 'We'll keep the questions to the point, OK?'

'Fine by me.'

'I don't want you running off at a tangent over some esoteric quiddity.'

'Thought they were a rock group.'

Troy was laughing already in anticipation. He spotted The Three Tuns where they were supposed to turn. Manoeuvre, signal, mirror. And there they were in Clover Street, Camel Lancing. Evens on his side.

'Could you look out for thirteen, Chief?'

Troy was not quite sure what he expected. Perhaps a tiny hunched-up hovel with a witch's hat on the roof, like one of the drawings in Talisa Leanne's storybooks. Or a grey, castle-shaped construction, sinisterly shrouded in mist. Number 15 Clover Street was a small, semi-detached house of outstanding dullness. Even the garden was so drab as to be almost invisible.

'This is it,' said Barnaby. 'Park by that laurel.'

Troy, quite overcome with disappointment, parked. But then, ringing the bell, he cheered up somewhat. First the door mat seemed to be covered in all sorts of mysterious signs and symbols and also the bell itself was in the form of a pregnant goat with green glass eyes.

'Chief Inspector Barnaby?'

'That's right. Mr Footscray?'

'We've been expecting you. And this is . . .?'

'Sergeant Troy,' said Sergeant Troy, producing his warrant card and having it waved away.

'Enter, please. Come and meet Mother.'

They stepped into a tiny hall on to a large rug featuring a lion and a unicorn, a crown and a begirdled woman holding a thistle. There was also a butler. He was a life-sized wooden cutout, badly if carefully painted and somewhat removed from the normal run of butlers in that he had full-feathered, floor-length wings with golden tips. There were some neatly folded newspapers on his tray and a notice reading 'Donations: Thank You.'

'They're here, darling.' George opened a door, then flattened himself against it so the two policemen could squeeze through. Then, to Barnaby: 'I expect you'd like some refreshment?'

Neither man replied. Just simply stood and stared. They had entered a shrine dedicated to the worship of one of the most revered deities of the twentieth century. Every inch of the walls was covered with plates, mugs, tins, photographs, drawings and paintings reflecting her image. Book-shelves held china figurines in her likeness. She adorned biscuit barrels and gestured from coaches of golden filigree. A glass case held a hairdresser's block supporting a lime-green, fur-trimmed brocade hat dripping with feathers.

In an armchair, peering from a swaddle of airy blankets, sat a tiny old

271

lady. Little puffs of hair like cotton wool seemed to have settled on her pale scalp at random. Not a scrap of her face was clear of wrinkles but her eyes were blue as periwinkles, bright and sharp.

'Welcome,' she said. 'Please sit down.'

The voice was a shock. It was quite loud and had a clackety rattly delivery, like a stick being drawn across railings. She was indicating a sofa, draped with a tapestry illustrating various royal residences. Barnaby sat on Windsor Castle. Troy got the mausoleum at Frogmore. Neither knew quite what to say.

'Hello,' said the old lady. 'I'm Esmeralda Footscray.'

Barnaby introduced himself and Sergeant Troy. There was some more silence broken by the sound of cutlery, off stage, as it were.

Eventually Troy, gesturing, said, 'Quite a collection.'

'From the moment of her birth.' She indicated several rows of box files stacked beneath shelves crammed with photograph albums.

'Must be worth quite a bit.'

'Money?' Esmeralda's disdain knew no bounds. As Troy said afterwards, he felt like he'd been caught farting in church. 'All these artefacts are saturated with sublunar energy to be transmitted whenever an urgent need arises. As you can imagine she needs constant recharging, especially after that last operation.'

'Sublunar energy, yes,' repeated the sergeant, just as if this was an everyday conversation. He stared out of the windows, which were heavily barred, and noticed that the door too had a quite an elaborate lock.

'This is our guidance source.' She stretched forwards with some difficulty and laid her hand upon a milky white globe. It glowed, the interior pulsating gently like an illumined heart. Troy looked around for the flex but could see none. 'Formulated and constantly sustained by my guide, Hu Sung Kyong.'

'That's very . . . er . . .'

Barnaby closed his eyes and shut his ears. He had had enough arcaneries, enough giddy convulsions of the spirit already in this case to last him a lifetime.

Troy became intrigued by some grey fluff at the corner of Mrs Footscray's mouth. Assuming it to be the beginnings of a moustache a closer look revealed small feathers. He found this rather disturbing. Surely she didn't eat birds. He'd always thought spiritual-type people were vegetarians. She was talking at him again.

'You must remember the last time she took the salute at Clarence House?'

'I'm not sure—'

'As she left the dais she stumbled?'

'So she did!' cried Sergeant Troy.

'I had become distracted – only for a moment, but it was enough. I apologised immediately, of course.'

'Was it sorted then?'

'Naturally. The power line was still open, you see.'

George came in, pushing a trolley. Fearing some witchy brew from entrails sown at dead of night 'neath a gibbous moon and nourished by the sweat of hanged men, the Chief Inspector declined.

'Sainsbury's Breakfast or Earl Grey, Sergeant?'

'Well, just a cup,' said Barnaby.

Troy was admiring the biscuits. Star shapes, about as big as ginger nuts, covered with white powder. He accepted one gratefully and took a bite. He had never tasted anything quite like it before. As he chewed he tried to name the strange spice that was now lingering in his mouth. Ginger it wasn't.

George, having fed and watered the visitors and seen his mother settled, now spoke.

'You wanted to talk to me about Ava Garret?'

There was a snort from Esmeralda as Barnaby replied, 'I believe you knew her quite well, Mr Footscray?'

'Indeed. I was Ava's mentor and the first person to appreciate her remarkable gifts. I oversaw her tutelage and accompanied her, for the first few months at least, to church meetings.'

George's voice was also unexpected. Very weak, it came out all quavery and wavery, as if he was a crotchety old man. Perhaps Esmeralda had made him like that over the years. Sucking his strength to nourish her own. Other people's lives, thought Barnaby, newly grateful for Joyce and Cully. And even Nicolas.

'You never doubted that she was genuine?'

'Not for a moment,' said George. 'After every service people would be waiting to talk to her, to say thank you. Often in tears.'

'What about seances? Private sittings?'

'As to that, she couldn't be persuaded. Ava believed she was born to be on stage.'

'And were you there the day Dennis Brinkley . . . um . . .?'

'Punctured the heavenly matrix? Certainly. And I can tell you, Mr Barnaby, it was a daunting experience.'

While George expounded on this Sergeant Troy made one or two brief notes. Truth to tell his mind was not really on the business in hand. It was dwelling rather on the strange confectionery he had recently swallowed. For no reason at all the film *Rosemary's Baby* came to mind. He recalled some strange root ground up by witches and fed to Mia Farrow that had been called something like aniss. Now, to Troy's alarm, a discreet burp was releasing the definite flavour of aniseed balls.

He stared accusingly at George, who was now describing his stewardship of the Church of the Near at Hand. Stared at his face. Long and oval like a stretched egg, it reminded Troy of that bloke holding his head and screaming that you saw on all the T-shirts. He stared at George's greyish

273

yellow strips of hair darkened by brilliantine. At his skin that looked as if it had been reclaimed from the sea. At the back view of his trousers, which fell directly from his waist to the heels of his shoes without obstruction. Troy remembered a bit of advice given to a female cousin by his mother when she started playing the field. Never trust a man with no bottom. Could there be anything in it? He also noticed that Footscray never quite closed his lips when he spoke and you could hear the tiny shift and click of his false teeth. It sounded like a mouse tap-dancing. Troy tuned back into the conversation, which had now become a three-handed affair.

George was saying, 'Mother's quite looking forward to going to spirit, aren't you, dear?'

'I am,' agreed Esmeralda. 'I shall know a lot more people over there than I do over here.'

'But we shall be in constant touch,' said George. 'It's not generally known but there is an excellent telegraphic system – Ariel Cobwebs plc from outer space to planet earth.'

'Really?' said Barnaby. He could never understand why people called it planet earth. Could there be another earth somewhere in the universe that was not a planet? George was still clicking on.

'Mother has a psychical opening at the crown of her head.'

'With a myriad connections,' explained Mrs Footscray, 'going back to prehistoric times.'

There was no answer to this and wisely Barnaby did not attempt to make one. Just smiled at the old lady, rose and was preparing to take his leave when she suddenly cried, 'The loop, George! The loop!'

The light in the illumined globe was weakening by the second. Fluttering too, like a huge trapped moth. George hurried to wheel a small table holding a portable television and video recorder to her side and pressed play. The Queen Mother appeared in all her cerise and gamboge glory, walking down a line of uniformed cavalry. Mrs Footscray pressed the middle fingers of her right hand to the lamp, the flat of her left hand to the screen and started humming. Then she began crooning: 'Divine love from me to you . . . divine light from me to you . . . divine strength from me to you . . .'

The others just stood there. George nodding gravely. Barnaby stolidly expressionless. Troy intently regarding the tea cosy – a lumpy tangle of pale brown string, strangely stiffened – and struggling to keep a straight face.

Suddenly the ectoplasmic intervention was over. Esmeralda beamed at everyone and said, 'Healing completed. She'll be all right now.'

'Until the next time,' sighed George.

'It can't be helped, dear. At her age one must expect it. I do hope,' she raised her voice as Barnaby showed signs of edging towards the door, 'we leave our earthly tabernacle on the same day. She'll need help settling in.'

'The hierarchy's different over there.'

'I'm a quid down on that gig,' said Sergeant Troy, driving away from number 15 Clover Street. In the hall he had been encouraged to take one of the newspapers from the butler's tray, only to have George blocking the way to the front door, clearing his throat and staring hard at the donations notice. Now he was stuck with the bloody *Psychic News*. 'You couldn't make them up, could you, people like that?'

'Anyone who could,' said Barnaby, 'is plainly in need of professional help.'

'Wish I'd got a spirit guide. I wonder what they actually do.'

'They tell you when to add the tonic.'

'A Chinese one would be brilliant.'

Troy's voice, delivering the wistful lead in, had a nudge in it. The DCI braced himself.

'Lo Hung Dong?' suggested Sergeant Troy.

Not a smile, not a flicker of response. Well, he'd done his best. And not for the first time. Maybe the moment had finally come to face the sad truth. He was working for a man who had no sense of humour.

Fortunately there were no passers-by to see the door to Appleby House flung open with such force it cracked on its hinges. Mallory Lawson came running out, his face frenzied with emotion. He flung himself at the Golf, tugging and wrenching the handle, then cursed and shouted, going through his pockets, slapping at them, pulling out the linings. Finally producing a key, he released the locks. The car screeched into reverse, shot out into the road and vanished.

Mallory had been thinking of nothing special when he picked up the telephone. His irritation with the police had disappeared. He'd had a vague idea of visiting the orchard, which had also come to nothing. Perhaps he might do a bit more unpacking. Perhaps he might read. Or he might just hang about perpetuating this state of easy indolence. He said, 'Hello,' and when a woman's voice said, 'This is Debbie Hartogensis,' recognised the name immediately. Saw the notice pinned to the basement flat door inscribed: 'Fforbes-Snaithe. Hartogensis, Lawson.' His flesh cold and shrinking, he cried, 'Polly?'

Now he was burning rubber doing a ton up the motorway, foul-smelling liquid brimming in the cup of his mouth and so hot he could have been melting away. He couldn't control his face, which kept shuddering and twitching. His hands, hot and oily, slithered all over the steering wheel. Terrified of losing control, he hung on till the knuckles almost pushed through his skin.

He had abandoned his daughter. He had not rung, he had not gone to see her. When he had gone he had not persisted. He had neglected her. Assumed she had gone on holiday simply because he heard it from Benny, of all people. Worst of all, he had forgotten her. Now she was . . .

275

That was the nub of his anguish – he didn't know. Debbie Hartogensis had talked on but he had been so paralysed with fear that all he could now recall was a jumble of key words. Flick-knife sharp they were too: dangerous terrible deep wasted reek tablets crying smashed tablets crying tablets.

Mallory's exit was coming up. He tried to slow down. He remembered the mirror. What use would he be to her dead? The traffic streamed and screamed behind him as he entered the slip road too fast.

He breathed slowly, braked hard, tried to calm his churning mind. It was a terrible time to be crossing London, but when was a good time and anyway it was the only time he'd got. What he simply must not do was get caught up in any provocation. No arguments. No cutting in or cutting up, no matter how desperate his awareness of time passing.

He was reminded of the last occasion he had driven in frantic worry to see Polly at Cordwainer Road, only to find she was absolutely fine when he got there. Why hadn't he listened properly to what this flatmate had to say? Asked some sensible questions, found out exactly what the situation was.

In the street where she lived everything looked exactly the same. Mallory realised he had been dreading the sight of an ambulance or police car. He skewed the Golf any-old-how on to a double yellow and ran down the basement steps.

The moment the door moved Mallory pushed it hard and bolted into the flat. Picking herself up from the hall floor where she had fallen on to her bicycle Debbie Hartogensis righted the machine and followed him.

'You pushed me over.'

'What?' Mallory was coming out of the bathroom and staring around. All the doors he could see stood open except one. He crossed to this last, started hammering on it and shouting: 'Polly!'

'Mr Lawson.'

'Polly, are you all right? *Polly*.'

'Don't do that!' Debbie seized his arm. 'What are you trying to do – frighten her to death?'

An image of Polly behind the door, cowering, stopped Mallory straightaway. He stared at the girl. This must be her, the person who had rung. He couldn't even remember her name.

'Come and sit down.'

'What shall we do?'

'If you'll just listen—'

'Why is she in there – shut up like that?'

'I tried to explain.' Debbie pulled him towards an easy chair and pushed him into it.

'Yes, I know. I just . . . couldn't take it in.'

'I came back from vacation two days ago. I knew Amanda would still be in Majorca. Polly's door was locked so I thought she'd gone off somewhere as well. Then, in the middle of the night, I heard somebody in the john. Boy, was I scared.'

'Who was it?'

'Jesus – you think I *checked*? I was shitting myself. I'd just crawled under the divan when they went into Polly's room and locked the door.'

'So it was her?'

'She was kinda moaning, then it all went quiet. Next day, when she realised I was back, she wouldn't come out. I had to go get bagels and milk and stuff. When I got back she'd used the bathroom then locked herself away again. I heard her crying.'

Crying! He could never remember Polly crying. Even when very small she had screamed rather than cried. And if there were tears they would be tears of rage.

'Did you talk to her?'

'I tried.' She shook her head. 'Zilch.'

Mallory went over and laid his head against the doorjamb. Listening, frowning.

'It went on like this – her only coming out when I wasn't here. Then I got kinda worried. Maybe she was really sick, you know?'

'You said something about tablets.'

'I'm coming to that. So, next time I went out – I didn't. Just slammed the door, came back inside and hid. After a while Polly got up and went to the kitchen. She looked really freaked out. I snuck into her place and it was just gross. Like that room in *Seven*? She must have been holed up there for days. I saw my sleeping tablets by her bed—'

'Oh God.' Mallory left the door but couldn't sit down again. Just shifted and moved about. 'Had she taken any?'

'Some.'

'Did you get a doctor?'

'No.'

'Why not?'

'She wouldn't let me in. You think she'd let a stranger?'

'But stuff like that . . . an overdose . . .'

'She'd been taking them to get to sleep.'

'How do you know? How do you know she didn't take them all at once? Christ, with no one looking out for her—'

'If no one's looking out for her, how come you're here?'

'You should have got in touch straightaway. I would have—'

'Hey, hey! Now you listen to me. I have run my ass off trying to help your daughter. I biked all the way to Parsons bloody Green. I knocked on every door trying to get your new address. I finally got the estate agent who sold your house. His solicitor gave me your number. Straightaway I ring you – and not collect, in case you hadn't noticed. Next thing you're crashing in here and knocking me over. And not even a fucking "sorry" never mind a fucking "thank you".'

277

Mallory stared at her. At Debbie Hartogensis who had gone to so much trouble to make the phone call that had practically put him into cardiac arrest. She was young. She had on combat trousers and a tight pink top with shoulder strings and little glasses with blue lenses.

Some of the panic drained out of Mallory. He was here and he would not leave. Whatever happened there would be no more terrible messages out of the brazen, heartless blue. Now only sorrow and gratitude remained. Sorrow for his daughter, whatever her plight. Gratitude towards this young girl who had done so much and could so easily have done nothing.

'I'm so sorry. Forgive me, please. I was distraught.'

'Yeah. Right.'

'I know Polly's mother also would wish to thank . . . to say . . .'

'That's OK, Mr Lawson.' Christ, he looked as if someone had pulled his insides outside and stamped on them. No kids, vowed Debbie for the millionth time. Absolutely no kids.

'Look, I gotta split.' She had picked up a black helmet and a pair of roller skates and was making for the door.

'Split?'

'I'm meeting someone. There's tea and stuff in the kitchen if you want.'

Surprisingly, when she had gone, Mallory found he did want. After knocking softly on Polly's door and getting no response he made some tea in two mugs and took it back to the sitting room. Then he tried again.

'I've made us a hot drink. Will you come out or shall I come in?'

In silence he waited. In silence he sat down again, drank his tea and waited some more. He was prepared to wait for ever to find out what had happened to Polly. To wait – how did the song go? – till all the seas run dry.

What had happened to Polly was this. After those final astonishing moments in Billy Slaughter's flat she had danced home. Gambolled like a child. Grabbed the vertical rail on a moving bus and whirled around, swinging over the road. Couldn't stop even when the conductor told her off. Pelted down the road to the flat and let herself in, still feverish with exhilaration. Unable to keep still, she had put on a Nineteen Gazelles CD and danced violently about, heedless of the insider information rattling around her mind like primed sticks of dynamite.

' ". . . Oh, fire flash of love . . ." ' sang Polly, swirling and twirling, ' "burn me away . . . burn me away . . ." '

There was a lot of time to kill. Hours, actually. There was no way she could enter the offices of Brinkley and Latham in the bright early evening. A curse on British Summer Time, cried Polly, but without rancour. She couldn't just hang around the flat. She would explode. She decided to go to see the latest Coen Brothers movie at the Curzon and buy something special at Oddbins on the way back to celebrate.

Polly finally set off around eight thirty for Baker Street, there not being a convenient Green Line. She caught a Metropolitan train to Amersham and was pleasantly surprised at the spacious, high-roofed carriage. It was more like a proper train than the Tube. Still simmering with happiness Polly gazed out of the window and, once Harrow-on-the-Hill had been left behind, became more and more charmed by the prettiness of the landscape.

She decided that she would buy a house in the country and that Buckinghamshire would be ideal. Such fresh, healthy air, so close to town. It would be a modern house, naturally. An airy structure of spun steel and glass. She would commission an architect. Not one of the stuffy old school. Chadwick Ventris, perhaps. Or Giles Givens. The house would almost certainly win an award. Polly saw herself at the ceremony in something backless and glittering, the architect at her feet.

Variations on this pleasant fantasy lasted until the train drew into Chorleywood. There were several taxi cards in the station phone box and a cab arrived quickly. Causton was about ten miles away. It was almost dark by the time Polly alighted in the market square.

Approaching the street door to Brinkley and Latham, she had deliberately refrained from looking over her shoulder but slipped the key into the lock, turned it and entered the building as casually as anyone with a genuine right to be there. Once in Dennis's office, just to be on the safe side, she drew the blinds down.

While finding her Market Maker and setting up her screen Polly thought about her father. She remembered the lie she had told after he had agreed to release some of her money. Her pretence that these disastrous speculations had really been for him all along. So that he could abandon a job that was killing him and be free. Mallory had believed her and was touched, Polly could see, almost to the point of tears. But what if . . . what if . . . this time *it was really true?*

The idea of using any special knowledge to benefit someone other than herself would normally never enter Polly's head. But this was something different. Something personal. Imagine being able to double the Lawson inheritance overnight. What on earth would they say, her parents? They wouldn't believe it, of course. Not at first. Polly imagined this disbelief. Then pictured her father's gradual amazement at the realisation that it had actually happened. Her mother would be pleased too. More money to throw down the bottomless pit of literary publishing. But it didn't matter what the stuff was used for. The point was that Polly would be helping them and – improve on this – at no cost to herself. Only down side would be an inability to take the credit for such a brilliant coup. For she could never reveal how she had stolen keys, entered offices illegally and broken into a file – even if it was one relating to her own affairs. OK, the first time there was some excuse. Then she had been in rapidly expanding debt, and desperate. But this time the reason was straightforward maximisation of profits. Or, as the self-righteous whingers denied access to the golden mile would doubtless put it, naked greed.

Of course it would soon become obvious that someone had been tinkering profitably with the Lawson finances. That should be fun, thought Polly. She wondered if Dennis would take responsibility but straightaway discounted the idea. He was far too honourable (i.e., sober, self-regarding and principled). No, eventually she would have to own up. And they would all see she had done a wrong thing but for all the right reasons. Satisfied with this conclusion Polly completed both her transactions and dispatched a heart-stopping amount of money. Even though she had watched Billy Slaughter transfer much, much more and had already seen a slight but definite increase in the share price, it was still a deeply frightening moment.

Anxious now to get away, she found a local directory and checked out a minicab. Careful not to draw attention to an unusually late call on what might be an itemised bill, she rang from a box in the market square.

Financially, she just made it home. She shouldn't have been short. Earlier, coming back from the movie, she had drawn out the permitted maximum from a cash machine (a humiliating fifty following an acrimonious snarl-in with the bank). But then, high as a kite on great expectations, a mighty wack of it had gone on a bottle of Veuve Clicquot. No matter: even though it was long past midnight when she arrived back in London with a few pound coins in her pocket, one of the night buses would get her home.

Polly had imagined that, like a spy or commando after the conclusion of a particularly dangerous mission, she would return fizzing with a mixture of elation and relief. She saw herself unwinding, playing a little music, drinking the wine. Walking about till the first papers were on the street. Until the whole financial world now knew what she knew. But, in fact, once the string of tension had been cut, she felt very tranquil. Tranquil but tired. She pulled off her dress, slipped into bed and within seconds was fast asleep.

When she awoke it was high noon. Polly couldn't believe it. How could such a thing have happened? The traffic, the phone that was always ringing, the passers-by clacking sticks against the railings, the yapping dogs – where were they when she needed them? Twelve o'clock!

While Polly fumed she was climbing into jeans and flinging on an old striped shirt. Into sneakers, grab keys, run from flat. The nearest newsagent a five-minute hurtle. She picked up the *Financial Times*. Gillans and Hart had made the front page.

Masood Aziz, giving change, was surprised to find his attention urgently drawn in the direction of the magazine rack. A young woman stood there. She looked stricken; about to fall. Sheets of pink-coloured newsprint slid through her hands and floated to the ground.

Mr Aziz shouted for his wife, who came quickly, threshing through strips of plastic curtain at the back of the shop. They found a stool and tried to persuade the girl to sit down without success. And when Mrs Aziz brought a tumbler of water it was pushed fiercely away. The girl set out for the door, stumbled, righted herself. People gathered in the shop entrance, watching as she staggered off down the road. At one point she stopped and vomited in the gutter. Mr Aziz picked up the newspaper, which was dirty, and started grumbling about lost revenue.

Polly had no recollection of returning to the flat. But suddenly she was there staring into the bathroom mirror, swilling sick from her mouth, cleaning her teeth with such force her gums began to bleed.

Consumed utterly by fear and rage, incapable of intelligent thought, she paced round and round the flat, punching the furniture, banging on the wall till her knuckles bled. At one point she stood in the middle of the room yelling, 'Bankrupt . . . bankrupt . . . bankrupt . . .' a wild ululation like a bird screaming in the jungle. Just after this the telephone rang and she ripped it from its socket and hurled it across the room.

Eventually, her throat raw, Polly wore herself out. At any rate physically. Her mind still ran at a lunatic pace. She sat down and, for the first time ever, wished she was more like her American pain-in-the-backside flatmate. Debbie was always doing what she called her 'practice'. Sitting on a cushion staring into space for half an hour at a time. Said it calmed her nerves; softened her edge. Polly should try it. Polly had no wish to try it. She wanted her edge honed as keenly as an executioner's axe. Enter the exchange with anything less and you deserved all you got.

However, even as she despised such inane and woolly thinking, Polly squatted on the floor and breathed slowly for at least five minutes. It didn't calm her nerves or soften her edge but she did start seeing things with just a shade less emotion. This led her to consider her next move. No doubt at all what that would have to be. The question was, how should she handle a confrontation with Billy Slaughter? What she couldn't do was what she longed to do. Go round there and stick him with an extremely sharp instrument. He was bigger and stronger and the whole business would no doubt end in her complete humiliation. And if, by some freakish stroke of luck, she did inflict any serious damage, the police would be called and she'd be in even worse trouble than she was now.

Polly flung a denim jacket over the scruffy clothes she had on, grabbed her credit card, plus the three remaining pound coins, and ran. On the bus she sat upstairs, leaning forwards, urging it ahead. Drumming her fists hard against thighs and muttering, 'Come on come on come on come on . . .'

Polly had given no thought to her appearance. She was unaware that her hair was sticking out all over one side of her head and totally flat on the other where she had slept on it. Or that the gamey, slightly unpleasant smell on the top of the bus was not coming from the old man sitting directly behind her. Or that there were splashes of vomit down the front of her shirt. So she thought nothing of walking straight through the swing doors of Whitehall Court and heading across the vestibule towards the lift.

One of the porters behind the counter called after her. The other came quickly around to the front and caught up with Polly at the lift gate.

'Can I help you?' The words and his voice were quietly civil but his eyes were not.

'I've come to see Billy Slaughter.' Polly rattled the handle in her impatience though the lift was already groaning downwards.

'Mr Slaughter?'

'Room seventeen.'

'Ah, yes. I'm afraid he is no longer here.'

'We'll see.' Grimly she stared upwards through the metal trellis. 'Get down here, you lazy fucker.'

'I wonder . . . would you happen to be Miss Lawson?'

Polly gave the man a suspicious stare. 'Why?'

'There is a parcel for you at the desk.' He stepped back, stretching out an arm, indicating that she should precede him. And, as the lift had suddenly stopped and now seemed to be returning to the stratosphere, Polly did so.

Joining his colleague behind the vast polished counter, the porter took a small Jiffy bag from one of the pigeonholes. Although neither man as much as glanced at each other Polly sensed what she was convinced was shared contempt.

'Do you have any identification, miss?'

Polly slapped her credit card down. She had now decided not to risk the humiliation of a journey in the lift to an empty flat. 'Do *you* have any idea when Mr Slaughter will be back?'

'Probably not at all,' said the second porter. 'He doesn't live here.' He observed Polly's suddenly white face with trepidation. The last thing they needed on the premises was a fainting female.

'Doesn't.'

'That's right. Just stays occasionally.' The first man took down a large, lined ledger. 'Being a friend of Mr Corder.'

'Corder?'

'Who does live here.' He opened the book and offered Polly a pen. 'Would you sign, miss, please? For the package.'

Polly found it hard to get a grip on the pen but managed to scrawl something on the page, if not actually on the line. She took the Jiffy bag and her card then, totally disoriented by shock, turned the wrong way blundered down another corridor and found herself in a large room with lots of comfortable chairs and low tables There was a bar at the far end and the place was full of people. Mainly men who began staring at her but not in the way she was used to. Polly realised why when she caught sight of herself in a long mirror. Staring, unfocused eyes, a tangled mat of hair, sick all down the front of her shirt. She looked filthy and mad.

Even so, she attempted, when leaving, to walk the walk. Her proud walk to the exit doors and down the steps to the street. But the force field of her confidence had vanished and Polly knew she appeared merely grotesque.

In the street outside, in the baking heat and dust surrounded by surging tourists in souvenir hats, she began to cry. Running dangerously into the road she flagged down several taxis, planning to dodge the fare by jumping out at the lights in Dalston. But though some of the cabs were for hire, none of them stopped. Polly turned, doubling back past the Ministry of Defence, turning towards the Embankment, looking for a cash machine. She found one in the Tube station but it flashed, in bilious green: 'Unable To Process This Transaction' and spat out the card.

She had to get home to open her envelope. Quite why was beyond her understanding but she knew that she absolutely must not realise the contents when other people were about. Though muddled and afraid, Polly was quite sure about that. Briefly she played with the idea of finding an abandoned underground ticket to brandish, waiting till the pushchair/ heavy luggage gate was busy and slipping through. But then she'd have it all to do again at the other end and might well get stopped. While she hesitated, the decision was taken for her when someone on the staff shouted, 'Oy! No beggars.'

Eventually she got home by catching a series of buses, travelling till the conductor came for her fare, then asking for a destination in the wrong direction. Flustered and apologetic she would then get off, catch the bus behind and repeat the procedure. The journey took five changes and lasted over an hour.

Back in the flat Polly prepared to open the package from Billy Slaughter. She had been gripping it so tightly her fingers had stiffened into claws. She sat down on the bed, reading her name, immaculately written in authoritative black script, again and again. Then she squeezed the bag. Tracing an outline of something hard and rectangular, Polly's breath caught in her throat. The news lately had been all about letter bombs; of certain ministerial departments where explosive experts were permanently on call to handle any suspicious mail. But such items were planted by stealth, surely? Not brazenly couriered by someone unmasked and known by name.

Polly tore the bag open and turned it upside down. A tape fell out wrapped in a sheet of A4. She smoothed out the paper and read:

My Dear Polly,
Remember these things. Rumours as to an upturn in commodities are easily started. Insider dealing is a criminal offence, whether loss or profit results. Computers tell the truth as much and no more than the person operating them. If you thought I bought shares in Gillans and Hart you were sadly deceived. Play the tape. And consider carefully before you ever speak to anyone in such a way again.
BS.

With trembling fingers Polly rammed the cassette into her Walkman. The first words recalled the occasion precisely, even though at the time they were spoken she had been very drunk. She had just begun to grasp how frighteningly deep was the financial pit into which she had fallen. When Billy Slaughter had read out the small print on the agreement she had so casually signed and pointed out her legal obligations Polly had laughed. She thought herself immune from the slightest form of pressure, let alone genuine unkindness or bullying. He was mad about her – everyone knew that. Then slowly, as the net tightened, she had begun to understand how things really were. It was shortly after this that he offered to cancel the debt if she would go away with him 'for a few days'.

Polly, consumed by disgust and rage at the thought of being at any man's mercy, least of all a revolting creature like Billy Slaughter, then made the telephone call to which she was now listening. She had rung him in the middle of a sleepless night encouraged by several glasses of Southern Comfort.

She had assumed he would be there and perhaps he was. Just not picking up the phone. Not giving her the satisfaction. Black hatred coated Polly's tongue with a dreadful fluency. She dwelled on his appearance – the sweating abundance of his greasy flesh, the graveyard stink of his breath, the ugliness of his thick-lipped, piggy countenance. On the fact that his arse was better-looking than his face and his genitalia were such as to make him a laughing stock wherever two or three women were gathered together in a City wine bar. She described the vile sensation as of crawling maggots when once his hand had brushed her arm. She jeered at his loveless existence. At the pretence that he chose not to have friends when the truth was that to know him was to loathe him. Take away his money and what was left? A noxious heap of stinking blubber, and so on and on and on . . .

Now she switched off the machine and sat on the bed, shaking. What a fool she had been. What a fool to think the straightforward repayment of a debt could draw the sting from an attack of such venomous ridicule. Of course he would seek revenge. And what a revenge. She had lost her entire inheritance. And more than that, and worse. She had lost money that was not hers to lose.

At this point Polly began to weep in agonised frustration. She howled and wept until she felt physically ill. Then tumbled into wretched sleep, woke for a while before escaping again into the dark. This cycle continued for what she recognised afterwards to be several days. She dreamed of revenge, longing for it in the hopeless, helpless way an abused child will. Drifting in and out of consciousness, picturing the form it might take. You could have people killed for as little as five hundred pounds – she had read that in a Sunday paper. Or, better still, maimed. Shot in the spine, Billy Slaughter could live for years, paralysed in a wheelchair. Better still, he could be blinded or scorched with acid or cut with knives so fiercely that people would shudder and turn away, crossing themselves at the sight of him.

Finally Polly woke, not to fall asleep again. She became aware of a horrible smell in the room, and a great yawning space where her stomach used to be. She walked shakily into the kitchen. There was nothing immediately to eat. Furry grey-green bread, sour milk, no cheese, no fruit. In the fridge a bottle of Veuve Clicquot. Polly wrestled with the urge to smash it into a large gilt mirror over the fireplace. How much worse could her luck be? Instead she switched on the microwave and put in a shepherd's pie from the freezer. Gobbled it down, burning her lips. Heaved it back up. Took a cloth and hot water to the mess. Shortly after this Debbie came back.

Polly disliked both of her flatmates for quite different reasons. Amanda Fforbes-Snaithe, a parliamentary secretary, for her disgusting allowance and boastful inside knowledge of what she kept calling 'the hice'. Deborah Hartogensis for her relentless optimism and common boyfriends. Of the two Polly would rather Amanda had come back first. Though, like lots of very wealthy people, tight as a tick when it came to parting with even a fiver, at least there would be money in her purse. And a mobile that worked. (Debbie refused to use one in case it gave her brain cancer.) But even as she struggled to picture herself talking to her bank, begging them for even a minute increase in her overdraft, Polly, now quite light-headed with hunger and exhaustion, slipped to the bottom of a dark well with no light anywhere.

When she came round it was to realise that her father had somehow materialised. That he was talking to her through the door. Talking gently and lovingly, not knowing she had recently done him an irreparable wrong.

Devastated, Polly blocked her ears. Lay with a pillow over her head. He didn't go away. The front door slammed. She dragged herself off the bed and peered through the curtains but it was only Debbie, biking off.

Gradually she recognised that Mallory had settled in for the duration. And that, sooner or later, she would have to face him. At least, if it were sooner, there would just be the two of them. Her heart full of dread, Polly made her slow, dragging way through the mess on the carpet. And opened the door.

CHAPTER TWENTY-TWO

Back once more at the station, the incident room seemed even more busy than when DCI Barnaby and Sergeant Troy had left. Feedback was still coming in from London Underground. And there was news about Ava's car.

'A Mrs McNaughton came into reception, sir,' WPC Carter explained. 'Parked near Camberley Street at just gone six. She was going to a film with some friends, then they were having dinner at the Hirondelle. Came back around half-ten only to find this red Honda stuck alongside so she couldn't get out. She was furious. Waited about five minutes and was just about to call us when the owner turned up.'

'Fitting Garret's description?'

'To a T. Mrs McNaughton started to let rip but then,' DC Carter applied herself again to the form. ' "I toned it down because I thought she was ill. She looked really bad, swaying about, though she didn't smell of drink at all. I said could I help her but she just got into the car and drove off." '

So that was that. One more thing they had pretty well guessed at was now confirmed. But where was the new stuff? Barnaby's fingers were crossed for luck with the posters of Ava, which should be all over the platform at Uxbridge by now, and inside the carriages. Add this to the exposure on the local TV news and daily papers and surely someone somewhere must have seen her, if only for a moment. Barnaby allowed himself the brief indulgence of a daydream where whoever sat opposite her got off at the same stop. The station was practically deserted. At the entrance someone was waiting to meet her. Yes, as it happened this fellow passenger could describe the man exactly. He even followed them along the road for a while. They went into a restaurant called—

At this point Barnaby had the sense to call a halt. It could happen, of course, though he knew what the odds against it were. He was also beginning to understand what the odds were against finding a motive for the murder of that scrupulously honest, quiet and inoffensive man Dennis Brinkley. Like everything else, it seemed to be in the lap of the gods. And everyone knew what bastards they could be.

A phone shrilled at a nearby desk. A uniformed constable answered, caught Barnaby's eye and said, 'Are you here, sir?'

'Who is it?'

'A Mr Allibone. He wants to speak to whoever is in charge of the investigation. Says he has some important information.'

'DCI Barnaby.' Barnaby listened. 'I see. I'll send someone . . . Then it'll have to be tomorrow, Mr Allibone . . . I do indeed . . . Can't be too precise as to that I'm afraid . . . as early as I can. Goodbye.'

'Can't we go now?' asked Sergeant Troy.

'No. My daughter and her husband are coming round at six o'clock. I haven't seen them for weeks. If I'm late I've been threatened with meatless meals for the next six months. And home-made meatless meals at that.'

'Did it sound promising though, Chief?'

'It sounded extremely promising. Which is why I'm going to put it right out of my mind until the morning.'

The fragrance enveloped Barnaby the moment he stepped into the house. Delicately it wafted, deliciously it filled the hail and stairwell. It was fish, he decided. But not as he knew it.

They were all in the kitchen where the fragrance was slightly stronger but still not strong enough to be called a smell. No one was slaving over a hot stove. Joyce, Cully and Nicolas sat round the table, drinking. They had got through one bottle of Prosecco and were well into the second.

'Come on, Dad,' said Cully. 'You've got some catching-up to do.'

'Hello, you.' Barnaby, overwhelmed with pleasure at the sight of his only child, sensibly attempted to conceal it. 'Nicolas.'

'Tom.'

'Nico's just done an audition, darling.' Joyce poured out the wine. 'For *EastEnders*.'

Barnaby took his glass, remembering the vows made not so many years ago when Nico was at the National Theatre and Cully at the RSC. No way would either of them ever, *ever* take a part in a soap. If they were starving they would not do it. And if one showed signs of weakness the other would threaten to leave rather than let them succumb. It puts you in the second rank straightaway, Cully had explained. You don't see Eileen Atkins or Penelope Wilton or Juliet Stevenson acting in soaps.

'What sort of character is it?'

'A cockney chancer who's a compulsive gambler and collects old motor bikes but really wants to be a chef.'

'Couldn't he be into gardening as well?' asked Joyce. 'Then, if the character disappeared, you could have your own show on BBC Two.'

'Four shows,' suggested Barnaby.

'It's going to be bloody tiresome,' sighed Nicolas. 'Being recognised wherever I go. Pestered for autographs.'

'He's gagging for it.' Cully laughed and taught her father's eye. 'I know what we said, Dad. Circumstances change things.'

They had recently bought a three-bedroomed house on the borders of Limehouse and Canning Town after selling a one-bedroomed flat in Ladbroke Grove. The house needed 'a lot doing to it'.

'And you can't do much,' explained Nicolas, 'on an Almeida salary.'

'Though we may well transfer,' said Cully. 'This new guy is brilliant. Everyone seems to think he'll do for *Blithe Spirit* what Stephen Daldry did for *An Inspector Calls.*'

Joyce, who had gone over to the stove, asked how Madame Arcati was coming along.

'Great. I play my own age, wear Dolce and Gabbana and there's no crystal ball. It's all astrophysics on a laptop.'

'Whatever next.'

'Lady Bracknell gets them out for the lads?' suggested Nico.

'Nicolas!' said Joyce.

'Picture Dame Judi—'

'I'd rather not, thank you.'

'D'you think any of these psychics are genuine, Tom?'

'I am a practical man, Nicolas. A policeman. What do you think I think?'

'Garbage, he calls it,' said Joyce, gently nudging the cooking with a wooden spoon.

'Don't poke!' Cully ran across to the cooker. Then Barnaby went over, and Nicolas too. They all stood looking down at a vast fish kettle containing a pretty vast fish.

'Sea bass with fennel, onion and lemon,' explained Cully. 'You've turned the gas up, haven't you?'

'No,' said Joyce.

'I told you. The liquid is just supposed to shiver.'

'Tremble.'

'Shut up, Nico. What do you know?'

'*I didn't turn it up.*'

'What are we having as well?' asked Barnaby.

They had wild rice and a salad of green leaves, one or two of which were quite new to him. The salad had a mustardy dressing made with walnut oil and white wine vinegar. Joyce opened a third bottle of Prosecco and amiability was soon restored.

'This is definitely one for the gastrocenti,' said Nicolas. 'We might almost be in Camden.'

'Not at these prices,' said Joyce.

'He's right, though.' Barnaby speared a large chunk of sea bass that almost melted off his fork. 'It's delicious.'

'So what's happening on the case, Dad?'

'Oh, not work,' cried Joyce.

'Very little, I'm afraid. We've found out where Ava left her car the night she died and that's about it.'

'Have you come across any weird and wonderful specimens for us?'

'With interesting physical quirks.'

'You're like a pair of cannibals,' said Joyce, 'sucking what you want out of people and moving on.'

'What else are we supposed to do?'

'People are an actor's raw material.'

'It's not as if they know they're being used.'

Barnaby was briefly tempted to offer up the Footscrays for his daughter's delectation. How entertained they would be, Cully and Nicolas. Poor George, into his fifties before he was out of his teens, and his deranged mother now struck Barnaby as more sad than comic. He decided it would be cruel to hold them up as a laughing stock. Even if they'd never know.

'Doesn't sound as if this Garret woman was much use anyway, Cully,' Joyce was saying. 'Your Arcati being so different.'

'True. She was a good character, though. I'll remember her.'

'And very convincing.'

'Oh, come on, Nico.'

'Look – she described the machine that killed him, what the room was like, the shape of the windows, the colour of the walls . . .'

'Someone must have told her then.'

Barnaby made a strange gurgling sound at the back of his throat.

'Tom?' Joyce came round the table. 'What on earth's the matter?'

'Sorry . . . gone down the wrong way.'

'Have some water.'

'Give him some more pop.'

'Thanks. I'll be OK, darling. Don't fuss.'

Pudding was clementines stacked in a perfect pyramid on a white china dish. And there were hazelnut and marzipan cookies, which had lumps of dark chocolate in as well.

'The fruit,' said Cully, sweet golden juice trickling from the corner of her exquisite mouth, 'is organic.'

'That doesn't make you immortal,' snapped Joyce. She was getting a bit fed up with suggestions on alternative living. Every time Cully rang there was some crisply delivered lecture. Massaging the back of her neck with ginger (headache); pressing a crystal to the tips of her ears (feeling grumpy); dried chrysanthemum tea (always forgetting where put glasses).

'It'll be feng shui next.' Joyce began to clear the plates.

'Now that is pretty well proven,' insisted Cully.

'Try it,' suggested Nicolas.

'If you'll move the piano.' Barnaby started on the biscuits.

'It does feel strange,' said Joyce, 'coming for dinner and bringing your own food.'

'We can't ask you to ours,' said Nicolas. 'Nothing's working.'

'When it's all fixed,' said Cully, 'you can come and stay.'

They went shortly after that. Cully had a rehearsal at ten with an hour of yoga and thirty minutes' meditation before she left the house. They surrendered the marzipan cookies but took the fish kettle. Barnaby carried it to the car and put it in the boot.

'What on earth do the two of you want with a thing this size?'

'We're always having people round,' explained Nicolas.

'There were sixteen for supper just before we moved.' Cully kissed her parents. 'See you at the first night if I don't before.'

Back inside, Joyce began to load the dishwasher. Barnaby thought about the fish kettle and the sixteen for supper. He pictured the kitchen in their new house full of theatricals. Laughing, drinking, gossiping. Tucking in. And felt a bleak sense of exclusion from his daughter's life, which was ridiculous because barely five minutes earlier he had been sitting with her at his own table laughing, drinking, gossiping. Tucking in.

'Some people are never satisfied.'

'What are you muttering about?'

'Oh . . .' He stumbled through a rough approximation of his smarting thoughts.

'Really, Tom.' She came to him; slid her arms around his waist. 'How often did we invite your parents round to meet our friends?'

'That was different.'

'No, it wasn't. Anyway – remember when Cully asked us to a party after *The Crucible* closed?'

'No.'

'You said you'd never met such a load of posturing ninnies.'

'Oh, that party.'

'They've asked us to go and stay, Tom. Think about it.'

'Mmm.'

'But until that happy day,' she kissed him, 'I'm afraid you're stuck with me.'

'You'll have to do then,' said Barnaby. And kissed her fondly back.

It was past seven o'clock before Mallory returned to Appleby House. By this time Kate had been through every emotion of which she was capable and quite a few she hadn't known existed.

The anger that had driven her out into the forecourt yelling after Mallory as the car zoomed away drove her back into house and straight to the telephone. She dialled Polly's number because, of course, this was to do with their daughter. Nothing else would have sent him haring off in such fear and anguish. Yes, fear. Kate had seen it on his face. Still he could have said *something*, she wailed, but silently, her throat already sore from screaming after him. The phone rang and rang and rang and rang. Eventually Kate hung up.

Neither herself nor Mallory had the number of Polly's mobile. She had refused to give it, saying it would make her feel like some juvenile delinquent being tagged and kept track of. The one thing Kate knew she definitely must not do was ring Mallory on the car phone. He had left the house at an alarming speed. She tried not to think what he could be doing on the motorway.

So began the long wait that proved to be almost six hours. Kate spent quite a long time picking and tearing at various cushions. Then emptying the linen cupboard, folding and refolding all the sheets and towels and pillowcases and putting them carefully back. Reading was out of the question. Television seemed occupied only by fools cackling with laughter and applauding themselves and each other. Gardening, which might have soothed, was not an option. Benny would almost certainly have come out to help and Kate would not have been able to conceal her misery and despair.

As the time dragged by she began to feel nauseous with an even deeper apprehension. Because whatever had happened to Polly was now beginning to seem like her, Kate's, fault. If only she had encouraged Mallory to visit the flat the night before their move. And why had she accepted without question Benny's suggestion that Polly had gone to Crete? She had never gone on holiday without letting them know before. To be honest, thought Kate with some shame, I was relieved. I was happy at the thought that we would have a couple of weeks on our own. And all the while . . .

By the time the car turned into the gates at nine o'clock Kate was almost hysterical. She had to force herself not to run outside but stood in the kitchen forcefully drying some already bone-dry cups and plates. As the front door opened she heard voices. He had brought her back.

Polly was alive. She had not died of some rogue virus or electrocuted herself or been run over, or killed during a break-in or by a jealous lover or a madman on the loose. She was all right. Kate took several deep and careful breaths, then, still dizzy with relief, stepped out into the hall.

Mallory was standing with his back to her, holding Polly. Kate's welcoming smile, half formed, now froze. She was too appalled to speak.

Polly, swaying on her feet, looked like a ghost. Her face was without colour but for the deep bruising around her eyes. Her hair, her lovely thick shining hair, hung down like a tangle of greasy string. Her clothes were unclean. She was crying, tears splashing on the floor at her feet.

Kate moved forward without hesitation. She couldn't help it. The armour developed against years of rejection, the training of herself not to care, the determined cultivation of indifference to slight and insult dropped clean away.

Polly turned from Mallory and, in a single blind movement, fell into her mother's arms. Kate held her gently for a moment then murmured, 'Come along, darling . . . come and rest.'

Slowly they stumbled upstairs, Polly's head resting awkwardly against her mother's breast; Kate with an arm around Polly's shoulder. She led Polly into the bedroom and found her a clean nightdress. Undressed her like a little girl, sponged her face with warm water, helped her into bed.

Late evening sunshine, faintly tinged with red, spread over the coverlet, shedding warmth on Polly's deathly countenance. Kate thought the golden

291

light beautiful but when Polly started to turn her head to and fro to keep it from her eyes she drew the curtain a little.

Then she sat by the side of the bed, holding Polly's hand until she fell asleep. Gradually Kate became aware that, stronger than the feelings of fear and anxiety about Polly's wellbeing, stronger even than curiosity as to what had brought her to this terrible pass, was a slow pervasion of happiness. Polly had turned to her. She had been needed. She had held her child in her arms. In these arms, thought Kate, touching them almost in disbelief. And so she sat on as one hour flowed into the next. In the moonlight and starlight she sat, surprised by joy.

CHAPTER TWENTY-THREE

Knowing the chief's first appointment that day was with the fishmonger in Causton, Detective Sergeant Troy was surprised, on picking him up at eight thirty in the station forecourt, to be told to drive to Forbes Abbot. Lucky with the traffic, it took him barely fifteen minutes.

The village was looking good, warming up in what looked like the beginnings of a beautiful day. Troy thought, as he often did, that he'd like to move out of his cramped terraced house in the seedy part of Causton to a place like this. Never, ever would that come about. The prices here were astronomic. And you couldn't blame weekenders for pushing them up. This was commuters' territory.

'Property, Chief – eh?'

'What?'

'It's a madhouse.'

'Yes. I wouldn't like to be starting out now.'

Troy knew he should be grateful that he was not starting out. Nine years ago he and Maureen had scraped and saved for a ten per cent deposit on their present house, seeing it as the first step on the property ladder. Three years later they had Talisa Leanne, Maureen gave up full-time work and their dreams of moving were over. Now there was no way Troy could have afforded even a dog kennel in the town where he was born.

'I should park close to the wall,' suggested Barnaby as they turned into the drive of Appleby House. 'They might need to take the Golf out.'

'I did actually plan to do that, sir.'

'Good for you.'

'This is Croydon.' Benny had come to her door, holding a magnificent tortoiseshell. She put it carefully down on the veranda. 'He was Carey's cat but he's mine now. Shoo, Croydon. Go and play.' The cat sat down, yawned and began to wash itself.

'Has anything happened?' asked Benny eagerly, when they were once more in her little sitting room. 'Have you made an arrest?'

'I need to ask you some questions, Miss Frayle.' Barnaby lifted his hand in a negative gesture towards Sergeant Troy, about to produce his notebook.

'Will it take long?' asked Benny. 'I'm having coffee with Doris . . . Mrs Crudge, at eleven.'

'That depends on how frank you are with us.'

'I don't lie.' Benny sat down quite suddenly. 'I answered all your questions the other day.'

'Not quite accurately, I'm afraid.'

'Oh I'm sure I . . . What . . . what do you mean?'

'I asked you if you saw the medium. Ava Garret in church at all. And, as I remember it, you said you were not very good at putting names to faces.'

'That's true.'

'True may be, but also misleading. Because you had a meeting with her, Miss Frayle. You gave her some money and she did you a service. Would you like to tell us about that service or shall I?'

Benny's heart beat faster and faster. She tried to speak but her voice was thick and jumbled and the words made no sense.

Barnaby continued: 'When Ava Garret pretended that Dennis Brinkley had "come through", as I believe it's called, she described very precisely the room in which he died. The white walls, the windows, the machine which killed him. She even knew the colour of the clothes he was wearing—'

'She was a medium,' cried Benny.

'She was a liar!'

Benny gave a little yelp and shrank back in her chair. Troy winced. It was like watching a kicked puppy. He had more sense than to intervene but then, mere moments later, her attitude changed. She seemed to rally becoming at once tearful and belligerent.

'It's all your fault!'

'What?'

'I asked you – I begged you to investigate Dennis's death. If only you'd listened instead of writing that horrible letter none of this need have happened.'

'At the time there—'

'What else was I supposed to do?' Benny still didn't look directly at Barnaby. 'What would *you* have done?'

'How much money was involved?'

'A thousand pounds. Five hundred before the Sunday service and five afterwards.'

'Did you pay it all?'

'No. She gave me a week to raise the second instalment but died three days after the service.'

'And if she hadn't?'

'I don't understand.'

'What was she going to say the following Sunday? When the murderer is supposed to finally reveal himself.'

'We were rather hoping to genuinely hear from Dennis before then.'

The chief inspector paused, sighed and rested his forehead in the palm of one hand. Rodin's *Thinker* without the muscles.

'Did anyone else know of this arrangement?'

'Neither of us would have wanted that.' Her admission over, Benny straightened up, looking relieved and much less intimidated. 'It all seemed to work out very well.'

'Doubt if Mrs Garret would agree with you,' murmured Troy.

'Oh, well,' said Benny, in quite an airy voice. She lifted and lowered her shoulders in a casual sort of way.

Any minute now, thought Barnaby, we'll be into omelettes and breaking eggs. Having got what he came for he felt annoyed and dissatisfied being forced to recognise that, far from being a piece of the main puzzle, this new revelation belonged nowhere. It moved nothing forwards. It shed very little light on what had gone before. It was as dead as the proverbial parrot.

'How d'you get on to that then, Chief?' asked Sergeant Troy, squeezing the car between a new Land Rover and a B reg. Metro van on Causton market square.

'Something my daughter said last night. I realised that if Garret wasn't genuine someone must have fed her all those details about the death scene.'

'And Benny Frayle was the only one with any reason.'

'Exactly,' said the DCI.

Mr Allibone, Fishmonger, was just opening up. His spotless green and white awning was unrolled and the man himself, boater tipped against the brilliant sun, was standing in the doorway.

'Chief Inspector? Good day to you.'

'Mr Allibone. This is Detective Sergeant Troy.'

A youth was filleting herrings inside the shop, sliding the guts into a slop bucket, scraping the glittering scales. Ice was everywhere. Blocks of it in the window and piles of it, crushed, between the fish themselves.

Mr Allibone proudly pointed out the lack of smell.

'You don't get any with really fresh produce. Him, for instance.' He pointed out a large, handsome crab. 'Couple of hours ago he was saying goodbye to the wife and nippers.'

Troy felt rather sad at this and was glad he didn't like shellfish. He'd been persuaded to try an oyster once. Like swallowing frozen snot. Stepping carefully over a stout, rather pungent old dog, he followed the chief and Mr Allibone up some narrow, richly Axminstered stairs and into a room crammed with old-fashioned furniture. A large vase of chysanthemums released a bitter smell.

'My lady wife,' said Mr Allibone. 'Alicia – say how-de-do to the CID.'

Mrs Allibone blinked shyly and smiled. She looked a little like a sea creature herself. Her hair, a cap of shiny orange red was cut close to her head in overlapping little scallops. Her small pink mouth pushed forwards into a pout of welcome. Troy decided she looked like a rather pretty goldfish.

'A little something, gentlemen?' She had the sort of voice that wore net gloves. A table nearby was laid with a silver coffee pot, milk jug and willow-pattern cups and saucers. Various luscious eatables had been carefully arranged on embroidered doilies.

295

'A bit too soon after breakfast for me,' declined Barnaby.

'I'll have some,' said Troy.

Mrs Allibone poured the drinks and added hot milk. She nudged one of the doilies murmuring: 'Sweetmeats?' Then, extending her little finger, began to sip her coffee.

'I believe you have some information for me, Mr Allibone?'

Mr Allibone responded by taking Barnaby's arm and leading him to a large three-sided bay window at the far end of the room. Each section had a padded window seat on one of which was a pair of binoculars, almost concealed by the folds of a heavy plush curtain.

'It is my habit,' announced Mr Allibone, 'to occasionally glance out of this window.'

'Understandable,' said Barnaby. There was a splendid view of the market place. 'All human life seems to be down there.'

'Exactly. A neverending panoply.' Reaching carelessly behind him Mr Allibone twitched at the plush curtain. 'And this is how I came to observe what I later decided to entitle The Mystery of the Brass Snake Lamp.'

'Troy?' snapped the chief inspector.

Sergeant Troy, cheeks bulging like a chipmunk's, hurriedly wiped his sticky fingers on a napkin and reached for his notebook. He wrote down, quickly and carefully, a mass of details about lights mysteriously going on and off. Utterly irrelevant as any fool could see, but his was not to reason why.

'My motto,' Mr Allibone was saying, 'as anyone who knows me will confirm, is, if you can't say anything nice about someone, say nothing. Correct, Alicia?'

Mrs Allibone, also packing in the sweetmeats, nodded and waved. Troy noticed she extended her little finger even when she was only chewing. Maybe she had arthritis.

'But I'm convinced that when poor Mr Brinkley told me those lights were on a time switch he was telling a porkie.'

'Why would he do that?'

'Ahh . . . that's the mystery.'

'Well, that's very interesting, Mr Allibone. And we'll certainly—'

'Oh, that's just the horse's doovers, Chief Inspector. Wait till you get your ontray.'

Barnaby settled himself on one of the window seats. Troy's pen ran out. He dug out a reserve and stared interestedly round the room. So much furniture you could hardly breathe. There was a mantel over the carved fireplace with lots of little mirrors. Bouquets of pale stone flowers under glass domes. Hundreds of ornaments in glass cabinets and even a stuffed pike. Talk about bringing your work home.

'We're Victorians at heart,' whispered Alicia Allibone. She picked up a framed photograph. It showed herself wearing a crinoline and her husband in frock coat and stovepipe hat, struggling to board a stagecoach. 'Eatanswill club's annual outing.'

As Barnaby sat, absorbing Mr Allibone's further revelations, he felt his scalp begin to tighten. The information was purely circumstantial and might prove to have nothing to do with Brinkley's murder but it was extremely interesting.

'So at around ten p.m. you saw her get out of the taxi—'

'Cox's MiniCabs to be accurate.'

'But how do you know she went into Brinkley and Latham's? There are flats—'

'The street door opened and closed. Couple of minutes later their office light was switched on.'

'You wouldn't have the actual time and date?'

'I certainly would. It was the day Neptune had his abscess lanced. Alicia – the appointments diary, if you will.'

'Neptune?' Troy looked round.

'Our dog,' whispered Mrs Allibone. 'He lives in the hall now. Being inclined to let fly.' She pronounced it 'lit flay'. 'It was Monday the twenty-third, Brian.'

'But that isn't the half of it, Chief Inspector.'

'Isn't it?' replied Barnaby.

'Believe me or believe me not, Mr Brinkley himself was around when this strange incident occurred.'

'Really? Where?'

'He was actually sitting in his posh motor in the square. Up the far end, close to the Magpie. Almost as if he was expecting something to happen.'

A finger of doubt touched the chief inspector. They seemed to be moving into fantasy land. Everything he had heard about Brinkley mitigated against him being the sort of person who would be loafing around outside a pub late at night spying on his own office. It just didn't hang together. Unless . . .

'How did she get in, this girl?'

'Had a key.' As if sensing a reduction of confidence in his performance Mr Allibone leaped into fervid description. 'Beautiful she was. Dark curly hair, lovely legs. Slim but plenty of . . .' He cupped his hands as if weighing ripe melons.

Yes, he was making it up. For who could observe someone in such detail when they were a good twenty yards away and it was dark. Disappointment pricked Barnaby into a sharp response.

'You must have cat's eyes, Mr Allibone. Or X-ray vision.'

'Pardon? Oh – no. I'd seen her before.'

'What?'

'A week or so earlier. I was just selecting some mackerel – for Lady Blaise-Reynard actually – when I happened to glance up and there she was. This same person storming out of that same building. She flung herself down on Reuben's steps.' He nodded towards the statue. 'And was she in a paddy? Kicking her feet about. And her face . . .' He leaned close to Barnaby who had to force himself not to lean back. The fishmonger was sweating heavily. Licking his chops over furtive visions of long legs and young breasts and curly hair.

'Full of fire. Pure hatred. If you're looking for someone capable of murder, Inspector, all you've got to do is find that girl.'

Sergeant Troy took a deep breath of carbon monoxide from the queue of cars at the traffic lights. It was deeply refreshing after being shut in the Allibones' sitting room for nearly an hour. The acrid smell of chrysanths mingling with the knock-out perfume from a bowl of fruit so ripe it had practically liquified had made him feel quite queasy. Then, as they reached the sleeping dog at the foot of the stairs, Neptune's bottom had backfired. This strenuous, intensely sulphurous explosion was so powerful it all but bowled them into the High Street. Here Troy started to complain that Alicia's date and toffee flapjack (which she had called 'marchpane'), now firmly glued to the roof of his mouth, had been far too sweet.

'Didn't stop you packing it in,' grumbled Barnaby. His envy when observing his sergeant's constant guzzling of highly calorific food was matched only by his resentment as Troy continued never to gain an ounce. Joyce had tried to cheer her husband up by saying that Gavin was cruising for a bruising by which she meant an unheralded heart attack or stroke. But though Barnaby had waited patiently for now almost fourteen years, neither had yet had the decency to show themselves.

When they reached the car he said, 'Check out the Magpie, would you? See if anyone remembers seeing Brinkley or the Lexus around here the night before he died.'

'Shouldn't I do that later – when we've got a piccy?'

'We're on the spot. It's worth a try.' Barnaby picked up his car phone, dialled the incident room and got DS Brierly.

'Audrey, can you get someone out to Cox's MiniCabs? A fare, a young woman, was dropped outside the NatWest Bank around ten p.m. Monday, the twenty-third of last month . . . That's right. Dig up what you can.'

Some minutes later Sergeant Troy returned, positively burnished with satisfaction. He climbed into the car, beaming. 'Got a result, Guv.'

'Could have fooled me.'

'Talked to the barman. Same guy who was on that Monday night. He says Brinkley came in, ordered a drink, then sat by the window, hiding behind a paper, at the same time keeping an eye on the street. This bloke asked him if he was doing a spot of surveillance and Brinkley tipped him the wink and gave him ten quid to keep shtum.'

'How did the barman know who it was?'

'He didn't then. But there was a photo in the *Echo* the day after the inquest. If Brinkley was expecting the girl Allibone spotted,' continued Sergeant Troy, 'she could have been a legitimate client.'

'Some client,' murmured Barnaby, 'with the keys to the office in her pocket.'

When the two policemen visited Brinkley and Latham for the second time Gail Fuller, leading them into the main section, whispered over her shoulder, 'We've got the full complement today.' Then, jerking her head in the direction of the rear cubbyhole: 'Put the flags out.'

Barnaby, looking, saw Andrew Latham looking right back. He got up and, before Leo Fortune had even had time to greet the two policemen, contrived to join them, explaining that as the firm's senior partner he felt he should be present.

Leo said sharply, 'This might be personal, for all you know.'

'But it isn't, is it, Chief Inspector?'

'We're here to continue our inquiries into Mr Brinkley's death.'

'Get on with it then,' said Latham. 'Time's money.'

Fortune gave an ironic laugh then, having started, couldn't stop. Finally he managed to say, 'Sorry about that. Are you telling us things today, Chief Inspector? Or asking us things?'

'Bit of both really, sir. What can you tell me about this business of the lights going on after—'

'Oh, no!' cried Latham, making a dramatic gesture of cowering horror. 'Not the lights!'

'Please, Mr Latham. If you've anything to contribute just tell us. We don't have time to mess about.'

'A few weeks ago that nosy old scroat over the road told Brinkley what presumably he's been telling you. And instead of telling him to mind his own business Dennis started worrying himself silly. He even had the cheek to ask if I knew anything about it.'

'And did you, sir?' asked Sergeant Troy.

'I was getting ratarsed at a Lions Club dinner the first time it was supposed to have happened.'

'And the second?' enquired Barnaby.

'At the theatre. *Mamma Mia*.'

'That good, was it?'

'And before you ask,' continued Latham, 'there were three witnesses—'

'But those were just the occasions Allibone noticed,' interrupted Leo. 'We don't know about the ones he missed.'

Barnaby, remembering the glasses, thought he probably hadn't missed much. 'How many of the staff had keys?'

'Just me and Dennis,' said Latham.

'What about spares?'

'Dennis had some. I didn't.'

'Surely the building has a back entrance?' asked Sergeant Troy.

'Yes, but you can't get through to here. There's an internal wall.'

'Did Brinkley discuss this matter with you, Mr Fortune?'

'Of course. We decided to get the locks changed as soon as possible. Turned out to be the following Wednesday.'

'The day after he died?'

'That's right. I still got the work done.'

'Leo felt it was what he would have wanted.' Latham's words were rich with syrupy admiration so plainly false that Fortune flushed angrily.

'And who has the new keys?'

'Both of us,' said Leo. Remembering Dennis had not wanted his partner to have them had made handing the keys over quite upsetting.

'What has all this to do with the so-called murder, anyway?'

'You don't think he was deliberately killed, Mr Latham?'

'Of course he wasn't. One of those bloody machines fell on him. As for the phantom switch-thrower – I'd say he was a figment of Allibone's overheated imagination.'

'Not at all. In fact the person was actually seen going in and out of the building.'

'And it's a she,' said Sergeant Troy.

Leo Fortune looked absolutely stunned.

Latham said, 'This is the most exciting day of my life.'

'Which is mainly why we're here.' And Barnaby explained.

'Allibone saw this person in the *daytime*?'

Fortune was frankly disbelieving until Barnaby repeated Brian Allibone's description, concluding with the angry flight across the market square.

'Oh – l know who you mean now. Her name's Polly Lawson. The family are heirs to Carey Lawson's estate. She was Dennis's client for many years.'

'And now the Lawsons are yours?'

'Only by default. They may already have a financial advisor for all—'

'Mr Latham!' cried Sergeant Troy. He had dropped his notebook and now sprang to his feet. 'Are you all right?'

'I'm sorry . . .' Latham looked ghastly. He was supporting himself against the doorframe. 'I have . . . have these attacks . . . sometimes. I just need to . . .'

'I'll get some water.' Leo Fortune pushed back his chair.

'No, no. It's . . . er . . . so close . . . some air . . . I'll be . . .' He stumbled from the room.

Fortune rapped on the glass, did an urgent help-that-man mime and saw one of the women approach Latham, who angrily waved her away.

'That happen before, Mr Fortune?' asked Barnaby.

'It's a new one on me.'

As Troy sorted out his notebook the chief inspector watched Andrew Latham collect his briefcase and a jacket. A moment later the door of the outer office slammed shut.

'So, back to Polly Lawson. Could you tell me what this visit to Mr Brinkley was about?'

'I'm afraid he didn't confide in me. And even if I knew . . . well, as I'm sure you appreciate, any client's business would be strictly confidential.'

'In a murder inquiry I'm afraid confidentiality goes by the board. Have you knowledge of the relevant accounts?'

'No. I've hardly looked at Dennis's files. Been too busy working with Steve Cartwright, who's taking over my own. I presume the girl's parents are ignorant of all this?'

'As far as we know.'

'Mallory will be so upset.'

'Who?' Barnaby frowned in recollection.

'Appleby House, sir,' offered Troy.

Of course, Appleby House. Where Dennis Brinkley was going for dinner on the night he died. Where Benny Frayle lived, who found his body. And Mallory Lawson who spent time with that body before the police arrived and cleared away what might well have been evidence, and burned the shoes he was wearing.

Was this the connecting thread, wondered Barnaby, that would lead him out of the dark labyrinth of motiveless muddle and into order and clear comprehension? If not the thread, it was at least *a* thread.

'Do you know if the girl lives with her parents?'

'I believe she has a place in London. Dennis said she was at the LSE.'

'Right. Talk to your staff about all this, Mr Fortune. See if there's any feedback. It might also be wise to check out other accounts. But I especially wish to be informed as to the state of the Lawsons' finances.' He handed over a card. 'This is my direct line. Let me know the result, even if there's nothing untoward.'

'It may be a few days—'

'By six this evening will do nicely.'

CHAPTER TWENTY-FOUR

When Polly woke she immediately prayed for a magical withdrawal into unconsciousness. That was all she wanted and she wanted it to last for ever. Or at least for several years. Pain fretted her nerves. Her skin scalded as if she had fallen asleep beneath a blazing sun. Muscles and sinews ached. She felt permanently nauseous.

Bright daylight poured into the room through a gap in the curtains. She dragged herself off the bed to close them, covering her eyes with her hand. Outside the birds' sweet singing hurt her ears. Looking round, she realised she was in her parents' bedroom. Where had they slept? How soon would they come to see how she was? Though the house was silent she felt the crushing weight of their concern pressing against the walls and the solid door. Imagined them downstairs, worried and fearful, speaking very quietly so as not to disturb her.

Polly could recall little about her homecoming. She remembered feeling strangely remote, as if her personality had somehow absented itself. She remembered being helped upstairs. And that was about it. What wouldn't she give to feel remote now.

There was a soft knock on the door. Even as she was tempted to ignore it and pretend to be still asleep Polly heard herself murmuring, 'Hello.' Still dazed she tried to stand when her mother entered, only to feel her legs giving way.

'I've brought you some tea, love. Don't feel you have to get up.'

'No – it's OK.' A quick glance at her mother's face and Polly had to look away. Kate looked older. The brightness in her voice sounded forced and shaky.

'Would you like a bath?'

'Yes,' said Polly. 'Thank you.' It would delay meeting the two of them together. How strange it was, and sad, that her father should be the person she most dreaded to face. She loved her mother (another jolting recognition) but the attitude of clear-eyed pragmatism with which Kate had always faced the world meant she would be the less deceived.

'I'll put some of my lemon verbena in. And get you something to wear.'

Polly sat for a while, then took her tea into the bathroom. She curled up in a basket chair, watching the water gush from huge brass taps into an enamelled bath. They were very stiff to turn off. The bath rested on metal feet gone green with age. She climbed in carefully, lay down, surrounded by acres of space, and stared down at her body.

How thin she was. Her thumb and little finger encircled her wrist with ease, like a loose bracelet. Polly closed her eyes and drifted, moving her arms and legs languidly, making soft splashy sounds. Then she took a deep breath and slid under the perfumed water. Sealed off from sight and sound, she rested. You could hardly call it a breathing space but the effect was the same. The world and all her troubles seemed to float away. She could have been at the bottom of the ocean. But very quickly the troubles floated back.

Just now her mother had looked sick with worry. Yesterday Mallory had been frantic with concern. But neither had shown a trace of the devastating rage and condemnation that had possessed them in Polly's nightmares. The only conclusion must be that they didn't yet know about the missing money. Did this mean that Dennis knew but hadn't told them?

Polly could quite believe that. He would remember her visit. Recall how desperate she had been to get her hands on the legacy and probably guess at the truth. He would try to talk to her first because he was a decent and kindly man whom she had despised as old and stuffy. Oh, why hadn't she taken the chance to tell him—

A terrified shriek made her sit bolt upright. Her mother stood in the doorway, her arms full of clothes. They stared at each other. Polly, water streaming from her hair, shocked and amazed. Kate, pale as death, horrified. They both spoke at once.

'Sorry, sorry.'

'I'm all right. Really.'

'So stupid. Sorry. I thought.'

'It's OK.'

'You looked . . . Ophelia.'

'I wasn't.'

'No, Sorry. This striped frock. All that I—'

'It's fine. Thank you.'

'I'll just put it. There's some underwear.'

When her mother had almost run away Polly got out and dried herself carefully. She put on clean pants and a slip but not the bra, which was much too large. The dress was pink and white and also too large, but that didn't matter.

Polly took a long while to do all this. A long while using her mother's toothbrush. She pinned her soaking hair up into some sort of knot without looking into the glass and went downstairs, barefoot.

She had been picturing her parents sitting together, waiting. Trying not to look as if they were waiting. An awkwardness would prevail. It would not be the right time to tell them what she had done. But then, when would be?

Kate was alone in the kitchen, arranging sunflowers in an earthenware jug. She turned and smiled as Polly came in. It was hard to hold the smile. Sleep had done nothing to fade the dark shadows around Polly's eyes. She looked lost in the baggy dress, which hung forward revealing her collarbones, sticking out like little wings.

'You must be ready for breakfast.' It was almost twelve o'clock. 'Or would you rather wait and have some soup?'

'Where's Dad?'

'In the garden with Benny. Watering stuff. Picking beans for lunch.'

'Right.' She had forgotten about Benny. No way could she confess to her parents with someone else present.

'I've just made coffee. Or would you rather have juice?'

'Coffee's fine, Mum.'

Kate lifted the percolator from the Aga, her hand shaking slightly. It was years since she had been called 'Mum'. As a young teenager Polly had gone through a phase of calling her 'Kate' and, once that stopped, nothing.

'Some toast?'

'Later, maybe.' The fact was that Polly, who had not eaten for days, had got to the dangerous stage of no longer feeling hungry. And in any case, until the truth was out of her mouth and into the open she knew she would be unable to swallow. She felt her throat closing up just thinking about it. How she would choke on the ugly words. How they would turn the sweet air foul.

'Hello, darling.' Mallory came in, carrying bunches of herbs and a lettuce as well as the beans. He moved in a dull, heavy way but smiled, attempting lightness. 'How are you now, then?'

Somehow Polly smiled back. Like her mother, he had aged. And if they're like this, thought Polly, just because I disappeared for a bit and got ill, what are they going to be like when they find out that I have stolen, gambled and lost money on the strength of insider information and am a criminal twice over? She couldn't tell them. She simply couldn't. But what then?

Polly considered the possible consequences of keeping silent. What could anyone prove? Her visits to Brinkley and Latham had been carried out at night. And if she had been noticed no one knew who she was. Perhaps she could go back and put things right. Take money from another account and somehow put it into her parents'. She still had the office keys. Here Polly's mind slipped its moorings and whirled into faster and ever wilder imaginings. Kate watched her with increasing concern.

Mallory, his back to them both, washing lettuce at the sink, saw a car draw up outside the house and groaned aloud, 'Ohhhh no. Not again.'

Within half an hour of Barnaby's visit to Brinkley and Latham's offices, the driver from Cox's MiniCabs, a Mr Fred Carboy, had been traced and had been persuaded, with some difficulty, to help the police with their inquiries confirming Mr Allibone's revelations.

Driving over to Forbes Abbot for the second time that day, Sergeant Troy sneaked a sideways glance at the boss and decided that all these little revelations were doing him the world of good. Look how he sat. Upright, leaning forward a little, fingertips drumming lightly on his knees. Couldn't wait to get there.

'I've been thinking, Chief. Two things, actually.'

'Run them by me, Gavin. I'm feeling lucky today.'

'First the cleaner – the link there being she worked for the Lawsons and Brinkley. She had keys both to his house and the office. And also, it was down to her Benny Frayle met Ava Garret.'

Tell us something we don't know, thought Barnaby. But he was feeling charitable so said simply, 'What's the other?'

'Remember Brinkley had something on his mind and wanted to talk to Lawson about it?'

'But died before he could.'

'We've only got Lawson's word for that.'

'Carry on,' said the DCI.

'What if they did talk and it was about all this? We know Brinkley saw Polly Lawson go in. Saw it was his office where the light went on. Wouldn't he check the accounts to see what she'd been up to? Anybody else – it would've been straight through to us and an arrest.'

'But because of their friendship—'

'Going back over thirty years.'

'He'd try and sort it out with her dad.'

'Who killed him to protect the girl.'

Barnaby leaned back now, relaxing. 'Yes, I think all that's certainly within the realms of possibility, Sergeant.'

Troy, lifting a leg so pleased was he with this encouragement, took second with a swanky flourish. 'Which means no way are they going to hand over her London address.'

'We can get that through the LSE.'

Mallory Lawson was peering through a window as they got out of the car. He looked vexed and resentful but, alas for Troy's imaginings, not at all apprehensive. He turned on both men with little ceremony.

'I don't wish to be rude, Inspector—'

'I'm glad to hear it, sir.'

'But we do have a houseful of unpacking here. I answered all your questions during our first interview. I've nothing further to add—'

'But I have something to add, Mr Lawson.'

Troy was gazing at a wreck of a girl slumped in a chair. Could this be the one Brian Allibone had described as 'absolutely beautiful with dark curly hair and lovely legs'? The girl full of fire and capable of murder.

She looked anorexic to him, all skin and bone. Her hair, piled up any-old-how, had started to fall down in black ratty tails. The eyes had a bluish bruised appearance, even her lips were violet-stained. The chief was addressing her but she didn't seem to take it in so he tried again.

'Are you Polly Lawson?'

When she still didn't reply her father said: 'Poll?'

'Yes.' Spoken on the breath. No more than a sigh.

'I have to ask you to come with us to Causton police station, Miss Lawson, where we shall put certain questions to you. If you would like a solicitor present—'

'What is this? What the hell is this?' Mallory Lawson, astounded, glared at the two policemen. 'Are you mad?' His face became suffused with blood. Even his neck seemed to swell. 'Get out . . . *get out.*'

'Mallory, for heaven's sake.' Kate took his hand, his arm. 'Please, darling, calm yourself. There's obviously been some dreadful mistake.'

'Mistake . . . yes.' He was swaying like a tall tree. 'Christ . . .'

'I should sit down, Mr Lawson,' said Barnaby.

Yeah, sit down mate, thought Sergeant Troy, before you fall down. He'd been watching the girl through all this, trying to make her out. There she crouched, barefoot, huddled in that stripy tent thing like some pathetic refugee. But what was she thinking? Could her seeming indifference as to what was going on be genuine? Or was it a cover for fear? Maybe she was just too shagged to give a toss. Looking at her you could well believe it. Her mother had brought in a pair of sandals.

'Try these on, darling.'

The girl looked up then and smiled. Or tried to. And Troy saw, just for one bright moment, what they'd all been on about.

'And you'll want a coat.' Kate realised too late what the words implied. It was hot or at least very warm now till late at night. 'Well, maybe a cardigan.'

'We must be leaving,' said Barnaby.

'I'll go in the car with you,' said Kate, kissing Polly. 'Dad can follow with the Golf. So there'll be something to bring us home.'

They all fetched up in a waiting room off reception. Setting up the interview proved deeply problematical. The Lawsons' family solicitor was on holiday and the next most senior member of the firm was in court. The solicitor on call at the station was roundly insulted, fortunately in her absence, by Mallory Lawson, whose wife argued for reason.

'Everyone knows the sort of characters who do this job. Incompetent, unsavoury, shiftless – people who can't get work anywhere else.'

'I'm sure that's not true—'

'Of course it's true. You think the police want crack lawyers sitting in on these interviews?'

'Mr Lawson—'

'Or they're warped. Get their kicks out of mixing with criminals.'

'I must ask you—'

'Well, my daughter's not a criminal!'

'If you're so concerned about your daughter why put her through all this?'

'*Me?*'

'The interview would have been well under way by now, perhaps concluded, if it weren't for your obstructive behaviour.'

Here we go. Sergeant Troy, aware of what was coming, felt his skin prickle. It wasn't often they were treated to the awesome spectacle of the chief losing his temper. Observing the intent cold gaze, sensing the rising anger, Troy stepped sideways.

Even then the explosion might have been averted if Lawson had shrugged and resigned himself. Sat down and shut up. But no – blind to the incipient whirlwind, he blundered on.

'And I demand to sit with my daughter throughout—'

'You *demand*? Mr Lawson, you are in no position to demand anything. I am in charge of this situation and I will tell you this: any further trouble and I will have you for obstructing a police inquiry. Should it be my humour I can hold you here until you come before a magistrate. And I shall not hesitate to do so.

'If you and your wife insist, on Miss Lawson's behalf, that your own solicitor is present at her interview that is your prerogative. But if you think she will be returning home with you until he is available you are very much mistaken. She will be detained here for however long it takes. Do I make myself clear?'

You could say he had, decided Troy. In fact, you could pretty much count on it. All the clattering keyboards and murmuring voices in reception had become silent under the need to give full attention to the power and volume of the chief's address.

Troy answered the telephone, listened, then said, 'Jenny Dudley's arrived, sir. Interview room three.'

'Miss Lawson?'

Kate, who had an arm round Polly, removed it and gripped her hand. Mallory, riven with doubt and fear, got up, then quickly sat down again. Kate started to cry. Barnaby had no patience with such emotional incontinence. Anyone'd think their daughter was going to the scaffold.

Polly didn't know how they'd found out. She didn't care. The discovery was all of a piece, somehow. Almost to be expected. Seduced by pride in her own cleverness and dazed by greed, she had flown too near the sun. And yet, even in the depths of mortification and misery a tiny shred of self-preservation still remained. So when during their brief private interview the solicitor advised her of her rights, including the right to remain silent, she decided to do just that. Guilty she may be but there was no need to hand herself over trussed up like an oven-ready chicken. So, when the older of the two policemen asked if she knew why she was there Polly said nothing.

Then the young one went through his notebook quoting dates. Stating that she had been seen entering the office premises of Brinkley and Latham on two separate occasions when said premises were closed. In both instances a witness was prepared to identify her and give evidence. As was the minicab driver who brought her from Chorleywood to Causton market place.

Then they wanted to know where she had got the keys, why she had entered first the building then Dennis Brinkley's office especially. What was she looking for? What did she hope to accomplish?

Polly tried to work out what was going on. Where Dennis came into all this. Who was this 'witness' prepared to give evidence? Surely not Dennis himself. He just wouldn't do it – go to the police behind all their backs. Perhaps it was that awful man Latham. They were off again.

'Where did you get the keys, Polly?'

So it was Polly now.

'Where did you get the keys?'

'Did you steal them?'

'Did you steal the keys to his house as well?'

'At the same time, perhaps.'

'Do you come down to Forbes Abbot often?'

'Were you there on Tuesday the twenty-fourth of July?'

At least this question was specific. Was she there? A backward glance down an unspeakably dark memory lane and she was being sick in the gutter, raging in the marble vestibule of Whitehall Court, weeping and screaming in her bedroom. Polly spoke briefly to Mrs Dudley and was reassured.

'No, I wasn't.'

'Prove that, can you?'

'Definitely.' The hall porters wouldn't forget her visit in a hurry.

'All day?'

'I didn't wake till lunchtime. Shortly after that I went out. I saw . . . some people. Then I came home.'

'Who are these people?' asked Sergeant Troy.

'I've no idea of their names.' Polly explained where they could be found.

'Was anyone in the flat with you?'

'No.'

'Then we've only your word that you slept late.'

Polly, who had believed herself to be totally bereft of energy or any spark of gumption began to experience faint stirrings of resentment.

'So? What does it matter when I got up? What's so special about Tuesday the twenty-fourth?'

Barnaby regarded Polly with disdain. He did not take kindly to someone insulting his intelligence. Or trying to play foolish games. His voice was deliberately aggressive when he said, 'You're surely not pretending you don't know?'

Polly shrank from this harsh approach; from the vigorous accusing stare. It was rather frightening. And surely a bit extreme. Technically she had broken the law and no doubt would be duly charged but it wasn't as if she had stolen anything that was not in the family, as it were. Or caused any damage.

'Polly?'

'I'm not pretending anything,' cried Polly. 'I *don't* know.'

Troy looked across at the chief. Noted the dark brow and tightening jaw. No wonder he was angry. Were they really supposed to believe that three weeks after Brinkley's death with his body as good as discovered by this girl's father she knew nothing of the matter? Given that it had slipped his mind to mention it, which frankly beggared belief, the bizarreness of the machinery responsible had ensured comprehensive coverage in the daily press. There had even been drawings of a trebuchet. The dramatic setting aside of the inquest verdict after Garret's murder had also been widely reported. No, decided Sergeant Troy, genuine though her bewilderment seemed, Polly must be having them on.

'You appear to be puzzled by this whole situation,' suggested Barnaby. 'Let me enlighten you, at least in part. One of the people who watched you enter the bank building on the night of the twenty-third was Brinkley himself.'

'*Dennis?*'

'You didn't see him?'

'No.'

'Surely he followed you in. Daughter of old family friend, acting very strangely. Not to mention illegally. He confronted you. Probably not angry – just wanting to understand.'

'I didn't –' Polly's voice rasped in her bone-dry throat – 'see him.'

'Stay down here that night?'

'I've already told you . . .'

'No matter. London's not far. Plenty of time to nip down to Forbes Abbot in the morning, get into the house, do the necessary and back to the Smoke. All ready to "wake up",' he poked two-fingered quotation marks directly at her face, 'at lunchtime.'

'Necessary?'

'Take the keys off the garage board, did you?'

There's a punch, thought Troy. Out of the blue, below the belt. The girl went even paler. The solicitor was solicitous, touching Polly's arm, murmuring advice. Polly shook her head. She was tired and just wanted it over.

'Yes.'

'When did you do that?'

'I had a meeting with Dennis in Causton . . .'

'Early afternoon. We know.'

Polly bowed her head. She was not surprised. Was there anything they didn't know?

'The bus back stops outside Kinders. No one was around so . . .'

'How did you know where the keys were?'

'I'd called there a few days earlier but he was out. I noticed them then. They had an "Office" label.'

'And the house keys?'

'Why would I want his house keys?' Her voice, weak to start with, was getting duller and slower – like a battery running down.

'Because I believe,' said the chief inspector, 'that on Tuesday, the twenty-fourth—'

'I've *told* you where I was then. How many more times? What does it matter anyway?'

'It matters,' said Barnaby, 'because, as I'm quite sure you're aware, that is the day that Dennis Brinkley was murdered.'

Polly recoiled at the sickening violence of his words. For a moment she seemed about to speak. Her mouth formed a strange shape, twisted to one side. Then she fell forwards, knocking the water jug over. The water ran everywhere, soaking her face and hair. Dripping off the table to form pools on the dusty floor.

Seated at his desk in the incident room, DCI Barnaby was getting outside his third cup of the very strongest, very best Bolivian coffee. He felt he needed it. More, he felt he deserved it. He was not a whiner or a shifter of blame. He felt the phrase 'it wasn't my fault' to be only a step away from 'they started it', and that both should be abandoned by adolescence at the very latest. But today, just for a brief moment, he had been sorely tempted to take refuge. Eventually he settled for the almost equally shifty, 'How was I supposed to know?'

Sergeant Troy, listening, tried to look sympathetic but only succeeded in looking rather stern. He'd spent enough years exposed to lectures on the importance of the open mind not to be mildly chuffed when the DCI had kept his own tight shut and fallen headfirst into a dump truck of crapola. Because if he'd thought there was a possibility, however slight, that the girl had really not heard of the murder of Dennis Brinkley it would have been counterproductive to fling it so violently into her face. Afterwards all hell had broken loose, with Polly sprawled over the table, the solicitor threatening harassment, the chief switching the tape off and cursing. Himself running to get help.

The Lawsons, who were still in the waiting room, heard the shouting and rushed outside to see what the matter was. Someone from Traffic came out to persuade them to calm down but the man especially would not be talked to. He started demanding to see his daughter and began

310

charging about opening doors. His wife, equally distressed, though more on his behalf, onlookers felt, than her own, was begging everyone in sight to tell her if 'Polly' was all right.

Into this turmoil Barnaby strode. Fatally deciding that the best form of defence would be attack he immediately squared up to Lawson.

'Why didn't you tell me your daughter was not aware—'

'Where is she?'

'What's happened?' cried Mrs Lawson as Sergeant Troy moving quickly, flashed through the pass door. 'Why is that man running?'

'Miss Lawson fainted. There's no cause—'

'You bastard.' Lawson swung a punch. It wasn't precisely aimed but there was a lot of rage behind it. It landed on Barnaby's face, crashing into the side of his nose and his right eye.

Not long after this the girl appeared to recover. She had so far not been charged. To the station's surprise Mallory Lawson had also not been charged, in his case with assaulting a police officer. Eventually the whole family, drastically sobered, had wandered off, together yet plainly quite separate, in the direction of the visitors' car park. Though relieved beyond measure to see the back of them, Barnaby thought he wouldn't mind being a fly on the wall when they got home.

All this was three hours ago. Now he sat trying to put the unpleasant and humiliating fracas from his mind and hoping for a result via the clattering keyboards and now less frequently ringing phones. Troy came over to collect his empty coffee cup.

'She never did cough it then, our Poll?'

'Cough what?'

'Why she was in the office in the first place.'

'I'm hoping Leo Fortune will find that out.'

I'm hoping to sleep with Cameron Diaz, reflected Sergeant Troy, and if the Lawson girl's half as smart as she's cracked up to be, I'd say the odds are in my favour. As he thought these lascivious and traitorous thoughts, Troy kept his eyes fixed on the chief's in-tray. Like everyone else present he was trying to avoid staring at what was plainly going to be an absolutely splendid shiner.

'Even if he does find out, sir, it won't help us solve Brinkley's murder.'

'Why not?'

'If Lawson didn't even know it had happened how could she have been involved?'

Before Barnaby could reply someone signalled from the far end of the room. He got up and quickly made his way over. 'What is it, Bruno?'

'Maybe you should take this call, sir. An Alan Harding from Northwick Park claims to have seen Ava Garret the night she died.'

'Him and half Uxbridge,' sighed Barnaby. There had been hundreds of calls already.

'This sounds like the all-singing, all-dancing version.' Sergeant Bruno Lessing passed over the receiver.

'Mr Harding? Detective Chief Inspector Barnaby – Causton CID . . . Yes, I am.'

Troy came over too. He and Sergeant Lessing watched and listened. Heard the DCI's voice quicken with interest as he asked questions.

'Would you be prepared to make a statement for us, sir? . . . No, no, at your nearest station. Or someone could come to the house, if you prefer . . . Excellent. Do we have a contact number for you?'

Barnaby hung up, seeming quite pleased. He was displaying what Troy always thought of as his 'sniffer' look. Nostrils flexing, mouth tightly closed but smiling a bit, head cocked as if listening to a sound no one else could hear. He seemed flushed too, though it was hard to tell, what with the eye and everything.

'This sounds like the real McCoy. Harding was on the same Metropolitan Line train as Ava Garret. He described her clothes, jewellery, even a handbag, which the poster didn't mention. He was sitting some distance away but could hear her talking to a couple of girls, teenagers. According to him she never stopped. She didn't receive or make any calls on a mobile but got off when he did at Northwick Park.'

'Brilliant,' said Lessing.

'He was well ahead of her at the exit so didn't see which way she went. But once we've nailed the exact time of the train's arrival we can put out an appeal. Not just for the teenagers but for anyone else who got off at the same time.'

'Wouldn't it be great if this "Chris" character had actually met her off the train?' said Lessing. 'And we got a description.'

'Wouldn't it just.' Barnaby recalled his recent fantasy, which might not be so fantastic after all.

'How about if he was in disguise?' asked Sergeant Troy.

'How about you giving up Agatha Christie for Lent?' said the DCI.

At just about the time that Barnaby was in receipt of a black eye, and the Lawsons were beginning their wretched journey home, Roy and Karen were getting ready to have tea with Doris. Karen had put on her second new top (the one with kittens in a basket), clean socks and the sneakers. There had been some attempt to constrain her hair in bunches with bright pink bobble things but it was so silky it wouldn't bunch and slid out and halfway down her back again. She was talking to Barbie. Roy could hear her through the bathroom door. Having managed for years with a lick and a promise he now had a bath every day. In fact, this was his second, he'd got so sweaty painting.

This visiting business, Roy told himself, was no big deal, right? Right. Yet somehow he had come to the decision that none of his clothes would do. They had looked OK before but they definitely didn't look OK now, so

312

he and Karen had earlier taken the bus to Causton and gone round the charity shops. They found two smart shirts and some khaki chinos at Oxfam. Plus a polo-neck declaring: 'Look Out World Here I Come!' in the disabled shop.

Roy had carefully ironed one of the shirts, turning the temperature up a bit at a time so it wouldn't burn. He had put on clean underwear and socks and his new trousers and was brushing his newly shampooed hair for the umpteenth time. Bringing his face close to the mirror over the washbasin he was convinced the ring holes in his nose and around the rims of his ears were definitely a little bit smaller. He knew that eventually they would close up completely because a girl had told him who'd had hers pierced. But there was nothing he could do about the tattoo around his neck. How he hated it – that dotted line saying 'Cut Here'. He'd thought it brilliant at the time, a real laugh. Worth the agony. Now he could see it just looked stupid.

Roy was not looking forward to going to the Crudges. Actually that was a bit of an understatement. When he thought of all the things he could say and do wrong, his heart stuttered and jumped with nervousness. The moment Doris had left the other day, his brief happiness, the disbelieving joy in being not just accepted but held and rocked and stroked, evaporated. He recognised that, briefly, he had been comforted but also understood that it was probably nothing personal. Women were just like that. You cried or got upset, they gave you a bit of a cuddle. Boys at the home were always boasting it was a sure way to get a screw. Maybe Doris fancied him?

One thing he simply must not do for his own safety was to confuse the experience with . . . Roy buried the word. The four-letter word. The worst, the blackest, the dirtiest. None of the others could compare in terms of cruelty.

From the time he could put a name to it he had seen examples everywhere. Leaving school, little kids waving drawings would run through the gates to be hugged and kissed by their mothers. The drawings were crap but you'd never know the way the mothers went on. Later, teenagers in pairs, arms round each other wandered past, smiling and gazing and dreaming into each other's faces. He'd assumed at the time this happened automatically when your voice broke and your balls dropped. Not to him. Oh – girls were available if you had money or dope or fags and even sometimes if you hadn't. But the smiling and gazing and promising and dreaming – all the stuff that mended you when you were broke – forget about it.

So this going round to the bungalow would, in the long run, prove to be just another con. Or maybe even in the short run. She was probably just a bit sorry for him. Still, he'd go along with it. A cup of tea, a bit of cake. What had he got to lose? But if there was any sign, the tiniest hint, the faintest suggestion that he wasn't wanted, he'd be off like a shot. A boy

313

called Toad had put him right on that one. Dump them before they dump you. At that stage Roy had still believed, in spite of all previous evidence to the contrary, that he would eventually be found wantable. What, he had asked, if they don't dump you? Man, Toad had replied, they always dump you.

'Are you ready, Roy?'

'In a minute.' He took off the new shirt and decided to wear the polo-neck. This would hide the tattoo and the slogan would give him confidence. He brushed his hair again, slapped on some cheap aftershave and wished he was taller.

'Roy! You look lovely.'

'Look Out World,' said Roy. 'Here I Come.'

Earlier in the day there had been a brief shower but now it was hot and dry again. Karen's feet, skipping, running ahead, running back, kicked up puffs of dust on the pavement. Doris and Ernest's bungalow, just five minutes away, was called Dunroamin'. The front garden was strange, made up of four large triangles of coloured stones and a pot with a spiky green plant placed in the exact centre. Barbie rang the bell, Karen lifting her up and pressing her astronaut's fingers against the button. Soft chimes echoed inside the house. Doris opened the door. Karen danced inside and Roy, adopting a slight swagger and already sick with nerves, followed.

It was a lovely tea. A marmalade cake and three sorts of sandwiches so small you could eat two or three at once and never notice. Not that Roy did. He seemed to be on what Doris described silently to herself as 'his best behaviour'. This was not quite the case. Roy only had one sort of behaviour. What he was on now was a frozen awareness of pending disaster.

'You all right . . . um . . .?'

'Roy.' He smiled nervously across at Doris's old man. 'It's French for king.'

'That right?' Ernest smiled back. 'I'm not very up on the parleyvoo, myself.'

He seemed a friendly old tosser. When Roy arrived he was watching the football, which meant at least there'd be something for him and Ernest to talk about. Assuming, that is, Roy stayed long enough. He had already let himself down. A sandwich had gone and slipped through his fingers on to the carpet. When the others were all talking Roy picked it up and stuffed it into his pocket.

'Would you like some salad, love?'

'Yes, please, Mrs Crudge.' Why had he said that? He hated salad.

'There you are then.' She had dished out a large helping including beetroot. Now everything was stained dark red. Roy took the plate, which looked as if it was bleeding. 'And you can forget the Mrs Crudge. It's Doris.'

'Aunty Doris,' insisted Karen.

That rang a sharp bell. Roy flipped back to the morning Ava died. The ambulance men. The policemen. How afraid he had been. Still was. What had they said – he and Karen – to save themselves from homelessness and separation? An aunty was coming. Her aunty. That night. Tomorrow morning. Any minute now. Soon. Definitely.

What if someone from the council checked up? He could fob them off once or twice maybe, but once they'd got a grip they'd keep coming round. But if he and Karen could actually produce one, and not just any old aunty – a grown-up, quite old aunty who was reliable and kind and living just a few minutes' walk away – what a difference that would make. All the difference in the world.

'D'you know,' she was saying now, 'I think this beetroot's a bit off.'

'Tastes all right to me.' That was Ernest.

'Sour, vinegary.' She put her knife and fork down. 'Can't eat that. Roy?'

Roy, mute, disbelieving, handed back his huge pile of salad. What a stroke of luck.

'How about a bit of cake? Take the taste away.'

Roy had two slices of cake plus a few more sandwiches. Ernest said: 'I like a man who knows how to eat.'

After tea Karen and Doris cleared away and the men went out the back. Roy didn't know what to make of the aviary. Ernest went right inside. Just stood there with the birds flying all round him, small brilliantly coloured tornadoes. And they didn't half squawk. Even the tiny ones made peeping noises.

'This is Charlene.' He took a small, pale yellow bird into his hand. 'She's been a bit poorly.'

'Sorry to hear that, Mr Crudge.' Roy tentatively approached the cage. The birds fluttered even more wildly and he stepped back.

'Not to worry, son,' said Ernest. 'They'll soon get used to you.'

A treacherous warmth spread across Roy's solar plexus at this hint of not one but many future visits. He gave it five, then said casually, ''Spect they will.'

Inside the house Doris and Karen were washing up. Doris washing, Karen rinsing and stacking. Doris's thoughts were full of what she would always regard now as the two children. Roy had been a bit withdrawn today and she totally understood why. Breaking down like that – in front of a woman too – he'd regret it afterwards. He'd backtrack, perhaps even pretend it had never happened. That was fine by Doris. However it was with Roy she wouldn't change and sooner or later – probably quite a long while later – he would start to trust them both.

'You're doing a grand job there.' She was taking such trouble, Karen. Holding the big plate with both hands under the cold tap before placing it carefully in the plastic rack. Doris had to slow down to keep up with her. This was not a cause for irritation. In fact, she had never been so happy.

She felt like one of the women in those telly adverts for washing powder, smiling and shaking her head at the little ones coming in from play all dirty.

Then she noticed the child was frowning and squinting. Screwing up her eyes as if in pain.

'Are you still having them headaches?' Karen looked frightened. 'It's all right, my lovely. What's the matter?'

'Nothing.'

'Put that down.' Doris gently took a cup away from the child and dried her hands on a tea towel. There was a battered old armchair next to the cooker. She sat in it, drawing Karen close. Then, burning her boats: 'You know I'm going to be looking after you, now?'

Karen nodded vigorously, tightening her arms around Doris's waist. 'Don't go away.'

'I shan't never go away. But if I'm going to be responsible you'll have to help me.'

'I will, I will.'

'So, are you still having the headaches?'

'Don't tell anybody.'

''Course I won't.' Doris, disturbed, way out of her depth, tried to sound calm. 'But we've got to do something to make you better. Find a doctor—'

'No!' The child twisted out of her lap. 'I can't. I mustn't . . .'

'Come on, you've been to the doctor's—'

'I never.'

'Now Karen—'

'Honestly, Aunty Doris.'

'You were probably too little to remember.'

'No. She wouldn't let me. It was for my own good.' She recited the last few words in a flat, monotone as if they had been drummed into her many times. 'Ava said . . . she said they'd . . .'

I wish I'd got that woman here, thought Doris. I'd wring her bloody neck. Karen looked terrified. Doris reached out and coaxed her close again.

'Tell me, sweetheart.'

Karen shook her head but climbed back into Doris's lap.

'Whisper then.' Karen shook her head. 'Go on . . . I won't tell anyone.'

'Promise?'

'Faithful and true.'

Karen whispered.

Doris felt dizzy and knew it was her blood pressure. When able to speak, her voice trembled. She said, 'That's a wicked lie. And you mustn't ever believe it again.' She kissed Karen's forehead, rocking her gently. 'Me and your uncle Ernest – we'd never let such a thing happen.'

Trying to keep the anger that flamed in her heart from marking her face, Doris eased the child into a more comfortable position and kissed her again. How to handle this? Doris's own doctor was on the point of retiring. She had been with him for almost thirty years and he had seen her through countless illnesses and minor operations. He was a kind man and very good at guessing what was really wrong, which was not always what you'd said. There would still be time to make an appointment and ask his advice about Karen. Perhaps he'd agree to make a home visit and talk to the little girl. As a family friend like, just dropping in.

If she really wasn't registered anywhere it should be sorted straight away. Dunroamin' would do as an address. And themselves, she and Ernest, as nearest relatives or next of kin. Better say they were officially fostering; all the details could be sorted later. Doris, for whom the word 'respectable' could have been invented, found herself ready and willing to spin as many lies in as many highly coloured variations as the occasion might demand. A child who was lost had been found, and must never be lost again.

The stifling weather had broken. After lunch it had rained, releasing the fragrant scent of flowers. The grass on the croquet lawn still sparkled and pollen dust floated through bars of sunlight.

Observing herself and Polly, in their long summer dresses and straw hats resting under the great cedar tree, Kate thought they must appear like characters from a novel set in the early twentieth century. *Howard's End*, perhaps. Or *The Go-Between*. Certainly the atmosphere was fraught and wretched enough to occupy either. There was a tray of lemonade, which Benny had made while they were out, but no one was drinking.

The journey back had been extraordinary. All of them had sat, silent, carefully upright, fearfully prescient, like people in a tumbril. Once home, Polly got out of the car and wandered into the garden, and Mallory followed. But Kate, already sensing great unhappiness to come and knowing the action to be pathetically childish, went into the house for her lucky beekeeper's hat. She found a frayed old Panama of Carey's in the back porch for Polly.

Now Mallory, who had been pacing about since they first arrived, suddenly stopped dead in front of Polly and said, 'Aren't you going to tell us—'

'Yes, I am,' said Polly. She was shivering with nerves. 'I was going to. I was actually on the point of it. I knew I must. Then the police arrived. I'm sorry.'

'Come and sit down, Mal.' Kate tugged a garden chair closer to her side. 'Looming over her like that.'

Mallory sat down but his energy and attention, unfaltering, continued to stream in Polly's direction. He didn't even feel Kate's hand on his arm. When Polly began to speak he listened intently while his world and everything in it fell slowly apart.

The aftermath was terrible. The gradual unravelling of how he had been deceived cut Mallory's joy and pride in his daughter into bleeding ribbons.

317

When she had finished he sat, humiliated, his gullibility exposed in the market place. A fool for love.

All the lies. How many he would never know. That was almost the worst part of it. Because now so many memories, right back into her childhood, were tainted. How could he have deceived himself that the mocking, self-centred and ruthless girl the world knew as Polly Lawson wasn't really Polly. Not his Polly.

He remembered the scene where she had led him up to explaining how it was he who had control of her legacy. Led him like a stupid donkey to admit something she already knew. How her eyes had widened with amazement. She had actually flung her arms around his neck and wept genuine tears. And then, to compound the lie, the pretence that she had only joined this syndicate in the first place to make money for him. So that he could leave the Ewan Sedgewick and be well again. How confident he had been then of her love; how overwhelmingly proud.

Endless recollections like this combined to leave him rigid with outrage and misery and shock. When, after a long silence, she tried to speak again he turned on her.

'I'm so sorry, Daddy—'

'Don't call me Daddy. You're not five now.'

'I'll pay it back.'

'And don't talk such rubbish.'

'I'll work hard—'

'You've cleaned us out.'

'I'll make money. In the city you can. Five years—'

'Don't lie. You've no intention—'

'I have. I have . . .'

'I'm sick of your lies.'

'I promise—'

'And I'm sick of you.'

'Mallory—'

'Still, there's always a bright side. At least we've seen the back of those grudging visits. You hardly bothered to take your coat off half the time.'

'Back of . . .?'

'Now we're broke I've no doubt we'll quickly be found expendable.'

'Please, Dad.'

'Mind you, there's still Appleby House,' said Mallory, stony-eyed. 'That must be worth a bob or two. Could be some while before you can cash in though.'

Polly dried the shining fall of tears on her pink-striped dress. She hadn't looked at her parents since the beginning of her confession. Now she began slowly to get up.

'Because I'm buggered if I'm going to die just to please you.'

'*Mallory – stop it . . .*'

Kate caught up with Polly near the terrace steps. She took her arm but

Polly gently disengaged it, shaking her head. She said quietly, 'Stay with him,' before going into the house.

That was hours ago. Kate and Mallory, willingly abandoning the now-tainted comfort of the cedar's shade, had moved to the terrace and were still sitting there under a darkening sky. A sudden cool wind ruffled the roses.

For a long tune Mallory had said little and Kate had said nothing. He was glad she was there. He didn't want to be alone but could not have borne anyone else to witness his mortification. Now she was taking his hand, kissing it, holding it against her cheek. The magnanimity of the gesture overwhelmed him. He thought of her life, what he had dragged her through. How modest her ambition had been: to live quietly and happily with her family and publish a few worthwhile books. And now even that was to be denied her.

'Listen,' she was saying, taking his other hand, 'everything we had yesterday we have today.' Then, when he looked incredulous: 'All right, we've discovered some things we didn't know—'

'Like our daughter's a thief.'

'But nothing important has changed.'

'I believed in her. I thought she loved me.'

'Darling – she loves us both as much as she's able. She's . . . Polly.'

Even the sound of her name hurt. How ridiculous. So his eyes had been opened: his illusions shattered. Wasn't it about time? A man of his age should be past such wistful imaginings. Ordinary common sense could have told him nothing lasts and things are never what they seem. Much better to view life from a clear uncluttered perspective. So it looks suddenly barren and drained of colour – he'd just have to get used to it. And it beat being rammed up to the eyeballs in a cesspit of deceit.

He remembered years ago his aunt saying that human beings are meant to live within certain limits. And if we do not live within these limits everything goes wrong. Had he unknowingly exceeded them in some way? Perhaps by too greedily embracing the happiness that had, at last, appeared to be his lot.

'How do you do it, Kate?'

'It's my nature.' She knew what he meant. 'So I can't really take the credit.'

'Do you think . . . this speculation . . .' The yearning tightened his throat. He could hardly get the word out. 'She was actually doing it for us?'

'Of course she was doing it for us.' Kate was amazed. 'Who else would she be doing it for?'

'I don't know. I don't know anything any more.'

They sat on in silence. The sky became an even darker blue. Pinpricks of silver light appeared.

Kate said, 'Look – the stars are coming out.'

319

And Mallory said, 'Not from where I'm sitting.'

Kate went into the house then to prepare supper. It was still and quiet. The kitchen smelled of sweet peas and the coriander Benny had chopped to sprinkle on the carrot soup that was never eaten. On the table was a note.

Dear Mum,

I have gone back to London. I plan to get a job and save as much as I can before September. I shall get a loan for my fees next term and also find a cheaper place to live. Please don't worry about me. I will send my new address. Thanks for everything.

Love Polly.

CHAPTER TWENTY-FIVE

By mid-morning the following day the appeal for passengers alighting at Northwick Park off the 6.10 p.m. Metropolitan Line train from Uxbridge on Wednesday, 8 August had been widely circulated. DCI Barnaby of Causton CID, the officer in charge of the case, appeared at the conclusion of the local television news at 1.30. His appeal was also broadcast from radio stations, both commercial and BBC.

'That should smoke him out,' said DS Troy as the chief returned from the press room, rubbing crossly at his face with what looked like a tea towel.

'I can't stand this stuff. What the hell does it matter if the light catches my nose?'

Sergeant Troy thought, at least they've covered up his black eye. He said, 'I'll do it next time, if you like.'

There was an immediate chorus of jeers and 'ooohhhs'. Sergeant Troy sneered silently back, noticed the lovely Abby Rose, who had not joined in the mockery, smiling sympathetically, and was struck afresh by her beauty. Having been true to his unconsummated longing for Sergeant Brierly for as long as he could remember Troy had lately noticed a definite coarsening in Audrey's features, a blurring of that matchless profile. Also, since her promotion to a rank level with his own, she had become overconfident, even a touch sarky. Admiration was definitely off the menu there. Respect likewise.

DCI Barnaby noticed the exchange of looks and hoped things would go no further. Fancying other people was human nature, and the workplace was often a forcing house for an attraction that, denied propinquity, could well die a natural death. The physical and emotional closeness police work often entailed made such situations especially hazardous. Barnaby himself had never been unfaithful, though there had been one or two very close calls. The second so close it had led to a request for a transfer.

Troy was turning away now, giving all his attention to the ringing of Barnaby's direct line. The DCI stretched out his hand and Troy handed the receiver over.

'Leo Fortune, sir.'

'Mr Fortune?'

Barnaby listened. Troy watched, trying to read the chief's reaction. Plenty of the old gravitas, some frowning. Now he was groping around for a pencil.

'That is remarkable. Will you prosecute? . . . What about the other files? . . . If you remember I suggested that you should . . . I am aware that tomorrow's Saturday . . .'

There was a bit more along these lines and the conversation ended.

As he hung up Barnaby said, 'The girl's practically emptied the Lawson account.'

'Crikey. What are they going to do about it?'

'Fortune's not sure. She didn't break in, did no damage and only took money belonging to herself and her parents.'

'Look bad for the firm if this gets out. Lack of security.'

'Exactly. What amazed him was that all the cash then went on shares that were generally known to be worthless.'

Troy, perching on the chiefs desk, gave a snort of satisfaction. 'So much for high-flyers.' He removed himself to be more comfortable in a swivel chair. 'How did she break into the account anyway? Aren't they supposed to have passwords?'

'These were all in medieval French. Brinkley believed this made them incomprehensible to anyone except a specialist scholar and left the disk in an unlocked desk drawer. As for the rest—'

'You think she's been stealing from other accounts?'

'Don't know. And won't know till Monday when the lazy beggars drift back into work.'

'Be fair, Chief. Even money men need a break.'

Barnaby was cross and impatient. Two murders had been committed here. One of a man who thought so well of his staff he had left them his share of the business. And where was this staff when the police needed them? Playing golf, shopping, swimming with the kids, visiting garden centres. Fortune himself was going to a wedding, offering the pitifully lame excuse that the groom was his eldest son.

'Cheer up, sir,' said Sergeant Troy, whose spirits always rose on seeing those of others fall. 'It's not as if it's urgent.'

During morning service at St Anselm's, Benny sat and kneeled and stood and sat again, all the time grappling with the jumbled desolation of her thoughts. She couldn't seem to sort her emotions out. Loneliness, keen as a knife, was paramount. She had tried to counteract this by flooding her mind with happy memories. Presently, as the vicar droned through his sermon, she was remembering the last time she and Dennis had been together. The turbot he had cooked so beautifully, the delicious chocolate pudding. And how they had talked about being involved with the Celandine Press and what fun it would be.

Now all that was gone. Anger against whoever had so cruelly ended a gentle, harmless existence was forever prowling on the fringe of Benny's conscience, seeking to get a grip. As a Christian she tried to fight this but the simple, unquestioning faith that had supported her all her life was crumbling. The idea that if you were good and kind and hurt no one God would look after you was plainly a lie. Which left prayers, always her first and last resort in times of trouble, no more than ashes in the mouth.

Now she stood for the final hymn, recited the meaningless words, then stumbled from her pew and up the aisle. Flinching from the vicar's flabby handshake and warm stare of compassion, Benny made her way to Dennis's grave. How bare it looked now the wreaths had been removed. How suddenly neglected. She must arrange for a stone. Sensing that people were observing her and wary of clumsy attempts at consolation Benny didn't linger.

But where was she to go? The obvious place, home, for the first time ever did not appeal. Something had happened at Appleby House. Something wrong, even bad. It had started when Mallory had gone tearing off to London and come back with Polly. The next day she, Benny, had been cutting back the first lupins when Chief Inspector Barnaby had come back. He had taken Polly away, holding her arm as if she might run off. Kate and Mallory went as well.

Distressed and bewildered, Benny watched for their return, instinctively keeping out of sight. She had stayed in the flat with only Croydon for company that night and all the following day, making a brief phone call so no one would worry. Pretending she had the beginnings of a cold and didn't want to spread it about.

Now, hesitating at St Anselm's lych-gate and suddenly drawn by the peaceful sound of rippling water, Benny turned from the big house and made her way to the banks of the stream. She sat down beneath a drooping willow, folding her hands quietly in her lap until gradually the turmoil in her mind gentled down to just plain sorrow. Then, to keep the disturbance at bay, began deliberately to plan for the future.

The whole orchard was resonant with the thrumming of wasps and bees. Mallory didn't know what he was doing there except that it didn't really matter where he was, so this was as good a place to be as any. Ladders still rested against the trees and half-full baskets of ripe apples, carefully labelled, were stacked on trestle tables. Peasgood Nonsuch, Coeur de Boeuf, Api Rose. The heat brought out their full, rich fragrance.

He would give anything to switch his mind off. Half his kingdom, as the fairy tales used to have it. The ones he read to Polly. Except now he had no kingdom. No financial kingdom and no other sort of kingdom either. Trust and happiness, the only riches worth having, had vanished. All right for Kate to say they could now all have a more honest relationship. She had lost nothing and gained everything. That this made Mallory jealous only increased his self-disgust. Mean-spirited it appeared as well as gullible.

Kate stood briefly in the opening of the blue door. Every now and then she sought her husband out, not always declaring her presence. There was nothing she could do but be there. Sooner or later things would change; he would change. Until then she would occupy herself with the ongoing development of the Celandine Press.

Kate was aware, though he had not put it in so many words, that Mallory now presumed this venture to be at an end. No money, no business. On the contrary. She was more determined than ever that it should go ahead. And they now had two titles to launch. She had written to the author of *The Sidewinder Café*, one of the outstanding novels that she had unsuccessfully recommended for publication, found the title still available and offered a tiny advance plus a high percentage of royalties. Any loss from this title Kate believed would be more than offset by *The King's Armourer*. Though there were no certainties in publishing she had been in the business too long not to sniff out a winner when it fell into her hands. Still no response from E.M. Walker but August was a holiday month so this was no surprise.

Last night, with Mallory slumped in front of the television – talk about back to square one – Kate had sat at the kitchen table sorting out their finances. There was Mal's pension, her own savings, their profit on the London house and twenty thousand a year in rent from Pippins Direct. Both pension and rent would be taxed but they could live reasonably on what remained.

The computers and printers had already been bought and Kate planned to edit and produce the books herself. Financially this would be well within their grasp. It was not printing books but their promotion and distribution that took the money. The big companies would spend thousands on publicity for a single title. Even bribing booksellers was not unknown. The Celandine Press's budget would be tiny. But Kate had a lot of contacts in the business and planned to make use of every one. She already had several ideas for a website and even thought of publishing 'taster' chapters in advance on the Net.

She was in good spirits as well as happy. Indeed, it was astonishing considering what they had all been through in the last couple of weeks, just how happy she was. Until it had been unexpectedly watered by Polly's tears Kate had not realised what a dry, enclosed place her heart had gradually become. Now, whatever happened, she would never cross that particular desert again.

Closing the orchard door she wandered back through the walled garden. The espaliered figs were so ripe, so luscious and bursting with juice that she picked one and held it, soft and warm, in the palm of her hand. She flung her head back and squeezed the rosy seeds into her mouth, then, wiping her fingers on her denim skirt, made her way to Benny's flat. She had already been round once but no one came to the door, which had been locked. Unsure whether Benny was still sleeping, nursing her cold or had gone to church, Kate had left, deciding to come back later.

But now was later and Benny was still nowhere to be seen. Becoming anxious, for morning service must have finished long ago, Kate hurried to the churchyard, half expecting to find her sitting by Dennis's grave. Guiltily she remembered her determined vow always to look after Benny. How long ago was that made? Less than a fortnight at the outside. The village shop would now be closed. Perhaps she had gone to visit Doris? Or really was at home but too ill to come to the door. By now seriously worried, Kate was just leaving the churchyard when she saw Benny sitting by the humpbacked bridge, gazing into the running water. Kate hurried over but before she could call out Benny turned, got up and immediately began a conversation. She had come to a decision. It was about the Celandine Press. Could they have a meeting as soon as possible? A business meeting, that was.

Kate, intrigued, smiled and said, 'Of course we can. Mallory's in the orchard. We'll go and find him straightaway.'

Troy stood over the whirring fax as the paper unfurled. Only a tiny percentage of his attention was involved in deciphering the details of Dennis Brinkley's telephone calls. Most of the rest was on Abby Rose Carter, sitting next to the machine. On the fragrance of her hair and the downy sweetness of the back of her neck. Sex was on Troy's mind a lot at the moment. Only last night he had dreamed of Nigella Lawson. She had been wearing satin pyjamas and standing in front of a towering silver fridge eating chocolate cheesecake. He had awoken in an ecstasy of longing, though whether for Nigella, the cheesecake or the pyjamas he could not quite disentangle, such was the bewildering fluidity of the dream.

'Details of Brinkley's calls, Chief.' He tore the paper off. 'Poor old sod. Half a dozen in as many weeks and that's pushing it.'

Barnaby held out his hand. He recalled his own bills, especially when Cully had still been at home. Once the damage had been so completely unbelievable that he had asked for an itemised breakdown and received seven pages of information so tightly packed he had gone nearly cross-eyed struggling to make sense of it.

Dennis's calls, made and received, were certainly few and far between. To Barnaby's mind this did not make him a 'poor old sod' but rather a person who lived simply and had found a measure of contentment in his own company. He was certainly not without the gift of evoking affection, as the interviews at Brinkley and Latham had clearly showed.

As Barnaby stared at the fax his fingertips began to tingle. A call had been made from Kinders at 11.17 p.m. on Monday, 23 July. Made after Brinkley had returned, having seen Polly Lawson illegally enter his office. Had he made the call himself? Barnaby thought it must be so. Brian Allibone had seen Dennis drive off, unaccompanied. It was pretty unlikely he would have picked up someone along the way and brought them home.

The DCI dialled the given number. He did not check it out, feeling sure it would belong to Appleby House. But he was wrong. The Lathams' answerphone responded. Gilda was presumably elsewhere, improving the shining hour; no doubt composing haiku, perfecting her butterfly stroke, deconstructing Milton, whatever. Latham himself, on the other hand, was probably lolling in the hammock, getting outside a few blue label Stolichnayas and wisely ignoring the call lest it give his prohibited presence away. Which suited Detective Chief Inspector Barnaby just fine.

He asked for the car to be brought round. Troy got this sorted in double-quick time, which was a shame as they had no sooner driven off the forecourt than devastating news arrived, via Leo Fortune, that seemed to blow the whole case wide open.

Andrew was packing. He had left all his stuff over the bed, careless of Gilda noticing. When he had spent years concealing every move he made and every penny spent, she had watched him, hawk-like, pouncing on each real or imagined misdemeanour. Now, as he slung the few good things he had managed to steal or wheedle out of her into a holdall she lay downstairs, becalmed on the huge sofa, guzzling a tub of Funky Monkey and ogling Kilroy.

Andrew checked his briefcase. Passport, plane ticket, English money plus euros and all the evidence of his recently opened private bank account. These documents, in the first instance sent to his office address, had then been stored in the garden shed along with seed packets and plant markers in an old biscuit box. There they rested secure from investigation by anyone who valued the shape and varnished perfection of their work-shy fingernails.

The cab was due in five minutes. He'd already opened the gates. Andrew had decided against taking the Punto because a) he hated it, and b) he wouldn't put it past her to report it stolen and set the rozzers on him. Hell hath no fury and all that jazz. Humming 'Come Fly With Me' he trotted down to the lounge.

'You'll be late for work,' said Gilda, still glued to the box.

'So?'

It took a moment for this to register. Then there was puzzlement followed by outright disbelief. Surely she must have misheard. 'What did you say?'

'I don't go to work, Gilda.'

'What on earth do you mean?'

'You surely don't expect me to exert myself for the pitiful scrap of money you dole out?'

'Don't worry.' Still gazing hotly at Robert the smooth, Gilda snorted her contempt. 'I never thought you earned it.'

'Not earn it? *Not earn it?* You try humping a lard mountain five times a week for ten years. You'd soon find out if I bloody earned it.'

She looked at him then all right. Turned her great moon face round, widened her little eyes so much the electric-blue lids all but vanished.

326

'No, what I do the minute you're not around is come back here to drink and watch the telly. And not always alone.' He smiled cheerfully. 'You'd be surprised the number of playmates available to a lonely man.'

Now her mouth was opening. Opening, closing, Opening, closing. Andrew affected concern.

'Don't worry, they were never serious. Just something to take the taste of you away.'

'Uz . . . uz . . . crawke . . .' Her lips were working now, jumping in and out like lively little sponges. 'Fay . . . fay . . .'

'What's that?'

'I . . . fay . . . foo . . .'

'Of course you've been faithful. What man in his right mind is going to fuck a woman the size of an elephant with one brain cell and a neck wider than her face?'

This time there was an even stranger sound. Rather like someone gargling on broken glass.

'Too late now to say you're sorry. And do close your mouth. The view from here is disgusting.'

Gilda was struggling now, rocking and wrestling with the sofa, trying to rise.

'Don't look at me for assistance,' said Andrew. 'I've suffered my last hernia. Get yourself a fork lift.'

More heaving and shaking and then—

'Oh, not tears? That's what comes of having your own way all the time. I've spoiled you – that's what I've done. But now I plan to make amends. I'm offering you your freedom. Think of it. You can do anything you like. You could do a tiny stroke of work for the first time in your useless life. You could find some other wretched bloke to torture. You could hire yourself out as a bouncy castle. The possibilties are—'

Damn. There was the cab drawing up and three-quarters of his long-nurtured eulogy still undelivered. With a brisk, jolly swing of his hand Andrew picked up the bag and prepared to leave. In the doorway he looked back, savouring the final moments of victory.

Gilda did not look at all happy. In fact she looked incredibly wretched and also rather ill. Andrew hesitated, then did something he was to regret for the rest of his life. He took the telephone from the far side of the room and placed it on a little table near her hand.

'Cheer up, fatty. Talk to someone – get it off that gargantuan coal heaver's chest. Try The Samaritans. Better still –' over his shoulder, closing the door – 'Save the Whales.'

It must have been about forty-five minutes after this that the police car drove up to the first set of electronic gates at Mount Pleasant and was admitted. Barnaby saw the ambulance, turning in the drive of Bellissima, straightaway.

'Bloody hell!' Troy pulled up as close as he could to the nearest flowerbed, leaving room for the larger vehicle to manoeuvre. The siren howled and the ambulance shot by as Barnaby got out and ran across the grass.

A youngish man stood in the porch. Pale, alarmed, smartly suited. Barnaby produced his warrant card and started asking questions. The man was Simon Wallace, a solicitor. The Berrymans' solicitor.

'Perhaps we'd better go inside,' said the chief inspector. Then, when they were, 'You look as if you could do with a drink.'

'Yes.' He helped himself to a whisky, his hands shaking. 'God – what a day.'

'What happened?'

'She had a heart attack.'

'Is Mr Latham here?'

'No one's here. We had a call from Mrs Latham. She sounded . . . extraordinary. Somebody had to come out immediately. She was almost screaming.'

'And when you arrived?'

'The front door was open. I found her on that sofa. She couldn't move.'

'So what was the call about?'

'She wanted me to bring her will over.'

'Did she say why?'

'The usual reason. To change it.'

'Was this a habit?'

'Not at all. It was made just after she was married. She'd meant to make a new one long ago. Just hadn't got round to it.'

'The details?'

'Oh, come on. You know I can't—'

'I'm involved in a murder investigation, Mr Wallace. We can go through the proper procedure but, to be frank, time is not on our side.'

'It's not as if I'm a senior partner—'

'Then I'll talk to a senior partner. Your number?'

'Well . . .' Simon could just hear them at the office. Unable to handle heavy stuff. Can't take decisions. Better not risk him on the new Ainsley account.

'She cancelled the will, which left everything to her husband. Then made a new one and signed it.'

'Leaving everything to . . .?'

'Charity. She couldn't think which one – she was in such a state. But it had to be animals. People were vile – those were her last words. I suggested the Cat Protection League, my wife and I being members of the Fancy.'

Blimey, thought Sergeant Troy, some mogs have all the luck. This place alone must be worth over a million.

'There was also mentioned a nuptial agreement drawn up years ago by her father. In case of a separation it was supposed to stop her husband getting any of the spoils.'

'But they're not valid over here,' said Barnaby.

'Mr Berryman hoped he wouldn't work that out.'

'So when did Mrs Latham become ill?'

'Directly after the business was concluded. To be honest I got the impression she was just hanging on till I got there. The ambulance men said things didn't look too good.'

'I see. Thanks very much, Mr Wallace.' Barnaby got up. 'You've been very helpful.'

'Can I go now?'

'Of course. But leave a card, if you would.'

Barnaby watched the solicitor's Mercedes negotiate the drive and the small but select gathering of neighbours just beyond the boundary wall. He thought human nature didn't vary much. Whatever the locale – run-down sink estate, neat suburban terrace or gated enclosure of the superrich, curiosity as to the business of one's neighbours seemed endemic.

'See what you can find out from that lot,' said Barnaby. 'I'll look over the house.'

He started at the far end in the larger of the four bedrooms. Men's clothes were strewn everywhere. Some on the bed, some on the floor, over an armchair. An empty suitcase lay by the dressing table with its lid open. Some drawers had been tipped upside down.

Barnaby tried to open the sliding wardrobes running the length of the room. He had just discovered the electronic button when he heard Troy running through the hall. Racing up the stairs.

'It's Latham, sir.' Troy stopped on the threshold staring at the mess. 'He's gone.'

'Tell me.'

'Hour, hour and a half ago. Left in a black cab carrying a large holdall. Cab was advertising Britannia Building Society.'

'Right. Get a search call out. Railways, air and seaports. Full description. And get a trace on the taxi.'

Troy seized the phone. Barnaby abandoned his investigation into the wardrobe and set about a more systematic search for Latham's passport. He started in the library. He knew it was the library because there were red and gold book spines glued to all the shelves. There was also a framed picture of Shakespeare, quill poised, gazing gloomily at an astrolabe. But he had hardly started on the Chippendale desk before Troy was calling out again. Tetchily the chief inspector returned to the bedroom.

'For heaven's sake, man. Can't you do a simple—' Then took in Troy's expression. 'What is it? What's happened?'

'I think you should hear this direct, sir,' said Sergeant Troy, and passed over the telephone.

The offices of Brinkley and Latham were almost deserted. The receptionist was still there, her eyes grossly red and swollen with weeping. A waste-paper basket at her feet full of sodden tissues. When Barnaby and Troy arrived she began to speak, then started to cry again. They made their way through to the main office.

Leo Fortune sat in his cubbyhole staring blankly into space. His desk was cluttered with papers and notes and letters as if, only moments before, he had been lively and busily engaged. There was also a cup of tea, stone-cold with a congealing skin.

When Barnaby said, 'Mr Fortune?' he brought his head up with great difficulty, as if it were a lump of rock. He looked years older than when they had seen him last, his mouth a miserable jagged line.

'This is a bad business, sir.'

'Have you found her?'

'Found . . .?'

'The Lawson girl.' His voice was cracking all over the place. 'Have you arrested her?'

'I need to clarify certain things. The message I got—'

'What's to clarify? You know what's happened. You know who's responsible.'

'I still need to—'

'Haven't you done anything?'

'Calm down, sir,' suggested Sergeant Troy.

'Calm down?' He stared at them both in turn, his face such a mask of absolute incredulity it verged upon the tragic. Which made it, to Troy's mind, also comic. He turned away, fumbling for his notebook.

Barnaby sensed the man struggling not to cry. He said quietly, 'If we could just take some details, Mr Fortune . . .?' Then sat himself squarely in the comfortable chair facing what used to be Dennis Brinkley's desk. His stolid, phlegmatic presence and the silence that gradually took over the room eased Leo Fortune back into some sort of composure.

'Money has been stolen from nearly all of the accounts held here. Thousands of pounds. Hundreds of thousands.'

'But you're insured?'

'Of course, we have to be. But this will still finish us. When you're dealing with other people's money once trust has gone you've had it. God knows what Mrs Latham will say.'

Barnaby thought this was perhaps not the time to pass on the news that Gilda was in intensive care and not expected to last the day.

'Have you any way of tracing the money?'

'It'll be out of the country by now. Some offshore slipperiness. Ghost accounts, more than likely.'

'Ghost?' Barnaby looked up sharply. 'How does that work?'

'It's an old scam. You find a child's grave, the child being the same sex as yourself and, had it lived, roughly the same age. Apply for a copy of its birth certificate. Using this and an up-to-date photograph, apply for a

330

passport. You can then open an account and start putting money in. And the owner of this account can never be traced because they don't exist. Hence, ghost.'

'Surely it's not as simple as that.'

'If it was,' decided Sergeant Troy, 'everybody'd be doing it.'

'There's quite a risk. Checking procedures have been tightened up a lot, especially when presented documents are copies. And you can be in serious trouble just for trying it on.'

Barnaby became briefly distracted then by the phone in reception. It had been ringing quite often since they arrived. He wondered if such frequency was the normal traffic of the day or whether the news of the disaster was already leaking out. With a dozen or so distressed staff on the loose it would hardly be a surprise.

'Are you going to close the office, Mr Fortune?'

'I can't decide. If I do it's going to look as if I've scarpered – like one of those dodgy types you see on *Watchdog*. And if I don't, when this really gets out we'll be practically lynched.'

'Aren't you going to tell people yourself?' asked Sergeant Troy.

'Of course.' He waved a sheet of foolscap at them. 'It's what I've been working on all day. Trying to warn clients that something untoward has happened without actually telling them how bad things actually are.'

'A fine line,' agreed Barnaby.

'So you see why I jumped on you about getting hold of the Lawson girl. Every minute counts.'

'We don't think Polly Lawson is responsible for this, sir.'

'Not . . .? But she must be. I mean – we know she did it. You said yourself—'

'We believe these thefts to be something quite separate and unrelated to the earlier incident.'

'How can that be?' Leo looked really sick. Terrible though things were, he had thought at least the police had a name. A point of entry to start searching for the money. 'I don't understand.'

'Do you remember when we talked here a couple of days ago? When Andrew Latham joined us and became extremely disturbed.'

'Of course.'

'And at what point in our conversation it happened?'

'You were talking about the fishmonger. How he'd identified the person Dennis saw breaking in here as Polly Lawson.'

'Why do you think that brought about such an extreme reaction?'

'How should I know?' Fortune put his elbows on the desk, covered his eyes with his hands and groaned. 'I don't know anything any more. I don't even know what day it is.' Then he looked up sharply. 'But I do know I haven't got time to play stupid games. So get on with what you want to say in a straightforward manner. Or just go.'

* * *

Latham was found before the day was out. The photograph helped. A happy smiling one of him and his wife taken years earlier. Gilda neatly excised, the police had it circulated within the hour. The lunchtime edition of the *Evening Standard* featured it on the front page. The black cab too had been quickly traced. Its driver had taken Latham to South Ruislip; the nearest Tube station to Bunting St Clare that connected with the main line.

There he was clearly remembered, having tried out his charm to poor effect on the female booking clerk. He had bought a ticket to London via High Wycombe. Apparently he was in exceptionally high spirits. You would have thought, suggested the clerk, he'd won the lottery.

Latham's complete ignorance as to any interest of the police in his whereabouts led to him travelling openly and, alas for Sergeant Troy's romantic imaginings, with no attempt at disguise. He was detained around four o'clock at Waterloo, attempting to board the boat train for Southampton. By six he was seated in an interviewing room at Causton police station, having rejected, with an air of complete bewilderment, the suggestion that he might like to have a solicitor present. Two plainclothes officers were also at the table, on which was a folder and a large, somewhat bulky envelope. They were the same two officers, he recognised sourly, that had turned up at the bungalow only days ago and dropped him in it.

If they'd known anything then they would have arrested him then. So what did they know now? What could they know? There were one or two details skilled ferreting could no doubt discover. But you had to know what you were looking for and they knew bugger all.

His rights had been read. He knew he could not be compelled to speak, which meant he was the one with the power. And there was nothing like the power of silence.

'Off on your holidays, Mr Latham?'

Andrew smiled.

'All on your own?' Barnaby paused. 'Perhaps you were meeting up with someone later?' Nothing. 'In France, perhaps?' Nothing.

'Where did you get the money?' asked the skinny red-haired one.

'None of your business.' Damn, that was a mistake. He should have said, 'What money?' How quick they were to trick and provoke.

'Enquiries have led us to believe that you earned no regular salary.'

'And that it was Mrs Latham who held the purse strings.'

'I believe she gave you an allowance every week.'

'A very small allowance.'

'So where did you get the money?'

'What money?'

The big man opened a folder and took out some papers, which Andrew immediately recognised. They had taken his travelling bag when he arrived, giving him a receipt as if that somehow made it acceptable. Obviously it had been searched. Surely that wasn't allowed without some special warrant. If they had bent the law didn't that mean any evidence so discovered would be inadmissible? Andrew wished now he had agreed to their suggestion of a brief.

He said, 'Are you allowed to do that?'

'There is a balance here of over four hundred thousand pounds.' Nothing. 'Did you have any special reason for opening an overseas account?' Nothing. 'Protection from the Inland Revenue, perhaps?'

Andrew shrugged. Having absorbed the initial shock of seeing the details of his recently obtained wealth made public he recognised anew the importance of silence. What he must not do was slide into some question and answer loop with them hammering away, looking for a slip or contradiction to pounce on. He would dig his heels in and keep shtum. God knew he'd had years of practice.

'What made you choose today to disappear, Mr Latham?'

'It was a disappearance, wasn't it?'

'Not just a trip to gay Paree.'

Gay Paree? Do me a favour. It was Cherbourg and a car, and motoring down to Provence and then across to Italy. Sorrento, Positano, Capri. All the places he had once pretended to own and manage property in. Except now the villa would be for real.

'Perhaps the investigation of Ava Garret's death was getting a little too close to home?'

'The *Causton Echo* was full of it.'

'How she met her murderer at Northwick Park.'

Andrew allowed an expression of utter stupefaction gradually to possess his features. This was difficult because it had, of course, been exactly this series of events that had provoked his flight.

'Sooner or later a witness will come forward who saw you.'

'Or your car.'

'Stands out, a yellow car.'

At this point a wondrously pretty uniformed policewoman came in with a tray of tea and a plate of shortbread biscuits. God – what a sight for sore eyes. Briefly Andrew's concentration slipped its moorings. He gave her a warm smile but she had locked on to the younger of the two investigators, who was giving her an even warmer smile. He said, 'Abby Rose, you're a star.'

Abby Rose! Andrew stored the lovely name away. He could afford her now. A girl like that.

The tea was boiling hot and tasteless. Ignoring it, the detectives shifted tack. Now it was Dennis who occupied their attention. Dennis the menace as he was turning out to be. If he had minded his own business he would be alive today. With a million missing quid to account for true, but alive.

What was this? Andrew was being handed some sort of printout from British Telecom. His number featured along with a few others. As did the time and date of the call. But that wouldn't tell them what had been said.

And without knowing that, such information would be meaningless. He smiled politely and handed the paper back.

'Quite a coincidence, Mr Latham.'

'Perhaps you remember discussing this very same evening with us recently in your office?'

'When you had that rather unpleasant turn.'

'Knocked bandy, as I recall. Sir.'

'You didn't mention this telephone conversation then.'

He hadn't been able to resist ringing, Dennis. Vindicated at last. Able to prove his fuss about the snake lamp had a sound basis in fact. Not triumphant – Dennis could never have managed that. But chuffed in his mild way. Silly, silly man.

Because he had seen who it was. He knew the woman. The family lived in Forbes Abbot. The matter, Dennis gave earnest assurances, could be safely left in his hands. But that was the last thing Andrew could allow to happen. There was far too much at stake. Money, naturally. Love too (though not for him). And most important of all, freedom, without which the first two were as ashes in the mouth.

Now he cursed his indolence over the past month. There had been time to plan his departure carefully. He could have got himself another passport. Another name. Created a totally different persona. But how was he to know that Dennis would decide to play Sherlock Holmes? Or that some stupid woman – and, boy, had she been stupid – would have a clairvoyant experience that would put the whole enterprise at risk.

The questioning had started off again; the hefty one repeating himself. Andrew frowned, cocked his head, faking a willingness to participate.

'And we believe that late telephone call—'

'Which you did not see fit to mention—'

'Led directly to his death.'

Prove it. Go on, I dare you.

'I suggest that after Brinkley left for work the following morning you entered the house and sabotaged one of the machines.'

Andrew couldn't help himself. 'Walked through the walls, did I?'

'No. We think you used these.'

The envelope was tipped upside down. It held a bunch of picks from the days when he was a petty thief. Gilda, having no idea what they were, had found them in an old box. Thought them 'all spiky and thrilling' and wanted them turned into a necklace.

Should he deny they were his? There seemed little point, for he hadn't been able to conceal a start of alarm when they had been tossed on to the table. Still, proving they were his was one thing. Proving he had entered Brinkley's house with them was something else. Andrew began some slow and calm breathing. The red-haired one replaced the picks in the bag using a clean handkerchief.

'They haven't been to Forensics yet.'

'We have high hopes of Forensics.'

'Apparently the lock on Kinders kitchen door had been oiled only a couple of days earlier.'

Now that was entrapment. Because it simply wasn't true. He'd been sure to check for anything that could transfer. On the handle too. And they wouldn't be able to come up with a surprise witness either. After parking on the very edge of the village overlooking an empty field he'd sat on a bench opposite the house, sheltering behind *The Times* till the coast was absolutely clear. Then in like lightning and doubly cautious coming out.

'Not a complicated business, modifying the machine, Mr Latham. You had, I understand, seen it before?' Silence. 'But what I did find difficult is how on earth Dennis Brinkley was persuaded to pull on the rope and release the weight that killed him.'

'Yeah – that really puzzled us.'

'He must have seen the trebuchet had been dragged out of place—'

'Marks all over the floor.'

'A mysterious, one might even say a suspicious thing to happen. Yet before any attempt was made to investigate—'

'When the alteration to the ramp might well have been noticed.'

'He reached out and tugged on the rope.'

'Now what on earth would make him do that?'

Andrew sighed and solemnly shook his head. It was plainly just as mysterious and suspicious to him. If only he could help . . .

Actually the key to the whole stratagem was Dennis's obsession with order, his compulsion to straighten and tidy. Andrew had left the rope caught up in a half-knot, the end hanging loose. Dennis would have been compelled to undo it. And to reach the knot he needed to lean directly over the machine and pull. It had been very precisely placed; just too high to get at any other way. Andrew was rather proud of this literally clever twist. The police would never work it out. And if they guessed, so what? When has a guess ever stood up in court? Solid evidence was what was needed and so far they'd got sweet FA. Which meant they'd either have to let him go, period, or release him on bail. In which case, Sorrento here I come.

There was almost another hour of this then they took a break.

His two interrogators having left the room, Andrew was offered something to eat. They had to do this apparently after a certain time. Sadly it was not brought by the gorgeous Abby Rose but by a spotty young constable who put the tray down and walked off, leaving the door of the interview room open. Andrew could just see him sitting on a chair in the corridor. The food was quite tasty: shepherd's pie with garden peas and a custard slice. He asked to use the toilet, small and windowless. So much for the great escape. Then spent the rest of his time alone, recapping on the story so far and bracing himself for the questions to come.

The Brinkley side of things looked pretty watertight. His only possible connection with the case – that final late-night phone call – the police had already discovered and it had availed them nothing. But Ava Garret? He could still remember with absolute clarity the moment in the radio interview when she started describing the death scene. The shape of the room, the tall narrow windows, the machines. She even knew what Dennis was wearing; the colour of his hair. If that child hadn't started crying . . .

Until then Andrew, sitting on a stool sipping his Lavazza, had been having a good laugh at the woman's expense. Then came the shock. So powerful it was as if a great fist had crashed into his chest. He fell backwards, gasping. Coffee flew; burning his legs, staining the floor. His fingers trembled so much they couldn't turn the radio off.

He picked up the broken cup and put it in the bin, then stood helplessly amid puddles of brown liquid, unable to get his breath. It was as if something large and fierce had entered the room and was eating up all the air. Clearly drawn before him as on a map, he saw the end of everything. Goodbye money and sun and sex and sand. Farewell golden, shadowless landscapes and licentious living happy ever after.

A genuine medium. He had never believed there was such a thing. But a little while later, when he began once more to think coherently, Andrew started remembering all sorts of instances when such people had helped the police with their inquiries. Had even found bodies.

Filling the washing-up bowl, getting bleach out of the cupboard to scrub the floor, he tried to subdue the panic that shock had left behind.

As Andrew saw it, his hands, morally speaking, were clean. Yes, he had tinkered with the giant catapult and nudged Brinkley into a dangerous situation but the final step had been taken by the man himself. Even obsessives had free will and he had made the wrong decision. No reasonable person would call that murder.

Even so this woman could put him away, perhaps for years. Years he hadn't got, thanks to the decade of spineless grovelling that Gilda's father had purchased with his scrap metal swag.

Dennis's death had taken place at one remove, as it were. Stopping Ava Garret would inevitably be more . . . the phrase 'hands on' came horribly to mind and was immediately rejected. There was no way he could physically kill someone. He just hadn't got it in him. He was not a violent man.

He sat and thought for so long he only just got clear before Gilda returned. It was while he was tucked away behind Bunting St Clare parish church waiting for going-home time that he remembered the methanol. He'd had it for years. Someone in the iffy circles in which he once moved had hinted at its efficiency and given him what had darkly been described as 'the leftovers'.

Andrew, interested and repelled in equal measure, had kept the unlabelled medicine bottle without ever asking himself why. Certainly he

336

would never have slipped the stuff to Gilda. Taking risks for no financial advantage was definitely not his bag. Perhaps he was keeping it for himself. For when he got too old and tired to philander; too creaky to leave the house. Shut up with Gilda twenty-four hours a day might drive the most patient man to top himself. Anyway, whatever possible reason, it was still in the garden shed on the weedkiller shelf.

The strange thing was, no sooner had he thought of the stuff than various schemes on how to use it came tumbling into his mind.

Astonished and impressed, for he was not normally an inventive man, Andrew decided to regard this fecundity as a good omen.

The first step obviously was to get hold of this clairvoyant. Using the nearest call box he tried Directory Enquiries, giving her name and saying that he only knew she lived in the Causton area. No joy. He tried the *Echo*, who gave him the number of her agent, a Mr Footscray. Even less joy there. Andrew had hardly opened his mouth before Mr Footscray hung up on him. That left the studio.

Even as he wrote down the number he recognised the chances of them handing out personal details about a programme guest were pretty slim. Then on the point of dialling (141 first, naturally), he had a brilliant idea. Why not pretend to be working for that honourable and world-renowned institution, the BBC? Surely a hack radio station run by teenagers who'd never make it and has-beens who'd already lost it was bound to be impressed. And it worked. There was a brief, awkward pause when they asked his name until Andrew noticed a framed advertisement for computer tuition right under his nose. He said, 'Chris Butterworth.' And the die was cast.

Having perceived Ava's grandiosity, hunger for attention and blinding lack of self-awareness during the interview, Andrew had no doubts that she would agree to meet him. Getting her out of the house had been a doddle. Likewise redirecting her via the mobile, catching her just before she boarded the train.

Where to take her had been slightly more problematical. Briefly, purely out of satisfaction at the symmetry of it all, he had been tempted towards the Peacock Hotel. The change in his fortunes had begun there just a few weeks ago, thanks to a chance meeting. How satisfying if the account could be closed there as well. But he frequented the place quite often and could be recognised. Common sense warned him off.

A long time ago, just before he met Gilda, Andrew had been vaguely seeing a woman who lived at Northwick Park. Suburban anonymous, as he recalled, which meant several anonymous places to eat. He decided to take Ava there. Naturally it had all changed, but there were still plenty of cafés and restaurants. Driving round he couldn't decide whether to look for a really busy one where they could both get lost in the shuffle, or somewhere nearly empty with perhaps just one waiter and a guy at the till to risk recalling their visit. In the end he hit on a little Greek Cypriot place, Cafe Trudos. There Andrew got the worst of both worlds as there was no one there when they arrived but by the time they left the place was packed.

Ava had talked non-stop. Andrew need not have worried about answering awkward questions regarding his position at the Beeb, length of service, actual programmes produced. The only time his opinion was solicited was on how best to present her. The sets mustn't be cheap and her support must definitely be a star of some magnitude. He was also instructed to contact Michael Aspel and explain that Ava was not comfortable with surprises.

After about half an hour of this Andrew no longer found himself somewhat embarrassed at the thought that he was about to dispose of another human being. The miracle, it seemed to him, was that no one had done it years ago.

He had been nervous about giving her the methanol. But his idea, to put it into his own glass – which he planned to conceal in his lap – then swap them round, worked perfectly. To distract her attention all he had to do was say: 'Isn't that Judi Dench over there?' (As if.) And there was Ava craning and gawping, twisting round, even standing up at one point before disappointedly flopping down again. Andrew apologised for his mistake but she refused to be mollified. He tried to make amends with some made-up gossip about Esther Rantzen but Ava would have none of it.

'Miss Rantzen is a personality merely.'

'She's very famous,' said Andrew. 'Got an OBE.'

'There is nothing,' said Ava firmly, 'like a dame.'

Sipping his tiny cup of sweet, muddy coffee Andrew then explained that they must think about leaving as he had to be in the studio by eight a.m. Ava took this very well and so she should, having just been offered the chance to front a new documentary on Victorian Spiritualism. Andrew paid the bill and the waiter helped Ava on with her coat. While she was so distracted Andrew flipped open her handbag and stole the mobile, which he later destroyed by running over it with the car.

As he led her towards the platform for the Uxbridge train he was concernedly watching for signs of illness. He'd had little time to bone up on methanol and had no idea how long it took to take effect. Maybe he'd been lucky to have got through the dinner without her falling into the feta saganaki. At the other extreme, if its make-up was not stable, the potency could have completely faded, in which case she'd wake up tomorrow morning with a bit of a headache and he'd have to start all over again.

Except that he wouldn't. He'd screwed his courage to the sticking place once, and once was enough. Though there was more money to come, he would walk – no, he would run away, as far and as fast as the wind would carry him.

The policemen were coming back. The older one, the chief inspector, came in first. As soon as Andrew saw his face he knew that something had happened. Something bad. He got up, pushing back his chair, which screeched and scraped against the concrete floor.

Barnaby stood at his office window watching the sun go down. The longest day was now nearly eight weeks behind them and the evenings were insidiously creeping in.

Sergeant Troy put on his jacket; checked his watch. He glanced across at the chief, wondering if a cheery word might not come amiss.

Barnaby's profile was not easy to read. Today it featured his enclosed, poker face. This inscrutability could be rather frightening, which was strange really, because there was nothing to see or read behind it to cause concern. It could be misleading too. Troy remembered once coming across the boss late one night sitting bolt upright in his leather revolving chair, showing this same impassive profile and inscrutably fast asleep.

Right now, though, he was probably simply knackered. Even Troy felt tired and he'd got twenty years on the DCI. Barnaby was, as Troy saw it, a scarred and battered old war-horse. Himself, by comparison, a jumping, prancing young stallion caparisoned by FCUK and with barely a scratch to his glossy hide.

It had been a dramatic, if ultimately barren, afternoon. After their break, when they had wearily eaten whatever was left in the canteen – warmish meat stewed to rags and green jelly with grapes in it – and Troy had seen off the remains of a packet of Benson's in the yard by the waste bins, they had returned to the interview room to discover that Latham had decided that he did, after all, want a solicitor.

Although this inevitably caused some delay the request pleased the chief inspector. It meant that, when it came to questions regarding the death of Ava Garret, Latham was not nearly as confident as he had appeared that morning. Not that his *modus operandi* changed much. Apart from the occasional murmured aside to said solicitor, silence continued to prevail.

As no answers to his questions had yet been forthcoming Barnaby decided to change tack. He would describe the matter and manner of Dennis Brinkley's murder as he supposed it to have been carried out and observe Latham's reactions.

He didn't learn much. The man listened with a slight smile, frowning sometimes or shaking his head. At no point did he look surprised. Only once was there an uncontrolled reaction. This was when Barnaby touched, for the second time that day, on the strange scene in Leo Fortune's office.

'What was it that upset you, Mr Latham? And so severely that you had to leave the building?'

Latham shrugged.

'Shall I tell you what I think?'

Latham did one of those resigned, open-armed gestures you get when returning substandard merchandise to an iffy market stall.

'I believe it was because you discovered that the person Brinkley saw entering his office the night before he died was Polly Lawson.'

At this Latham became excessively pale. Globules of perspiration broke out across his forehead; dark crescents bloomed in the armpits of his shirt.

'And not, as you had assumed, the woman who was your accomplice.'

Latham produced a handkerchief and mopped his face.

'It might also interest you to know that Ava Garret had no clairvoyant insight into Dennis Brinkley's murder. She was able to describe the scene of his death only after being fed this information by a member of the public.'

Latham was now as white as paper, swaying slightly as if from a gentle push. His solicitor became attentive; asked for a drink.

'So how does it feel,' persisted Barnaby, 'to have killed two people for nothing?'

Here the solicitor's protestations were interrupted by a uniformed policemen with a message. Sergeant Troy asked him to fetch some water and Barnaby, having read the note, indicated that the tape should be turned off.

'I'm afraid I have some bad news, Mr Latham.' He used the phrase automatically as he seemed to have done a thousand times in the past thirty years, the job being rather conducive to such situations. Invariably what followed provoked sorrow and despair. Fear, sometimes. Rage, often. But anguish as tormenting and exquisite as was presently in his power to bring about was something new. His voice showed not the slightest shadow of sympathy as he continued, 'We've just heard from Great Missenden that your wife has passed away.'

Barnaby did not leave it there. He explained the circumstances of her admission; related his conversation with the family solicitor. Latham was made aware that he had been the only beneficiary in Gilda's will; a place now seconded to the Cat Protection League. That her health was such as to encourage imminent collapse. And that if he had walked away from the marriage the circumstances were such that any court in the land would have granted him recompense.

By the time the chief inspector had finished speaking Latham was practically unrecognisable. It looked, Sergeant Troy remarked afterwards, as if all the blood had left his body. All the blood but not the bile. A few seconds later and, quite without warning, yellow liquid arched into the air and all over the tape recorder.

'Sir?' Troy brought the present back into the room. 'D'you think we'll get witnesses for whatever happened at Northwick Park?'

Barnaby was sure of it, 'Photographs of them both are well circulated. And details and pictures of his car. Wherever he took her someone will remember.'

'No wonder he panicked when we locked him up.'

'At the moment he's a broken man. Lean a bit and he'll probably snap. Also there's the matter of this accomplice. We can dangle a possible sentence reduction under his nose if he's prepared to betray her.'

Sergeant Troy, having fastened his jacket, unfastened it, then fastened it again. He examined his shirt front, rubbed the toecaps of each shoe on the backs of his trousers and began to comb his hair.

Barnaby laughed. 'She taking you home to meet her mother?'

'I'll thank you not to mention mothers,' said Troy. 'Or the word Sproat.' He sniffed inside his jacket.

'Don't do that. It's like the monkey house at the zoo.'

But Troy was already gone, quickly, without even a good night.

Barnaby returned to his position by the window and his perusal of the sky, darkening at the end of the day. He was still struck by the melancholy beauty of that phrase despite it having become such common currency that a journalist on the *World at One* recently referred to it as 'the ee of the dee'.

Though he tried not to dwell on it, his retirement was more and more on his mind. He was taking the earliest option available without losing out on his pension. Another five years could be served but Joyce had got very upset when he had mooted the idea and Cully had fiercely backed her mother up. He saw their point and would not have had it otherwise. Love meant other people had claims on you.

Though the date was a good six months away he was already being asked around the station what he would do. Barnaby never knew how to reply. He would have liked to say 'nothing' but knew this would be considered strange. Everyone had a story about someone they knew who had tried this. Physically in good shape, economically comfortable, psychologically they were dead men. Pushing up daisies within six months was the favoured tag line.

Barnaby did know what he wouldn't do. He would not become a collector. He would not become enmired in the wasteland of silicon chip technology. Neither would he begin wearing shorts and a reversed baseball cap and start behaving like someone half his age. No marathon running or ball games or, God forbid, golf. No bridge or anything else that involved sitting still for long periods and bickering with grumpy elders. No plastic surgery – his double chin could stay where it was. And, above all, no bowls.

He knew people who did some or all of those things. Only the other day he had run into a former colleague. They had exchanged a few words and Barnaby suggested a quick half in the Magpie to catch up on each other's news. The man declined. Boasting that he had never been busier he riffed through all the things he still had to do before bedtime, then disappeared like the white rabbit, agitating his wristwatch and bringing it up to his ear.

Barnaby felt vaguely depressed after this encounter. He knew he could never cram his life with things that would normally give him no pleasure just to escape aimlessness and boredom. What an arid, starveling prospect. And all to avoid facing the fact that the hourglass was running out.

Things were handled differently in the East. Apparently the first third of their lives out there was spent learning how to live, the middle section by becoming a householder and raising a family. Finally they retired to a hut in the forest to meditate on the meaning of life, gradually dissolve the ego and learn how to die. Cully told him all about it one evening. He was grumbling about having to take blood pressure pills and she was trying to persuade him that deep relaxation was a safe alternative.

Barnaby had a vivid image of himself sitting cross-legged, clad only in a loincloth under a spreading chestnut tree. He snorted with laughter, liked the sound of it and laughed some more. It did him the world of good.

About to turn from the window, a movement on the station steps caught his eye. Detective Sergeant Troy was leaving the building accompanied by WPC Carter. They walked, their heads close in earnest conversation, towards Troy's beloved Ford Cosworth. Aby Rose climbed into the passenger seat but seemed unable to fasten her seat belt properly. Troy hesitated then, about to close the door, reached across her lap to help, staying in that position rather longer than was necessary.

Barnaby turned away before he could become at all saddened at what such an incident might foretell. His thoughts leaped forward twenty-four hours. Tomorrow night he and Joyce would be driving to Limehouse for supper *chez* Bradley. Cully said they must celebrate their very first visit by choosing whatever they liked to eat. Joyce had decided on her favourite starter: chunks of jellied beef consomme and Boursin's Pepper Cheese on hot toast. Barnaby fancied steak and kidney pudding with cauliflower and new potatoes. An apricot sorbet, they both agreed, would round things off nicely. Already Barnaby's stomach rippled gently in anticipation.

Oh, lucky man! Happiness beckoned. He switched off the light and went home.

AFTERWARDS

AFTERWARDS

CHAPTER TWENTY-SIX

Just over a month had passed since the man arrested on suspicion of the murder of Dennis Brinkley had been formally charged and remanded in custody to await trial at Aylesbury Assizes. Forbes Abbot's outrage at the doing to death of one of its own having been suitably assuaged, the village, briefly glamorous and in all the papers, once more subsided into its usual comfortable, unthreatening routine.

Autumn was almost upon them. Bonfires were crackling and huff was being taken about the smoke and the breaking of 'not until dusk' by-laws. The Horse and Hounds darts team were setting up match schedules with neighbouring villages. A quiz in aid of multiple sclerosis took place at the village hall and the last cricket match of the season was being played out on the green. Preparations for the Christmas Fayre were already being mooted. The competition at the September meeting of the WI was Your Best Ever Mincemeat Recipe. And rumour had it that Mrs Lattice of Mon Repos had already secretly weighed out in readiness for the making of her notorious puddings.

Mists and mellow fruitfulness were the order of the day and fruit came no more mellow than the beautiful apples now being carefully graded and packed in the orchard of Appleby House. Over the last couple of weeks fewer and fewer pickers had been needed and now the final handful were being paid off.

David and Helen Morrison of Pippins Direct were helping to load the last boxes into the back of an open lorry to be driven to the market at Seven Dials. Mallory watched, hovering awkwardly. He had got to know the Morrisons slightly over the last few weeks but inevitably, given the convulsive events in his own life and the extreme business of theirs, it had been very slightly. Feeling he should be there to see them off he stuck it out, smiling and waving until the lorry finally pulled away. They would return once the leaves had fallen, David had explained, to start pruning.

Alone now, Mallory drifted back into the deserted orchard, grateful for the space and silence. Grateful even for the sensation of rotten, wasp-infested fruit squelching beneath his sandalled feet. Ambling vaguely about in the weak light of the setting sun he yearned for consolation while simultaneously despising himself for weakness and self-pity. During these evening wanderings he struggled to concentrate on the smallest thing, however ordinary, which lay directly under his nose. He knew, of course, that the intensity of this endeavour was prompted by a need to hold at bay bitter memories of what he still saw as his daughter's deception and betrayal. He knew Kate thought he'd be better talking about it but he just couldn't and she was sensitive enough to let things be.

She had spoken with Polly. Just over a week ago she had been saying 'goodbye' on the telephone when he came into the room. He heard ' . . . of course I will, darling,' before she hung up. Then she had turned to him smiling and said: 'Polly sends her love.'

Mallory couldn't speak. He had hurried away across the terrace and into the shrubbery where he began pulling out fistfuls of tall weeds, violently, without discrimination. At one point he had gripped a long bramble and wrapped it round and round his wrist, tugging and ripping until the roots came out. Tearing with it the skin from his hand.

Mallory was choosing to spend the larger part of every day outside now, weather permitting. There was never any shortage of things to do and he had to learn as he went along. Occasionally he would ask Benny's advice but mainly he'd look things up or muddle through. He remembered Kate telling him once, when all else fails we must cultivate our gardens. She'd said it was a famous quote; he thought it was bloody silly. He'd thought a man would have to be desperate to engage in such an incredibly pointless and boring activity. Now he was not so sure. Sometimes, gently lifting and separating papery tulip bulbs or collecting lupin seeds in a small envelope Mallory became aware of a momentary lightening of the heart. A fleeting sensation, even, of peacefulness.

Polly had fallen comfortably on her feet, landing in a top-floor flat off Eaton Square. The owner, an elderly, extremely wealthy Brazilian with a wife as young and lovely as Polly herself, had homes in Paris and the Costa Esmeralda as well as a ranch in Kentucky, Virginia where he bred horses. They were hardly in London at all.

Polly got the job through an agency. When told her wages would be four hundred pounds a month she gaped at the interviewer in astonishment and got up to leave. Then sat down again. There must be extensive perks going with such a derisory salary and this indeed proved to be the case. The job was light, to put it mildly. She was to forward any post and telephone messages to an office in the Boulevard Haussman in Paris. The apartment was to be kept clean and tidy. All bills would be paid and if any problems of a domestic nature arose she was to inform and liaise with the porter. She was not expected to house sit. Once these simple tasks were performed her time was her own. Naturally references were required. Polly obtained one from her tutor at the LSE and forged the other on House of Commons notepaper stolen from Amanda Fforbes-Snaithe's briefcase. She was always sure this was the one that swung it.

She was not sorry to leave Dalston. Though ultimately grateful for Deborah Hartogensis' earlier intervention, Polly felt uncomfortable in the girl's presence. No one likes to have be seen grovelling and incapable. Deborah seemed to understand this and mainly kept out of Polly's way, smiling tentatively when their paths happened to cross. But she did forward a small package of mail, which included a splendid view of the French Alps. Ashley wrote to say he was getting better every day. Better and stronger. He was looking forward very much to seeing her again. He sent his love. Polly found it almost impossible now to even remember what he looked like. She threw the card away.

Her room in the new flat was quite small, windowless and plainly furnished. The other seven were stuffed with antiques and ancient statuary rather in the manner of William Randolph Hearst's castle at San Simeon but minus the packing cases. The bathrooms and kitchen were magnificent.

Once settled Polly looked around for a way to earn some money. She took the first job available that was within walking distance, thus saving on fares. This was at Calypso's, a wine bar on the King's Road. Meant as a stopgap, the place proved so congenial and the owner so accommodating as to hours that Polly decided to stay on working as and when, after the new term began. The wages were rubbish but the tips outstanding. Some days it seemed every other man at the counter wanted to buy her a drink; one week she took home nearly three hundred pounds. A meal was included in every shift, which was another bonus.

Being busy helped her through the first few weeks back in the Smoke. She sent her new address to Appleby House and had talked to her mother a couple of times on the telephone. Soon Kate was hoping to come to London. So far there had been no word from Mallory. Polly totally understood this and was even relieved at the enforced separation. Though she missed him she now saw clearly that his constant and uncritical support – emotional, psychological and financial – for whatever she chose to say or do had been seriously damaging. It was not his fault. He loved her and wanted to see her happy. But what makes you happy, as Polly had bitterly discovered, does not necessarily make you wise.

She had already obtained a loan for her final year and was stubbornly set on not taking a single penny from her parents. The wrong she had done them was still fresh and raw. And with the City in the state it was, her vow to repay now seemed just so much empty rhetoric. But she could at least get a good degree. No more slacking, no more drugs, no more speculation.

Speculation especially was off the agenda. Though as determined and ambitious as she had ever been, Polly had changed in one important respect. Excessive greed had left her, taking with it the will to chicane. Cheating and lying now seemed abhorrent. Also fractured beyond repair was that of which she had been most proud – her precious edge.

But, hearing herself so described, Polly would have made one thing very clear. There had been no Damascene conversion. She still did not have an altruistic bone in her body and probably never would have. Polly would not be seen putting her intelligence and training to the service of the poor on some unspeakable housing estate. She knew only too well what that sort of thing could lead to.

Billy Slaughter was always in her thoughts. She struggled to remain free of him, to draw his sting but found it impossible. Constantly she imagined him walking into the wine bar, even though Calypso's was nowhere near the City. The fact that she had no idea where he lived only added to Polly's anxiety. What if it were Knightsbridge or Sloane Square? Or, worse, one of the supremely grand, monstrously priced wedding-cake villas directly off the King's Road.

At night, before a full-length mirror in the master bedroom, she sometimes practised how she would behave when they met. Polite, withdrawn, uninvolved. One time, raising and lowering eyebrows in aloof enquiry, she laughed at herself. Something she could not remember doing her whole life long.

But all these rehearsals were in vain. Billy Slaughter did not come to the wine bar nor did she see or even hear about him during her final year at the LSE. Even when she started work in Gracechurch Street, in the hub of the City, his name was never mentioned. And when Polly became confident enough to bring it up herself no one recollected him at all. Eventually, her fancy running riot, she began to wonder if he had been some demon spirit fired into life by an unknown benevolence then dropped squarely in her path, forcing her to change direction. And in the cold light of day this notion still appealed. For Polly saw quite clearly now what sort of person she would eventually have become had they never met.

If you'd asked Roy Priest where he lived at the moment he'd have had his work cut out to tell you. He was cool with this, mind. No worries. Mrs Crudge had worked out a system and he was happily mucking in. Her plan covered every eventuality. If Roy was on nights Karen slept at Dunroamin' and he'd go there straight from work (Doris and Ernest didn't like the idea of him going back to an empty house). Other days, he would see Karen safely on the school bus and one or the other of the Crudges would see her safely off at teatime. Weekends, Roy and Karen floated. Sunday lunch at the bungalow for sure. The rest of the time, fifty-fifty.

Rainbow Lodge, now Roy had finished painting and decorating, was a picture. On his day off some part of the time was always spent cleaning it and sorting out the back. Ernest was a great help in this respect. His own garden being pretty much taken up with a wooden shed, a small but pretty summerhouse and the aviary, he welcomed the chance to, as he put it, 'get a bit o' dirt under me fingernails'. He brought his *Reader's Digest Year Book* round and he and Roy pored over it, checking out what could be planted now and what should wait until the spring. They might order a few raspberry canes, suggested Ernest. And some daffy down dillies. After they'd dug and cleared a section they'd clean up and walk over to the Horse and Hounds to wet their whistles.

Roy felt awkward the first few times. He'd stand, clutching his half, on the fringe, as it were, speaking only when spoken to. Then, gradually, he began to join in. Wary of even the mildest confrontation he would agree first with this person, then that. When the football was on he did let rip a bit but so did everyone else so that was all right. Last Wednesday he'd thrown a few darts.

He continued to pay the rent on Rainbow Lodge, in cash, at Causton Council Offices, reckoning that if someone in the Crescent was going to shop him they'd have done it by now. And the longer he lived there, never in arrears, keeping the place smart, the better chance he'd have of staying should the penny eventually drop. If it did and they made him go, well – that would be pretty bad but not, as he had believed only a little while ago, the end of the world.

Because Roy had a family now. He told himself that every time he lay down to rest in what was now unrecognisable as Ava's room. 'I've got a family,' he would murmur, over and over again, and sometimes even in his sleep. More and more he was believing it until gradually, over the years, he came to know that it was true.

In the fullness of time Her Majesty Queen Elizabeth the Queen Mother departed this earth. Esmeralda Footscray, informed simultaneously of the event by her spirit guide gave a great cry: 'A million beams of light attend Your Majesty!' jumped on to a passing beam herself and hurtled after.

George, lowering a crenellated macramé fort into a bath of glue, a special order for a child's birthday, heard the cry but paid it little mind. She was always calling out for something or other. A cinnamon stick to burn, brandy to pour on aching gums, sausages to roast over the electric fire. All activities primed for disaster. Only the other day she had set alight a bowl of feathers and he'd had to clean up the mess.

To tell the truth, George was discovering a certain steeliness within himself and the discovery was not unpleasant. He didn't run quite so fast to her every beckoning and calling. In fact, he no longer ran at all. Occasionally he sauntered. More often he affected not to hear.

It wasn't difficult to recall the first apprehension of this harsher version of his previous self. It had surfaced during the memorial meeting for Ava Garret. Recalling her cruel and insulting dismissal barely a week earlier he could hardly get through the address without spitting. But by the end of the service malice had been transformed to satisfaction at the dark immediacy of her comeuppance. George, finding it hard to keep a straight face, had had to hide in the gents, where he muffled joyful yelps of laughter by stuffing a handkerchief into his mouth.

Now both of the women who had contrived, one way or the other, to make his life a misery, had gone. Untethered, George felt very strange. So that he would not float away entirely he continued to structure his days in the usual manner, looking after the house, himself and the Church of the Near at Hand. This last proved to be a mixed blessing.

349

Sympathy there was in abundance, which was no more than he expected. What he wasn't prepared for were stiflingly genteel romantic overtures. These took many forms. Gifts of food, invariably described as being more than enough for two would arrive, often with an offer to pop round and heat everything up for him. Secretarial help was also proposed, and here George was briefly tempted. After his mother's death was reported in the *Psychic News* he had received an escalation of cards and letters. They contained mostly straightforward expressions of sympathy but a fair proportion also included messages or more often instructions purporting to come from Esmeralda herself. George began to get a feel for these missives. They were longer, for a start, and one or two correspondents did him the favour of delivering the extraterrestrial stuff in differently coloured ink. He binned them all, unread. Other members of the Near at Hand kept asking how he was coping with the shopping, as if he hadn't already spent half his adult life hurtling round the aisles of Asda.

Ladies – George always thought of women as ladies – who did not want to do something for him wanted him to do something for them. Dripping taps, sagging shelves, sticking doors, blocked pipes. What, George couldn't help wondering, had they done all the years up until now? He was also asked if he could mow a lawn, run someone to the chiropodist and take a pensioner's elderly dog, Elaine, on a final visit to the vet. The reason for this last, explained the distressed owner, was that if she herself did the deed the spaniel might feel betrayed. George, feeling that calling a male animal Elaine was more than enough betrayal already, did agree, on this one occasion, to oblige.

There had also been several offers to help sort through his mother's things. These came mainly from the Buckinghamshire section of the Worshipful Bowes Lyon Society, (hermaj/bolyon@co.uk). Esmeralda was not a member, though when the news of her collection got out the secretary had written urging her to join. It was, the missive seemed to imply, no more than her duty. When she declined, invitations to view the treasure were angled for and once even demanded, but also without success. So it was not entirely a surprise to George when, a few days after the funeral, a fierce rapping at the front door introduced the chairman of the group, Fabian Endgoose.

Surprisingly young, with cropped fair hair, Mr Endgoose wore Himmler glasses and a floor-length black leather coat. A silk scarf showing the QM's racing colours was twisted tightly round his neck. He had hardly opened his mouth before George attempted to close the door. Mr Endgoose wedged a heavily studded boot in the gap. George threatened to call the police. It had all been most unpleasant.

Later, sitting in his mother's armchair beside the now extinguished milky globe, he struggled to decide how best to handle matters. First, to ease the immediate pressure, he wrote to the society fibbing that his mother's collection would be shortly going in its entirety to Sotheby's.

350

However, after posting the letter, it struck him that an auction might actually be quite a good idea and he spent the next few days writing to all the main houses to suggest this. Awaiting their response he locked the door of her room and was immediately overcome by such feelings of relief and happiness that he didn't open it again until the day the archives were finally handed over.

He used the dining area to sit in, throwing out the ugly fumed-oak table and straight-backed chairs, then treating himself to a lovely striped sofa with a pouffe to rest his feet on, plus a large television set and matching video. These improvements made the faded wallpaper look so shabby that George decided to have first the room, then the whole house redecorated. To prepare for this he made a bonfire of all the old furniture including the butler, whose wings were the last to burn.

Sorting through Esmeralda's personal belongings had an unexpected outcome. Having thrown most of her stuff straight into the bin, George was then left with assorted clothes and shoes. These were in beautiful condition, largely because his mother had lived for the last two decades wrapped in just a nightdress and a fluffy blanket. Unsure what to do next, he rang Help the Aged, who handled the house insurance. They suggested their charity shop in Uxbridge.

Carefully folding the mothballed dresses, George was especially attracted to what his mother would have called a tea gown. Grey georgette with a frilled hem and covered with splashy, peach-coloured flowers, it suddenly seemed to him quite irresistible. He took off his suit and shirt, unlaced his black Oxfords, removed his socks and put the dress on. It slid easily down his body as he was very thin. Unfortunately he was also very tall and it only came to . . . well, George blushed to look. He found a floor-length one, which was more respectable, and walked around in it for a while. It was amazingly comfortable. He couldn't recall when he was so relaxed. In fact it was beginning to dawn on him that he had never before understood what the word really meant.

After he had delivered the rest of the clothes to Help the Aged he reconnoitred the other charity shops and department stores. Inventing a housebound sister ('very tall, about my height, size twelve') he found all sorts of nice things, though shoes proved impossible. Eventually he bought a man's pair in soft cream leather, pointed and elegant with little gold tassles. Unisex, really.

From then on George spent every evening in what he quickly came to think of as his real clothes. He grew his hair, throwing away the brilliantine, using instead fragrant shampoo, conditioner and an excellent hot oil treatment. He upgraded his dental fixative so his teeth stopped clicking and bathed every day in scented water. A CD player revealed the delights of light music, which quite eclipsed his previous passion for macramé. Sometimes George would dance, romancing the night away to Cole Porter. Other times he would favour a haunting, bitter lament from the pavement cafes of the Argentine. As the anguished violin begun to sob he'd tango across the carpet with long, loping strides, snatching his head round sharply at the skirting board before loping back. All performances were usually rounded off with a glass or two of champagne.

Finally, tentatively embracing the twenty-first century, he ordered an answerphone. This turned out to be the solution to all his problems. It certainly settled the hash of the Church of the Near at Hand. People rang and left a message. He didn't respond. They rang again, he didn't respond. They rang again, then gave up. Bliss.

Doris was not really sorry when her hours at Appleby House were cut right back. To tell the truth, so much had happened in such a short while she was glad of a breather. She had four people to look after now instead of two and it was amazing how much extra work they made. Not that she minded. Doris had taken to her mother hen role with calm assurance. It was as if, she suggested to Benny during one of their now less frequent get-togethers, she had been in training for it all her life.

The real surprise had been the way Ernest had adapted to this new domestic situation. From the beginning he'd supported her a hundred per cent but he was a man in his sixties who liked a set routine and a bit of peace and quiet. As Karen began to spend more and more time at Dunroamin' with Roy not far behind, Doris had pictured Ernest escaping from the house rather more often than was usual. Disappearing into the backyard to converse with his birds. Pottering in his shed.

Not a bit of it. He was completely involved from day one. He'd get Karen's tea if Doris was tied up. Sit with her to watch television, try to comment on the pop stars and aliens, even though he was often unsure which was which. He even tried to help with her homework. She seemed to have an awful lot, and soon he and Doris became sharply conscious of the absence of books about the place. Ernest had a few about birds; Doris, some light romances plus cookery and knitting magazines. That was about it. They attempted to remedy the situation. Ernest found an encyclopedia in the church jumble; Doris joined the mobile library. They had a lovely range. Also she discovered that you could order any book you liked and they'd get it, though that service wasn't free.

There were hiccups, of course. And strangenesses. School was one area which proved surprisingly complicated. In her ignorance Doris had thought children went in the morning and came home in the afternoon, that being the end of it. Not so. She soon discovered there were also projects and special trips, after-school activities, pre-school activities. Sports days, end-of-term plays and concerts. Raffles, charity drives and something called the PTA. Karen, aware and ashamed that her real mother had never once shown her face, was proudly dragging Doris into any and every extracurricular activity.

Doris did her best. So far she had collected stamps for *Blue Peter* and made cakes for the guide dogs. She had agreed to help produce costumes for the choir's October concert and collected branches from six different trees or shrubs for the nature table. Only the fact that she couldn't drive and Ernest no longer risked it after dark kept them off the filing rota for the school and village archives.

Even then, Ernest did not escape entirely, having been persuaded – bullied he called it – into painting a gold and silver turreted fort for the end-of-term entertainment. This was eventually described in the programme as King Wenceslas' last look-out. So far the play was called, *Holly and Ivy's Big Adventure* but Karen said that could easily change as they were writing it as they went along. Only once had Doris felt compelled to refuse a request, drawing the line at three lizards coming to stay over the Christmas break.

Money was a little bit tight at the moment, but would be easier when Karen's allowance was properly sorted. The social services, who were considering an application to foster 'very positively', explained that this would be backdated. And Roy had given Doris over four hundred pounds, which he had found in Ava's room. She and Ernest had decided to put half of this in a Post Office account for Karen and use the rest to give her and Roy really nice Christmas presents. Food wasn't much of a problem. Doris did all her own cooking, not holding with what Ernest called 'cobbled-up factory junk', and it didn't cost all that much more to double upon the amounts. Plus Roy was always bringing contributions from Tesco. Chops or fruit and suchlike; yesterday a lovely box of dates; last weekend, a beautiful ready-stuffed chicken.

Sadly the expected dividend from Doris's small amount of shares in Brinkley and Latham had come to nothing. The firm collapsed shortly after the death of Mrs Latham. No one had explained the ins and outs to Doris and she didn't want to know. What she did know, and told anyone who would listen, was that it would have broken poor Mr Brinkley's heart.

However, in spite of this and other small disappointments, Doris had never been so happy. But happiness, as any parent could have told her, always comes at a price. In her case this was a continual anxiety over Karen's health. Mainly pushed to the back of her mind during the day by sheer busyness, in rare periods of rest the worry would gather into a dark ball and roll around usually settling in the pit of her stomach. Sometimes she would even dream about the child and the dreams always ended sadly.

Karen's headaches had not gone away. Gently talking around the idea of a visit to the doctor had not worked. After the terrible threat the child's mother had made in this direction Doris was not surprised. She then tried bribery, which had always done the trick with her nephews and nieces, but that didn't work either.

Not that Karen ever admitted to feeling bad. The fear equals doctor equation was too firmly established. But Doris noticed her screwing up her eyes sometimes and only last week she had her hands clamped over her ears and was trying not to cry. Overcome with worry, Doris had talked to her sister, who was convinced it was a brain tumour and that every minute counted.

Doris became desperate. She could not bear to put at risk the new and extremely precious relationship between herself and Karen. Imagine the damage, the breaking of all trust, if she attempted to trick the little girl into a surgery. And what if it was then decided that she needed an X-ray? Doris pictured the child somehow being forced 'for her own good' to go through this distressing experience, surrounded by strange machinery and getting more and more panic-stricken.

Then, just a few days ago, Karen caught a cold. A late summer wheezing cough and cold. Something had to be done. Doris booked herself an appointment with Dr Dickenson, now in his last couple of weeks with the practice. She said it was an emergency and was fitted in at the end of morning surgery. She told him everything from the very beginning, struggling to remain calm, not always succeeding.

The doctor said there were almost as many reasons for persistent headaches as there were headaches. He said that brain tumours were extremely rare in adults and even more so in children but that, of course, Karen must be seen by someone. He suggested Doris registered her with the practice as soon as possible and that he would call at Dunroamin' on his rounds that afternoon. He had an idea, which Doris would perhaps consider, on how the visit might be handled.

So around four o'clock Dr Dickenson arrived, leaving his bag in the hall. Ernest, primed, made some tea, took the tray in, with instructions to Karen to pour, then made himself scarce. As Karen gave the pot a stir, wondering if it was strong enough Doris rolled up her sleeve and had her wrist gently palpated.

'Why is he squeezing your arm, aunty Doris?' asked Karen.

'Don't say "he", Karen. It's rude.'

'I'm your aunt's doctor,' said Dr Dickenson. 'I'm afraid she's got a bit of a sprain.'

'Oh! Does it hurt?'

'Could be worse,' said Doris, truthfully. Then, getting carried away, 'Shall I have to wear a bandage?'

'Rest is the thing, Mrs Crudge. And I can see you won't be short of a helping hand.'

'She's a good girl.' Doris smiled as Karen poured milk into rosebud-patterned cups. 'I don't know what I'd do without her.'

Passing a plate of ginger parkin round, Karen started to cough, covering her mouth with her hand as Doris had shown her.

'You want some Buttercup Syrup for that,' said Dr Dickenson.

'There's no such thing.' Karen was uncertain, not sure if she was being teased. Whether it was all right to laugh. 'Is there?'

'Get it at the Co-op.'

'Made from buttercups?'

'I had that years ago,' said Doris. 'My mum used to swear by it.'

They ate and drank comfortably for a little while, Dr Dickenson sitting back, smiling and munching, as if he had all the time in the world. Doris watching Karen without watching. Suddenly Karen sprang up.

'Uncle Ernest hasn't had any tea.'

'I'll get it.' Doris heaved herself out of the armchair. 'Do me good to move about.'

'What about your arm?'

'I can manage a tray.' Doris brought a mug in from the kitchen, filled it then cut a large square of cake. 'You look after Dr Dickenson, Karen.'

'Actually, I have to be going in a minute.' But he didn't get up. Instead he asked Karen if she watched a lot of television. Then, when she said, 'No,' asked if she wore glasses and when she asked, 'Why?' said she seemed to be screwing up her eyes a lot and he wondered if it could be eye strain.

'Um . . . I get headaches sometimes,' said Karen. Then, quickly: 'That is, I used to.'

'My grandson – he's about your age – gets terrible headaches.'

'Can't you make him better?'

'I did, actually. Took some time – he had to have all sorts of tests.'

'Did they hurt?'

'Heavens, no. But it was bad news.'

Karen gaped and her eyes grew round.

'Turns out he's allergic to chocolate.'

Doris, moving about in the kitchen, doing nothing special, listened to the low voices. Once Karen laughed and Doris sighed with relief. Surely that meant it was going to be all right? They talked for quite a bit longer, then she heard Dr Dickenson heaving and puffing his way out of the sofa and went back into the lounge.

'Karen's going to come and see me about her cough.'

'That's a good idea,' said Doris.

'Can I have some more parkin?' asked Karen.

'You'll eat me out of house and home.' Doris showed the doctor into the hall and opened the front door. 'Not that she can't do with putting a bit of weight on.'

On the step he turned towards her and Doris saw his face clearly in the harsh sunlight. It was grave and sad. Her hand flew to her heart. Gasping, she cried out.

'What is it? Tell me.'

'I don't know—'

'*Tell me.*'

'Please. She'll hear you.' He backed away into the front garden. Doris stumbled after and, when they reached the gate, stood against it blocking the way.

'I'm her mother. I have a right to know.'

'I'd like someone else to see her. A specialist.'

'Is it a brain tumour?' Doris seized his jacket, her eyes dark with fear. 'Will she have to have an operation?'

'No. I'm pretty sure it's nothing . . .' He hesitated. 'Nothing like that.'

What could he say? He was not capable of accurately diagnosing mental illness, though, God knew, he had seen enough seriously disturbed children in his time. He knew it could be linked to poverty, abuse or inadequate parenting. That last could certainly be a factor in this case. It could be genetic. It could spring up with devastating and frightful results in a formerly sunny-tempered child with a loving home. There was no accounting for terrible things.

'So – what sort of specialist?' Doris was saying.

'There's someone at Princes Risborough. A woman doctor, specialising in child care. She's young, very sympathetic and I'm sure Karen will "open up" to her, as they say.'

'Open up?'

'Talk to her.'

'What about?'

It was a perfectly reasonable question that Dr Dickenson found extremely difficult to answer. What he would have liked to do was reply, 'Her headaches,' and walk away. Plainly that wasn't on. Yet if he was honest as to the true nature of Karen's anxiety he would be laying a heavy burden on this poor woman. He paused, thinking around and about the matter. Seeking perhaps an alternative. Wondering if he had perhaps been too hasty in his conclusions. Wishing and hoping that might be true. Noticing how much worse bad things seemed when you put a name to them.

He began to backtrack, telling himself he had been too hasty; attempted to look at what he had been told from a different point of view. A layperson's, for example. Unburdened by any medical knowledge, what would they think of Karen's strange ramblings? The answer came quickly enough. They would think she was making it up. What an imagination, they would say. And if it all went a stage further? Would they see this as genuine derangement, as he had done? Probably not. They would say she'd been watching too much telly. Or eating cheese before bedtime.

Hot in his tweed jacket, and becoming unreasonably annoyed in the face of Doris's panic, Dr Dickenson eased his way through the gate, pausing only to suggest that it would be unwise to put pressure of any kind on the child.

'To do what?'

'Um . . . discuss things.'

'As if I would.'

Doris was indignant. More bewildered now than before he came she was still glad to see the back of him. Her only regret was that they didn't have the name of this specialist. At least then they could maybe get some idea of what they were looking at. As things stood, now all they could do was wait.

In the library at Appleby House Kate was editing *The Sidewinder Café*. Yesterday the author had come down to Forbes Abbot for lunch. It had been an exhilarating experience for them both. The writer, joyful and excited at the thought of publication, had drunk nearly a whole bottle of Rosemount Chardonnay, whereupon Kate, quite overcome with pleasure that a simple action of hers could bring about such happiness, opened another. They'd ended the afternoon toasting the recollection that it was a small (if not exactly unknown) publisher that had scooped Harry Potter when all the big boys turned it down. And that an even smaller one had published last year's winner of the Booker Prize.

Presently calm and sober, Kate still felt great. She had lots of energy these days and wondered if it was because she was so happy. It seemed an oversimplistic equation. Anyway, whatever the reason, it was just as well as there was an awful lot to do.

Regarding the Celandine Press, Mallory was of little help. He came to all the meetings, listened carefully to what was said and took his turn in reading the handful of manuscripts that were still dribbling in. But mentally he was permanently somewhere else and Kate accepted this. The business was, after all, her baby, her dream and she just buckled down and got on with it.

There was still no reply from E. M. Walker, though she had now written twice to the accommodation address in Slough. This left Kate in something of a dilemma. Plainly the man – she was sure it was a man – wanted his novel published, otherwise why submit it? But could she just go ahead and do this without a properly signed contract? She decided to ring her old employers and talk to someone in the legal department about it.

The unexpected element in the new enterprise was Benny's input. Kate was now discovering what Dennis had always known. Given room to breathe, freedom from pressure and the confidence of someone she respected, Benny proved surprisingly capable. Alarmed at first by the presence of computers, she was persuaded to attend a basic Word Processing weekend at Causton Tech. Quickly recognising the advantages over her old typewriter, she threw out the Imperial and was soon producing standard letters on her AppleMac to enclose with any rejected typescripts.

She kept a book with details of all submissions and dates of their return, and also an account of all expenses. Kate had had a new business line installed. The number had not yet been given out but she could hear Benny's soft little flute of a voice rehearsing ('The Celandine Press. Benny Frayle speaking. How can I help?') when Benny thought no one was listening.

There had been only been one really awkward situation that Kate had found difficult to handle. Unfortunately it involved that most raw and painful of subjects, money, which meant she could not talk it over with Mallory.

A short while ago Benny had approached Kate, anxious to discuss her own position in the company. It seemed, Benny explained, that the few simple tasks she was hoping to carry out when the business was up and running were disproportionate to her owning a third share in it. Kinders had already been valued for a quite breathtaking sum and when it was sold Benny wished to invest half of the proceeds in the Celandine Press. To become, as she put it, 'a sort of semi-sleeping partner.'

Kate was overwhelmed. She knew the offer was not made in any knowledge of the financial disaster that had so recently overtaken herself and Mallory. Benny, though she must have noticed the coming and going of the police and Polly's rapid departure, had never referred to these things. Good manners and kindness of heart would not allow it. Kate had expected nothing else but was still grateful. And now this.

She thanked Benny saying, truthfully, that she was overwhelmed by such a generous offer, adding that it might be a good idea to postpone a decision until after the first publication, when they would be able to see more clearly exactly how they stood. Benny was happy with this and hugged Kate, not at all tentatively.

Kinders was on both women's minds at the moment. Benny vowed she would never enter the place again. Indeed, went to great pains to avoid even walking past it. Kate absolutely understood this. On the other hand, Dennis had willed not just the house but its entire contents to Benny and things had to be sorted.

Surprisingly the machines had been the least of their worries. Kate had had them professionally photographed and faxed the results to the Royal Armouries Museum, which had been astonished and delighted at the opportunity of owning such a collection. Neither London nor Manchester, they admitted, presently had the space to display but the machines would be disassembled and stored until a proper exhibition could be mounted.

That still left a flat full of furniture and books and paintings. Kate had already packed up towels, bedding and Dennis's clothes and taken them to Oxfam. She decided to do an inventory, which Benny could then check and decide if there was anything on the list she wished to keep. The kitchen and bedroom had already been covered. Benny had chosen the blue Le Creuset casserole that Dennis had used to cook their lovely turbot supper, but when it arrived she became very distressed and urged Kate to take it back. Kate didn't. She hid it in one of the cavernous kitchen cupboards at Appleby House, feeling sure that at some point in the future, even if it was a long way away, Benny would regret having nothing to remember her friend by.

This coming afternoon Kate would be tackling the sitting room and then the job was done. She drove round to Kinders with lots of newspaper and boxes in the Golf to fill with books and other small things.

Just before she left Benny had said she wouldn't be wanting any furniture. She had the wing chair in which Dennis always sat and that was enough. Gilbert Ormerod, Dennis's solicitor and executor, had already removed any personal papers, which he had had instructions to burn.

So, thought Kate, now wandering shoeless over the glowing Chinese rugs, it's largely books and paintings. The latter were all illustrations of scenes of conflict. Soldiers in the great war leaping back from the recoil of a massive gun. Spitfires spiralling through the air, trailing smoke and flames. Hand-to-hand fighting by men in helmets and skirts, with halberds dripping blood. A blow-up of a still from the original film of *Henry V*: the great front line of cavalry, poised to charge. Violence in waiting, banners and armour shimmering in the heat. A print of Turner's *The Fighting Téméraire*. An ornately framed oil showing the Field of the Cloth of Gold.

Kate could not imagine Benny wanting any of these. She took them down, turning their faces to the wall. The books were nearly all in the same vein. War stories, soldiers' memoirs. *The Illiad* and Penguin Classics by warriors long gone to dust. *Sieges Through the Ages*. Biographies of Churchill and Montgomery, Nelson, Alexander, Napoleon. A few volumes on cricket.

Kate began to take them down, quickly filling all her boxes. She began to list the few small ornaments. There were also some beautiful enamelled bowls which, only the other day, she had cleared of dead hyacinths and freesia. About to throw the bulbs away, Kate suddenly decided to take them home. She had planted them in the shrubbery in a place apart from the massed daffodils and bluebells, marked by special bronze tags.

The inventory was quickly completed. All Benny had to do now was check it through and Kate could ring the antique dealer from Amersham to get the place cleared. There were some beautiful pieces, which should fetch beautiful prices. And one or two oddities that were harder to classify. A soldier's trunk, for instance, lacquered a rich burgundy, bound by webbing and displaying a raised regimental coat of arms. Kate gripped one of the leather handles and lifted. The trunk seemed empty but it was sensible to check. Unbuckling all the webbing seemed to take ages and when she finally looked inside there was nothing but a few old newspapers.

They were quite yellow and foxed with brown markings. Kate took them out carefully. One or two were over a hundred years old. The headlines all spoke of war. The Boer War. The Crimean. The Great War. The Second World War. More stuff for the museum. Kate was going up to London the following week to see Polly. She felt, given the state of the paper, it might be best to deliver them personally. An artist's folder would probably be best to carry them in.

Underneath the final copy was a large unsealed envelope. It was quite heavy. Kate turned it upside down and a stack of A4 paper, punched at the side and threaded with pink legal tape, fell out. The pages, over four hundred, were handwritten in black ink. The letters, beautifully shaped, were inscribed in such an orderly and balanced manner as to gradually cause feelings of harmony to steal into the heart of the fortunate observer. Intrigued and bewildered in equal measure, Kate settled down in an armchair and began to read.

In his wonderfully comfortable private room on the top floor of the Clinique pour les Maladies Tropicales, Ashley Parnell was getting his confidence back. And with it his looks. He knew this without checking in the mirror. It showed in the gradual change in his nurse's attitude. She touched his body now in a slightly different way. And after taking his pulse, her hand would remain for a moment, the fingers supporting his wrist, the thumb pressing lightly into his palm. Most days she combed his hair though they both knew he could do it quite well himself. Then his scalp would tingle and not only from the gentle friction of the comb. None of this was in the least blatant. She rarely looked directly at him and her smile was coolly professional.

Yesterday, at his request, she had brought in some postcards, the usual exaggerated panorama to dazzle the folks at home. A sky impossibly blue, mountain peaks perfectly iced, clean goats nibbling on velvety grass and wild flowers. Now written on and signed by himself and Judith, the little pile lay on his bedside table. The nurse offered to post them. Ashley thanked her, removed another card from inside a book he had been reading and passed it over.

Nothing was said but her face changed. She smiled and he could see she thought this secret card was to his mistress. When asked if there was anything else before she left, Ashley said he would like some fresh water. As she moved towards the bathroom he noticed her walk was different too: looser, more indolent.

A full-length mirror was fastened on to the back of the bathroom door and he could see her reflection. She put the freshly filled carafe aside and studied herself in the glass, stroking her hair smoothly away from her forehead. Then she slowly undid the first two buttons on her uniform and loosened the collar, easing the neckline.

As he watched the tawny sun-marked skin transform to creamy white Ashley became aware that she was also watching him. At that moment his passivity fell clean away. Aware for some time of vague, unfocused feelings of sexuality, he now felt overwhelmingly hot and needful. When she came back into the room and leaned over the bed to smooth his pillows Ashley slipped an arm around her shoulders, drawing her down beside him. Kissing, undoing the rest of the buttons, pushing aside silk and lace to encounter warm, yielding flesh . . . It was all quite a shock to a system that had almost forgotten just how marvellous sex could be.

* * *

Some small distance away, on the third level of a beautiful terraced garden, Judith Parnell sat sipping fresh orange and pomegranate juice. The drink had been beautifully served: the glass in a pitcher of crushed ice itself enfolded by a linen napkin, whiter than snow. Powdery sugar was in a silver bowl. Pale yellow rosebuds finished off the presentation.

And yet, Judith was not satisfied. She was discovering that when you had money you were easily displeased. Things that cost a lot should be perfect. More than perfect, in fact. The orange juice was not quite as sweet as it could have been. No doubt that was what the sugar was for but naturally sweet fruit could surely be found?

The Hotel Mimosa had been chosen purely for reasons of proximity to the hospital. It took barely fifteen minutes to walk there and, if that didn't appeal, cabs were always available. Judith visited Ashley two or three times a day. Three-quarters of the other guests were also alone and she assumed they were staying at the hotel for the same reason. The management asked each visitor on checking in if they would care to share a table at dinner. Judith had refused and was glad of it. She did not wish to partake in the hopes and fears of strangers, being already in thrall to more than enough of her own.

As Ashley got better and better, Judith struggled to come to terms with her reaction to this wonderful development. The very speed with which it seemed to be happening caused her to fear it might be temporary. Then she wondered how she would feel if this rapidity did mean an early regression.

The answer should be clear enough but, to Judith's acute distress, this didn't seem to be the case. Emotion clouded her head at the very suggestion. She tried to isolate and clarify her thoughts, one at a time, by rigorous self-examination. Wasn't this extraordinary recovery just what she had been working and praying for for months? She remembered very clearly when it all started. That terrible morning when Ash, after struggling with acute lethargy and dizzy spells for weeks, had woken up too exhausted even to get out of bed.

But it had been wonderful having him at home, even with all the money worries. As neither was involved in village affairs, hardly anyone came to the house. She had him to love and look after all by herself. Now there were other people. Judith either resented or disliked them all, even the specialist, an elderly and compassionate man, infinitely approachable and friendly.

If asked to single out the person she disliked the most Judith would not have hesitated. Of all the nurses in and out of Ashley's room – and they were in and out even when she herself was visiting – Christiane Blonde was the one she feared. The acknowledgement brought her up short. What was she thinking? Did she really mean 'feared'?

Judith sensed an intimacy between the nurse and her husband that she kept telling herself was merely her imagination. It was true she had nothing solid to base this assumption on. Well, almost nothing. There had been one incident not long after Ashley was admitted. Visiting in the early evening Judith had come across them both walking towards her down a long corridor, the nurse holding his arm. The late sunshine poured through the huge windows and Ashley paused to lift his face towards the sky. He smiled, then, preparing to walk again, stumbled. She put an arm around him and he leaned briefly against her before righting himself. That was all. If it had been anyone else . . .

What was it about Frenchwomen? She wasn't young, especially. She was probably Ashley's own age but there was something about her. Nothing artificial. Though her complexion was flawless she appeared to wear no make-up. She was just one of those rare people, Judith concluded unhappily, that could suggest beauty by a turn of the head. Or the resting of a hand against the cheek.

As Ashley recovered the bleakness vanished from his gaze and his sluggish skin began to glow. His eyes were once again warm and lively and when Judith held his hand his own grip was strong.

Loving him constrainedly for so long she now fell in love all over again and couldn't help wondering how soon it would be before they slept together. Every night she would sit on the balcony of her room, picturing how it would happen. What they would do. What they would say. How passionate his caresses and kisses would be.

There were some boutiques in the atrium of the Mimosa, full of horrifically priced merchandise, and she had bought a semi-transparent nightdress of smoky grey lace and chiffon, loosely tied with satin ribbons. Unable to resist showing it off she had taken the box along on her next visit to the hospital. Folding back layer upon layer of silvery tissue with trembling fingers Judith had drawn out the lovely thing and held it against her heart, the gossamer folds tumbling to the floor. She couldn't quite make out Ashley's reaction. For a fraction of a second, (blink and you'd miss it) she could have sworn he looked alarmed. Then there was a certain awkwardness, which Judith was quick to reason away. It had been a long time; he had been very ill. She should have been more patient. Then he said something nice, though the feeling of uncomfortableness still came through. She had forgotten the exact words.

But eventually it would all come right. It must or she would have cheated and lied and turned her whole life over to the bad for nothing. White-collar crime, they called it, as if this made it somehow cleaner than the other sort. As if stealing money by tapping a keyboard wasn't as serious as grabbing some old woman's handbag and frightening her half to death. Frightening people by remote control must inevitably be less traumatic.

Anyway, it was half expected these days, the way things were. Every day, workers with pension funds woke up to find they had halved in value, if not worse. Insurance companies actually trained staff in how to avoid paying out. Honest investors lost thousands through companies still paying their directors obscene bonuses. If that wasn't theft, what was?

And surely the reasons behind a crime should be taken into account? In her case they were admirable ones. She had stolen for love. It had seemed to her a matter of life and death.

Not so her partner. She had regarded his involvement as purely a matter of greed. He denied this. For him the robbery had been a question of freedom. 'Call me a freedom fighter!' he had shouted, laughing and half drunk, not long after their first meeting in the Peacock Hotel.

He had delivered her from a terrible assault. On the pretence of setting up a business meeting a repulsive man had lured her there; wedged her into a tight corner and urged her to have sex with him. When she'd refused he'd almost climbed into her lap, all the while pouring depraved and filthy suggestions into her ears.

Shaking and on the verge of tears, she'd caught the eye of someone about to buy a drink, who saw the man off. That was when it all started. Overwhelmed by gratitude she was surprised to find her rescuer knew who she was. He had seen her, apparently, at Carey Lawson's funeral, though they had not been introduced. Somehow this seemed to make it all right to talk to him. A couple of brandies later and Judith had told him everything. She had described Ashley fading away before her eyes; clients disappearing, her desperate need for money. How she had sold nearly everything they owned that was sellable and now there was only the house and that was mortgaged.

He too had a tale of woe. Married to a gorgon of a woman who doled out pocket money for services rendered and if he couldn't she didn't. Humiliated by being forced to sit in an office all day, pretending to be of use when everyone knew it was only because his wife owned half the business he was there at all. The other half – well, he assumed Judith knew Dennis Brinkley? Could there be some way she and himself could help each other? Why not start by sharing their strengths and weaknesses?

This didn't take long. It quickly became plain that Judith had all the strengths while Drew, as he had asked to be called, owned up to all the weaknesses. However, as the conversation developed, both terms proved inappropriate. Knowledge, it seemed, would be the counter with which to play the game.

There was little Judith didn't know about offshore accounts, tax dodges, stock exchange fiddles and money scams generally. All accountants pick up such information along the way. Only the bent ones make use of it. And computers held no mystery for her. She had been working with them all her life.

Drew knew nothing of such matters. What he had to offer was access to lots and lots and lots of money via a key to the street door and main office of Brinkley and Latham, plus the combination to a safe that held the passwords for all the main office accounts. For good measure he also threw in cautionary tips on how to avoid detection. Mainly this seemed to involve keeping a sharp eye out for the nosy fishmonger opposite when entering or leaving the building. And speed, once inside, must be of the essence. Shift a lot of stuff in two or three visits max, casting the net wide. Smallish amounts from lots of accounts, suggested Drew, soon mounted up and were less likely to be detected. Judith explained that detection would take some time anyway, as false entries would have to be made to cover the debits, however small. Drew was impressed.

They talked and talked, getting more and more exhilarated. He bought a bottle of cheap sparkling wine. They saw it off and Judith ordered another. Later, though, getting out of her car and stumbling up Trevelyan's garden path, the intoxication began to drain away. And by the time she had taken off her coat and drunk several glasses of water, she could not imagine what on earth had possessed her. God – she must have been mad.

Running a bath, pouring in lots of scented oil, she attempted to wash away the dirt from the infected early part of the evening and the insanely dangerous fantasy of the final two hours. Eventually she crawled into bed, falling into an uneasy sleep. Her last thought was, he must be feeling just like this. It was the drink talking. Tomorrow it will all seem like a crazy dream. But in the morning, when the phone rang and he asked if it was still on she said 'yes' straightaway.

They met only twice after this although they spoke several times on the telephone. Everything worked smoothly. As Judith did not have access to Dennis Brinkley's private office, his fatal accident hardly caused a blip on the screen of her activities. But as the police had been involved, albeit tangentially, she decided it would be safer to extricate a final amount to bring them near to their aimed sum for balance and quit.

Not reading the local paper, which she rightly described as illiterate rubbish, Judith had missed entirely the fact that a self-styled medium, boasting a knowledge of Dennis Brinkley's death, had herself passed away in somewhat mysterious circumstances. This item hit the national press as she and Ashley were boarding Swissair at Stansted. And even if the news of what would soon be recognised as a double murder had been brought to her attention, she would never have linked it with the man she knew only as Drew. Judith had sized him up pretty thoroughly at their first meeting. Weak, desperate, good-looking in a faded, second-division soap star sort of way. Wouldn't hurt a fly.

The new owners of Kinders considered the name rather an affectation and restyled the building the Old School House. He was a banker, she did graphic design, working from home. They had three children and a live-in nanny. Their architect had transformed the place. Four bedrooms, two bathrooms and living rooms, and a crescent-shaped kitchen that ran halfway round the ground floor. The arrow slits had been bricked in and replaced by huge windows. The interior was now flooded with light and there was a shiny new red front door.

Everyone said to Benny, 'You wouldn't know the place,' but of course she always would. Her last visit had been impressed, as with a branding iron, on to her conscious mind. She accepted that this was so and would always be so. She understood too that the agonising, sharp-edged pain to which her heart had, at last, been gently opened would blunt and soften in time. Even so, she remained glad that the larger half of life's allotted span was now behind her.

After her cruel awakening to the self-protecting lie that had seemed to promise happy ever after, Benny forgot all about her talisman. The frantic craving for security that had obsessed her every waking moment simply vanished. Why yearn for something that didn't and couldn't exist?

Happily, love and friendship were still present in her life. Mallory had always been reciprocally dear but Benny was gradually becoming more and more fond of Kate, who was tremendously kind and supportive. She seemed to sense when Benny needed to talk – only recently ever the case – and when she wished just to be quiet. And both she and Mallory urged Benny to sleep at Appleby House if she was ever lonely.

Benny, on the deepest level of her being, was always lonely, though she derived great comfort from their kindness. But to her surprise it was the business, the Celandine Press, that helped her most through the first months after the court case and successful prosecution of the man who had caused Dennis's death.

There was so much to do in the office, most of it quite alien to Benny's previous experience. But Kate explained things clearly and was always on the spot if a problem arose. It was plain from the outset that both she and Mallory had complete confidence in Benny's ability to cope. And so Benny coped, calmly and even with a certain *élan*. She was especially good at handling distressed authors, of whom there were many. It was not at all uncommon for Kate or Mallory to pick up the phone, only to have whoever was on the other end refuse to speak to anyone but Miss Frayle. After the hoped-for conversation, the writer, although nothing definite about the reception of his or her manuscript had actually been said, would hang up, feeling both consoled and valued. Mallory asked Benny once how she did it and Benny replied simply, 'I know how they feel.'

Every day at five, when the office officially closed, she would go to the churchyard. Actually, this present afternoon she was a little late, easing open the lych-gate with some difficulty, balancing her folding stool, a small hand fork and a damp cloth.

Containing only his ashes, Dennis's grave was barely half the size of the others. With permission from the vicar it had been edged with very old barley-sugar tiles from the garden at Appleby House. Benny had hoped to plant some rosemary too, for remembrance, but the Reverend Johnson had demurred, saying it was rather a strong grower for such a small space. So instead she usually included one or two sprigs with whatever other flowers she brought along.

The leaves had just started to fall. Tough, leathery ones, glowing ruby and bright amber, they covered the grave. Benny picked them off, loosened and removed a single weed, which had appeared overnight, opened her folding canvas stool and settled down.

It was a good time to come, the hinge of the day. There would rarely be anyone around, even in the summer. If there was she would talk to Dennis silently. She had already told him about the discovery of *The King's Armourer*. About how Kate, dazed with disbelief, had brought it home from Kinders. The excitement it had raised: the happiness, the sorrow. Now Benny described briefly how the editing was going. Kate had said there was hardly anything to do, barely a cut to make. The book raced ahead of you, was how she described it. Vivid as a dream.

To ring the changes Benny would also talk about the nonbusiness part of her day. Small domestic matters – ordering Madonna lilies from the new de Jaeger catalogue; Croydon's injured paw, now coming along nicely after antibiotics from the vet. A pair of new linen curtains for the kitchen window patterned with forget-me-nots, blue as the sky.

Occasionally she would touch on village affairs – quarrelling in the church choir, yet another appeal to the Lottery Commission for a new village hall. Other times she would just sit, quietly crying out her grief, while the rooks wheeled and shrieked unnoticed above her head.

Quite often Dennis would be present. Not in any weird or mystical way – Benny had had no further truck with the Church of the Near at Hand – but just kind of solidly there. Asked to explain this she wouldn't have known where to start. All in the mind people would have said, though Benny knew that wasn't true. If it had been she could have conjured him up at any time. As it was, there was never any warning: just a sort of gathering of energy that slowly intensified. Her ears would hum a bit. The air changed, becoming warm and so close there was even a slight feeling of pressure. Then she was no longer alone.

Whenever this happened Benny would experience an overwhelming rush of gratitude. She always remembered to thank God in her prayers for such a gift of grace. To have had thirty years of true and loving companionship was blessing enough, but to still be aware of his dear presence . . .

Benny took several deep breaths and sat up straight. She could hear voices. An elderly couple were coming up the path with some chrysanthemums and a watering can. She folded up her stool, took out her cloth and carefully removed some specks of dirt from the stone on Dennis's grave. It was of pale grey marble, veined with cream. The description, in plain gold letters, read simply:

DENNIS BRINKLEY
WRITER
1946–2001

Karen was now quite used to Dr Dickenson. She had visited his surgery several times, once with her bad cough, now completely better, but also after falling from the parallel bars in the school gym and hurting her leg. Aunty Doris had gone with her to hospital where they'd taken a photograph of it and put the picture up on the wall for her to see. Another time they'd had a different sort of look at her head and that was called a scan.

The best part, the most important part, was that it had been absolutely true what the doctor had promised. She had told him the very thing that frightened her most, the thing she had promised Ava never ever to tell anyone, and it had been all right. Nobody had come to take her away. Or lock her in a cupboard and throw the key down a bottomless well like Ava told her they would. All the doctor said was he knew a special person who would be able to help Karen and that he'd arrange an appointment as soon as possible.

It seemed ages before they heard. Karen wasn't worried; for her the worst was over. But Aunty Doris was. Karen noticed her all the time looking for the postman. When the letter finally came she nearly ripped the envelope to bits getting it out. When she'd read it she went very quiet and gave it to Ernest. Later, Karen found Doris crying. She climbed on to Doris's knee and hugged her, saying that she mustn't be sad because now everything would be getting better. 'You'll see' – Karen was solemn and assured – 'soon all the hurting will go away.'

Although the letter had been signed 'Dr Barbara Lester', and the appointment was at a proper clinic, when the day finally came the room where Karen found herself was more like a nursery than a surgery. There were squashy armchairs, a sofa and a whole range of things to have fun with. Shelves full of soft toys and dolls and others holding tanks and planes and Action Men and Lego. Lots of coloured pens and paints and paper were on a low table and a computer stood on a desk by the open window next to a stack of boxed tapes. There was even a doll's house.

'Where would you like to sit, Karen?'

Dr Lester didn't look much like a doctor either. It wasn't just that she didn't have a white coat or a thing round her neck for listening to your chest, she looked, well . . . a bit like Karen's PE teacher. She'd got quite a short denim skirt on and one of those shirts that tied up in a knot round your waist. Her bare feet were in white sandals. She was already sitting down, on the puffy yellow sofa. Karen sat in the nearest armchair, which had a large box of tissues balanced on one of the arms.

'Can I put this on the floor?'

'Of course you can.'

'Only my cold's better now.'

Karen watched intently as the doctor put some glasses on and took a folder from a briefcase resting on the carpet nearby. There didn't seem to be much in the folder. She read it in what Ernest would call 'the shake of a lamb's tail'.

Dr Lester was rather surprised at the picture the little girl presented. Having been a child psychiatrist for thirteen years she had come across every attitude in the book and quite a few others you wouldn't believe but Karen's was most unusual. In the first place, her expression was totally unworried. She appeared confident, happy even, sitting forwards eagerly on the edge of her seat, as if expecting some entertainment to begin.

'I've been waiting ever such a long while to see you.'

You and a hundred others, dear. And already the clock was ticking their time together away. The doctor's notes told a familiar story. Physical neglect, psychological abuse, no love to speak of. And unfortunately no grandparents to buffer sorrow. But now the mother had died and the child was being fostered, very successfully, by all accounts. She suffered constantly from noises and chattering and pains in her head.

Dr Lester was not surprised to note the GP's suspicions of early schizophrenia. Even laypeople jumped to this conclusion, given such symptoms. However, there were other early signs and these were not present. One also had to make allowances for the imagination. Wretched and lonely children will struggle to conjure alternative worlds in an attempt to escape the horrors of the real one. Karen's fantasies were incredibly inventive.

Dr Lester smiled, offered some sweets from a glass bowl, suggested Karen called her Barbara. They talked for a few minutes about the successful present. How kind Aunty Doris was. Uncle Ernest's birds. Roy's beautiful new dog, Dancer.

'And I'm in a higher class at school. We're going to talk French.'

'You like school?'

'It's great. I was in the Christmas play.'

'I played Aladdin once – in a hospital pantomime. How did you get on?'

'I couldn't really learn it very well.'

'Because of your headaches?'

'That's right. It's hard when everyone's talking at once.'

'I believe they started just after your mother died?'

'That's *why* they started. I explained to Dr Dickenson.'

'Yes. But there can be other reasons for headaches, Karen. For instance, if we cry a lot—'

'And she didn't just die. Someone gave her poison.'

'Really?'

'Like Snow White.'

'That's a fairy story, isn't it?' Dr Lester paused, waited. 'Do you like fairy stories?'

'No.' Karen remembered pricking her finger and waking up without a prince. 'They're all lies.'

'Do you find it difficult to tell the difference?' Karen looked puzzled. 'Between what's true and what we make up.'

Karen shook her head and the gossamer hair lifted and floated in slow motion, like thistledown.

'I'd like to talk about when you were little, if that's all right?' Karen shrugged. 'How far back do you remember?'

'For ever.'

'Tell me the first thing.'

'You mean when I was born?'

'A bit further on. Playgroup, say.'

'What's a playgroup?'

'OK, when you went to primary school. Did you make friends there?'

'I've never had a friend.' This was delivered without a trace of self-pity. She could have been saying: I've never had a mobile. Or a bicycle.

'What about imaginary friends?'

Karen stared at Dr Lester in amazement. She couldn't help thinking that it wasn't herself who didn't know the difference between what was true and what people make up. Then she wondered if it was a trick question. Or perhaps a joke. It was certainly pretty funny. She said politely: 'You can't have *imaginary* friends, Doctor . . . um . . . Barbara.'

'Why not?'

'Because you couldn't play with them or go for walks or round to their house or anything.'

'You can do all those things in your imagination.'

Karen frowned. She was beginning to look anxious. 'I don't understand.'

'The mind can fool us in all sorts of ways, Karen. And one of its tricks is the ability to make things that don't exist seem totally real.'

Karen's air of bright confidence was dimming by the minute.

'Look . . .' Dr Lester glanced down at her notes. 'How would it be if we—'

'I thought you were going to help me.'

'Before anyone can help you your illness has to be diagnosed. Seeing me is just the first step.'

'I'm not ill.'

Define illness. Not always easy on the physical level, mentally you were in a minefield. Take out the unmistakably mad and there still remained thousands of afflicted souls suffering from simple depression, if it ever was, through to torment so wild and strong that the sufferers had to be confined for their own safety and that of others.

Having read the report on Karen, Dr Lester was pretty sure that the headaches were psychosomatic and directly linked to the extraordinary

369

fantasy that the child had woven about herself. Not that these imaginings were in themselves harmful – far from it. If you don't have a dream, as the song says, how you gonna have a dream come true? Dr Lester had come across several adults admitting to a very freaky fantasy life, which hadn't stopped them going successfully about their daily business and harming no one. Alas, Karen didn't fall into this category.

At this early stage there was little point in challenging her story. The way forward was gradually to lead her to a place where she would be secure and confident enough to begin to dismantle the whole structure, eventually accepting that none of it was true. There were various techniques that could be used to bring such an understanding about. It was just unfortunate that the scenario was so grotesque and frightening. No wonder she had headaches. The miracle was she had so far avoided a breakdown.

Dr Lester glanced at the Mickey Mouse clock over the door. Ten minutes to go. Suddenly she shivered. A breeze seemed to be flowing directly through the open window, cooling her neck and arms. She got up to close it and the metal latch was clammy to her touch. Fastening it securely she noticed a butterfly clinging to the curtains and stood on tiptoe to get a closer look. It was extraordinary. Totally black; not just the velvety wings but even its body and antennae. Surprised and delighted, Barbara studied it for several seconds, even agitating the fabric gently to see if it would fly. When she sat down again Karen regarded her with a mixture of apprehension and yearning.

'So, Karen – these people you told Dr Dickenson about. What are they like?'

'Ordinary.'

'When did you first see them?'

'I've always seen them.'

'Where?'

'Everywhere. Well, not in the house. At the shops, on the bus, just walking about.'

'And have you always talked to them?'

'Only if they talk to me. It got me into trouble, though.'

'What sort of trouble?'

'I was outside and one of them, an old lady – she was ever so nice – asked me to take a message.'

'Who to?'

'Elsie next door. She was in the garden. They don't ask unless the person's present.'

Dr Lester held back a smile. The detail, everything fitting, every impossible aspect so rationally described was impressive, to say the least.

'I'd never actually done it before. I thought I'd try but then Ava came rushing out. She got hold of my hair and dragged me inside. She was ever

370

so angry. She said if the neighbours heard me talking to myself it'd be all round the village I was mental.'

'But you weren't talking to yourself.'

At these words something happened to Karen. Her brow became smooth, her thin bony little fingers stopped plucking and pulling at her skirt and, interlacing, came to lie quietly in her lap. Her shoulders relaxed, which made her neck look longer. She held her head in a delicate, assured way. Her eyes, unclouded now, glistened with happiness. She smiled.

'I knew you'd understand.'

Dr Lester experienced a moment of deep misgiving. Had the decision to appear to accept Karen's story been a mistake? If so she was stuck with it, for there could be no backtracking. The important thing was that the child should grow to trust her.

'I tried really hard to explain,' continued Karen. 'Ava wouldn't listen. I didn't know what to do. But then she met this man, George, at a club. And suddenly everything got better.'

'I see.' Nothing about him in the notes. 'And what was George like?'

'Really nice. He gave me a little bag made out of funny string. And some Smarties.'

'So . . .' For now she gave this unknown sweet-giver the benefit of the doubt. 'He was Ava's friend?'

'Yes.'

'Did he ever stay at your house?'

''Course not.' Karen laughed. 'He lived with his mother.'

'So how did he "make things better"?'

'Well, she asked him round to Rainbow Lodge for tea. He was on the patio when this old man walked round the corner.'

'One of your . . .?'

'That's right. He gave me some messages for George but I got frightened and ran inside. The old man came after me. I didn't know what to do. So I told Ava. I went on and on and on to make her listen. I knew she wouldn't hit me with somebody else there.'

This was incredible. The child was so convincing Dr Lester actually found herself leaning forward.

'And then what happened?'

'She said she had high hopes of George and didn't want him thinking she'd got a kid what was round the bloody twist. I promised I'd never, ever do it again if she'd just help me this one time.'

'And did she?'

'Yes. She made out she'd had this dream. All about an old tramp, trying to tell her things. But when she said what the things were George started shaking and crying. It was awful. She thought he was having a fit. Than he ran off shouting, "I have to tell Mummy. I have to tell Mummy." '

Belatedly Dr Lester realised this last scene was not in her notes and scribbled a couple of lines.

'Carry on, dear. Carry on.'

'Ava believed me after this. She said we had to have a serious talk because a gift like mine was from God and should be really worth something. Later on, George rang up and said he knew a lot about the . . . um . . . parasomething . . .'

'Paranormal?'

'Also, he belonged to this Church and said for her to go along with him.'

'Where was it, the church?'

'In our village,' explained Karen, patiently. 'It's called the Near at Hand.'

That the place could really exist Dr Lester knew. Occasionally fantasists create a dazzlingly unreal universe as a background for their imaginings but mostly they would use genuine places. Often these will be inhabited by famous people flitting in and out of the action. Well-known landmarks too can be casually relocated to accommodate the plot. Pointless to argue as to authenticity. Try showing a globe to a member of the Flat Earth Society.

'And did she go?'

'Yes, but she couldn't do anything.'

'Because you weren't there?'

'Yes!' Karen glowed the glow of the appreciated. More, of the totally understood. 'Back at home she kept walking up and down. I went to sleep and when I woke up she was still doing it. She said she was racking her brains.'

This time Dr Lester did smile. Couldn't help it. The total wildness of the invention combined with Karen's fervent sincerity should have been disturbing, yet, because she was so young, the anodyne phrase 'make believe' was never far away.

'Then she got this amazing idea. I told the doctor.'

'Yes – it's all down here.'

If the invention had been wild up till then it now spiralled totally off the wall. Ava apparently hit on a seemingly foolproof method of exploiting Karen's 'gift'. Concealing the child behind curtains she had set up a microphone through which messages from all these strange and invisible people could be relayed. Ava then received them via an earpiece and passed them on to the waiting congregation.

What Dr Lester found somewhat unsettling about this extraordinary tale was the amount of common or garden detail mixed up in it. Karen described precisely the shop in Slough where they had bought the equipment. And how her mother paid cash so she wouldn't have to give her real name. The assistants had laughed behind her back when she'd tried to swear them to secrecy if they were ever questioned.

'And you were happy with this arrangement?'

'It was brilliant. They came into my head, I passed the messages on and they went away.'

'I see.'

'But she'd only tell people happy things. There were terrible stories as well.'

'Thank you, Karen.' Dr Lester smiled, slipping the notes back into her envelope file. 'But we'll have to leave those for another time.'

'What do you mean?'

'I'm afraid our sessions only last half an hour.'

Karen stared at her. 'You said you'd help me.'

'And I will—'

'You said you'd find someone to talk to them. Like Ava did.'

'I don't think—'

'They're coming all the time – going on at me. They never give up.'

'I can give you something to help your headaches.'

'*They're not headaches*,' screamed Karen. Her arms shot out with such force they seemed to be jumping from their sockets. They flailed the air, beating and flapping as if fending off some great bird.

Dr Lester, shocked at the suddenness of this explosion, hesitated. Her immediate impulse was to try and restrain the child but even as she started to get up Karen became calm again.

The change happened so quickly Dr Lester was immediately suspicious. Yet she could have sworn Karen was not manipulative and had not been acting. A draining paleness had come upon her. The milk-white skin now appeared almost translucent. Her hair, that floss of dazzling light, stirred slightly, though there was not the slightest breeze. Her colourless lips drooped at the corners in disappointment.

Barbara was glad the session was at an end. Glad too it was the last of the day. It had been a difficult one and she was very tired. They had already overrun by nearly ten minutes.

She said carefully, 'Are you all right now, Karen?'

'Yes. Thank you.'

Karen sat quite still, absorbing this new understanding that had so unkindly presented itself. Dr Lester, in whom she had put all her faith, was not going to help. Karen had a moment of panic, of frail crying inside, then deliberately let all hope in that direction go.

But what to do now about the clamour in her head? She couldn't go on like this – she just couldn't. She'd go mad. If only she was older. If she was grown up they would all understand. Even now it would only take one person . . .

Dr Lester picked up her briefcase and put the file inside, then pulled out a cardigan, throwing it casually over her shoulders. Almost immediately she shook it off and put it on properly. How cold her arms were. Almost goosepimply.

'Brrr . . .' said Dr Lester.

Yet the sun was still out. She could tell because it was shining through the trees, throwing lovely reflections of pale grey leaves on to the office

373

wall. The soft shifting and drifting of this shadowy mass was quite hypnotic. You could easily be drawn into a consoling reverie. Dr Lester rested in this peaceful thought for all of a minute, then got to her feet saying firmly, 'Time to go home.'

She set her answering machine, closed down the computer, locked her desk and checked the windows. The child hadn't moved but stayed, still and quiet, staring at the floor.

'Now, Karen—'

Karen jumped up and ran across to the sofa, placing herself exactly where Dr Lester had been sitting. The doctor hesitated. Doubtless the quickest and most sensible way out of such a situation was to bring in the woman who had accompanied Karen and ask her to take the child away. Psychologically, however, the idea was not feasible. This room, this space now belonged to herself and Karen. Over time it was where they would hopefully build a secure relationship. Introduce an outsider, even a friendly one, and any future feelings of closeness would be that much harder to establish and maintain.

'What's worrying you, Karen? Are you afraid that if you go you might not be able to come back?'

'No.' Laying a hand on the cushion next to her, half patting, half stroking it.

'Good.' Dr Lester sat down. 'Because I've already got your next appointment in my book.'

Karen was regarding her closely and the doctor gave another friendly, if slightly strained, smile. What an odd little creature she was. Such strange eyes: the silvery rings encircling the pupil so bright. Indeed, as Dr Lester watched, they seemed to glow with a stronger and stronger intensity, becoming almost luminous. She noticed the extraordinary quality of the silence that had stolen into the room. So deep she could have been at the bottom of the sea. So dense it was almost stifling.

Karen stared across at the wall with the trembling shadows, then looked back, encouraging Dr Lester to follow her gaze. To the doctor's annoyance – for her intention had been to ease Karen towards the door in a firm but kindly manner – she was drawn to do this. The wall looked the same. Almost. Perhaps the shades of grey were a little deeper. The leaves and branches dancing in a slightly more vigorous fashion. Then she noticed one tiny leaf, darker than the rest. Nearly black. It moved in an almost three-dimensional way, apparently lifting from the wall to transfer itself, branch to branch. She looked again and recognised the butterfly.

Two things happened next, it seemed simultaneously. A freezing current of air slid across the floor, curling around her ankles, coating her bare feet in icy sweat. And there was a muffled rustling: a harsh susurration as of rough silk on silk that appeared to be coming from all corners of the room.

A closer look at the wall saw it transformed. The delicate pattern had thickened into a more solid mass and, smoke-like, was shifting and swirling about. Suddenly it seemed to gather itself, intensify and advance into the room, though leaving a rounded emptiness in the middle, like the mouth of a cave. Then, at the very centre of this hollow cell, half concealed by a gossamer web of drifting vapour, an insubstantial white form arose.

The cold was now so intense that Dr Lester found herself unable to move. Her limbs were heavy as lead. She tried to breathe but nausea overcame her. Her heart seemed unnaturally still. Then a powerful smell pervaded the room, as of freshly turned earth. And with this another recognition. She had mistaken the rustling. It was, in fact, whispering.

A galvanic shock made her cry out. She stared down at her arm, fearing a cut or sudden burn. But it was just the child, laying fingers gently across her wrist. Now Karen's face was kissing close, her breath further cooling Dr Lester's already frozen cheek.

'Don't be frightened.'

'I'm . . . I can't . . .'

'It's all right, really.' The fingers tightened. Her voice had an open, yawning quality; the words unnaturally extended. 'Do you understand what I'm saying?'

'Yes.'

'I have a message for you. From Alice.'

'Aahhh . . .'

'Your sister is happy. She sends you and your mother her love. She asks about Henry.'

'He ran away. Alice . . . Oh! Alice . . .'

'She can't hear you, I'm afraid.'

'But . . . she can hear you?'

'Oh, yes.' The uncanny lustre of her shining eyes deepened. Karen released her grip and sat back, satisfied. Confident. Vindicated. 'She can hear me.'